C000023819

Patricia Mullin trained at the Central School of Art and Design. She has had a successful career as a designer and illustrator and has exhibited widely. She moved to Norfolk from London fifteen years ago where she lives with her husband and two children. *Gene Genie* is her first novel.

Acknowledgements

I would like to thank: Peter Brinsden the Medical Director of Bourn Hall Clinic and his staff; my brother, Chris Mullin MP; Charles Clarke MP; Dr Ian Gibson MP; Sarah Woodhouse; Café Writers. I am indebted to many friends for their constant encouragement, wise counsel and passionate criticism.

The author has tried without success to contact the copyright owner of the quote by Tom Parks and would be pleased if he or she would make contact.

Gene Genie

Patricia Mullin

the STONE press

Published by the STONE press Norwich 2005
www.thestonepress.co.uk

Second edition

ISBN 0 9550035 0 4

Printed in Great Britain by
Biddles Ltd., King's Lynn, Norfolk

Designed by
Remark Design Ltd., Norwich

For my children Amiria and Kupa and
in loving memory of my father L. R. Mullin 1920 – 2004

"Family is the anvil on which the soul gets beaten out."
Tom Parks

February. A clinic, London, thirty years ago.

Michael sat on the stained bench of the cubicle staring uneasily at the magazine that had been placed there for him.

He didn't generally use soft porn, he had no need; medical school provided a steady stream of young women eager to sleep with a student doctor. Not that Michael was promiscuous – he had a regular girlfriend, a nurse, Sally. And whenever he needed to please himself, by himself, he only had to imagine undressing her; it was all the stimulus he required.

Dust to Dust

It was a grey, miserable day. There was no rain but the sky was oppressive. It was left to the undertakers to carry Marion Laing's coffin into the church and the smell of leaf-mould and damp earth entered with them. Nigel had thought that his father Gerald might suggest that they both shared in this sad duty. Instead he settled for handing out the order of service and greeting ageing aunts and uncles, suggesting they filled the pews at the front; they weren't expecting a crowd.

The vicar, Roger Elmswood, an enthusiastic man with evangelical pretensions, had made clear his dismay regarding the choice of hymns – he thought 'Dear Lord and Father of mankind' especially downbeat and maudlin, and was no happier with 'Breathe on me breath of God'.

"I expect he'd like something you can strum a guitar to," Gerald muttered gloomily. "Apparently it's a celebration of Marion's life, not a funeral. Is it any wonder nobody bothers going to church any more? All this unrelenting bloody cheeriness, it's enough to put anyone off."

No family member volunteered to lead a tribute to Marion, so the vicar stepped in and said a few words about her contribution to the world. As this had consisted solely of fussing over her son Nigel, having dinner on the table by six and keeping the house spotless, the vicar took as his theme 'an ordinary life', reminding the mourners that in God's eyes each and every life was *extraordinary*.

"Marion Laing", he said, "was a devoted mother to her only child Nigel and a loving and loyal wife to her husband Godfrey." A murmur ran round the congregation at the misnaming of Gerald, but the vicar pressed on undaunted, "And, I can assure you, God will be pleased enough with that."

Nigel bit his lip. Poor Marion. It all sounded a little strained and patronising, this tribute from a man who had scarcely known her.

He looked up at the dust and cobwebs that had collected high up in the nave roof. She would certainly have admonished the vicar for such lax standards and suggested fetching a ladder as soon as possible.

Outside, as his mother's coffin was placed in the hearse ready for the journey to the local cemetery, Nigel busied himself by reading the condolence cards attached to the small cluster of flowers and wreaths. 'Rest in Peace' and 'God Bless', was all that was written on them, there were no poems or testimonies to Marion's goodness nor expressions of unendurable loss. Hers had been, apparently, a life lived without blame, ambition or incident.

"You were everything to your mother, Nigel." Aunt Dorothy, tall and plain, stood beside him. "She went through more than most," she added softly, the words catching in her throat.

Nigel, surprised at this unexpected expression of emotion, put his large comforting hand on her arm and squeezed it lightly. "I know."

"Do you, Nigel? Do you?"

Question Time

Michael Barton MP, newly appointed Minister for the Family, only just reached the studio in time. He had been rushed about all day from one meeting to another. He thought this frenetic pace would stop once he was a minister with a department of his own, but his diary secretary could still overbook him and make his daily life hell. Today had been particularly bad and he'd arrived everywhere late – and not fully briefed.

The floor manager hurried him straight through into Make-up, and as he finally took his seat David Dimbleby – already behind the desk and having his microphone adjusted – greeted him by name. Soon the title music was playing and the introductions were made.

"Good evening, ladies and gentlemen. Tonight 'Question Time' comes to you from Great Entworth, a village in an area sometimes referred to as the breadbasket of England: East Anglia. I should like to extend a warm welcome to our panel tonight: Geoffrey Blythe-Simpson, a prominent member of the Countryside Confederation; Estelle Mallory, editor of 'Future Families', a magazine that addresses the concerns of those in less conventional families; next an especially warm welcome to Janet Emerson, vicar of the parish of Frensham, who has bravely stepped in because Gavin Enderby, the Liberal Democrat MP, has 'flu; Susan Fipps, who needs no introduction as the plain speaking shadow Minister for Health; and finally to Michael Barton, MP for Wynshore and Minister for the Family." The camera focused on each panellist in turn while the audience applauded politely.

"In a week that has again seen hunt supporters state that they will not obey the law – and indeed that the law is unenforceable – rural issues are again in the spotlight. This evening we have a number of questions that reflect the public concern for the rural economy and traditional family values. And the birth of a baby girl to a lesbian couple who bought semen on the Internet from a donor with an exceptional IQ and used a surrogate, makes us ask, what then is the family today?" Dimbleby paused, and turning to camera three continued:

"Can we any longer define the family as husband and wife rearing their own offspring? Should modern fertility techniques be freely available to those with the money to pay for them? And the nation's health; a study suggests it is income, rather than anything else, which determines an individual's future well-being. Has this government done anything to address this and other inequalities? These are just some of the questions tonight. Our first questioner, please."

Michael was perfectly at ease on the set, in a radio car, or on the 'Today' programme. It was, by now, second nature. He knew his stuff and was generally well briefed. What he disliked was being caught off guard – unlikely here on 'Question Time'. He knew with a degree of confidence which questions were likely to be asked, and a review of the week's newspapers could be as good a guide as any to the topics raised.

Blyth-Simpson had hotly defended hunting and argued that the legislation was unenforceable. "But don't forget," he said, "The Countryside Confederation is about far more than blood sports."

"If that is the case," Michael interjected, "why does the Confederation appear to allow every meeting to be hijacked by the pro-hunting lobby? We've heard precious little about the very serious problems of decline that rural communities face: loss of transport, post offices, schools, hospitals and affordable housing." Michael drew a muted round of applause for this comment.

"That's a bit rich coming from a government that had done nothing except alienate rural communities and send honest hardworking farmers to the wall!" Susan Fipps countered. Her comment drew robust applause and she sat back with satisfaction. She was a worthy opponent; Michael had a sneaking admiration for her despite her right of centre views. The public liked Fipps. She spoke her mind and was quick witted. A little, wiry, elderly woman, usually described in the press as diminutive or frail, but in reality as tough as old boots, she'd devoted her life to politics. Michael had

5

found to his cost that you couldn't catch Susan Fipps out. She was the nearest any politician was ever likely to come to being a national treasure. Smiling charmingly across at her, Michael outlined the government's position, such as it was. He took care to keep his own views out of the discussion.

"This country's responsible citizens will be criminalised and the countryside turned into a theme park for the benefit of city dwellers," Susan remarked to more fulsome applause.

The vicar, Janet Emerson, was against hunting in any form. She took the line that such treatment of one of God's creatures showed a lack of respect for the natural world that He had provided for us. The audience listened politely. Estelle Mallory on the other hand simply considered hunting of any sort backward and unscientific. In the days of clean, licensed abattoirs and sophisticated pest and vermin control, what possible need could there be to set hounds upon deer and foxes? There was, she proposed, nothing fundamentally wrong with the killing of foxes, it merely lacked a modern scientific approach which would, in her view, sanitise the process and make it more acceptable.

Estelle, Michael had decided, was pretty dotty, and only on the panel to add colour, which she certainly did with her low cut, flimsy, turquoise outfit, more suitable for a night-club. There was always one guest who could be guaranteed to enliven the proceedings and lately all sorts of pop stars and unlikely panellists had been foisted on the programme in order to widen its appeal. Tonight, he suspected, Estelle Mallory was there to fulfil this function.

Dimbleby took a firm line and turned hurriedly to the funding of technology schools. This caused less acrimonious debate. Then a homely-looking woman in the front row of the audience asked the Vicar for her view on the availability of donor sperm on the Internet, in the light of the recent case of the lesbian couple who bought sperm from a biochemist, a member of Mensa.

Janet Emerson didn't mince her words:

"Children," she said, "should be born from love and they require devotion and selflessness from their parents. I'm deeply perturbed that neither of these women wanted to give birth to the baby, and that they consider IQ, a questionable measurement of talent and ability, so important. I don't see this as a sign of two people who will love a child unconditionally. And I share the misgivings of the questioner, although I am not sure such arrangements can be legislated against. Scientists seem to have carte blanche." She paused and turned to Dimbleby, "They used a surrogate from the United States, didn't they?"

"So I believe. Michael, what is your view on this type of arrangement? And what exactly is the family these days?" Dimbleby asked, turning to face him.

Estelle Mallory, clearly irritated and tapping her pencil, leaned forward and butted in: "What are you suggesting? That the only right and godly way to rear children is in a heterosexual relationship? That's ludicrous! Lesbians and gays have just as much right to rear children and they make equally good parents. Now, at last, we have the technology to allow others to bear children for us – it would be silly not to use it. I understand this couple are in their forties and they considered it safer for the baby to use a younger surrogate. As for the accusation that they want intelligent children – don't we all?" She threw herself back into the chair and swivelled, agitated, from left to right.

Dimbleby held out his hand, inviting Michael to reply.

"I have never considered having children a 'human right'. Children, as Janet says, are a blessing, not a right," Michael insisted.

There was a ripple of applause.

"So are you against IVF and such treatments?" Dimbleby asked.

"Goodness, no! The pain of childlessness is, I know from my experience as a GP, unbearable for many couples, and where it is at all possible they should be helped to have the children they so desperately want. But the children's needs remain paramount and from what I've heard of this couple, I don't believe they will put the child's needs above their own."

"Lots of selfish heterosexual people have children!" Estelle leaned forward and turned to Michael. "So what are you suggesting? Some sort of aptitude test for those using donor eggs or sperm? A test that is only applied to those who are unfortunate enough not be able to get pregnant by screwing."

"No, I can't see that being practical, although I wouldn't reject it out of hand. After all, it has always been accepted that to adopt a child a couple will undergo vigorous investigation which, in my view, is only right. This child has three mothers, one social, one genetic and a surrogate! I do understand the level of public disquiet about some of the more repugnant medical advances."

Michael knew as soon as it was out that he had made a dreadful slip.

"Repugnant!" cried Estelle. "So the thousands of children born every year in this country, with aid of IVF, donor sperm, eggs and modern scientific methods are repugnant! And that from the Minister for the Family!"

She sat back triumphant.

*

Michael didn't have to wait for the papers to cross his desk the following morning. Logan, the Prime Minister's press secretary, was on the phone to him at six a.m.

"Let me read you some of the more lurid headlines, Michael. 'REPUGNANT!' That's *The Sun*, with a delightful picture of a Tamsin Shelton, four days old and conceived through an egg sharing scheme. Page two, a picture of Mum and Dad, Cheryl and Mick, cuddling little Tamsin. By all accounts they've been trying unsuccessfully for ten years to conceive. 'How could anyone say such a thing about our beautiful daughter? She's everything we've ever wanted and has made our lives complete. We are as good as any other parents.' " Logan paused for effect. " 'Minister backs assessment for parenting,' *The Daily Record.* It tacitly supports your proposal, but wants to know who could take on such a role? Social services, you remember, having such a poor reputation with regard to adoptions and children in so called 'care'. They've also dragged out Professor Kenton again – sorry, Lord Kenton – and we all know his views on the matter. Oh, and the leader column in *The Guardian* is devoted to the subject. Suffice it to say, Michael, there is not one national daily that is not running with this story in one form or another. The Prime Minister is due at the European summit tomorrow and you've hijacked the media with a comment which in no way reflects government thinking and which, for the foreseeable future, is unlikely to lie down and die!"

"Now hold on a minute," Michael interjected. "This quote had been distorted until it's unrecognisable. Did you actually watch the programme?"

"I've just seen the tape," Logan replied, clearly exasperated.

"I did not say that children born through fertility treatment were repugnant and that most certainly is not my view. I sent countless couples forward for IVF in my time as a GP. I do, however, believe there are some highly questionable practices..."

"God, Michael. Leave it, okay? 'Today' have asked for an interview with you: you're unavailable. And when you're doorstepped by the press, turn it around and promote our new policy on paternity leave. Otherwise just smile and make yourself scarce," Logan instructed.

"Very well," Michael said wearily.

No sooner had Michael replaced the receiver than the phone rang again. It was Julia, his wife.

"I've had Frank Smite from *The Daily Record* on the phone. He wanted to know if the views you expressed last night were in any way related to your being a Roman Catholic."

"But I'm not a Roman Catholic! I hope you told him that," Michael said, sounding drained and irritable.

"Of course I did."

"Don't say anything else to any of the press, and get Breeda to ferry the girls to and from school. You'd better tell the headmistress that they might be bothered. What did you say exactly?"

"Just that I am a Catholic and so are our children. You, however, are not," Julia replied calmly.

"Good. If any others ring or turn up on the doorstep, just politely but firmly refuse to comment and don't be drawn. Is that clear?"

" Michael, darling, I do know how to handle a few hacks, you know."

"I'm sorry. I know you do. It's just I've had Logan on the phone slapping my wrists. Did you see it, 'Question Time'?"

"No, I went to bed. What happened?"

"Less than you would think, given all the fuss. A remark I made has been twisted. It'll blow over, these things do. I love you," he added. "I'll try and get home early on Thursday so we can have a meal together."

"That would be nice. And the girls will be pleased to have your company for a change, my suppertime conversation gets a bit repetitive," Julia said with feeling.

"Until Thursday then, and I'm sorry about all this."

"All what?" She laughed. "Like a shower, it will pass."

3

Like father like son

Nigel had never felt quite right. For a start, his name was wrong. He didn't feel like a 'Nigel' – and his middle name was Kenneth so that was no consolation. Sometimes he felt as if he had been beamed from another life to co-exist with people with whom he had nothing in common.

As a child he had always been inappropriately dressed. He was put into smart well-pressed shorts, white ankle socks and the sort of shoes the Prince of Wales had worn when small. For family gatherings he wore a shirt and tie.

"Just like your Daddy! What a grown up boy!" Nigel was three.

His father Gerald – Gerry to his friends – was often exhorted to admire Marion's handiwork.

"Look, Daddy, doesn't he look quite the young man?" she would say, pushing Nigel forward.

And Gerald would drop the newspaper down a fraction and made a snorting noise, "Humph."

By the time he was seven, Nigel was aware that the behaviour of his besotted mother also irritated other family members. Nigel was 'advanced', as Marion put it, with a precocious talent for music. He played piano and clarinet and Marion would make him display these talents at every wedding, christening and even funeral, whether he was invited to or not.

"'Ere we go, bleeding Eine Kleine Nachtmusik again," Nigel once overheard his Uncle Stan say despairingly.

Nigel never got dirty; it wasn't permitted. Marion was forever picking fluff, stray hairs and crumbs from his jumper.

"We can't have you looking like no one cares, now can we?" she would remark every time. He found it unbearable and would pull away from her and shout "*Don't!*" with unintended aggression. Often he took what refuge he could by burying his head in a book. Consequently, he was remarkably well read.

During the late seventies, when glam-rock was at its height and girls and boys on every high street teetered about on ludicrous platform shoes, Marion was horrified.

"Their poor parents, they must be so ashamed. Promise me, Nigel, that you will always make me proud of you?"

"Humph," replied Nigel, rather like Gerald. It seemed enough to satisfy his mother.

Nigel passed his eleven plus with ease and Marion rang round all the relatives to tell them that Nigel was off to grammar school, the first of the Laings to achieve such dizzy heights.

"I don't know where he gets it from, this remarkable intelligence. I think it must be from Gerald's side, don't you?" Marion, in just one sentence, managed to offend her every relative, while Gerry, ambling past the telephone muttered:

"Well, that would be a bloody miracle."

Gerald worked in Local Government. He didn't have much to do with Nigel and would just ruffle his hair occasionally when passing, and sometimes he would inquire about Nigel's homework. Nigel had no idea what his father did every day. His parents always remained at a distance from one another and his father showed no interest in standing on the touch-line shouting encouragement like the other dads. Not that Nigel was exceptional at sport, although he did play rugby; he was big for his age and he could run well. It was enough to stop him being bullied and called Mummy's pet.

When he was little he used to wish for a brother or even, when desperate, a sister. Once he asked his mother why he was an only child. She had replied that it was 'God's will,' and the matter was never referred to again. Like all unhappy children, he often believed that he had other parents from whom, through some inadvertent disaster, he had become separated. He imagined they would one day return to claim him. Yet when he looked in the mirror, he thought he saw a resemblance to Marion, the same curly pale hair – not blonde, not brown – and her grey-blue eyes.

By his teens Nigel realized he would just have to work hard and escape to university as soon as possible. He took eleven GCSEs and passed them all with top grades. His A levels were the same and, consequently, he embarked on a degree at the Guildhall School of Music in London, later taking a postgraduate teaching certificate. His mother was delighted. It was all she had ever wanted for him and her happiness was complete when he was made the youngest ever head of music at an independent boys' school in Maidenhead. She died later that year of bowel cancer, having kept the seriousness of her illness from her family for as long as possible, not wanting a fuss. The end, when it came, was mercifully quick. Nigel was twenty-nine and engaged to a scientist, a petite dark-haired girl named Sarah.

For several weeks after his mother's death, Nigel took the train to Brentwood each Sunday to visit his father. They usually ate a packet lasagne, chips and frozen peas and then sat at either end of the living room with very little to say to one another.

This particular Sunday it was different.

"Is there any little memento of your mother's that you'd like? Something for Sarah perhaps, a bit of jewellery?"

"I don't know Dad, I hadn't thought. I'll have a look, shall I?"

"Only I'm selling up, taking early retirement. I've always fancied Malta."

"Malta!"

"There's nothing to keep me here now – no family as such."

"There's me. And who knows? Sarah's keen to start a family, so perhaps grandchildren."

Gerald drew his hands over his face and eyes as if to wipe away the strain.

"Nigel, I have something to tell you. Something, which in my view you should have been told years ago." He paused, and then said hoarsely:

"You are not my son."

Nigel sat motionless, looking at him.

"I am not your father," Gerald repeated.

Nigel continued to stare, uncomprehending. Finally, he said:

"Then I'm adopted."

"Well no, not that either, I'm afraid."

4

Mistaken Identity

Nigel sat on the train wondering whether he had heard all this correctly. Or whether the sense of loss at his mother's untimely death had rendered him incapable of understanding what Gerald had just told him. It made no sense – and yet absolute sense at the same time. It explained everything and nothing, all at once. The facts, such as they were, went round and round in his head and they seemed to mingle with the motion and the noise of the train until he felt giddy. When the conductor came to ask for his ticket, he sat trying to make out in his own mind what, exactly, the word 'ticket' meant.

"Your ticket, sir. Small piece of card, says where you're going and when, and proves you've paid. I stamp it. A ticket, get it?"

"Oh…sorry. Yes." Nigel rummaged in his pocket.

When the train pulled into Liverpool Street station, Nigel sat staring blankly out of the window.

"Come on, Sunshine, let's be having you, this is the end of the line." The conductor was altogether more kindly now, having decided Nigel really wasn't quite right in the head.

Nigel still had to cross London on the tube and make his way back to Maidenhead but he wasn't sure he was capable of navigating what was, by now, a familiar route. He bought a cup of coffee and perched awkwardly on a café bar stool, watching the thronging people hurrying to platforms and greeting old friends or relations – people who knew who they were, people with a clear sense of self, people with a complete identity.

Sarah let herself in with the key that Nigel had given her. She had moved in with Nigel, having sold her own studio flat, which would have been be far too small for the two of them. She'd been to Tesco's. With the wedding only a few months away all her free time was spent preparing for it. She was trying to make a decision about the cake. Square or round? Fruit? Did anyone like fruit cake? Nigel usually helped, giving his opinion when it was asked for, but always making sure that it was Sarah who had just what she wanted. It hadn't been easy, Marion being so ill and then dying when she did. They had discussed a postponement but Nigel and his father were adamant; nothing would have given Marion more pleasure than to see Nigel happily settled with Sarah.

She found Nigel staring into space in the twilight.

"It's very gloomy; why haven't you put the lights on?" she asked. "You know, you'd think people would have better things to do than spend Sunday in the supermarket. The place was packed. How was your father?"

Nigel didn't reply.

"Nigel? How was your father?"

"Oh. Fine. Father – Gerald – is selling up. He's going to live in Malta. He won't be at the wedding."

Sarah stopped unpacking, a bunch of bananas dangling from her hand.

"What do you mean, he won't be at the wedding? Is it grief?" She paused. "I thought we should have waited," she continued, almost to herself.

"No. No, not that. I don't think he felt much when she died. They've been going through the motions. He hasn't cared... not for years anyway." Nigel gave a heavy sigh which seemed to come from deep inside him and ended in a small nervous shudder.

"It's only in May. Just two months. He won't have gone by then," Sarah tried to reassure him.

"He seems very determined and he's got it all worked out. He's going to put the house on the market."

"But surely he'll want to be at his only son's wedding!" Sarah's voice rose in alarm.

"That's just it – I'm not his son."

There was complete silence.

"Say that again."

"I am not... his... son."

"I don't believe it!" Sarah collapsed into a chair, still holding the bananas.

"Oh, I do. It explains a lot."

Julia switched on the answer-phone. She had decided to stay at the back of the house and turn out a cupboard or two. That way none of the press, who were huddled outside on the road, would be able to get a glimpse of her. The phone rang repeatedly. Hacks from the local paper and a couple of other tabloids had joined Frank Smite on the stakeout of the house. Silly really, they should know by now that they wouldn't get anything out of Julia, but the fuss over Michael's supposed outburst was not going away quite as quickly as he had hoped. The doorbell rang and, without thinking, Julia walked up the hall. It was a long, insistent ring. On the other side of the glass she could see the outline of Frank Smite. She hesitated and turned back towards the kitchen.

"Mrs Barton, Julia, please. I was just wondering is there any chance of a cup of coffee for me and the lads. It's a damp cold day. Just a drop of something to warm us up?" Frank was on his knees and calling through the letterbox. Julia continued to walk away. Nice bum, thought Frank.

The last time the press staked out the house was when the government had changed the tax laws to make marriage more of a disincentive than ever. They had wanted a quote, and the press corps knew that Michael's department was at odds with the Chancellor on this policy. There were still those in the party who, it seemed to Julia, had undue influence and were completely out of touch with public opinion. They considered any and every arrangement and grouping of people a family. Michael was uneasy with the way in which the traditional family unit was sidelined and disregarded, and he had said as much. He argued with conviction that all the evidence showed that children thrived in traditional family arrangements. There was also a wealth of evidence to prove that young people went off the rails due to the mounting tide of family breakdown and disintegration. And that this happened more frequently when the parents were not married and were cohabiting. In a veiled statement Michael made his view known. The press loved it. They saw it as a feud between the two departments and the media were keen to see any disagreement as a party split. Julia had been photographed taking the children to school and unloading the supermarket shopping. She had just smiled pleasantly, taken out tea and coffee on a tray, as she had been asked to do today, and confined herself to commenting on the weather. Nevertheless, a delightful photograph of Julia smiling appeared on the inside page of several papers. 'The beautiful Mrs Julia Barton takes her family shopping,' the headline read. Michael had said it was a lack of more interesting news that had precipitated the article. Julia had tried not to be offended.

"Sure, it's because your wife is so lovely and photogenic, you old fool," their friend Finn had reprimanded Michael, and Julia liked him for it.

Now Frank Smite let the letterbox spring back and stood up to rub his aching knees. There was to be no coffee from the lovely Mrs Barton today and he was getting on a bit for this sort of lark. He should by rights leave this game to the youngsters. But he couldn't settle for an office, desk and computer. Computers! He hated the bloody things. Gone were the days when you legged it to the nearest phone box and rang in with your copy. Now, with mobile phones, there was an advantage, he had to admit – but it took the action and the edge out of the game. Often in the old days, he'd be first in with a scoop because he had got hold of a telephone ahead of the rabble. He'd sweet talk some old dear into letting him use the phone while the rest of the hacks would all be fighting for the phone box. Frank would slip the old dear a tenner to supplement her pension, have a cup of sweet tea and be back in the office before the rest had even filed the story.

Smite trudged back across the road and joined Tonkins from *The Echo* and a very young girl, Samantha, from the local rag, *The Wynshore Gazette*, who didn't look old enough to make tea.

"Any joy, Frank?" Tonkins enquired.

"Nah! All I was after was cuppa and a photo, but she's holed up at the back of the house. I got the lovely sight of her pretty bum, for what it's worth! Poxy little story anyway. No sign of a vice girl or a bit of tasty corruption. Who gives a toss how the great British public spawns it offspring?"

"I think quite a lot of people do, actually," Samantha piped up, in her perfectly clipped vowels. She eyed Smite with contempt. He was a repulsive little man. Samantha was far too young to know of Frank Smite's legendary journalistic coups. He and Johnny Clarke had been the Woodward and Bernstein of their day. But when a motorway pile-up killed his wife and two young children, Frank hit the bottle. This job was a favour called in by an editor who respected Frank for what he once was, a serious investigative journalist. Now he was reduced to door stepping benefit fraudsters, reality TV contestants or, on a good day, a politician on the make or the take. It had been a long time since he had got a trace of anything juicy and he had had to settle for tedious stake-outs in thin drizzle, any copy relegated to the bottom of page ten.

Smite sniffed. It was a long, bubbling, disgusting sniff.

"Give it half an hour and I'm off," he said, ignoring Samantha completely.

"What's it got to do with the wife anyway?" Samantha pressed on, failing to recognise that she had been snubbed.

"Gawd give us strength," Smite said, rolling his eyes. "She's a Catholic, ain't she?"

"So?" remarked Samantha tetchily.

"Well, darling, it's like this. Half of this lot are old school, 'what about the workers', only they're not allowed to say so. Gagging order, see. And the rest are smooth suited bastards who want to ram bio-technology, alternative families and poofs down our throats." Frank adopted the voice of a pantomime dame to express this last part. "And then they tell us how effing good it is for us all, while certain individuals make themselves a bloody fortune. Somewhere in the middle are the people of conscience, represented by the likes of your local GP turned MP, now Minister for the Family, who says what he thinks and talks a lot of common bloody sense. Now you're not allowed to talk common sense these days, it all has to be okayed by the spin-doctors first. I reckon Barton's given Logan a few headaches in his time."

"And Mrs Barton, Julia, what has any of this got to do with her?"

"It's what's called an angle, dear," Smite went on sarcastically. "Unusually, in this increasingly secular society," – Smite took on the tone of a high-brow leader writer – "we've got three members of this cabinet with devout wives, a Catholic, a Baptist and a Jew. Does this have an influence? Religion and bio-ethics – is there a conflict? Of course there is, but we'll…"

"She's a looker," Tomkins butted in.

"Ah, yes, isn't she? And that is really why we're all here, this damp spring morning. The Minister's wife is a beauty in what could be described as the late Grace Kelly mould, so a picture of her pretty face outside her charming Victorian villa and any quote will do. Because when all's said and done, call it what you like, bio-what's-its-name is very dull. And Mrs Barton is gorgeous."

"Oh, very twenty first century!" snapped Samantha.

"Darling, what did you expect?"

Smite gave a dismissive snort.

With her head in the cupboard under the stairs, Julia faintly heard the voice of her friend Breeda on the answer-phone. She hurried to the telephone to intercept the call.

"Julia, it's me, Breeda. I just wanted to say that Michael is quite right. 'Repugnant' is exactly what all this sort of scientific meddling is. A baby is a blessing from God, not something you mix up in a petri dish. And…"

"Breeda. I'm just hiding from the press," Julia said, breaking into the message.

"Shall I come over, keep you company?" Breeda offered.

"No. No, I'm fine. I'm just cleaning out the cupboard under the stairs. I'll just keep a low profile and they'll give up and go soon. It's silly nonsense. I don't know why on earth they're still running with this – lack of any more interesting news I suppose. Anyway they've taken Michael's comment completely out of context."

"I thought he was marvellous, saying what we all think. Sure, if more decent honest people spoke up we could put a stop to a lot of this scientific hocus-pocus and we'd all be a lot better for it." Praise indeed from Breeda, Michael's fierce critic. "Now I'm off to the shops – is there anything you need? Bread? Milk?" Breeda spoke with her gentle Irish lilt and at her usual terrific pace.

"Thank you, Breeda, but I'm all prepared. We could survive a week's siege if necessary."

"You don't think they'll be there for that long, do you?" Breeda sounded concerned.

"Goodness no", Julia laughed. "They'll be gone by midday, sooner if it rains hard."

"Saint Swithun is the patron saint for weather! I'll say a prayer. He'll know what I'm after. I'll drop the girls off for you, after school, just in case the press wolves are still lurking."

Julia smiled to herself. Dear Breeda, always the first to offer to help even with all the running round she had to do for her own family.

"Thanks, Breeda, that'll be a big help. I'll see you about four. Bye." Julia put down the phone and returned to the cupboard. She unearthed a particularly nasty pair of trainers and consigned them to the black bin bag.

*

Tess had just stormed upstairs the moment Michael put his key in the door, but Katherine ran to greet her father. She was ten, and she adored her daddy. She looked rather like him too.

"Daddy!" She flew across the hall and into his arms. "I've missed you! Have you missed me?" Michael swung her round and then planted a kiss on her cheek. As soon as he put her down she began to rifle through his pockets looking for the small gold mints he usually saved from the restaurant car.

"What a question! I always miss you, all of you! Hello, darling, you all right?" Michael gave Julia a hug as she came through to warn him about Tess's ill humour and to take his bags from him.

" Fine. Except number one daughter has flounced off to her room. She had plans for this evening and having supper with us didn't figure in them."

"Ah. Shall I pop up and have a word, or is it safer to stay down here with a glass of wine?"

"There's definitely safety in numbers and the wine is open," Julia advised.

"How have two such reasonable people managed to produce such a tigress?" Michael said jokily.

Tess, who had suddenly appeared at the top of the stairs, called down to her father:

"I heard that!"

"Well, come and give me a hug and explain what it is that my arrival home is spoiling," Michael called up.

Tess had the same pale hair and golden skin as her mother, but she was both beautiful and truculent. How could such angelic beauty house such a maelstrom of hormones and temper one moment and devastating charm the next? Tess sashayed down the stairs in the manner of a catwalk supermodel and reluctantly kissed Michael's cheek. She was wearing very tight green satin trousers and a minuscule top. Michael was struck by an overpowering smell of cheap perfume.

"Well, what better offer have you had than eating supper with your some-time father?" They made their way towards the kitchen, where Julia put a glass of Merlot in Michael's hand.

"I was invited to eat at Beatrice's house and we were going to do our French revision together," Tess replied haughtily.

"Really!" Michael remarked sceptically. "And French revision clearly requires that you adopt the costume of the sort of girl one might encounter loitering late at night on the Champs Elysées, does it?"

Julia winced visibly and waited for the explosion. It didn't come. This surprised her because, after all, suggesting to your twelve year old daughter, whom you hadn't even seen for four days, that she was dressed like a French tart wasn't the tactic that Julia would have employed to get a reasoned response. This sort of remark, which Michael thought amusing, could go either way with Tess.

"Honestly, Daddy, you should be ashamed of yourself. How can you be so horrid? I'm not one of your political opponents. And if you want me to, I'll buy some more suitable clothes at the weekend. You could take me shopping with one of those nice credit cards you have." Tess snuggled up to Michael, laying on the charm.

Julia laughed.

"Touché. Now let's eat, shall we?" she said, and ladled the lamb casserole onto the plates.

"Only if Tess rings Beatrice and puts off this pressing engagement. After all, I've rushed home for a re-match of 'Don't Panic'. I was badly beaten last week. I think you girls have been fixing the categories. I only seem to get dog breeds, nothing I ever know anything about."

"It's just that you're out of touch, Daddy. Good on current affairs, science and music, but boy bands, no, footballers, no, and pie fillings? Only apple and rhubarb in sixty seconds! You completely forgot savoury. Face it, Daddy, you're hopeless!" Tess twined her arms around her father's neck.

"At least I don't cheat!"

"And when have I ever cheated?" Tess enquired, taking mock offence.

"Monopoly, every time – you move my hotels onto your property when I'm not looking. And your cheating at Scrabble is legendary. I haven't forgotten 'xenophobe'!"

"It's a perfectly good word. You ought to be impressed by my vocabulary."

"Darling I am, but that still doesn't make it spelt with a Z, however much you might want it to be."

"Well how silly of it to be spelt with an X when it sounds like a Z. It's a stupid letter anyway; apart from x-ray and Xmas when is it ever used? And silly of you too, imagine forgetting where you built your hotels. He'd never make a property developer, would he, Mummy?" She planted a good-natured kiss on her father's cheek. "Can we go shopping on Saturday plee…ease?"

Michael looked over to Julia for approval. She nodded in agreement.

"Go and ring Beatrice and we can eat," Julia instructed as she placed the plates of steaming casserole on the table. She grinned at Michael. "She has you wrapped right around her little finger."

"I know," Michael replied tenderly. "Lovely, isn't it."

From the hall Katherine called, "Daddy, there aren't any mints!"

"No darling, I'm early, so I get to eat with my family instead of on the train for a change. Don't tell me you'd rather have free chocolates from the restaurant car than my company at supper!"

"No of course not. Both!" Katherine replied with a grin as she slipped into her seat.

"I'll tell you what," Michael began, "we'll all go out shopping Saturday morning and have lunch at Stoddards afterwards. Let's make a day of it. We haven't done that for ages."

"That would be lovely," Julia replied – and highly unlikely, she thought. She knew full well what the morning would bring. She had checked Michael's diary with Geraldine, his secretary, enquiring whether there were any known lunatics on his appointment list. This common hazard had resulted in the police being summoned to the last constituency surgery to deal with a martial-arts maniac who had pinned Geraldine to the wall with one of the trade union banner poles. Quite what his gripe was no one could determine.

The day would start at seven a.m. with a breakfast interview from the local radio car parked outside their house, and then Michael would be whisked to some far-flung corner of the constituency for a meeting with the Police Consultative Committee. Later there would be a brainstorming session on urban regeneration projects. He would run late all day, having refused a ministerial car, believing that taking taxis gave him the common touch but forgetting how impossible they were to find when it was raining. He also shunned a pager, though this Julia found more understandable: being elusive afforded him much-needed breathing space. Finally, he would arrive late at his surgery. His staff would ring at about 5.30 p.m. advising Julia of a delay because another meeting had been tacked on, and Michael would arrive home hours after he had intended. If he didn't spend Saturday opening a new medical centre, or joining in a fundraiser, then his constituents' problems would seep into the weekend, keeping him desk bound or on the telephone for hours.

It would certainly keep him from going shopping with the girls.

*

Sarah made Nigel a cup of tea and sat on the floor opposite him. The flat was modest and comfortable and was furnished with bits and pieces that Nigel had picked up from local second hand shops. A

23

stranger would have recognised at once that this was a home created by a solitary male. Sarah hadn't liked to make any alterations. She was conscious of this being Nigel's territory and there would be ample time for decorating their own home. They would sell this flat and buy a little terraced house with two bedrooms, one as a guest room or for a baby when one came along. That, at least, was what Sarah had imagined; but this was before Gerald had made his shock announcement. She had an awful sense of foreboding.

With her back to the bookcase, Sarah sat drinking her own tea. She didn't know quite what to say or ask. Nigel appeared to be in shock. She considered calling the doctor, but then that seemed ridiculous. What could a doctor do? Her mother always made tea in a crisis. There hadn't been too many of those in Sarah's well-ordered life but all the same, they had drunk gallons of tea.

She looked across at Nigel, dear, dependable Nigel. They had met at a party and she had liked him at once. He was attractive, very tall and well built, with curly hair, a sort of mousy colour that was really rather nice. He had quite rugged features but there was a softness to them that matched his personality. He was clever, an intellectual, with a passion for music matched only by his talent. And the love of his subject made him an inspirational teacher, so it was no wonder that he had risen so quickly to such a position of responsibility. Sarah had, by now, attended a number of the school concerts and they were outstandingly professional. There was talk of the school orchestra recording an album and Nigel had started a mixed jazz band, staff and pupils together, which played local venues. And he put in extra hours training the rugby team. He was certainly dedicated. It was clear that he had never really fitted into his family, yet he had never belittled nor dismissed them, even though it was obvious he found his mother stifling. Sarah decided it was impossible to imagine Marion having an affair.

She shifted uncomfortably and asked:

"So if Gerald isn't your father, then who is?"

"He doesn't know," Nigel replied.

"And now because Marion is dead," Sarah surmised, "it will be harder… But someone will know, she'll have confided in someone surely, Aunt Dorothy perhaps."

"My mother didn't even know," Nigel stated flatly. "No, it's not what you think. She wasn't loose or molested, nothing like that," Nigel said. "Father was, is, infertile. I was conceived as a result of my mother receiving sperm – donor sperm."

Sarah didn't say anything. She was struck by Nigel's curious use of the word 'loose'. It was such a quaint term and sounded so like something that Marion would say.

"It doesn't matter, darling. It doesn't alter anything." Sarah realised as soon as the words left her lips that this was the wrong thing to say.

"It matters to me. And it changes everything…my entire life to date."

Nigel got up from the chair and walked out of the room.

Sarah sat in the gathering darkness. Rain had begun to slant against the bay window. She didn't know what to do. Should she go into the bedroom and console Nigel, or take herself off to a friend's house and give him the space to try and come to terms with this astonishing news? In the end she decided that she couldn't leave Nigel alone like this. Clearly he was shattered by this discovery. And just as clearly Gerald, the man he had believed was his father, cared for Nigel not one jot, or he wouldn't be walking out on him just after his mother had died and as he was about to marry. Was it possible he could be so callous? Admittedly, Gerald had always come across to Sarah as distant and somewhat detached, but she knew herself that sometimes those who are very shy often appear stand-offish and vague. Especially men of a certain age; they just couldn't do the small talk that women seemed to use to good effect in difficult social situations. Gerald talked about routes and whether the A11 was a better bet than the A140 on a bank holiday, how best to avoid the contra flows and the merits or otherwise of various motorway service areas on the M4. However, he had always made an effort and been perfectly pleasant to Sarah. He had tried to show an interest in her research on the fatty acid chain, and he was also very encouraging about her PhD studies. He was clearly impressed that Nigel had attracted a fiancée who was so intelligent and capable. He thought them well suited and said as much.

"I can't have done too badly then," he had remarked once, allowing himself a small congratulatory smile. When Sarah thought about this comment now, it took on a whole new meaning. It was not what Gerald had actually said, but what he had left unsaid: "considering I am not his father". Perhaps this would have been how Gerald would have finished such a sentence had the truth been known.

What could it have been like for him all these years, bringing up a child who was not his own? And at the same time harbouring this secret, unable to express his true feelings, watching Marion groom and fuss over Nigel and believing that he didn't have the right to interfere because Nigel wasn't really his. Although no blame could attach itself to an infertile man, that might not be how Gerald saw it. He might have felt emasculated, or useless and empty. Nigel was right; it explained a lot.

They would have to go and see Gerald, together.

5

Things Can Only Get Better

"So you can see, Minister, how meditation, introduced into the prison service for both officers and inmates alike, could be of the most enormous benefit."

So far Michael had been able to keep a straight face. Life as a minister and as an MP was certainly varied, but nothing had prepared him for this meeting with two members of the Levitation Party. They were, in all seriousness, suggesting that the Home Office set up a controlled study of meditation for criminals. Senegal, they went on to explain, had seen its recidivist rates drop dramatically and apparently this was all due to the alteration of the alpha rhythms in the brain during meditation.

He couldn't wait to get home and tell Julia over a good bottle of Shiraz. Julia had an excellent sense of humour and he always enjoyed sharing the more amusing incidents of parliamentary life with her. Michael hid his mouth under his hand and nodded sagely. He couldn't quite trust himself not to laugh. No one would have imagined looking at this neat, unremarkable couple that they could possibly be proponents of anything more unusual than herb tea.

"So you are saying that when – in Senegal, is it? – there was a mass meditation, the crime rate for the whole population fell. Now, wouldn't that be because everyone was occupied meditating?" he asked. The woman, in a neat green dress, began to correct this mistaken and cynical suggestion.

There was a tap on the office door and Michael was rescued by Tim. After some time Tim or Geraldine always popped in to hasten a speedy conclusion. Michael had found from experience that after twenty minutes of putting their case, people just began to repeat themselves by which time he invariably had enough information to know what action, if any, he would take.

"Excuse me," Tim nodded to the two visitors. "Your taxi is waiting, Michael. You are due at your next venue in five minutes."

Michael promised to consider their suggestions seriously and stated firmly that he was in favour of anything that reduced stress. In another couple of minutes they were ushered out. They did not appear unhappy with the response from the Minister.

It was the end of a long day and a hard week, and Michael's next call, an hour and a half later than planned, was home, Julia, and the girls.

*

Michael had met Julia on a children's ward where she was the hospital teacher, her first job. She ensured the chronically sick or long stay children weren't bored witless or falling too far behind with their schoolwork. It was her voice that caught his attention. She was completely hidden from view, behind a curtain, drawn around the bed of a young girl awaiting a life-saving bone marrow transplant. She was reading from a poetry book, Roald Dahl's 'Revolting Rhymes'. It was a silly poem about an anteater. Its humour relied on a convincing American accent to muddle the distinction between ant and aunt. She read it brilliantly. The child laughed, a small hopeful laugh. Michael stood on the other side of the curtain, absorbed. The voice was steady and soothing and quite unlike any other voice he had ever heard. He was captivated. He moved away as soon as she had finished the Dahl story, embarrassed to be caught eavesdropping on what was obviously a private moment. Later, as he was attending another child further down the ward, Julia emerged from behind the curtain and he saw that her looks were a perfect match for the extraordinary loveliness of her voice. She had shoulder-length, naturally fair hair that turned up slightly at the ends, and beautiful almond-shaped green eyes. Her lips were full and when she smiled her face came alive with a translucent, beatific quality and the delicacy of a Renaissance painting. Fleetingly she looked towards Michael. Then she turned and left the ward, although her presence remained, like the tracing of an angel.

After this Michael couldn't stop thinking about her. She appeared in his dreams, and on his ward rounds he would think

28

he heard her and turn suddenly to greet her. But the voice he was hearing was in his head. For two weeks he saw no sign of her. He began to think she must be a visitor; a mother, an aunt or friend. He resorted to asking the ward sister and discovered she was a teacher. Michael inquired about her movements and then contrived to be on the ward at the same time. He failed miserably and always seemed to be looking wistfully after her. When he did finally speak to her, he fluffed it hopelessly. He felt a red flush rise up his neck. Julia was easily ten years younger than he was, and it occurred to him that perhaps his attentions would be unwelcome. Eventually they happened to be at a case conference together and at last he had the opportunity to ask Julia out to dinner. Michael knew then that he was going to marry her.

Their wedding took place on a bright, clear June day at the Catholic Church on the hill in Bishop's Stortford. The photographer captured Julia under falling rose petals, head thrown back and laughing, looking perfectly beautiful. Michael, barely able to comprehend his good fortune, counted himself the happiest man alive.

They had both anticipated a large family but Julia had a dreadful time delivering Katherine: the placenta had come away and she had haemorrhaged badly. Etched forever in Michael's memory was the terrible night when she had woken him to say she felt sure that her waters had broken. But when they turned on the lamp and pulled back the duvet, the bed was drenched in blood and his beloved Julia was already grey. Though the baby survived, Julia lost her womb and the hope of more children. It was three weeks before the fragile Katherine was pronounced fit to leave the special care baby unit, and it was a miracle they came through such an ordeal at all. Michael remembered this as a twilight period in their lives. Days and nights were spent camping out at the hospital. Their friends Breeda and Finn had scooped up Tess, just over two years old, settling her in with their own brood for the duration. Michael had often stood looking out of the seventh floor window, having just left Katherine – a fragile life – in her incubator, looking down in reflective wonder at the distant streets below, where the ant-like people hurried about, unaware that above them lay tiny scraps of humanity wired to machines, new lives hanging in the balance.

There would be no son for Michael. He would remain a solitary male in a family of women. He told himself he should be grateful, he had both his wife and daughter. Yet often playing like a film at the back of his mind was a screening of Michael and this boy, the son he would have taken camping, cheered from the touchline and taught intricate fingering on the piano. He and Julia grieved quite separately and it took Michael time to accommodate the loss of this rumbustious family and this mythical child that he had conjured up in his mind's eye.

*

"So tell me again, darling, what exactly do they want you to do?" Julia asked whilst dressing the salad.

"Yogic flying, probably in the House of Commons," Michael joked.

"Now, now, don't be unfair. After all, if it works it could save taxpayers a fortune. The prison population can't go on growing inexorably," Julia joked.

Michael slipped his hand around her waist and kissed her softly on the nape of her neck.

"It could be handy, I suppose. If we teach inmates to levitate you could probably fit more men to a cell."

"Oh, Michael, you're dreadful..." Julia slipped away and put the salad on the table. "That well-intentioned couple are your constituents too and you should treat them with consideration."

"In fact, darling, they're my opponents. They are, after all, a political party, which is where the problem lies. I feel sure you could introduce a programme of meditation into prisons, but not as a political party. That would be seen as drumming up business."

"Pity. I could see it working," Julia mused.

"What? Creating more bed space?"

"No, silly. Relaxing inmates, helping them review their lives, even changing their behaviour."

"I think, Julia, I should warn Father Frank of your conversion. Before we know it, you'll be sitting in a white room on a cushion humming and chanting."

Julia hit him playfully with the dishcloth, and added laughingly, "My lot do that already, it's called going on a retreat!"

*

Michael was an accidental MP and he had always considered promotion unlikely. He was a bit of a maverick, his own man. He could be somewhat opinionated and occasionally, in interviews, he didn't trot out the party line. Often he didn't know exactly what the party line was. It got him into trouble. He unfairly gained a reputation for being outspoken when, in fact, his pronouncements were merely his own notion of common sense.

"No, of course the NHS couldn't fund operations on request. Transsexuals, for example, should clearly pay for gender reassignment themselves. I even understand NHS surgeons have been chopping limbs off body dysmorphics!" he blithely told a women's magazine which was featuring MPs at home. "And some of the advances in IVF treatment are clearly beyond the public purse. Given their high failure rate and questionable merit, in my view some techniques are unethical and immoral and prey on vulnerable, desperate people, at the same time lining the pockets of doctors who should know better. A lot of these fertility guys are millionaires, you know."

"In what way unethical and immoral? Our readers would be interested in your views, especially as you were once a GP – at the sharp end, so to speak," the pretty young journalist asked.

So Michael, warming to his theme, continued at length.

Once again he was taken aside by Logan, the press secretary, and strongly advised that should he have ambitions of a post in Health he would have to curb his tongue.

"Good God, man, such careless talk could bring up that whole issue of rationing again!"

"There has always been rationing in the health service," Michael retorted.

"Yes, but Joe Public doesn't know that and now is not the time to tell him," Logan countered.

"So what am I to say when asked such a question?" Michael

enquired.

"You answer a different question. You turn it around, and put the government in a good light – tell them how the waiting lists are coming down," Logan replied, clearly exasperated. "Talk about our initiatives on cancer, and heart disease, and the targets we're setting – and meeting. For goodness' sake, Michael, you must have heard that tactic often enough on the 'Today' programme. It was only a bloody woman's magazine. It's not as if you were being interviewed by Jeremy Paxman!"

"Well then, you had better behave," Julia had advised as she rubbed his weary shoulders, "if you do want something in Health."

"Wretched spin doctors, putting their slant on everything. I can't stand Logan – he's such a smooth bastard. And he's always slicking his hair back, he gives me the creeps," Michael complained. "The general public may value freedom of speech, but it's not a privilege I enjoy, not any more."

When Michael was invited onto a parliamentary committee he realised that this was where the effective work of parliament took place. Gradually he began to feel he was of some use and that real change was now, finally, possible. Nevertheless, it came as a complete surprise to both Michael and Julia when, later that year, the call came from the Prime Minister's office and Michael was offered the post of a junior minister, not in Health, but in the brand new Ministry for the Family. After two years in this role, Michael's elevation to Minister came about after a tragedy; Jennifer Wentworth stepped down, her teenage son having suffered a serious and disabling accident, and Michael was appointed her successor. It presented an exciting challenge and he threw himself into the role with enthusiasm.

It had never been Julia's intention to marry young and have her first child at twenty-five. She had methodically planned her career. Her interest lay with vulnerable children with special needs, hence her work at the hospital. She hoped to go on to train in specialist learning support and had become very interested in brain function and visual perception. She was hoping to combine that study with teaching and later a PhD, but then she hadn't bargained on meeting someone extraordinary like Michael. She had been slightly in awe of him and when he proposed to her, she wondered whether the age gap would matter. She asked her mother's opinion. Rosalind was adamant; she approved of Michael.

"If it were the other way round," she said, "it might matter. But older men have always married younger women. You get a husband with experience and an established career, and twenty-four to thirty-six isn't too much of a gap. Think yourself lucky, you won't have to struggle to make ends meet. And Michael is a delight, Julia. After all, none of us knows what life has in store. Your father and I were the same age, yet he dropped dead of a heart attack at forty-seven! Perhaps God plans to take you before Michael. We just don't know. I wouldn't give it a second thought," she added briskly. Typical of Mother, thought Julia, bringing up death amid the wedding preparations.

And it didn't seem to make a difference, the age gap, not for years anyway. If she were honest, she would have to say that now Michael tired more easily and he could be a little impatient with the girls. Tess, twelve, had a boyfriend; it was nothing really, just a friend who happened to be a boy, a nice lad from school named Steven who had taken her to the cinema a couple of times. But Michael was cautious and tended to be overprotective. Tess and he had rows about make-up, nail varnish and skirt lengths and Julia had to arbitrate. They didn't get out much as a couple either, so she had to be content with her activities for the church and outings with other mothers.

Julia was torn between her efforts to establish a near normal family life and the unsettling notion that opportunities were passing her by. Visits to the cinema and theatre were a distant memory. Occasionally they drove to Hanbridge, which had a concert hall and was an hour away. But Julia didn't find a concert a sociable occasion. Looking up at the soloist giving her all, Julia felt guilty when, inevitably, she drifted off into her own world and she would tick herself off mentally when she found herself making shopping lists and worrying about labelling gym kit. A glance in Michael's direction found him utterly lost in the music, totally enraptured. But then Michael always had a love of the classics; he played the piano wonderfully and he could have made music his career. The only fixed engagement Julia insisted upon was the monthly Sunday lunch with their four oldest Wynshore friends, Breeda and Finn, Andrew and Moya. It kept Michael in touch with the real world. Julia had returned briefly to teaching when Katherine had started school, but it was hopeless. With Michael away all week, she spent most of her salary on childminders to cover her absences for meetings and parents' evenings. Tess, then seven, started to wake at night and the children couldn't depend on seeing much of either parent. After two terms Julia gave up the job and resigned herself to the role of full-time mother, with occasional forays into art classes at the local adult institute as well as chair of the Parent Teachers Association. Her days were spent running the girls to and from their various activities, planning events such as the Christmas Fayre and fitting in Beginner's French, all against the background as an MP's wife.

Julia tried to console herself with the thought that Katherine would probably be off to university in eight years and that she would, by then, be only forty-six.With luck it wouldn't be too late to get her career back on track.

6

Ordinary People

"I'm not really in the mood for this you know," Michael complained mildly to Julia, who was basting the chickens.

"You always say that and then you enjoy yourself. Anyway it does you good, brings you down to earth. If it weren't for these lunches you'd never come into contact with normal people," Julia countered.

"And since when has Breeda fitted in the category 'normal'?" Michael was easing the cork from a bottle of Shiraz. "For reasons I don't understand people who practise aromatherapy and that sort of nonsense always seek out a doctor to harangue! Now I'm a minister as well, I'm a sitting duck. I swear Breeda only comes here to pick an argument with me. For some perverse reason she always seeks my opinion, which she then dismisses completely out of hand."

"Because, not only are you a doctor – and Breeda believes that doctors conspire with the multinational drug companies to pump us full of pills we don't need – but she sees you as a direct line to the seat of power. She imagines you putting her views to the PM over a cup of tea at Number 10. Anyway, darling, you really shouldn't tease. Breeda is very kind and I judge her by her children, all of whom are a delight. Quite an achievement when you have five." Julia defended her friend gamely. "Remember what a wonderful support she's been to us over the years."

"You're right as usual," Michael agreed and, clasping Julia by the waist, he snatched a kiss.

They had made these friends, Breeda and Finn McLarty, Moya and Andrew Carlton, soon after arriving in Wynshore. In fact, Breeda had been one of the first people to welcome Julia, and she had always been grateful for that. They were pregnant together, and Breeda's introduction of Julia to the mother-and-toddler group in the church hall had been an instant inroad into the community.

They helped one another move furniture, turned out garages and sheds, ferried children to and from Woodcraft Folk and swimming, scooped them up in emergencies and put them into a sleeping bag and a spare bed. These friends were the warp and weft of Julia's life and they bound her to Wynshore, gave her a sense of belonging and kept her sane and happy.

Breeda and Finn's house was full of extraordinary and eclectic finds as they were very good at picking up bargains at sales. Breeda collected the cast offs from de-consecrated churches, any denomination, she didn't mind. "I'm very ecumenical," she would say, laughing. Statuary, gargoyles, pews, offertory boxes with rows of candles and her triumph, a Blessed Virgin Mary six feet high and with her arms outstretched to a group of children dressed ready for an Enid Blyton adventure. "Five Go Mad With Mary," Michael called it. The Blessed Virgin stood on a very large window ledge at the top of the stairs in front of some late Victorian stained glass. Hard to ignore, the Madonna stared down with gentle beneficence. When all Breeda's children came thundering past Mary trembled, as each one slapped her upturned, paint-flaked palm rather in the manner of a 'high five' and then mumbled, "Holy Mary, Mother of God" very fast.

Who knows what their priest, Father Frank, thought? He was often invited to share a meal and a drop of the Irish.

"I see the Blessed Virgin remains in pole position," he would say to Breeda with a twinkle in his eye.

Julia just didn't have the knack when it came to auctions, she often paid too much and never noticed the terrible stain or wonky leg until she got home, and only then realised that she had paid over the odds. Michael liked fine furniture, which they bought from the local antique dealers. "You're mad, Michael, to pay their prices!" Breeda would exclaim.

The meal prepared at these friendly gatherings was always much the same, a roast, except in high summer, when they would all decamp to the garden for a barbecue. There were, however, certain strictures regarding this informal gathering; the meat, and all the produce for the meal had to be organic, as Breeda didn't allow her family to eat anything else. Once, Michael tried to ignore this regulation but was soon caught out by Breeda's inquisition as to the supplier.

"Have you seen the price of this stuff?" Michael had once railed. "Eight quid for a chicken and with Breeda's tribe we need two, if not three! And how on earth can they afford to pay that when there are seven of them?"

Julia heard a car on the gravel.

"That'll be them now. Good, the vegetables are almost done."

Andrew arrived first in the kitchen with Breeda as they had shared the car journey. He kissed Julia lightly on the cheek. Breeda was re-plaiting her long auburn hair.

"Sorry. Father Frank wanted to bend Moya's ear about a family he knows – a bit of free legal advice, child custody or some such and you know how he can talk. Is that Michael playing, or a record?"

"It's Michael. Get yourself a drink and join him." Andrew helped himself to a glass of wine and wandered off towards the drawing room. "Where's Moya?"

"Oh, she's just out in the car changing her shoes, and Finn's getting the wine from the boot." As Andrew left by one door, to go and listen to Michael, Moya and their son Tom arrived through the other. Tom was the image of his father, tall, blonde and fair skinned with a scattering of freckles across the bridge of his nose mingling with his acne. He was fourteen, an awkward age in a boy, made worse by being an only child with little opportunity to mix. He preferred the company of adults.

"Tom, the girls are up in the attic with Breeda's lot, if you want to go up. Can you tell them all to wash their hands in five minutes and then come down." Tom smiled meekly and shuffled off.

"Sorry, I couldn't get away. Father Frank," Moya began apologetically.

"Yes, Andrew said he'd collared you. Drink?" Breeda stood ready with a glass and bottle in hand.

"Just what I need. Julia, where do you want this?" she asked, offering a cheesecake. Dessert was a shared responsibility, and the cheesecake joined the chocolate mousse in the fridge. "Is that

Michael playing, or a record?"

Julia laughed.

"That's just what Andrew said, word for word. And it's Michael."

"Oh God, we're becoming one and the same person. When Father Frank asked us about this child custody case we both said in unison: 'It will be hard to offer an opinion, Father, without knowing the full circumstances'. Can you believe it? That's what seventeen years of marriage does to you!"

Gradually the group drifted towards the music. Michael was just finishing playing 'Moonlight Sonata'. Their friends were draped casually around the room. Andrew sat on the arm of a wing-back chair that Moya was comfortably settled in. Breeda sat on the sofa, her legs curled up under her, having kicked off her shoes. Finn was leaning against the marble mantlepiece sipping his wine. Julia smiled contentedly. Good friends, a good family and Michael seducing them all with his gifted playing – what more could she ask for?

Michael finished the sonata with the lightest touch. Julia put her glass down and joined in the gentle applause.

"A joy to listen to, as ever, Michael! Beautiful."

"Thank you, Breeda, and how are you?"

"I'm well, Michael. And yourself?"

"I'm as good and as busy as ever." Michael surveyed the room full of friends. Breeda had on her Sunday best, an outdated floral Laura Ashley dress. It hung oddly on her and had probably been used as a maternity dress in the past. Breeda was rarely seen in a dress except for church. She worked part-time at an organic food co-operative, and jeans and a baggy shirt was her uniform. She was a lovely looking woman with quick, flashing green eyes and creamy skin, her hair pre-Raphaelite in length, colour and texture. She wore it plaited or twisted up and she would often plait and unplait it whilst talking.

"Are you set to become a star in the next reshuffle and get your dream job in Health?" Breeda asked mischievously.

"That's as likely as Father Frank giving up celibacy," Michael said.

Julia sent him a reproving look.

"I'll call the children down. Can you give me a hand, Breeda?" She asked in an effort to separate them. Breeda uncurled her legs and, slipping her feet into her shoes, moved towards the door.

"You never know, Michael, more than once I've seen Father Frank with a twinkle in his eye. He might surprise us all. I believe a married priesthood is inevitable, you know. Now there's a lively topic for our lunchtime chat!" Breeda smiled wickedly and ducked out of the doorway.

"I can see it's separate ends of the table for the naughty children who argue all the time," Moya admonished Michael lightheartedly, as she rose to see to the children and help Julia. "It's not the House of Commons, you don't have to be combative."

"Lively debate, Moya. Just a bit of fun." Michael winked.

"Ah, but does Breeda know that? Anyway, I shall leave you men to your bit of fun."

"That's me told off," said Michael, turning to Andrew and Finn.

Michael liked Moya, she was an intelligent woman. In her he found someone with whom he could converse about pressing issues of the day without acrimony. She would weigh up the pros and cons of any argument and evaluate the merits of each without prejudice. Michael valued her opinion. She was small, elfin and lively. She had close-cropped fair hair and a tiny waist. Moya wore expensive casual clothes, often trousers, but was always smart, neat and tailored. She was a partner in a local firm of solicitors; her field was criminal law. Mostly she seemed to plead for the disaffected young men who were constantly in front of the bench for stealing cars or TWOC as they referred to it, taking without consent. They moved on from such petty crime to drugs and general thuggery. Moya took it all in her stride, always appearing cheerful and confidently at ease.

Andrew, a gynaecologist, was equally likeable.

"So, Michael, what about these proposals for recruiting nurses?" Andrew asked without hesitation. It was obviously on his mind. "Without foreign nurses the Health Service will be on its knees. Have they no idea the havoc this will cause?"

Michael considered that one of the many hazards of being an MP was that at any social occasion, even good friends would lambaste you for any hare-brained scheme the current administration put forward.

"I know, Andrew. Believe me, it's not a proposal I endorse. But half of these nurses only stay six months, or a year at most. They almost never complete their contracts and often they are desperately needed in their own countries. Now that's not right. It was only ever supposed to be a short term measure and it's costing the earth," Michael concluded.

"You know that the solution to recruitment lies in pay and conditions. Girls today have a million other better opportunities," Andrew persisted.

"It's not even my department; my opinion isn't sought and my recommendations certainly wouldn't be followed," Michael stated firmly and then, changing the subject, he turned to Finn.

"How are you, Finn? Have they fixed that flat roof yet?"

"They're leading me a merry dance – I'm threatening solicitors for all the good it'll do. Every time it rains we're out with buckets. It's getting Breeda down. She wants me to get in someone else and she blames me in the first place for taking the cheapest quote."

"It's their responsibility to put it right. Threaten them with the trading standards authority."

Finn disliked accepting any offers of assistance from Michael, the man was only trying to help but sometimes he came across as condescending, a touch too paternalistic. Finn sensed that a casual arrogance had crept in. The business of politics encouraged it.

In the kitchen the children, who were being fed first, were wolfing down roast chicken and all the trimmings.

"So there's water pouring through the ceiling, and buckets and washing up bowls all over the shop, and what does Finn say? 'The forecast for tomorrow is dry.' 'Dry!' I said, 'I'll give you dry.' He has a week to sort it or I'll get someone else in."

"Builders are impossible!" Moya agreed.

"And roofers are the worst; they know full well you can't see what it is you're getting for all that money, and you'll only find out when it pours with rain, which it holds off doing until they've had your money and long gone!"

"We need to have this kitchen done – I hate this pine, it's so dated and shabby," Julia said. "And it's far too small. We should all be able to eat in here together."

"Dated we just have to live with," Breeda said briskly.

"It's not just that. Half the drawers are falling out and the doors don't stay shut," Julia added defensively.

Julia disliked the way she found herself either hiding or justifying every purchase to Breeda. They were comfortable, but nothing like Moya and Andrew; with the dual income of a lawyer and a consultant they really were well off. They lived in an interesting white, nineteen thirties house on a smart road on the outskirts of Wynshore. The house looked liked a liner. They both had very modern, cutting-edge taste though Michael maintained it was cold and austere. For some odd reason, Breeda never questioned their wealth, at least not openly. It was the idea that Michael was being paid out of the public purse – taxpayers' money – that Julia suspected irked Breeda, as if somehow Michael didn't earn his living but was kept!

"Call the men in, would you, Breeda?" And shooting a desperate glance to Moya, Julia said, "I hope we're not treading on eggshells today."

"Just stay clear of home renovation, education, religion, and any government initiatives and it should all go swimmingly," Moya laughed.

*

"God, you're lovely," Michael said in that slightly lazy manner he had after drinking good wine. Julia was slipping out of her dressing gown, having taken a long bath. He was observing her from his vantage point on the bed.

"Darling, come here." He held out his hand and pulled her gently down onto the bed beside him. The palm of his hand ran lightly over her shoulder and down onto her breast, caressing and stroking her tenderly. "Your skin's so soft and warm…you know I'm such a lucky, lucky man…the luckiest man alive."

"You don't think this might be the wine altering your senses?"

Julia asked softly, as she bent to kiss him lightly on the mouth.

"Why would I need wine to alter my senses when I have you?" Michael kissed her and guided her on to him. Julia rose up and down steadily and rhythmically.

"Oh….Julia…" he moaned.

Finally, when Julia was wrapped in his arms with her head on his chest, and thinking it was a fitting finale to a wonderful day he whispered softly into her ear:

"Aren't we lucky to have such good and kind friends?"

"Mm..." she agreed sleepily and snuggled even closer, "You're drunk."

"I love you, Julia." Michael kissed her head gently and together they fell deeply asleep.

February. A clinic, London, thirty years ago.

"*What, the lanky one? Ooh he's very nice; he wouldn't have to fill a specimen jar for me. He could just use the good old tried and tested impregnation technique!*" *Nurse Carol Roberts was reporting back to her good friend Mandy on the current 'talent' she had observed sitting outside in the waiting room.* "*And clearly a very productive stud, from the look of all these little fellows romping around in here,*" *she added, having taken a quick look down the microscope.* "*So who's the lucky lady?*" *She turned to the wooden board holding that afternoon's client cards.* "*God, never in a million years would you put those two together!*"

"*The wonders of science,*" *said Mandy.*

7

Family Values

The brouhaha over what exactly the Minister for the Family had, or hadn't, said on 'Question Time' died a sudden death in the media. It was the shock news that Hugo Amery, the elected Mayor of London successfully fielded by the opposition, had, prior to his selection and subsequent election, provided an influential member of the selection committee with an evening's lavish entertainment that included the attentions of a leggy blonde, Miss Carrie Sobel. Carrie had, in the nineties, appeared in several tawdry films with titles such as 'Teacher Knows Best', 'Teacher's Pet' and 'Bunny Gets the Cane'. Carrie wore a gown, mortarboard and not a great deal else. Her speciality, corrective instruction to overgrown public schoolboys. Carrie counted barristers, judges, politicians and several peers of the realm amongst her clientele. A picture of Carrie in full regalia, standing triumphant over a be-suited male, her foot pressing into his back and the whip in her hand tilting his neck towards the camera, graced several of the tabloid editions. Next to it featured a photograph of the disgraced Mayor being driven away by his long-suffering wife to their country retreat. Sleaze was once again back on the agenda.

Michael couldn't help a small grin of satisfaction spreading across his face when he read the headline. Hugo Amery was overdue for such a fall. He had spent years getting away with double dealing and duplicitous acts that bordered on the criminal. Thanks to this sudden and spectacular fall from grace, Michael could get on with his work.

*

Sarah and Nigel visited Gerald the following Sunday. As it was a bright spring day they walked from Brentwood station, hand in hand and lost in thought. They arrived at the modest detached house, built in the nineteen thirties, the exterior part pebble-dash. It was well maintained and orderly, like Gerald himself. It had an old world, musty air and its furnishings were dated; it could have belonged to a much older person than Gerald. Reaching the porch they waited under its round brick arch. Sarah turned to Nigel and asked quietly:

"All right?"

"Yes, fine," Nigel replied. Clearly he was anxious. Sarah had no idea how the meeting would go, she was worried for Nigel. He had barely spoken all week. Occasionally Sarah would put forward some hypothesis to explain Gerald's behaviour and Nigel would register her suggestion with a brief nod, a 'maybe', or a 'perhaps'. But apart from that, he would say nothing and he appeared withdrawn. She wondered how he was managing at school.

She rang the doorbell and, after what seemed an eternity, Gerald appeared behind the mullion glass in the door and opened it.

"Hello, you two," he said genially. "Come in. Good journey?"

"Not too bad," Sarah replied and pecked him on the cheek. They ate shepherd's pie and peas for lunch. It turned out that Gerald had made it himself.

"What do you think, Sarah? Not bad, eh?"

"I think it's excellent, Gerald, and I think it's great that you took the trouble to cook it yourself," Sarah replied, genuinely impressed.

"I've joined a cookery club at the local college. I can't live off packet food for the rest of my life and I enjoy the company – keeps me out of mischief." Gerald smiled and looked very pleased with himself.

"That sounds like an good idea, doesn't it, Nigel?"

"Yes. Yes, very good," Nigel agreed absently.

Gerald liked Sarah. He'd always thought she and Nigel were well suited. She was a pretty girl in a rather unassuming way. Her hair was dark, almost black, and worn in a neat bob, and she dressed well though she had to be careful with money. She was only getting paid a modest salary for her work at the research centre while studying for her doctorate. He had met her parents in the run up to the wedding and they seemed a very nice couple, educated, comfortable and decent sort of people. Gerald thought Nigel had done well, rather better than he had expected. With Marion as a mother, Nigel had been fussed over all his life and could have easily turned out queer, or gay as it was called these days. In fact, that was really what Gerald had expected. He was surprised he had become such a fine young man given the mollycoddling he had received. Perhaps it really was all down to his genes? Previously, it was considered that your environment formed your character. Now, all that had been turned on its head. They seemed to have found the genes for all sorts of traits, talents and defects. This possibly explained Nigel's intellect and remarkable musical ability, because it certainly didn't come from Marion, and Gerald had left the boy's upbringing to her, believing it wasn't his place to interfere. Perhaps he had been wrong. Certainly now, when babies arrived in all sorts of extraordinary ways, he wouldn't feel the level of embarrassment that he had when Nigel was conceived. Now he would be an involved father, or so he imagined. He had always felt that there was another presence in the family. He hadn't ever been able to express this to Marion but it was there, quite distinctly. Nigel was, and always would be, another man's child.

They ate ice cream with chocolate sauce for dessert. Gerald explained that puddings came later in his cookery course, so Nigel and Sarah would have to come for lunch again. Sarah was pleased, as she took this to mean that Gerald had reconsidered dashing off to Malta. They cleared the table together and Sarah offered to wash up and make the coffee. It would give Nigel and Gerald an opportunity to talk alone.

"I wanted you told from the outset – from babyhood so to speak," Gerald maintained. "And even your mother believed that it wasn't a good thing to start out a new life with a lie. But then you were born and your Uncle Stan and Auntie Agnes peered in the crib and started on about how like me you looked and what a proper little Laing you were and wasn't I proud? And I was proud of you, Nigel, I still am. It just seemed easier not to say anything, to go along with it all. And Marion had read somewhere that ten per cent of babies aren't fathered by their father, if you see what I mean, and no one knows the difference. So why would it matter?"

"But it does matter," Nigel stated flatly. "Not because you weren't a good father to me, you were, you are. But I want to know who my real father is." Nigel paused lost in thought for a moment. "I used to think I was adopted but then I saw a likeness to Mother. I never expected this, not in a million years. I shouldn't exist, not in any normal world. Babies are made at the very least by the coupling of two human beings, even if they loathe one another. But I'm the product of farming meets science fiction. My family is artificial. My entire life to date is based on a falsehood, a lie. Why? Why have me at all? I can't imagine my mother doing this, being inseminated with the sperm of a complete stranger. It's unbelievable. *Mother!* Of all people!"

Gerald shifted uncomfortably and said in his wife's defence:

"It was all she ever wanted, a family. And, after all, it was my fault."

"How?" Nigel asked.

"Well, by not having any... you know, none that worked anyway," Gerald added rather uncomfortably. "She had to have lots of tests before they realised it was me. It was very demeaning. You must realise, Nigel, that in those days, lots of women didn't have careers, not women like Marion. It might not seem that long ago but believe me the world was a very different place to the one we live in now. With only a handful of 'O' levels in domestic science, needlework and religious education, most women just had jobs as shop assistants or filing clerks, only the very brightest girls went to university. If Marion didn't have a family, then all she would have been was a housewife looking after me, not exactly fulfilling. A lifetime of putting the tea on the table for six o'clock and cleaning a house that never got untidy with only the two of us in it. She was very down, depressed. And the doctor was quite definite: with a sperm count as low as mine, conception was out of the question. We looked into adopting, but babies for adoption were hard to come by and it took forever. She did try to reconcile herself to being childless but she was miserable. And then she read an article in some medical magazine that she found in a dentist's waiting room. It was about sperm donation and how you could have a baby with sperm that another man had donated. I was dead against it at first, shocked that

47

she could suggest such a thing. But she got so low in the end that I gave in."

"Where did you go? How did you know what to do?" Nigel wanted any shred of information, anything at all that might help him understand.

"We went to our doctor, who was very sympathetic. First he put her on some pills but they didn't do any good. They didn't think to check on me – not in the beginning. Eventually he said he knew of a chap in London who might be able to put us onto someone, not in Harley Street but just around the corner from there, Wimpole Street I believe it was. It was very expensive. Marion had to have various tests and an examination and then she was referred to this clinic. I say clinic, but it was just a large private house."

"Where was it?" Nigel asked urgently.

"North London, somewhere quite posh," Gerald replied vaguely. "Hampstead, I think."

"Hampstead? You don't sound too sure."

"Oh, I didn't go. I was hardly going to go along for the ride. Marion went on her own, right time of the month, you see. She just had to lie down and have it…you know. I think she said they kept her lying down for an hour, to give it all a better chance to work and then they gave her a cup of tea and she came home."

"And that was it? I was conceived?"

"Oh no." Gerald said. "It didn't work. You were third time lucky and a good deal later on. It was expensive and I had said that if it didn't work first time then that was it, forget the whole thing. But when Marion found out she wasn't pregnant, she sobbed as if her heart would break. She was crying when I left for work in the morning and I found her sobbing when I came home that evening. Her face was all swollen and eyes were red and puffed up and she'd try and stop herself, get control of herself, but these terrible sobs would just come up from deep inside her. I couldn't see her suffering like that and the doctor said that I was being unrealistic and to give it a fair chance. He said if we were doing it the usual way, I couldn't expect it to work first time, which was right."

Gerald's eyes filled with tears. He coughed and then, regaining control, continued, "I said we'd do whatever it took and, as I say, third time we struck lucky. It was worth it just for the look on Marion's face when she held you. Radiant doesn't begin to describe her." Gerald ran his hands back through his hair, let out a sigh and relaxed visibly.

Nigel looked at him and for the first time saw him as he was. A man edging into old age, thick at the waist, his hair showing the first signs of thinning and his cheeks flushed and veined. This must have been a speech he had gone through in his mind a thousand times over the years, preparing to explain to his son why he was not his son, how his very existence had come about, why he was here at all. They both sat in silence. Finally, Nigel asked:

"And you never thought of doing it again, trying for another baby?"

"No. I wouldn't have agreed to that," Gerald replied.

"Why? You'd done it once."

"The cost was one reason, an important one too. It was more than we could afford and it put us in debt and for the only time in our lives, I might add. I felt we should be grateful to have you, a lovely healthy baby and we wouldn't get the same sperm again. These days I believe they can do that, but back then it wasn't done; so your brother or sister would have had another father – and three fathers in one family! It didn't seem right to me. Marion accepted that decision and, in truth, I don't think she would have wanted to go through it all again, the pull on the emotions was just too much for her."

"Did you ever talk about it?" Nigel asked.

"A bit. The first few months we were very sensitive and we expected people to guess that you weren't mine. I think Marion did for the rest of her life. She only ever told Dorothy. She was forever saying how like me you were in front of people, it used to drive me mad. How I didn't just lose my temper and blurt it out one day I'll never know. Everything from your musical ability to the dimple on your chin was put down to my side of the family! She fussed over you and preened you, though I could see you hated it."

"Why did you never say anything – tell her to stop?"

"It wouldn't have made any difference, Nigel. It was her way of coping and, as you weren't actually my son, I didn't really feel I had the right." Gerald paused. "Funny thing is, you know, if there was an outsider in our family, it was me, not you. I didn't want to interfere because I never wanted your mother to turn round to me and say in anger that you weren't my son. I never wanted you to hear it that way."

The living room door opened.

"How are you two getting on?" Sarah asked rather too brightly, as she carried in the tray of coffee. She set it down on the table and looked up expectantly.

"Dad has just told me the story of my creation. I can still call you Dad?" Nigel asked.

"Of course, if you still want to." Gerald was leaning forward to take a cup from the tray. He helped himself to sugar still avoiding Nigel's gaze.

"I know this is very difficult, Gerald, but we really want you to come to the wedding. Will you come?" Sarah asked, tucking her hair behind her ears.

"Yes, but only if you're both sure you want me there. I rather thought that Nigel might have strong feelings…" His voice broke and trailed away. Sarah reached over and gave his hand a squeeze.

"Of course we want you there, don't we, Nigel?" Sarah looked to Nigel for reassurance.

"You're the only father I've got. Please come," Nigel replied.

He could have put it better, Sarah thought.

"Good, that's settled then," she said.

*

Breeda and Moya were slumped, exhausted, in Julia's kitchen; it was Tuesday, and they had just had a game of tennis.

"I thought I was fit, but will you just look at the state of me?" Breeda, red faced, clutched the glass of water Julia had provided and took occasional sips. "Running around after all these children – you'd think I'd be able to manage an hour of tennis without going into a total state of collapse, now wouldn't you?"

"It's different muscle groups. Besides you have to keep running around the court for an hour." Julia turned and took off her navy track-suit top and flung it over the back of a pine chair. She switched on the kettle.

"We'll feel better for it really and, if we played two or three times a week, we'd be as fit as a fiddle in no time," Moya said.

"Lessons would help. I know for a fact that I still don't bring my arm back far enough and also when I miss-hit, and the ball doesn't come off the centre of the racquet, it sends a dreadful pain up my arm," Julia admitted, dropping into a chair opposite Breeda.

"There's no money for lessons," Breeda said. "And no time either. I wonder sometimes are other women as exhausted as I am?"

"If they've five children, very probably. I don't know how you do it."

"Ah, but I do have Finn to help and I know I complain about him all the time. But he is an extra pair of hands when I need them, bath time, meals, that sort of thing. You're a single parent with Michael away all week and, let's face it, when he's home he's not wanting to do chores and help out, now is he?"

"Hardly. I don't think he has any idea how this house is run or what I do during the week. Actually, that's the one thing I hate about Michael being away from home so much, he loses touch with the mundane necessities of daily life," Julia said. "Our Sunday lunches serve two functions, keeping Michael in touch with his friends and the real world, all at the same time." The kettle boiled and she got up to make coffee.

"That's why politicians make such a bloody awful mess of everything. They start off well intentioned and then, after a few years of living in that glorified boys' club, they forget what the real world is all about," Breeda commented. "I bet half of them don't even know what a supermarket check-out looks like."

"There are a lot more women MPs now," Moya remarked, stirring her coffee.

"And do you think that's made a difference? Because I can't see it. They might be more pro the family, I suppose. At least we've a politician who is a good example to our children. I'm sick and tired of explaining to Seamus and Aislin that these torrid goings-on are not the way decent people behave. Seamus was asking me, after that business with Amery, 'Why would a grown man want to be dressed up as a schoolboy and be caned! Where was the pleasure in that?' he asked."

"Oh yes, Finn told me about that – he thought it was a hoot." Moya laughed.

"Did he now?" Breeda said, wondering when they could have met.

"It's not easy bringing up children these days, is it?" Moya said.

"Don't get me started! The things they come out with, even on the children's news. You have to watch everything they watch. My parents never had to do that, and at home," – Breeda always referred to Ireland as 'home' despite having lived in England half her life – "we were playing out all the time in the fields or the street, and we were only ever allowed into the house for meals and bed. Now the streets aren't safe with all this traffic, and you're worried there's a pervert around every corner. I don't care what they say about the statistics being the same; there are more of those monsters about than ever there were."

Julia sensed the conversation taking a difficult turn. Soon Breeda would bring Michael into it, whereas Julia wanted to keep Michael's work where it belonged, in London, and not have it colour her friendships.

"So are we booking the courts for the same time on Tuesday next week? It seems to be a good time for you both."

"I know, I'm about to go on and you're right to stop me." Breeda got up and moved painfully towards the back door, stooping to pick up her racquet as she went. "Next week's fine, if I can still walk, that is! I'll see you later at school."

"Bye, Breeda, see you later."

"See you next week. I think you should partner Louise," Moya called after her.

"It would at least put me on the winning side…" Breeda's voice trailed away as she walked around to the front of the house.

Julia poured out more coffee.

"For what it's worth Julia," Moya began. "I know what Michael was getting at on 'Question Time', and he's right. Michael's comments provoked a lively debate at home!"

"Oh dear, that doesn't sound too good. I wouldn't like to think that Michael had been the cause of any marital dispute," Julia commented, tongue in cheek.

"No, it wasn't like that. But did you know that women who can't afford treatment are asked to donate their eggs to women with none? Then they get their own treatment free. Now surely that is unethical? It's blackmail!"

"What does Andrew think?" Julia enquired, trying to divert the conversation away from Michael. Friends, even close ones such as Moya were apt to try and make a point to Julia in the hope that she could somehow influence Michael or even government policy; it was an irritating fact of life, and the wife of a minister had to be careful.

"Andrew says considering the state the Health Service is in, he has far more important things to worry about and he believes there's still a mountain to climb."

"I'm sure he's right. I really don't want to get into the politics, Moya. One politician in the family is more than enough. Much of what we read in the papers doesn't go on in this country, it isn't allowed. It's just sensational tabloid headlines. Michael is very grateful for this Amery business, he says he can get on with some real work rather than being reprimanded by Logan and plagued by the press. To the media, politics is just a game."

"I just loathe all this silly point scoring. It's such a distraction. As if there isn't enough to put right in this country," Moya said.

"Absolutely." Julia brought the discussion to an end. "More coffee?"

"No thanks, I must go. I've a million other things I should be doing and this is my precious morning off. Whilst I'd far rather sit and talk to you, I have to pick up the dry cleaning and other vitally dull chores!" Moya collected her things together. "I'm not sure about tennis next week, I may be in the magistrates court. I'll ring you."

"Fine. Take care, Moya. Bye."

Suddenly the house felt empty. Julia tidied away the coffee pot and cups. Lately she had noticed just how quiet the house seemed when the girls were at school. When they were younger it had been such a relief to be alone and she had valued and enjoyed any spare time. Now she often felt the days stretching endlessly before her. The ticking of the clock in the hall only served to emphasise the silent emptiness of the house and her life.

The telephone rang, making her jump. It was Rosalind, her mother.

"What have you been up to, darling?" .

"Not a great deal. Oh, I played tennis this morning and Moya and Breeda have just left. They're busy people."

"You sound a bit flat, Julia. Is everything all right?"

"Yes. Everything's fine, I've nothing to complain about. I just wish something would happen, something different or exciting. Anything really."

"Be very careful what you wish for, Julia," Rosalind commanded. "Wishes can have a nasty habit of coming true."

"Perhaps," Julia replied doubtfully.

"You're very lucky. You've Michael, the girls, no financial concerns and a lovely home," Rosalind told her, ignoring a distinctly heavy sigh coming down the telephone line from her eldest daughter. Rosalind adored Michael, partly, Julia believed, because of the loss of Tom. The five-year gap between her daughters, Julia and Imogen, had contained another baby, a son. But he had died at four months from a congenital heart condition that the doctors had missed. Michael was exactly how Rosalind imagined Tom would have turned out had he lived, and in her eyes he was the ideal husband for Julia who had a lot to be grateful for.

"Imogen rang me yesterday," Rosalind continued. "She's in the Netherlands and then flying on to San Francisco. She has to lead some conference. It all sounds very exciting, but I hope she gets some rest, she overworks you know."

"Travel," Julia said wistfully, "That's another thing I haven't done much of."

"Julia, really! No one is ever content any more. The grass isn't greener, it just looks that way. Imogen envies you the children and you envy her her career. I'm sure if you each swapped lives for a week or two you'd soon see how very lucky you both are." It was impossible for Julia ever to question her mother's notion of the perfect life she had ascribed to her. With the two appalling tragedies in Rosalind's life, the death of her baby son and later her husband, any other concerns paled into insignificance. Julia's problems could never compare with the pain her mother had suffered. Rosalind often forgot that Julia had lost a brother and father herself.

Julia remembered Tom only vaguely, like a dream. She had made a mobile out of cardboard for his cot with her father – planets and stars. She had spent hours colouring them in. She delighted in playing the role of little mother; when Rosalind fed Tom, Julia fed her dolly. Visitors came and cooed over his cot and brought presents and slipped Julia a bar of chocolate, telling her how lucky she was to have such a lovely baby brother. Then Tom stopped feeding, lost weight and colour. Her parents took him back to the hospital and he never came home again. So they got rid of the cot along with the planets that Julia had made to dance above it. Gradually she learnt not to mention her dead baby brother because it made her mother cry. Even television adverts for nappies made Rosalind's eyes fill with tears. Julia's abiding childhood memory was of her mother's rigid back as she left the sitting room, a wet handkerchief screwed into a tiny ball in her fist.

"Keep busy darling, that's what I've always done," Rosalind suggested before ringing off.

8

Pandora's Box

Michael went into the strangers' cafeteria of the House of Commons where Tim, his local party agent, had already bagged a table. He waved to Michael, who went over to join him. The cafeteria was busy, buzzing with conversation, and many of the big guns from both sides of the House were there. This only happened when something big was going down and the Amery affair was the talk of the House, bars and terraces. The opposition leader was circulating, meeting and greeting. He had come under a good deal of pressure since Amery had been exposed, yet again accused of poor judgement. He was trying to shore up his position and authority, but the knives were out. No one was quite sure how he had managed to hang on as party leader in the light of the last electoral defeat, so his position now was perilous – it could only be a question of time. He was a friendly chap, witty, and the little group around him burst out laughing as he clapped a fellow MP on the back.

"So, Tim, what news from the wilds of Wynshore?" Michael enquired.

Tim had no time to answer. A hand had planted itself firmly on his shoulder, a hand with great sausage-like fingers and a powerful grip.

"Excuse me!"

"Giles! Good Lord! How are you? It must be nearly thirty years." Michael exclaimed.

"Michael!" the voice boomed. "I was wondering if I mightn't run into you here! How are you, old man? Sorted out the Health Service for us yet?" Giles Strumpshaw grasped Michael's hand and pumped it up and down. "Great to see you, dear boy."

He turned and commandeered a chair that a Liberal Democrat MP, Lorna Greenway, was just on the point of using. "Sorry, my dear, didn't see you there," Giles boomed again, and making no offer to return the chair, he sat on it.

"Whatever brings you here?" Michael asked.

"Aha." Giles laughed, tapping the side of his nose with his finger in the gesture that implied secrecy. He hadn't changed that much. Michael would still have recognised him despite the addition of a couple of stones in weight. He wore exactly the same style of suit, shirt and tie. The tie sported a huntsman and hounds racing across it. He still had a crop of thick black hair, possibly dyed, and the same quick darting eyes. It was the sort of face that might have been beautiful as a baby but, as it had never lost that ample fleshiness, was now a caricature in corpulent middle-age.

"Like the tie, do you?" Giles beamed, seeing it had caught Michael's eye. "It's in memory of the local hunt." He waved the end of it, which was just poking out from his beneath his waistcoat, showing off his watch and chain in the same movement.

"Are you still in medicine?" Michael asked and, realising that he hadn't introduced Giles, he turned to Tim. "I'm sorry, Giles, let me introduce you. Tim Nash…Giles Strumpshaw. Giles and I were at medical school together years ago, Tim is my hardworking party agent in Wynshore," Michael added.

"Ah. Deal with all the peasants' woes and worries, do you? Jolly good," Giles remarked dismissively.

"So what are you doing now, Giles?"

"Well, I don't practise any more. I'd had quite enough of renal failure, gallstones and angina I can tell you, so I got out. No, I head up a biotechnology company, 'StemShaw', and that what's brought me here. We've got a lobbyist on board to promote our industry – I say promote, more like save it. As you know, Michael, it's see-saw. The legislation can't keep pace, and there is all this scare mongering in the press and the UN vote against us. It's a worrying situation. This sort of technology – stem cell work, therapeutic cloning, genes and the like – has huge potential for saving lives as well as for the economic development of the country."

From the far side of the cafeteria a slick looking young man called out to Giles. "Got to go. I'll be in touch, Michael. We're having a meeting with Trade and Industry but your department would have some interest in this, I feel sure. I'll get laddie there to fix something up. So nice to have met you, er…"

"Tim." Tim filled in his name.

Giles stood up.

"Same wife on the go, Michael?" Giles asked, extending his hand.

"Yes, Julia, and two girls, Tess and Katherine," Michael replied. "And you?"

"On my third – gorgeous, twenty nine, an absolute corker, scattering of offspring, costing a bloody fortune in school fees and maintenance."

"Giles. We must make a move." The slick young man, who Michael recognised from the lobbies, had come across the room to hurry things along.

"Sorry, Michael, would love to stay and catch up. I'll be in touch."

Michael sat back and watched Giles leaving the tea-room.

"Well, well, well," Michael said quietly.

"An old friend?" Tim inquired, one eyebrow raised sceptically.

"That," Michael replied, "was the man who very nearly got me sent down from medical school." They both sat looking at the now empty doorway.

"Do you know I'm not altogether surprised by that," Tim replied with an impish grin.

"Should he ever try to get hold of me…" Michael began.

"You're a very busy man."

"I'm a very busy man," Michael repeated.

*

Sarah was standing in Marion's bedroom, folding her dresses neatly, reverently, and then laying them in a tidy pile on the bed. Nigel was sitting on the pink bedside rug emptying the dressing table drawers onto the floor.

Nothing can ever prepare you for going through the effects of a dead parent. Sarah considered a parent's life contained an element of mystery; it was in the nature of the relationship. There were bits of the past that, as a child, one simply was not privy to, and that was as it should be. If she felt uncomfortable handling Marion's clothes, then how much harder for Nigel? He was taking out the jewellery from the leatherette box Marion had kept in the top drawer. There, instantly recognisable, were the clip-on pearl earrings with a matching brooch she had worn the day that Sarah and Nigel had celebrated their engagement. They had been out to lunch at the Golden Fleece with Sarah's parents. Marion had come downstairs and asked for Sarah's opinion.

"You don't think they're too flashy, do you, Sarah?"

"Not at all. I think they're very discreet, very tasteful." Sarah watched as Marion glowed with delight. This is the wrong way round, she had thought. I should be seeking her approval, my future mother-in-law. Marion had been rather in awe of Sarah's parents and she was clearly nervous. She needn't have worried. Elizabeth and Bob were happy with Sarah's choice of husband. They had really taken to Nigel and it would have taken a lot to put them off, far more than a slightly ill at ease in-law. Elizabeth had said to Sarah afterwards:

"They're dull, but you're never going to have any trouble with them." And then, as if she knew, "How on earth did Marion and Gerald produce a gem like Nigel?"

They had been engaged for almost a year now, a year in which Nigel and Sarah had seen his mother's health decline until finally she was unrecognisable as Marion. At first, the drugs kept her puffed up and looking fairly normal, so much so that no one realised that Marion's diagnosis was, in fact, a death sentence. Sarah felt guilty about that; she should have spent more time with her but with the preparations for the wedding, her free time was spent with her own mother, shopping for the dress and deciding on the flowers. In fact, Marion's death was sudden. She seemed to have rallied and was looking far better, but then she got a chest infection that turned into pneumonia. Finally, her heart gave out. The doctor said this was a blessing and had saved her a great deal of pain. He was probably right.

"Should I pack them into this suitcase? Is that why Gerald left it out?" Sarah asked.

"Yes. He wants me to take them to the Oxfam shop."

"We'd better take them to the one near us in Maidenhead.

He doesn't want to run into anyone in Brentwood wearing your mother's clothes – that would be dreadful."

"I doubt he'd notice," Nigel said.

"Well, just in case. He's a lot more upset than he shows. And this other business – it's all taken a toll." Nigel's curious parentage was now often referred to as 'the other business'.

"I wonder what he will want to do with these?" Sarah had brought out a shoebox from the bottom of the wardrobe.

"What are they?" Nigel asked.

"Diaries, look. Going back years." Sarah lifted some out, small neat little leather bound books with a strip of faded ribbon to mark the place. She held open one of the books, from nineteen eighty-five.

"Look, Nigel. Shorthand. They're written in shorthand. I didn't know Marion did shorthand."

"She didn't. Not as far as I knew," Nigel replied, surprised.

"How strange. Do you think Gerald knows?" Sarah wondered.

"I wonder if he even knows they exist? How far do they go back? What year?"

"Nineteen seventy-four. No, hang on, there are more. Nineteen sixty-nine..." Sarah carried on rummaging.

Nigel spied another box at the back of the wardrobe.

"Look, more. They go back years and years but some of these aren't in shorthand. This is before they were married. Look for the year I was born – no before, nine months before. Here, nineteen seventy-two. God, I'm shaking." Nigel opened the diary; it was in shorthand.

"What are we looking for? Even Marion didn't know who your father was," Sarah said gently.

"Anything. How she felt, where she went, a clue."

They sank onto the counterpane on the bed. Nigel sat turning over page after page of the script that he could neither read nor interpret. After a long silence, Sarah asked:

"What are we going to do with them? Should we ask Gerald?"

"No. I'm taking them with me. I want them translated."

Nigel got out the Yellow Pages as soon as he and Sarah returned to the flat. He marked several typing and secretarial services. On Monday morning he phoned the school saying he was sick and sat down in earnest to find a translator and to read the earlier diaries that were not in shorthand.

Sarah was standing up gathering together bits and pieces for work, quickly drinking down the last of her tea. If she didn't get a move on, she would be late. She was worried about Nigel. She felt she should stay and help him, but she was also concerned about the amount of time he was taking from work. Nigel was utterly dedicated and would never jeopardise the pupils; several of the older students were preparing for exams and they would need Nigel's support.

"You'll go in tomorrow?" she queried. Nigel looked up at her, coolly dismissive.

"That all depends on whether I find someone to do this," gesturing to the diaries, "today."

"It might be better to use a personal contact," Sarah suggested. "A secretarial service might consider them, well..." she paused uncomfortably. "Private, not yours to read."

"Then they would be wrong," Nigel replied briskly. "I am, at least, Marion's next of kin."

"And Gerald? We should ask him, don't you think?"

"I don't think a translator will have the problem with this request that you seem to, Sarah." Nigel remarked with uncharacteristic coldness. "After all, I shall be paying them. And no, I will not be asking Gerald. This really has nothing to do with him."

Nigel went straight back to the telephone directory. Sarah felt a small physical pain twist inside her. Nigel had never been dismissive or cruel to her before. She had never had a terse or cold response from him in all their time together. Her eyes filled with tears, which she fought to suppress.

"I'd better go," she said, her voice fractured.

Nigel didn't look up, merely calling his goodbye after she had shut the door to the flat.

*

Julia sat on the end of the bed. She was in Tess' room, tidying up. It's what she spent Mondays doing. Every Monday. She had a pile of laundry next to her and was matching the stray socks. There was a picture of a boy band on the wall, but it was coming away at one corner and flapping forward. Julia had meant to bring up some blu-tack and fix it back in place. She had been meaning to do this for a month now but probably she would keep forgetting and, in time, Tess would fall for another band and consign this poster to the bin. Quite without warning, she began to cry. She buried her face in a pile of laundry and sobbed. After about five minutes the tears stopped and, feeling better, Julia went through to the bathroom and splashed her face with cold water. She felt terribly old and weary.

"Really, you silly woman, whatever is the matter with you?"

*

"Do you ever feel, Moya, that there must be more to life than this?" Julia was twisting the end of a scarf in her hand.

Moya, who was wiping down the draining board, turned and smiled faintly with just a hint of condescension.

"I have my work. As far as I'm concerned, there really aren't enough hours in the day."

Julia felt crushed. Intentionally or unintentionally, she really couldn't be sure. A few days later she tried the same question on Breeda.

"God, yes! When I have the time that is. My life is a constant round of school runs, lost underwear and PE kit, and food: buying it, cooking it and scraping it off the walls and floor. Seven people never stop eating, for which you need shopping. God, the place is a madhouse! But, you know, when this insanity stops and they've all gone off to college or whatever, I shall miss them all terribly. Now isn't that the crazy thing?" All this was said with Breeda's enviable breathless zest for life. "I have my days at the co-operative, of course, and they stop me losing my mind altogether…" She was all set to carry on until she saw that Julia was weeping.

"Julia, what's up?" Breeda moved a box of Kleenex tissues onto the table.

"Oh, I don't know. I'm just being silly." Julia sniffed and then blew her nose. "It's just that I sat on the bed the other day matching up socks and it just…it just all seemed so utterly pointless."

"Well, you silly eejit, matching up socks is utterly and totally pointless, you know! You'll just be doing the same lousy job next week and no one will thank you for it. But they'll complain soon enough if they're all mixed up and there are no clean socks. You're very low aren't you? You're on your own too much, Julia. Couldn't you get a job?"

A tear ran very quickly down Julia's face. She daren't speak for a moment for fear of really breaking down.

"I tried that once before, remember? And it was a disaster. I can't work with Michael away all week, and the girls rely on me. And, anyway, my skills are all hopelessly out of date. I'd need to re-train or refresh, whatever you call it," she added.

"What about part-time? I've found that working at 'Eco Foods' is just perfect, flexible hours that fit in with the school day."

"That's just it. I'd happily go and do a couple of days a week on a supermarket checkout, but that's hardly appropriate as the wife of the sitting MP and Minister. Michael would have a fit."

"Well, it looks like that old standby – voluntary work!"

"Now you're just trying to make me even more miserable." Julia blew her nose again.

"Now, now, Julia Barton, you'll have me praying to Saint Jude," Breeda chided.

"Saint Jude?" Julia queried.

"The patron Saint of Desperate Situations," Breeda concluded.

It did the trick. They both began to laugh.

"I'm quite worried about her," Moya was saying. She had just bumped into Breeda outside the post office. "I think she's clinically depressed, and should see her doctor."

"She has a doctor for a husband, for goodness sake," Breeda replied briskly.

"Exactly. As I can testify, when there's a medical man in the family everything goes untreated…'the cobbler's children go unshod'. Anyway, Michael hasn't practised for years now and he's never at home long enough to notice what is, or isn't, happening in

Julia's world. Devoted to the girls and Julia of course, but inevitably he always has his head in a red box."

"But that's just it – she has too much time on her hands, rattling around in that pristine house with the girls at school all day and Michael in London. She needs something to do. Something Michael would approve of."

"What though?" Moya asked thoughtfully.

"Julia would be quite happy to do a couple of days on a checkout but Michael wouldn't hear of it."

"She could hardly work in a shop! Michael's a minister for goodness sake!"

"Why ever not? I do." Breeda replied sharply.

"Yes, but that's quite different."

"I don't see how."

"Michael's right. Julia has a position in the community, and anyway, people would bother her with their problems," Moya stated firmly. Breeda's sensitivity on this matter irritated her. "Perhaps that's it, perhaps she should work for Michael, do something in the local party office. I'll suggest it to him."

"Mightn't it be better to talk to Julia first?"

"There are times when the subtle approach is more effective. I'll get Andrew to take him out for a drink and have a quiet word," Moya said patronisingly. Breeda fought a shocking compulsion to slap her…neat, petite, clever, well-dressed Moya, with her brilliant son, her talented, consultant husband and a BMW for a second car.

"Well, I can't stand here all day talking, I've a mountain of things to do." Breeda bent down and collected up her bags, and saying her goodbye over her shoulder, strode off angrily.

Honestly, thought Moya, Breeda's so touchy it's no wonder Finn seeks solace elsewhere.

*

Sarah hadn't felt like coming home. She had hung about in the laboratory doing trivial chores and killing time. She hesitated on the

64

stairs, unsure what kind of mood Nigel might be in. He was right, this news had changed everything. It had certainly changed Nigel. Usually they spoke on the phone during the day. He would ring from the staff room at break or lunchtime, just to see how her day was going and to discuss who would cook and whether they needed to pick up any shopping. He seemed remote now. Sarah knew that he was embarking on a quest to find out who his real father was, and she also knew it would prove fruitless. Anonymous donor sperm was just that – anonymous. Nigel would never find out his origins, and coming to terms with that was clearly going to be painful. This was the first such test they had encountered as a couple and she felt she wasn't meeting the challenge at all well. After all, in a few months she would be making her vows. She would be promising to look after Nigel no matter what the circumstances, in sickness and in health, for richer or poorer. At the moment Nigel clearly felt he didn't have her complete support. She must remedy that. She took a deep breath and turned the key in the door. Nigel was sitting on the floor surrounded by an enormous pile of books and journals and he hardly glanced up to greet her as she came into the living room. He appeared to be studying in earnest.

"What's all this?" Sarah asked, trying to sound interested and not alarmed.

Nigel looked up, his face bright and eager.

"I'm going to find out who my biological father is and I want you to help me," he announced.

Sarah tucked her dark neat hair behind her ears, something she did habitually when anxious. When she had collected herself, she said:

"Nigel, mightn't that be impossible? How could you begin to trace him? He may not be traceable. It was years ago. The clinic probably doesn't exist any more."

"I'm not the only one, Sarah. By now there must be thousands of us. It's *my* right to know my paternity. What right do other people have to know and keep it from me? I've been to the library and on the Internet and have found all sorts of stuff on IVF but very little on artificial insemination by donor. They've changed the law, but not for people like me – only those conceived from now on.

But someone must know how it worked, the way they stored the stuff, how it was distributed, where it was collected from. There are records, there must be – sperm is a medical commodity like drugs or blood, it would be logged in, booked out and they would have to keep tabs on who got what. What if there were birth defects, genetic deformities, mental incapacity? Someone has those records."

Sarah looked at him, the man she loved. This Nigel was a driven man, burning with a passion greater than he could ever feel for her. She wanted to return to her wedding plans, discuss guest lists or place cards, decide on champagne or sparkling wine, worry about how the three-year-old bridesmaid might behave.

"I imagine if the birth was trouble-free and the baby well, then they would destroy them." In front of her, Nigel visibly crumbled and became smaller.

"You don't really think so, do you?"

"We're talking about nineteen-seventy-two, Nigel, or earlier, depending on how long they would keep sperm to use. And the whole process wasn't regulated, it was in its infancy. I really doubt that there is anything left to find. The records will have long since been destroyed. I'm sorry. But I couldn't bear to see you set off on some utterly fruitless search." For a moment they both sat in silence.

"I'm going to try anyway, Sarah. However slim the possibility, I must try and find him. And you're a scientist so you can help me, lead me through the processes and jargon that I don't understand." Nigel looked at her, pleading. "Please say you'll help me, Sarah."

Sarah's heart sank. Swallowing hard she put on a smile and said:

"Of course I'll help you, Nigel." After a pause she added, "You must be very careful not to let this jeopardise your career though."

"Oh, I'm taking three weeks leave, it's all arranged."

"Leave? How can you take leave? What about your students?"

"Compassionate leave."

"On what grounds?"

"In case you had forgotten, my mother has just died," Nigel replied, with a slight edge to his voice.

"Of course, I'm sorry. But it could take a very long time and in the end may simply be impossible. I just don't want to see you hurt any more."

She saw he wasn't listening. She suddenly felt very tired. She pulled herself up from the sofa and went into the bedroom. When she looked back at Nigel, he had his head in a book, oblivious to her retreat.

www.spermdonors children of

Sarah had never thought of Nigel as obsessive. Yes, he was passionate about his music and he was a dedicated teacher who lived for the school, yet in every other way he was relaxed, urbane, easy. This rather surprised Elizabeth, Sarah's mother.

"Isn't it curious," she had remarked, "that Nigel is so unperturbed and steady, when Marion's so anxious and ill at ease, and Gerald is so...removed."

Now, whenever Sarah put the key in the door, she found Nigel either buried in books and journals or making copious notes. He didn't ask about her day, nor enquire about the preparations for the wedding. On this particular evening he merely looked up and said:

"Often a website that looks like it might help the offspring turns out to be a clinic trying to push post-it sperm!"

"What! You can't buy sperm just like that?" Sarah asked, amazed.

"Yes you can! From America, here...look!" Nigel handed over sheaves of paper.

Donor #0075 was listed at the top of sixteen columns, each containing the details of the donor available. It went on to list availability of sperm, blood group, ethnic and territorial extraction, height, weight, skin colour, colour of eyes, hair colour, curly or straight, and the qualifications or studies donors were undertaking. Some on the list said 'Sophomore/Finance', others 'BS/Architecture' or 'Freshman/Computer Science'.

Sarah looked through the list in blank astonishment.

"They're all students; they're obviously doing this for the money. There can't be any other reason. This isn't altruism – this is to pay their way through college," Sarah added, shocked. "They can't possibly realise the full implications of what they're doing. How many of these young men would do this if they didn't get paid?"

"And look at this, this is a donor essay." Nigel handed over another sheet with a list of questions and answers on it. It asked some rather banal questions such as: 'What is the funniest thing ever to happen to you?' And, 'What immediate family member do you closely identify with, and why?' Saddest of all, the very last question was: 'When, and if, you have children, what would you like to pass on to them?' Donor#0048 had replied: 'A strong sense of self-pride, and understanding that success comes to those who work for it'.

"I find this dreadful. Heartbreaking," she said.

"Look at this! It's a selection register and search engine. You fill in what you're looking for and then it finds them for you, and, here at the bottom, it found thirty seven donors matching my criteria and now it tells me I may add donors to my 'shopping cart'." Nigel handed over another printout from the computer.

"My God! This is like shopping on-line at a supermarket!" Sarah sat down heavily in a chair. "What exactly were you hoping to find?"

"Other people like me – donors' children who feel as I do, deceived and betrayed. There will be some sort of agency or pressure group. I can't be the only child who has been lied to, only to discover the truth about their so-called parents years later."

"But surely many of the children are just that, children. They will either have been told from the outset and are happy with the explanation, or they aren't yet old enough to consider the full implications. Marion, you know, must have been one of the first women to use donor insemination." Sarah got up from the chair to go and make some tea.

"That's just it – this isn't a new technique. They've been at it for years; apparently some woman doctor in the nineteen-thirties started to make the connection between the insemination of cattle and decided it would probably work for women."

Sarah stopped filling the kettle. She looked startled.

"So there are what? Hundreds, maybe thousands, born this way who don't even know?" she asked.

"Since nineteen-ninety-one more than twenty five thousand children have been born this way, so I imagine if you go back further there are thousands more."

"You could end up marrying a relative, a half-brother or sister."
Sarah grimaced. "Yuk, that's appalling."

"Ah! The Yuk factor," Nigel repeated. "You might be interested
to know that in the House of Commons in April nineteen-ninety-
nine," he began reading out loud, "Lord Longford used that very
phrase and Lord Stallard said then that 'ethical judgement is rooted
in moral sentiments such as repugnance'. He recommended this
should be the guide, and warned of the psychological effects on
children." Nigel sat back with his hands behind his head and with
his long legs stretched out in front of him, looking very pleased
with himself.

"They could hardly legislate retrospectively, not if the donors
only agreed to donate anonymously."

"Whose side are you on, Sarah?"

"Yours, of course. But I can see that a donor may never have
told his family, so you couldn't just open the files and let all these
children rush off to find their natural parents. That wouldn't be fair
either."

"Adopted children can do just that. Hit eighteen and bingo, you
get to see your file and are even offered help and counselling to
make contact. So why not for donor children?"

"It's not quite the same, is it? An adopted baby was often given
up reluctantly, whereas sperm donors aren't expecting to ever meet
their child, they're doing the childless a favour. Or rather that's how
they see it, don't you think?" Sarah suggested.

"I think society has its priorities totally wrong when it produces
children for gain, who have no right to their own genetic or family
inheritance, who are lied to and deceived." He handed her a pile of
papers.

Sarah leafed through the fifty or more pages. It was fantastical,
science fiction turned fact and deeply disturbing. And worse, it was
part of their lives. Nigel came and put his arm around her. It was the
first time he had touched her in days and she turned up her face to
his and smiled. Nigel leant down and tenderly kissed her cheek.

"Sarah, I've been thinking. Perhaps we should postpone the
wedding, just for the time being, until things are more settled and I
can find out a bit more about myself."

"What!" Sarah pulled away, horrified. "Nigel, what are you saying? How could you suggest such a thing? The church is booked, the reception...my dress. This hasn't made you doubt us surely?"

Nigel looked at Sarah; dear good Sarah whom he loved. She looked so slight, vulnerable.

"It's me I doubt, not us." he said.

"I don't understand." Sarah began crying. "You love me, don't you? Nothing's changed."

"You know I do," Nigel replied softly.

"Well then, why? What possible reason could there be for postponing the wedding? And everyone agrees it would be what Marion would have wanted."

"I can't get married just because it was what Marion would have wanted," Nigel snapped.

"Nigel! How could you say...what do you mean?" Sarah pulled away from him and fled into the bathroom, slamming the door and bolting it.

"Sarah. Sarah, please listen, you've misunderstood," he called, rushing after her. He could hear her sobbing loudly. He'd never made Sarah cry before.

He looked up and caught sight of himself in the full-length mirror. He had placed it at the end of the cramped hallway to create the illusion of space – a false perspective. He stared at the outline of this man silhouetted against the light from the living room window. He studied the size, the physique, the manner of this person, as if meeting for the first time. Then he slid down to the floor, his back pressed hard against the bathroom door, his long legs pushed up against his chest and his feet wedged up against the front door. This flat is too small to have a row in, he thought. He turned over his hands. They were very big, square and strong with long fingers. In fact, the span of his hands had been one of the things that had made playing the piano easy. His piano teacher had compared them to the hands of Liszt, who apparently had the hands of a giant and could easily span an octave. And yes, he did look rather like Marion, his eyes and colouring. But he now realised that he must also look very like someone else, his other family, his biological father, a term used in all the literature. As if somehow giving a father the adjective – biological – changed anything. Out there somewhere was a middle-aged man with perhaps a family of his own, Nigel's half-brothers and sisters. His real father.

He threw his head back against the wall and shut his eyes. He knew then that he was about to cross a moral line of his own, he was about to behave in an underhand and manipulative fashion in order to get his own way. He loved Sarah deeply and didn't want to hurt and deceive her, but he needed her help if he was ever to find his father and his true self. He called softly through the locked door.

"This affects us, you know. Not just me." Sarah had stopped crying, and he could hear her blowing her nose. "When we have children we might need to know what our medical and genetic history is. And we don't know mine." He stood up as he heard Sarah unbolt the door.

"What do you mean?" she sniffed.

"Just that when you're pregnant they ask lots of details, don't they? About your family history; if there are any abnormalities and that sort of thing?"

"Oh, Nigel, there couldn't be, could there?" Her face was pale and her make-up was smudged by tears. "I mean, surely they check for that when they take the sample?"

"I rather doubt it. Back then, I bet they just relied on whatever the donor chose to tell them."

"Oh my God!"

"I'm sorry. I hadn't realised the implications of all this. But don't you see, half my genetic history is completely unknown."

"I haven't been much help, have I?" After a long pause, Sarah said, "I won't let you go through this alone. I'll help you."

Nigel kissed her on the forehead."I'm counting on you."

"I will help. Of course I will, but it's two and half months to the wedding and we are not postponing it. I love you, Nigel, whether I know your genetic history or not. I know the person I'm marrying to be a loving, thoughtful, gentle man. If, in a few weeks, we haven't got anywhere, then we call a halt until after the honeymoon... please?"

"Agreed."

"And I am not going to take any time off work. One of us has to save up for a house, if only to have somewhere big enough to row in." Sarah smiled and snuggled up closely to Nigel's shoulder. "So where do we start?" she asked.

"Wimpole Street." Nigel replied.

*

Julia was looking around Stoddards, Wynshore's idea of a department store. A small family owned shop with pretensions to be something altogether grander. She'd been upstairs to the coffee shop, where she surprised Moya and Finn who were having a chat and a cappuccino.

"You'd better be careful, you two, this is Wynshore – people will talk," she said jokingly.

Finn drained his cup rather hastily and stood up. "I must get back."

This pleasant interlude had killed half an hour and now she found herself amongst the fitted kitchens looking at the modern units that did all sorts of clever things. There were larder units, and little cupboards for storing oils and condiments. She admired the metallic racks and the under-cupboard lighting. Why did they still have that shabby, old pine kitchen? It had come with the house and was probably quite modern at the time but now it had aged to a nasty orange and most of the varnish had long since gone. Bits of it had faded where a much-loved child's painting had once been displayed. Food had stuck to it too, and you could never get it off, even with a pan scourer. It clung on resolutely, and so you ended up sanding down the wood all around it yet never shifting the offending item. The rest of the house was very smart, classical and stylish; the kitchen, by contrast, was simply appalling.

"Do you need any help, madam?" A pleasant looking young man lifted his head from some drawings and calculations.

"I was just wondering what all this might cost? Our kitchen is terribly dated and shabby."

"It depends on the range. This German range is excellent, and it does have a lot to offer, with some very clever design features.

73

And our own range is similar and excellent value for money. Would you like a catalogue?" he offered.

"Yes," Julia replied hesitantly and then said, "Yes, I would. And perhaps you can tell me what the process is? If I decide on something where do I go from here, what next?"

"We would come and do a site survey. Do you think you would need any structural work? Or would you just be replacing the kitchen in the same arrangement?"

"I wouldn't mind extending to give us room for a bigger table," Julia replied thoughtfully.

"Well, you might need to consult your builder regarding any structural work; but we can survey the kitchen, which costs fifty pounds, redeemable when you order. Or alternatively, for the time being you could bring in the measurements and I could prepare a rough estimate just to give you some idea of the relative costs. You will need a site survey, but that can come later when you have finalised the plans." The young man had warmed to his theme.

Funny, thought Julia, how people say 'your' builder, 'your' plumber as if every household kept someone on a retainer.

"Can I take this with me?" She held up the catalogue.

"Please do, and here is my card. Should you have any queries, do ring." He handed her a business card.

"Thank you, you've been most helpful."

"Not at all."

By the time Julia reached the car park, she had a plan.

"This is what you need, Julia Barton," she said to herself, slipping the key into the ignition. "A project, something to get your teeth into."

"Whatever is this going to cost?" Michael said in a concerned tone.

"I really don't know, not until we decide what we want and get an estimate," Julia replied.

"I can't see what's wrong with what we've got."

Julia was unaccountably irritated and found that she wanted to say, 'Can't you, Michael? Well, then you're blind.' Not at all the sort of comment she would usually make. She curbed herself and settled instead for:

"It's dated, shabby and horrible to work in. And the doors have warped – they keep falling open."

"Oh well then," Michael replied mildly. "Get some quotes and we'll take it from there." I can always put my foot down when the quotes come in, he thought to himself. The last thing I need is the disruption builders would cause. He shook an annoying crease out of the newspaper and returned to reading an article on a possible treatment for Alzheimer's.

Julia turned back to the brochure and smiled, a quietly satisfied smile.

*

"Julia seems much happier, more like her old self, doesn't she, Moya?"

Breeda was draining carrots whilst Moya was helping lay the table. Michael came in to Breeda's kitchen looking for the corkscrew.

"Oh hello, Michael," Breeda said brightly. "I was just saying to Moya how much happier Julia is, now she's something to get her teeth into." Michael looked blank. "The plans for the new kitchen?" she reminded him. "A while ago she was very low," Breeda went on, ignoring Moya, who behind Michael's back was drawing a finger across her throat in a gesture intended to silence her. Michael stopped searching for the corkscrew and said testily:

"And how would you know Julia was 'feeling very low,' as you put it? Or have you become a psychoanalyst as well, Breeda?"

"Actually Michael, you don't need to be an analyst when a friend breaks down in tears in your kitchen and says that she finds her life utterly pointless. Anyone could tell she was depressed."

"If Julia were depressed I would know. Not only am I her husband and better placed to judge, I am also a doctor. What Julia doesn't need is a lot of half baked quackery peddled by a foolish…" He stopped mid-sentence, realising that he was rapidly losing his temper and he was about to say something he would regret.

"Ask Moya," Breeda suggested implacably, as she poured the gravy into a jug.

Michael turned to Moya expectantly.

"She's certainly been at a bit of a loose end lately," she replied.

"A bit of a loose end, Moya? Oh come on..." Breeda cried. "When I met you outside the post office you described Julia as clinically depressed, and when I said this man here would know, seeing as he's a doctor, you were quick to point out that Andrew is a doctor and you knew to your cost that with a doctor in the family no one gets treated! 'The cobbler's children go unshod', to quote you exactly."

Michael turned again to look at Moya, an eyebrow raised.

"I think we both agreed," Moya began, "that Julia needed something to occupy her, some sort of rewarding work. I thought she might do something for you at the constituency office, Michael." Breeda disliked the emphasis Moya had placed on the word rewarding; she had already made it quite clear that Breeda's work at the food co-operative could never fall into that category.

"Well, thank you both, very much, for your wise counsel. When I need your advice I shall ask for it. Now if you don't mind, the others are waiting for a drink." He pulled the cork from the bottle and turned and left the room, shutting the door firmly behind him.

"And thank you too, Moya," Breeda said with heavy sarcasm.

Moya folded her arms tightly across her chest and leaning against the sink said:

"Why is it, Breeda, that you feel that the only way to deal with anything is to make a drama out of it? When will you learn that if you choose the right moment you can have far more impact and actually be of some help! Andrew, as Michael's friend, is far better placed to talk to him. I don't know just what it is you think you've succeeded in doing but it certainly won't help Julia. You always have to get your point across. I guarantee that your insensitive comments will cause a row over this. Now, if everything's ready, I'll go and call them in." Moya marched out of the room.

"Sanctimonious cow," Breeda said under her breath. Then, looking heavenwards, muttered, "Sorry."

There was a strained atmosphere during the meal. Moya encouraged Julia to talk about her plans for the refurbishment. The latest idea was to extend out into the garden which meant major structural alterations to the rear of the house, and Julia talked excitedly about them. Michael contributed very little to this conversation but made a mental note to put his foot down and tell Julia any plans to renovate were definitely off. Finn, who had a wealth of awful builder stories to relate, kept them all entertained so, with the hubbub from the children, there was too much noise for Julia to notice that Breeda and Moya weren't speaking to one another.

*

The translation of Marion's diaries took a little over a week. They yielded some insight into the turmoil Nigel's mother had felt after she had discovered that Gerald was infertile. She went into a deep depression and her doctor put her on some tablets. These she took for a month, not really knowing what they were and then, one day, she simply flushed them down the toilet. The very next morning she enrolled on a secretarial course at the local college. This she had kept from Gerald, who even now had no idea that Marion was, or had been, a shorthand typist with a Pitman's First Class.

"Poor Marion," Sarah said. "I think Gerald would have been quite proud of her if she'd told him. Why didn't she say anything?"

"She didn't think she'd pass," Nigel stated. "She had no self belief."

And that was just the problem. Marion had absolute faith in being a good, loving and caring mother but not in being a secretary. Despite her excellent qualification, she couldn't cope with the job interviews. She was awkward and timid and every application failed.

Nigel sat by the window in the Oxford Street John Lewis's, A Place to Eat. He had in front of him a fruit scone and butter. There wasn't enough butter in the little plastic tub with a foil top to cover both halves of the fruit scone. With the coffee there was a choice of milk or cream, again in plastic tubs and instead of a spoon, he stirred his coffee with a long thin plastic implement. I bet it wasn't like this in Marion's day, he mused. There would have been smart

77

young girls in black with crisp white aprons and a notepad to take down your order. None of this self-service nonsense with open sandwiches wrapped in cling-film.

He looked out of the large high window down to the square below. It wasn't lost on Nigel that this was the very course of action that his mother might well have taken twenty-nine years earlier.

Arriving early for her appointment in Wimpole Street she could easily have popped into John Lewis for some sewing thread, a knitting pattern, or a cup of coffee to steady her nerves. Marion wouldn't have felt out of place in there. Even today there were still a scattering of older women who would have been Marion's sort; they would beg one another's pardon, comment on the weather, the difficult train journey or how crowded London was compared to the suburbs that they inhabited. The demise of Lyon's Corner House would be mourned and a few carefully chosen comments might be passed about the lowering of standards of dress, the absence of gloves and hats. But on the occasion of her visit to Wimpole Street, Nigel imagined that Marion would be nervous, not chatty, dreading the ordeal ahead.

Nigel finished his scone and drank the last of his coffee and set off down the back stairwell and out through the doors that led to Cavendish Square. Ahead of him lay Harley Street and beyond it Regents Park. To the right stood the Post Office Tower, appearing curiously dated for a building with such futuristic intent.

He set off up the street past the elegant houses with their brass plaques and black iron railings hung with attractive displays of bedding plants. In the parking meter bay, leaning on an array of expensive cars – Mercedes, Jaguars and the occasional Rolls Royce – was an assortment of chauffeurs and minders, some heavily built with dark glasses and the bulk that showed they meant business.

Turning left down Queen Anne Street, which was being dug up – the noise and the smell of tar was overpowering – he turned right and arrived at Wimpole Street. It was a similar mix of Georgian and Victorian houses, some with the addition of pretty wrought iron lace balconies on the upper stories. At number fifty Nigel observed a blue plaque denoting that Elizabeth Barrett Browning had once lived there. His own heart began to quicken as he stood outside the very consulting room where nearly thirty years ago his conception had been planned with Doctor Edward Leatham. Nigel thought it unlikely this doctor would still be practising; but he hoped for some thread that would help him unravel the mystery of his existence.

The exterior of the practice was gracious and imposing. Poor mother, Nigel thought, she would have been petrified and intimidated coming here. She would have felt small and worthless, not good enough. The building had broad marble steps that led up to a wide black door with a large brass letterbox and an equally large shiny doorknocker. The door was so well painted and glossy that it reflected Nigel's image back at him. He looked at the plate listing the practitioners in order. There, to his surprise just under Peter Schultz, was the name Leatham, not Edward but Godfrey. A son perhaps? He took a deep breath and pressed the porcelain button.

"I have an appointment to see Doctor Leatham," he lied into the intercom. It worked: the door clicked and he was able to push forward and open it. He arrived in a fine wide hallway with an antique table below a large mirror. On it was an enormous bunch of stylishly arranged flowers. Reception was in a room to the right and he made his way there. There was just one client waiting, a small bird like woman, impeccably dressed in a camel coloured suit trimmed with black. It was belted, which emphasised how tiny her waist was. She looked about forty and had a great deal of heavy gold jewellery. Her shoes were high and pointed and gave the appearance of the talons of a bird of prey.

The receptionist, a woman in her thirties, was immaculate, and wore a smart navy tailored suit, her heavy blond hair held back with a padded Alice-band in blue velvet, wrapped over with seed pearls.

"Mr ...?" she queried with a brisk businesslike smile.

"Laing," Nigel replied. The receptionist looked at him sceptically and turned to the details on her computer screen.

"I have no record, Mr Laing. You say you have an appointment? With whom? This is not a clinic usually attended by men!"

"I don't have an appointment as such. I am making enquiries for

my mother, Mrs Marion Laing. She was, I believe, treated here."
The receptionist raised one eyebrow.

She could, Nigel decided, make his task very difficult if she chose
to. He would have to turn on the charm if he were to get anywhere.
Nigel smiled his most winning smile and thought that she thawed
a fraction.

"I'm sorry; I know that this is a little unorthodox but you see
I married only recently and I need some details regarding my
mother's treatment for my wife, who is pregnant. Am I right in
thinking that Godfrey Leatham is the son of Edward?"

The receptionist was tapping Marion's name into the computer.
She stopped.

"Just how long ago was your mother treated here, Mr Laing?
Doctor Edward Leatham has been dead for ten years!"

"Rather longer ago than that I'm afraid." Nigel produced an
endearing grin for the purpose.

She smiled, faintly amused this time. "We have some very old
notes in storage, but by no means all."

"All I want is an address of a clinic. I believe it's in Hampstead.
I thought Doctor Leatham might remember. Just two minutes of
the Doctor's time, that's all. Please. It's a possible genetic problem."
Begging with charm, that's what this is, Nigel thought.

She softened visibly. "Very well," she replied reluctantly. "Doctor
Leatham is writing up his notes. I'll see if he will spare you a couple
of minutes. But that's all it will be – he has another appointment in
five minutes."

Nigel beamed gratefully, as Miss Efficiency hurried off to make
the request for an audience.

He saw the bird-like woman was peering at him over the top of a
copy of 'The Tatler'. When Nigel caught her eye she shot her head
back down to the text and this added to his earlier appraisal of her,
giving her the appearance of a bird pecking.

The receptionist returned with instructions and a strict time limit.
Nigel would be allowed to ask the Doctor a couple of questions
only if they would not breach patient confidentiality. And it must be
stressed that it was unlikely that, given so much time had elapsed,
he would be able to provide information of any value. After all, the

Doctor had never met Mrs Laing.

Doctor Godfrey Leatham was everything a Wimpole Street consultant should be, blessed with the looks of a matinee idol, a beautiful speaking voice and, no doubt, an excellent bedside manner. From the lavish comforts of the consulting room, he was obviously raking it in.

Nigel came straight to the point. He was recently married and his wife was pregnant, but there was some question mark over his genetic history, his mother having died recently of cancer. He wanted the name of the clinic where his mother had been treated. Doctor Leatham listened carefully and then said:

"Over the years, Mr Laing, my father would have referred his patients to many different fertility clinics. Some have closed down or been taken over. We have some notes but a lot were destroyed to make space." This last part was, in fact, untrue. His father had been meticulous in the maintenance of all the notes and records, due in part to his growing curiosity about the nature versus nurture debate. He shared this interest with his good friend Emanuel Levison, an eminent psychologist. In fact the late Doctor Edward Leatham believed that one day the information contained in the notes of the women sent for donor insemination could open the door to the understanding of environment over genetics. That a study of the donor, the social fathers, and the child would yield insights into whether talents, such as artistic ability, musical or sporting flair were the result of genes or environment. He firmly believed that the study of the thousands of children born through donation would be far superior to any of the limited studies of twins done in the past. Sadly, the untimely death of Doctor Levison meant that this wealth of information lay unused, stored in an old air raid shelter at the back of the building. But Edward Leatham never gave up hope that he might eventually embark on this fascinating research. And somewhere at the back of his mind, Godfrey Leatham had also appreciated its value and so could never bring himself to destroy the records. Only last week he and the practice manager were struggling over the thorny issue of what precisely to do with all this material. He had actually instructed her to look into the cost of renting more appropriate storage facilities. He couldn't shred it all. Now a young man sat before him in obvious need and his request confirmed to Doctor Leatham that these records remained valuable.

Nigel detected a hesitancy. Was the doctor lying?

"My mother was referred by your father to a clinic somewhere in Hampstead. I will track down this clinic. All I'm doing in asking you is saving time." He looked steadily at the doctor.

"Very well."

"I want the address and the name of the doctor, please."

Doctor Leatham considered Nigel for a minute.

"Just a moment." He rose from his desk and left the room. What seemed like an eternity passed. Nigel even imagined the doctor might be calling the police. But when Leatham returned he held in his hand a tatty buff folder. He brushed some dust away from the cover with a tissue from the large box on the desk. Nigel's heart was thumping hard, as he realised that these must be his mother's notes.

"They were a husband and wife who worked together," Doctor Leatham pointed out. He did not add that they might be long dead or at the very least senile. He watched Nigel carefully weighing him up. "One thing I do know. Whatever you are looking for, you should remember that you can never turn the clock back and, equally, you can never un-know something. Once the genie is out of the bottle there can be no putting it back."

Nigel had taken out a small notebook and a pencil from his pocket and, from the other side of the desk, Doctor Leatham saw his hand tremble. He felt sorry for the young man.

"Mightn't it be best to let it lie, given the impossible nature of your quest? Many notes have been destroyed, you know. These are just your mother's – only one half of the jigsaw," he pointed out kindly.

Nigel took in a deep breath.

"I can't," he replied.

The folder lay tantalisingly on the desk. The doctor sat thoughtfully for a moment. Then he opened the file and copied down the address, handing the paper to Nigel. On it was written, 'Doctor James and Doctor Diana Temple, Dean Heath House, Hampstead, NW3. Tel: 0170 547381'. The telephone number was clearly out of date, the code was wrong.

The buzzer went and the receptionist informed the doctor that a pharmaceutical rep was waiting. The Doctor weighed up the buff file in his hands, sat back and, gazing steadily at Nigel, he replaced the notes carefully on the desk.

"In that case, Mr Laing, all I can do is wish you luck. I have to meet a pharmaceutical rep in reception." The doctor rose from his desk and passing Nigel he placed his hand on his Nigel's shoulder indicating that he should remain seated. "This might take a couple of minutes, take your time, Mr Laing, to recover your composure. Do please excuse me. Good day." For a fleeting moment their eyes met and Nigel hoped that in that one brief glance he could communicate his heartfelt thanks. Because he found he could not speak.

As the door closed he took the file into his trembling hands. He scanned it very quickly, thankfully it was a thin document. His eyes moved over the details of Marion's treatments, hesitating only over the letter outlining Gerald's sperm count and the impossibility of natural conception. There they were, the dates of each of the three attempts, and beside them two letters and a string of six numbers. Carefully Nigel copied the code into his notebook. Next to the code there was a note, a description: six foot three, light brown hair, and then the anticipated delivery date of the baby. That was all. It was enough.

Nigel found himself outside in the brilliant afternoon sunshine, feeling immeasurably sad.

10

Digging the Dirt

Frank Smite was in The Muck and Rake. His drinking companions, fellow hacks, had long since called it a night and gone home. 'No bloody stamina, these kids,' he thought to himself. Frank had been on pints of best all evening but his bladder wasn't what it was, so he switched to Scotch. He had been propping up the bar but, as he was beginning to feel a bit unsteady, he headed for a booth in the far corner where he could comfortably stretch out.

The booths had high comfortable bench seats covered in a tasteless pictorial tapestry fabric. Above the bench seat was a green velvet curtain suspended from a substantial brass pole. It gave a false sense of privacy. If you spoke in nothing but a whisper then, naturally, your conversation remained private. However if, as with the three men in the booth next to Smite, you were a bit the worse for drink as well as a hooray Henry with a booming voice, then no chance – your every utterance could be heard and you wouldn't know if anyone was listening to your conversation.

At first Smite was barely listening. His mind was on the result of the forthcoming football match, he had a bet on and he'd be down a hundred if Liverpool lost. But then something caught his attention, the name of a lobbyist he knew, Mark Stanton. Stanton would feed him little bits of information and gossip picked up from time to time at the House of Commons; nothing much, nothing big. But Smite would pass the gossip on and either earn himself a bit on the side, use it to gain a favour, or get himself out of the shit with the editor. Handy, knowing someone like Stanton.

Smite returned to the bar for a refill as an excuse to get a better look at the three toffs. The one with the loud voice was a big fella, a great pink, pudgy thing with black hair that appeared dyed, and he looked like an angry baby. He wore one of those horrible, big dark pinstriped suits, the type City boys were so fond of, even down to the sickly-puce handkerchief popping out of the breast pocket. Smite couldn't get such a clear view of the other two without making it obvious. They were thinner and not as loud and one of them was quite short with red hair. He returned to the booth and sat down. Strength regained, he twisted himself round, putting his feet up on the bench and propping himself up against the wood-panelled wall behind him. Through a crack in the curtain he could just see the fat hands of the big bloke and an open briefcase on the desk. Lying on top of the papers in the case was a glossy colour brochure. 'StemShaw' it read in large, blue type.

"Anyway, Giles, if they don't pass this legislation, then we're going to be hard pressed to complete this work. Finance will dry up and our sponsors will melt away. It puts our plans for expansion in jeopardy. The UN vote was a disaster – a declaration banning human cloning, even the therapeutic cloning of embryos, is hardly what we needed. If we're not careful we'll be back in the medical dark ages."

It was the red-haired chap talking, he sounded like an educated Scot. A fancy accent. Edinburgh, Smite guessed.

"Stanton is all very well. I respect him and I know that he's going to do his best but for us. But, frankly, we need a miracle if this research is to get a licence. The government may have been keen on the bio-tech industry when it came to power but, to be honest, policy is being driven by votes and they're running scared of the 'leave-it-all-to-nature-and-God' brigade. There was a lot of flak after this last vote. What we need is real influence. We need to get to some of these people."

By 'these people' Smite assumed he meant the MPs and ministers.

"I've got one chappie whom I can 'influence'," Giles declared with a suggestive and unpleasant laugh. "Michael Barton, GP, Minister for the Family. We were at Med school together and young Michael got into a spot of bother and I think you can guess who helped him out of it." He gave another laugh full of innuendo. "I rather doubt his wife has been apprised of his earlier activities and, given some of the pronouncements he makes and his voting pattern, well, let's just say I feel sure he will agree that he owes me a favour or two. I can be very forgetful if I have a vote in the bag." All three laughed.

"I think it's time to renew his acquaintance, don't you?"

Smite wrote down 'StemShaw', 'Giles' and then 'Michael Barton' on a page of his pocket book. Slyly he watched as the group gathered up their belongings and left the pub. He sniffed. There was a story here, a nice juicy story. In the meantime he'd do a bit of digging over the background of Michael Barton and see what he could come up with. Funny really, he thought of Barton as one of the good guys. Mind you, he would have been a student in the late sixties or early seventies and that could throw up all sorts... free love...LSD...the lot!

"Let's hope it's not as dull as 'having inhaled'!" Smite scoffed under his breath and slipping his notebook into his pocket, he set off into the night in search of a taxi.

*

The day of Nigel and Sarah's wedding dawned bright and clear. It was late May and the first Saturday of the half-term break, so Nigel could take the following week for the honeymoon in Paris without any further disruption to his teaching.

Sarah, who was entitled to feel the tingling nervousness of any young bride, was aware of the extra tension created by Marion's death and Gerald's revelations.

"At least he doesn't have to make a speech," her mother Elizabeth said, as she adjusted Sarah's veil. "Don't you worry about Gerald. We'll look after him and you know what everyone will say: how beautiful you look and what a shame Marion couldn't be here and how proud she would be of both of you." She knelt down on the floor to straighten the heavy silk skirts and smooth out the creases. "There are always secrets in families, darling. It's just that this one is a little unusual, that's all. So unusual, in fact, that no one would ever guess. Now, let me look at you. Oh you look so beautiful. I'll call your father." Both mother and daughter had tears in their eyes. "You can't cry, darling, it will ruin your make up!"

Elizabeth pinched Sarah's cheeks to restore a little colour and set off down the hall to fetch Bob and to check on the bridesmaids, who were changing in the spare bedroom.

The service went without a hitch, and the wedding party was soon settled into Sayers Hall, a large country house hotel where the reception was held. Sarah had caught sight of Gerald out of the corner of her eye as she walked up the aisle on the arm of her father. She was delighted to see that he was smiling and appeared genuinely happy for Nigel. Her mother was right; no one would have thought that Gerald was anything but Nigel's very own father. And a great many of the relatives remarked that Marion would have been so proud. Sarah's father, Bob, made a very nice reference to Marion in his speech and the best man, a fellow teacher at Nigel's school, was witty and thankfully not too risqué. And before she knew it, Sarah was tossing her bouquet into the air and she and Nigel were waving out of the car window as they sped away towards the airport.

"Happy, Mrs Laing?" Nigel asked.

"Blissfully, Mr Laing," Sarah replied as they kissed.

*

The plans for the extension were progressing at a steady pace. There were, of course, delays but Julia was enjoying the process. She liked the feeling of accomplishment that successfully designing and selecting the modern features for this refurbishment entailed. But the whole project had turned out to be considerably more costly than she had anticipated. She reasoned that if she was going to have all this disruption, then she might as well have what she had always dreamed of. The back wall of the house, where once the sink had looked onto the garden, was to be knocked through and a large steel beam placed there in order to support the end of the house. The drains would have to be taken up and repositioned. And Julia had frequent discussions with the architect about the planning consent and building regulations.

Michael relented a little, and agreed to meet the initial costs of the plans; he then requested a thorough breakdown of all the costs.

"We're only assessing the cost, Julia," he said sternly. Julia took no notice though and delighted in the preparation of what she called a 'design board' on which she secured cuttings from interior magazines and specialist appliance suppliers who might be part of the final plan. It was late May now and, by the time summer was in full swing, she would have a wonderful kitchen with space for a large table and double doors opening out onto the garden.

"You know, I think I'm quite good at this sort of thing," she said to Michael. "Managing projects, pulling things together. There must be a job I could do that would use these skills?"

"Yes," agreed Michael vaguely. "You have style. You could do a bit of interior design."

Julia felt crushed.

"I was thinking more of project management."

"Darling! Project management really is a term that is used for those clever bods who have an in-depth knowledge of computers or business analysis. And you just don't have that sort of knowledge. Anyway, you've got your hands full here, where you manage wonderfully." He bent down and kissed Julia lightly on the forehead as he went to pour another drink.

Flushed with anger Julia rose out of her seat and left the room abruptly.

When Michael turned round, having poured himself a large gin and tonic, he found the room empty. It didn't occur to him that his comments were in any way a contributory factor. He reminded himself that he really must sit Julia down and explain about the impossibility of such a scheme. In his ministerial role, Michael was now far too busy to cope with the level of disruption that construction work and remodelling the house would entail, and he certainly didn't want his summer recess blighted by builders. It was the only time that his family life was free from the tyranny of the blessed ministerial red boxes.

*

Nigel and Sarah spent a wonderful week's honeymoon in Paris. The weather was perfect and Paris was as romantic and enchanting as ever. They spent their days drifting through art galleries looking at their favourite Impressionist paintings and their evenings walking in Monmartre trying out enticing little bistros. Nigel insisted Sarah sit for one of the many artists who worked the tourists. But when the young man discovered they were on honeymoon he would accept no fee. The picture, in pastels, was a chocolate box image of Sarah and they laughed happily as they wandered on through the late evening sunlight, the exaggerated, showy sketch furled up under Nigel's arm. Sarah knew she would treasure it always. There was no discussion of Nigel's discovery, however, and for that one week they lived as if nothing had changed. They were happy.

But when the pilot came over the tannoy and announced the weather conditions at Heathrow – low cloud and rain – Sarah turned to Nigel and it was as if the change in temperature could be measured on his face; that haunted look had returned. It meant only one thing, he was deep in thought about resuming the search for his real father.

Nigel didn't have a plan as such. The three weeks allocated to the search for Marion's records were insufficient, he had barely scratched the surface, although his visit to Hampstead hadn't been entirely wasted. He had left the train at Hampstead Heath station, turning right up South End Road. He walked past the same small parade of shops that Marion would have passed. Later as the houses grew larger Nigel imagined her apprehension at the course of action she was taking.

At first, he thought he must have missed the clinic. He strode up the hill, the heath itself a sward of green on his right hand side. As he reached the summit he saw a group of beautiful bay-fronted villas. Each had its own wrought iron balcony adorned with clematis or honeysuckle. He looked along the row at the names of the properties. None matched the name he had been given. A postman emerged from behind a particularly pretty *daphne odora* shrub in one of the gardens. Nigel stopped him.

"I wonder if you could help me? I'm looking for Dean Heath House," Nigel asked.

"You're right outside it mate. Here, look." And the postman took him by the arm and turned him around to face the house.

The house was so grand and unusual that Nigel had completely dismissed it. It wasn't at all what he had expected. Behind two white wrought iron gates stood as fine a home as you could imagine. A large stately house with two magnificent oriel windows the full length of the three storeys, with white louvered shutters each side. The bays were not tacked on, as they would have been in any lesser house; the curving brickwork was integrated into the form of the building and the window, in what must have been a fine drawing room, was almost fifteen feet long. Curving around these bays was a mature wisteria in full bloom, every one of its long mauve fronds almost two feet in length. Beneath it sat a white painted bench looking out over the lawn and gardens.

Nigel went towards the gates and, realising they were chained and padlocked, set off around the perimeter of the garden looking for a way in. The entrance, once he found it, was in a lane around the corner. The front door, reached through a side gate, was covered by a wooden canopy running along the house. A charming edging detail on the canopy gave it the appearance of a turn of the century railway station.

He took a deep breath, walked up to the door and pulled the handle connected to a bell somewhere a long way off in what once were the servants' quarters. He stood waiting for what felt like eternity and then, just when he was about to ring the bell again, he heard small quick steps approaching the door. The door opened and behind it stood a small, neat foreign woman with shining black hair and equally black eyes. From her uniform Nigel assumed she must be the maid. Her English was limited and all that he could discover was that there was no Doctor Temple there and that as far as she knew the present owners, Mr and Mrs Schulz, were lawyers who had resided there for ten years. She was brisk and efficient and when she had passed on this inadequate information, she politely shut the door.

Nigel set off towards Heath Street past the up-market mansion blocks and another remarkable Gothic home. Finally, stopping on Hampstead High Street at a coffee bar for a cappuccino and an opportunity to collect his thoughts, he considered his poor mother as he spooned the froth from his coffee into his mouth. Hampstead had always been for the smart set, and Marion would have felt like a fish out of water. As if to illustrate this point, an elegant woman drew up in a gold Mercedes coupé, stopped on the double yellow lines outside and without a thought popped out to have a chat with a friend she'd seen sitting drinking at a table on the pavement. When a traffic warden appeared she persisted in her conversation and blithely tossed the ticket into the back of the car. Then, in a disdainful and cavalier fashion, she drove off.

A few days later Nigel contacted the 'Family Records Centre' where the census returns for the area were held. These documents gave up the following information: listed as past residents in the house were a husband and wife, both doctors. The doctors, James and Diana Temple, remained living at that address until ninety seventy-nine. These, then, must have been the very people who had brought Nigel into being. He felt both a curious mixture of triumph at having secured their names, and a powerful burning resentment. How could anyone so casually bring a life into being and then, with equal disregard, prevent that being from knowing who they really were? What did they think they were doing? Where were the rights of the child in all this? It was accepted that adopted children often suffered terrible psychological damage from their hidden past, and that the mothers who had given their babies up were often tormented by the lack of information as to their subsequent happiness. Adopted children, rightly, had access to documents about their birth parents but they was being withheld from Nigel and others like him – and it was wrong.

The breakthrough came, although at first Nigel didn't recognise it as such, when he contacted the Land Registry. Under B: Proprietorship Register, were two names, Gustav Lasson and Terence Matthews. Matthews and Lasson were also doctors and had taken over the Temples' clinic. It was some weeks before Nigel discovered that their tenure lasted just eighteen months, the house remaining in their ownership until nineteen eighty-one. If, as Nigel hoped, the clinic had expanded and moved to larger premises then Marion's records might be held at another clinic. But for now further investigations to trace the two doctors would have to wait.

Nigel felt he needed to resume his teaching and put his efforts wholeheartedly into his pupils and department. The headmaster, a wise and genial man, had welcomed him back and said that he hoped Nigel would now return to the school in spirit as well as body. Nigel knew he was right. Since his mother's death and the discovery it brought with it, he had been absent to some degree. His mind was not on his work. If he wasn't thinking about his mother or Gerald or the bizarre circumstances of his creation, then latterly he was occupied with some aspect or other of the wedding arrangements. It had helped that he and Sarah had invited the headmaster and his wife to the wedding. Nevertheless, with the honeymoon over, it was time for Nigel to knuckle down and help his pupils successfully through their exams and plan next year's expansion of the curriculum. The summer holidays therefore would be his next opportunity to investigate further.

*

"Julia! These plans are fabulous! You must be thrilled!" Breeda hovered over the large drawing that the architect had provided and then lifted the corners of the swatches of fabric and paint samples from the board. The perfume from some particularly heady white lilies drifted in on the breeze. "Will you smell that scent from your lilies…Mmm, now this truly would be my idea of heaven, an English flower garden in a gentle sun with the scent of the flowers, the bees collecting nectar and a bird or two singing for the sheer joy of it all! Just think, soon you'll be able to throw open the doors and step out into this paradise of yours."

Julia brought over a jug full of Pimms brimming with cucumber, mint and fruit.

"If it was going to be mine, I would plan a party to launch it as if it were a fabulous new liner. You've a great plan here, Julia, Michael must be really proud of you. There's not many men who have a wife as capable."

Julia didn't reply. There was an awkward pause.

"Michael does like it, I take it?"

"Yes, I think he's pleased. But he hasn't really shown a lot of interest. He's always busy," she added by way of an explanation. "That's part of the problem of him being away so much. I rather hoped it would show him what I was capable of," Julia concluded forlornly.

This was the first time Breeda could ever remember Julia voicing any criticism of Michael over and above the usual domestic failings of a husband.

"Everything is all right between you and Michael?" she asked gently.

"Gracious yes. Of course it is. It's me, I'm the problem. I have everything a woman could want; a husband who's loving, kind and adores his children, is in a well paid secure job, where redundancy only comes from total indiscretion or at four or five year intervals, a lovely home, two fine girls… But I'm thirty-eight, thirty-nine this year, and what, if anything, have I achieved? I haven't followed the usual career path of a woman of my generation. I really do need to get some training and get back into work or study. Anything." Julia moved away from the window and began to fold up the architect's drawing.

"But what? You said yourself that you can't manage the girls as well as a full time job," Breeda replied, coming over to the table and settling in one of the old pine chairs.

"I'd really like to go into some sort of management. Michael says I'd need computer skills. I'm ridiculously out of date. I can't afford to be this out of touch with technology."

"So you've talked this over with Michael?" Breeda asked, a hint of surprise in her voice.

"Well, no. Not as such. Actually, I'm trying it out on you, as an idea," Julia replied laughing. The Pimms was beginning to take effect.

"Go for it Julia, that would be my advice. Get yourself off to the local college and find a course, there's that women's business group who could put you in touch with the right type of training, I've got their number somewhere. I wish I'd done it years ago. We're not like those clever career women, you and I, we missed the boat somehow. Unless you're a medic or a solicitor and can afford a string of nannies, au pairs and cleaners, it's all too easy to fall off the rungs of the career ladder. We wanted to rear our own children – that was our big mistake," Breeda acknowledged. "You turn round and suddenly you're forty and no one wants to know. I tried looking up something on the Internet the other day, on the kids' computer. I nearly took a hatchet to the damn thing."

"But you have Finn," Julia reminded her, rising from the table and placing the folder together with some catalogues on range cookers.

"God! You'd think having a computer specialist for a husband would help. But if he does show you how to do something, it's keystrokes as quick as a flash and you've not even seen his hands touch the blessed keyboard, never mind know what he's done or why. I'll tell you, to have your husband teach you about computers, well, it's worse than having them teach you to drive!"

Julia threw back her head and laughed again. Her earlier melancholy had vanished.

"Oh, Breeda, thank you," she said.

"Thank me! Whatever for?"

"Making me laugh. I needed a laugh."

"You don't think that might be the Pimms?" Breeda replied.

*

No sooner was Sarah inside the flat than Nigel picked her up in his arms and whirled her round and round until she was giddy.

"Guess what! At last I've found Lasson and Matthews!"

"Oh, Nigel, that's wonderful. Where? How?"

"Morton Manor; it's just outside St Albans apparently. They bought out the Doctors Temple and eighteen months later they'd expanded the clinic and moved. It's now part of a big international group, doing all sorts of procedures as well as assisted-reproduction stuff." Nigel by now was holding Sarah firmly by her shoulders and was kissing her quickly on the mouth.

"And the records?" Sarah asked.

"Must be there."

"Let's hope so."

Even if they are, Sarah thought, Nigel will never be allowed to see them.

11

Altruistic Act

Nigel sat in the blue hire car outside the gates of Morton Manor. The journey had taken him almost three hours. He had pulled into a convenient lay-by just beyond the barrier and was watching people come and go. The cars were mainly occupied by couples, some relatively young but many more in their late thirties or forties. Nigel wondered how many of them were there for the express purpose of commissioning a child from donor eggs or sperm. Would they at some future date be telling this child how they were conceived and explaining that they were specially chosen?

He turned on the ignition of the car and it sprang to life. He drove through the barrier and along the gravel drive from which he could see mature conifer trees scattered across the velvet lawn. Finally, around a corner the magnificent building came into view. Morton Manor had once been a grand Jacobean country house and its imposing facade stood proud and elegant against a summer sky decorated with candyfloss wisps of cloud. In the car park a neatly painted sign in cream and blue lettering pointed him in the direction of reception. He locked the car, took in a lungful of the fresh country air and set off in the direction of the front entrance.

Nigel had given very little thought as to what he was actually going to say or do once he'd arrived. He considered this the first visit in a 'long game' played out in several stages, quite what those stages would be he had no idea. He followed another couple up the steps and in through the heavy and ancient front door. The reception hall was so dim in contrast to the strong sunlight outside that for a moment he was lost in the darkness. Gradually, he was able to see the high vaulted ceiling, the sumptuous sofas and the modern reception desk. Behind it several impeccably dressed women were variously dealing with clients or checking appointment times on the computer. The whole atmosphere was one of efficient, courteous hospitality. It could have been a country club.

He approached the reception desk and was greeted by a smart older woman with greying blonde hair swept up in a French pleat.

"Can I help you?" she asked.

"I hope so," Nigel began somewhat hesitantly.

She beamed a smile of encouragement.

"I haven't an appointment, but my wife and I are having difficulty… You see, we want to start a family and… Well, as I was in the area," Nigel continued. "I…I just want information really."

"So you haven't had any contact with Morton Manor before?"

"No. No, I haven't."

"So you won't have had one of our information packs." She reached down behind the desk and took out an expensive folder. This she arranged in front of Nigel and set about showing him the introductory booklet and several other brochures which were contained inside.

"Everything you need to know at this stage is here. So if you would like to take this home, you and your wife can look at it at your leisure. Usually an initial appointment will be made through a letter of referral from your doctor." The young man before her looked, she considered, nervous and slightly lost. "We have a cafeteria for clients," she said gesturing to a doorway in the far corner. "If you would like to have a coffee and read through these booklets then, if you have any queries, I'm sure I could find someone to spend a few minutes explaining things."

"Oh, thank you." Nigel brightened visibly.

The receptionist had already slipped out from behind the desk to direct him towards the cafeteria.

"Oh, I almost forgot! Could you sign in here." She took Nigel by the elbow and turned him back to the desk. He quickly thought of the name of a school-teacher colleague and signed 'Sam Black' and, with his visitor's badge on, he was directed to the spacious café overlooking another fine aspect of the garden.

There he tucked himself into a corner with a cup of strong black coffee, took out the various brochures contained in the folder and read them. Pictures of happy couples chatting with doctors littered the glossy pages. Tucked away at the end, after the statistics on cycles and success rates, was an outline of the law. Whereas in the past donors had been anonymous, now the children would have access to donor information on their eighteenth birthday; 2023 would be the date when these children would finally find out who their biological parents were. Nigel felt a curious and compelling resentment, for he guessed that somewhere in this building lay the answer, the identity of his real father, and for him there would be no legal entitlement to that information; the change in the law was not retrospective.

The café was empty save for a black couple in army combats. He leafed through the information. It was all reassuring and upbeat, giving the success rate statistics for the last available year and running through a summary of procedures. There were also helpful maps of the area and colour photographs of smiling staff interspersed with other photographs of a lone sperm and a developing egg. Nowhere could Nigel find a guide to the cost. A couple of young women came in – staff, Nigel decided – and sat at the table next to him. He listened in to their conversation. One was complaining to the other about her workload. Apparently she was a data input clerk.

"I've got a backlog of work that makes me want to weep. I've told Janice and all she'll say is it's not her fault. We've two girls on maternity leave at the same time and the position is going out to agencies in a couple of weeks."

"At that rate we won't have anyone before August," her companion grumbled.

"Tell me about it! I've got a fortnight on Crete booked for July and I am not changing it, not for anyone!"

"Well, that's just it, isn't it? Janice never thinks things through or plans ahead. Why should maternity leave come as a surprise? You do get several months warning, just as you know that in summer people go off on holiday. And yet here she is writing the perishing job description now! This should have been organised as far back as April!"

A thought occurred to Nigel. He felt a sudden deep excitement. He drained his coffee cup, returned his badge to reception, signed out and left.

He decided he would ring personnel.

Sarah had just returned from the cinema with a friend. Nigel hadn't wanted to go to see the film, he had work to do. There were a number of changes in the curriculum for the next academic year and, unless he sorted these out soon, it would blight the summer break.

"Good film?" he enquired as she dropped down onto the sofa.

"So-so," Sarah replied.

"How much holiday have you got left? Only, school breaks up on July the fourteenth." Nigel spoke as casually as he could.

"A couple of weeks, why?"

"I just wondered."

Nigel had been meaning to make a very difficult request for several days – and he'd been carrying an application form around in his briefcase for over a week.

Sarah went to fill the kettle.

"Did you have anything in mind? We could possibly have a couple of days in a bed and breakfast; that wouldn't break the budget," she suggested. "I've never been to Lyme Regis. If the weather turned fine we could go there. What do you think? Nigel?"

Nigel was rummaging through his briefcase.

"Actually, Sarah, I need your help." He produced the application form and handed it to her.

"What's this?" she asked cautiously.

"It's an application form," Nigel stated flatly.

"Yes, I can see that. But what for? I have a job," Sarah countered suspiciously. She turned the form over to face her. At the top of the box marked for employer's details, it read 'Morton Manor'. A small crease appeared above the bridge of Sarah's nose. She was disconcerted.

"What exactly is this all about, Nigel?" Sarah demanded. "If it's what I think it is, I have to tell you right now that I'm not doing it."

Nigel knew he would have to play this very cleverly. Sarah was apt to dig her heels in, and it was asking a lot of her. It would, he concluded, be better if he appeared injured rather than show his real feelings – anger at any refusal to help him.

"You said you'd help me."

"Yes, I did. But this would be a criminal act. I would be lying in order to get the job. I'd need fake references and probably wouldn't get it anyway."

"They're desperately short of staff."

"Oh thanks," Sarah replied sarcastically. "And just supposing I do get into the building. These files aren't going to be on computer, are they? They're ancient and they must be under lock and key somewhere, if they haven't already been shredded! So you expect me to snoop about, stealing keys and creeping around – I'll get caught, Nigel, that's what will happen – I'm not a private detective! I can't do it, I'm sorry. Anything else, anything legal that is, but not this. Anyway, why don't you try a private detective agency?" Sarah brightened at this obvious solution. "They're used to going undercover, or whatever they call it."

"For that very reason – it is illegal. They operate within the law. I checked."

"Well then, you'll understand that a criminal record would do nothing for my career," Sarah stated firmly and then added, "I'm sorry."

"But you would only need to be there for a couple of weeks and if you were found in a restricted area, you could just plead ignorance. It's only a maternity leave cover; they're not going to check you out so thoroughly. We could give your parents and Gerald's address for the references and intercept the letters. They'd never know."

"You've got this all worked out, haven't you? How do you know that this is just covering a maternity leave?" Sarah asked.

"I've been there and I overheard a conversation between two of the staff."

"And how do you know that Marion's records are even there?" He had been without telling her. She felt cold suddenly. He had been to this place without telling her and this search had become an obsession.

"Well, the Human Fertilisation and Embryo Authority don't hold them. I've asked; her records are too old. And Lasson and Matthews went from the Hampstead clinic straight to Morton Manor, they will have taken them with them."

"I still say they will have destroyed them," she said.

"They aren't allowed to."

"I'm sorry, Nigel, but the answer is still no." Sarah handed back the application form. "I'm really sorry but this would jeopardise everything I've worked for. I can't do this." She got up quietly and left the room. As far as she was concerned the subject was closed.

*

Michael and Julia had just finished supper and were now having a gin and tonic in the living room.

"How much? Julia, you can't be serious?" Michael had just been told the final quote from the builders and kitchen planner. It totalled almost thirty five thousand pounds. "Out of the question."

Julia hadn't expected this response.

"But you agreed I could go ahead with it," she declared.

"No. No, I said you should get some estimates. Now you have, I can see that we can't possibly afford such a scheme. I was expecting something more in the region of ten thousand, an altogether lower amount."

Julia felt her neck flush as she suppressed a furious explosion of anger.

"I think, Michael, that you're out of touch with the cost of everything these days." She felt tempted to add that this was because Michael never found himself in a shop anymore, as either she or one of his flunkies tended to his every need. But she stopped herself, realising that this tactic would merely result in Michael becoming entrenched and vetoing the plan.

"Julia, we simply don't have this kind of money to spend on a kitchen."

"Well, we'll re-mortgage or get a loan. That, Michael, is what most people do when they need a large sum for renovations. After all, the mortgage on this house is minuscule relative to its value, and you're on a minister's salary, so we can easily afford it," Julia stated boldly.

Michael stood staring at her, he had never known her be so insistent and dictatorial.

"That," he said provocatively, "would take my agreement. You forget, Julia, we still have a very large mortgage on the flat in London."

"I don't believe I'm hearing this, and you on a minister's salary with all those deductible expenses and allowances!" Julia's voice rose unpleasantly. She pushed the plans and estimates back into the folder labelled 'Kitchen Project' and stormed out of the room.

From her vantage point on the landing Tess had listened to the developing argument with rapt fascination. Her parents hardly shared a cross word, let alone quarrelled, although she sometimes wondered if this might be because they were so seldom together. In the kitchen, she could hear her mother crashing pots and pans about in fury. What on earth could have caused the trouble? Instinctively she knew better than to go downstairs and ask. She had noticed lately that her Mummy didn't seem as cheerful as usual, but she never dared to ask why. She slipped back into her bedroom and settled down to complete her maths homework.

*

Giles Strumpshaw had tried on several occasions to get an appointment with his old friend Michael Barton, all to no avail. He had written explaining the need for the new Scientific Research Bill. Without the freedom to experiment the chance of finding cures for cancer, Parkinson's disease, or Alzheimer's would be lost. He received only the standard reply from an underling: 'The Minister would give his views due consideration.'

Giles rang the department. Michael's diary secretary was vague and elusive. And at the constituency office the Minister's agent, Tim, gave Giles to believe that it would be months before he had a spare moment for lunch.

"The Minister does eat, I take it?" Giles had quipped, irritated. And so, in the end, he had sent in an envelope a rather crude picture of a nineteen fifties' big- breasted starlet, on the reverse of which he had written, 'WANKBANK!' Followed by the suggestion of a meeting over lunch to talk about old times.

12

Embryonic

It hadn't occurred to Sarah that anything out of the ordinary was taking place inside her. Adapting to married life had been easy enough. After all, she had been living with Nigel before the wedding. She was more comfortable at the flat. She felt happy making minor adjustments; it was fun replacing an old worn-out cushion with a new one that they chose together. Of course she was very careful to keep a tight rein on the budget, she was determined they would move to a small terraced house of their own within two years. In eighteen months she would have completed her PhD and she could get a real job with a better salary that would allow them to take on a larger mortgage.

She hadn't really considered her own needs since the wedding. So she was surprised when, during a visit to her parents, her mother had suggested she was looking a bit peaky.

"I'm fine. A little overtired maybe. Some of my lab work hasn't been going too well and I've been putting in a lot of extra hours. I was even in the lab last Sunday because a whole lot of results had been contaminated and I had to set up the entire experiment again."

"Nothing else to report?" Elizabeth hinted.

"What are you getting at, Mum?" Then the penny dropped, "Oh goodness no, that's all taken care of. We need a house first and I need my PhD. But don't worry, you'll be the first to know after Nigel."

A few days later Sarah suddenly felt unwell as she stood in a hot, crowded compartment on the train and she had to fight her way out at the next stop to rest on a bench. But it was only when she opened the bathroom cabinet looking for something to soothe her stomach that she realised that the symptoms of extreme tiredness, slight nausea and unaccountable hunger where not just those of overwork…they could also be those of early pregnancy. And now she came to think of it she had missed a month, possibly two.

Doctor Krishnamurthy confirmed what the blue panel on the predictor test from the chemist had already announced.

"About ten weeks at a guess. Does that seem right to you?" she enquired.

"This is rather a surprise. It's an accident."

The doctor gazed at her evenly.

"You're recently married and it might be a little sooner than you had hoped, but be pleased. You're young and fit; these 'accidents' often turn out to be the best-timed babies. I'll book you in at the hospital for your antenatal appointment and your first scan." She stopped.

Sarah was crying.

"I've my PhD to finish," she sobbed. "And we only have a tiny flat…I'm not ready for this, it's too soon."

Doctor Krishnamurthy took Sarah's hand in hers and said gently, "Women have had babies in flats and finished their studies before, you know. It's a shock, give yourself time to get used to the idea. Then tell someone who you know will be delighted for you, apart of course from your husband, who I'm sure will be thrilled. Future grandparents are rather good." The doctor handed Sarah a tissue, who nodded meekly, gave a thin smile and then left the surgery clutching some leaflets advising on the merits of giving up smoking and abstaining from alcohol during pregnancy.

*

Frank Smite had been ferreting around for weeks and had come up with nothing. If there was any dirt on Michael Barton then he couldn't find it. He went down to the constituency to dig around, questioning the agent, Tim, a funny little chap with a gammy leg. He even found an old room-mate from Barton's student days – nothing. The Minister for the Family came up squeaky-clean every time. He was plain speaking, good looking and women fancied him. Men respected him and everyone thought he did a good job both as a GP and MP. It made Smite sick.

"A bleedin' MP that the public like! Unique, apart from our Mo, but then she packed it in!"

There was nothing for it but to worm his way into this company 'StemShaw' and see if he could get a sniff of it from this fat toff that he'd overheard in the pub. And he'd buy that fellow Stanton a drink, see what he knew. First he'd check out their website, get himself some free information.

"Computers...hate 'em," he announced yet again, as the crisp modernist graphics of 'StemShaw' flicked onto the screen.

*

Sarah stopped outside a baby wear shop and looked at the window display. "I'm not ready for this," she repeated, "it's too soon." A harassed mother brushed past her as she left the shop with a screaming toddler and a baby in a pram. She was yanking the toddler roughly by the arm calling, "Belt up, Jade! And stop your whining!" Sarah turned away abruptly and set off home.

As usual Nigel was on the computer. He was on the trail of an Internet support group that he had heard of, but he had no definite name or web address and he was searching under any likely combination. As donor children were so rarely told about their origins it was proving difficult. Some sites for parents existed but there was hardly anything for the children. Each evening Sarah found him tapping away at the keyboard while she spent the time busy with her studies and, though this could sometimes be quietly companionable, tonight she felt angry.

"Nigel..."

"Mmm..." Nigel only vaguely acknowledged her, he was so engrossed.

"Nigel!" Sarah cried more sharply than she had intended. "I have something to tell you." Nigel looked up, surprised by her tone. "Please, come away from the computer," she added more softly.

"Sarah, what is it, what's wrong?"

Tears had welled up in Sarah's eyes.

"It's, you see I've missed...it's an accident...I'm...I'm ten weeks pregnant!"

Nigel made a reasonable job of showing the delight and enthusiasm of a first time father-to-be, even arranging time off to attend the first antenatal appointment. But when the flickering image appeared on the screen Sarah and Nigel looked on with wonder. There was this tiny being. The radiologist pointed out details to them; the heart clearly beating, a tiny pulse, the spine looking like a minuscule fish bone and then most startling of all, the sockets for the eyes and nose that seemed to form a face full of expression, a character, a distinctive little individual. The baby wriggled and squirmed as it was prodded.

"Is it possible to tell if it's a boy or a girl?" Nigel inquired, still holding tightly to Sarah's hand.

"Only if the baby's in the right position, and your little one has a thigh covering the vital area. It's not a hundred per cent either. Amniocentesis is though, but really you will only need that if there are any concerns about the baby from your first set of tests." She started to take the measurements of the skull, spine and pelvis. Nigel squeezed Sarah's hand. There was so much they'd left unspoken, so many questions lay between them and this scrap of humanity.

"I don't think I want to know the sex," Sarah said. "It would be nice to have a surprise."

"A lot of people feel like that," the radiographer agreed. "It's a sensible approach. You only ever need to establish the sex beyond doubt if there is a hereditary condition that runs in the male or female line."

Sarah looked alarmed.

"And how would you know that?" she asked urgently.

"Family history. We take detailed notes and test for whatever we can but these conditions are very rare," she concluded, aiming to reassure. "Don't worry," she said, taking a final measurement, "baby looks fine. It's perfectly natural to worry, especially the first time."

"So you can't find everything from a scan and tests?" Sarah pressed. "What if you don't know your genetic history? My husband is...adopted."

The moment it was out Sarah felt like a traitor. Why had she lied? Did she feel that sperm donor was some kind of stigma? Nigel looked astonished but he didn't correct her.

"Mention it to the doctor and please don't worry. There are all sorts of reasons people don't have a full family history. Apart from anything else, in previous generations problems were often kept hidden. Remember that the vast majority of babies in this country are born perfectly well and healthy. Let's print out a picture and I'll give you a few minutes to sort yourself out."

By the time they left the clinic an uncomfortable silence had fallen between Nigel and Sarah. As they walked through the endless hospital corridors Nigel kept just a step ahead of Sarah; but it felt like a mile.

Out in the patients' car park, the summer heat was beginning to build. It was going to be a sweltering day. The interior of their ancient car was already stifling and, without a word to one another, they each wound down a window. Nigel went to turn the key in the ignition.

"I'm sorry," Sarah said.

"Why? Why did you say that? Adopted." He was feeling hurt.

"Only that adoption sounded more normal, I suppose. It was a stupid thing to say."

They lapsed into silence; Nigel made no move to start the engine.

"Nigel, do you still have that application form, the one for Morton Manor?"

"Yes."

"I'll fill it in as soon as we get home. I want to know, for our baby's sake. I want peace of mind."

Nigel squeezed her hand. When Sarah turned to look at him, his eyes had filled with tears.

"Thank you. I love you, Sarah, and I haven't told you that lately. I'm so sorry for all this."

"Oh Nigel," Sarah pressed his hand in hers. "We're going to be all right. We will get through this."

*

The interview at Morton Manor was ludicrously simple. Sarah formed the impression that they would have employed a monkey if it had the necessary computer skills, so desperate were they to fill these temporary posts. Sarah was interviewed by Janice, her direct superior, and then introduced to the medical director, who was on her way to a meeting. They shook hands briefly and, not for the first time, Sarah was referred to as 'the cavalry'.

Nigel had arranged to intercept the references and forge the particulars. Sarah was to use her mother's maiden name, McFadden. He booked them both into a small family-run bed and breakfast in St Albans. That first morning Sarah was so terribly nervous that Nigel had to button her shirt because her hands were trembling so much. He dropped her at the main entrance at eight-thirty, giving her a chance to calm herself as she walked up the long drive.

She was greeted at reception by Janice, a middle aged woman in a smart grey suit. She was led along a corridor that stretched from the original building through to the modern extension and up a flight of stairs. Janice pointed out rooms and areas of interest that Sarah might need to know. Sarah took careful note of the layout. Next Janice showed her where to stow her handbag, which desk and computer she would use and where she could find the water cooler with plastic cups, and the staff rest room.

"You can have your lunch in here or you can buy sandwiches from the cafeteria downstairs and you may eat there if you want to. But you have to remember that there are clients using that facility and they take priority – and take care what you talk about, you can be overheard."

Sarah was issued with a badge to show at reception and given a set of keys to desk drawers, and was then introduced to two other younger women, Shirley and Angela. Shirley was tubby and Angela was slim and prettier, with fair hair. They both greeted Sarah warmly and made yet another joke about the cavalry having arrived, Angela gesturing to several piles of A4 manila folders lying on a table beside the window.

She intended to get on with the work swiftly and efficiently for the first few days and not to ask a lot of unnecessary questions, reasoning that if she was seen to work quietly and effectively then she would arouse less suspicion. Later on she could probe more deeply. Angela was charged with spending an hour explaining to Sarah exactly what data from the records needed to be transferred to the computer, and what to leave out; also where on the hard-disk it was stored, as well as access and security codes. The files she was transferring were those of couples who had successfully completed IVF treatment the previous year. The treatment programme, what drug therapy they had had, and number of treatments were all part of this data, as were details of any embryos, eggs or sperm that were still kept frozen and, additionally, whether they were willing to donate any of these to other couples. Sarah's fascination with this information dwindled as she concentrated on typing in the details as fast and accurately as possible.

It was important that she was seen to be competent and it was a slow process, given that she had to tabulate across to the appropriate boxes on the form each time. It was simple work but painstaking and dull. At the end of the day she was exhausted and thankful to be walking once again down the long drive.

Nigel pressed Sarah for every detail. Had she taken careful note of the layout? Could she draw him a diagram? How strict was security? Did she have any inkling as to where old records were kept?

She told him what she knew.

"Nigel, please. Enough! I'm exhausted. It's actually a very draining job, you have to concentrate on the details and be certain you get them all right. These are medical notes after all, I can't afford to make any mistakes or I'll be out."

"You're doing brilliantly," he said encouragingly and kissed her.

It was on her third day that a breakthrough of sorts occurred. Shirley suddenly exclaimed: "Oh, look, another piece of ancient history has surfaced!"

Angela and Sarah both looked up.

"What have you got there then?" Angela asked.

"Stray files from a clinic in Kent found in an old filing cabinet which was about to be dumped."

"Does that happen often?" Sarah asked from behind her monitor.

"Yeah. You'd be amazed where people store and lose medical records. We've even had some found on a rubbish tip!"

"You haven't seen the Dungeon," Angela laughed.

"The Dungeon?" Sarah queried.

"The cellars under here. As you can imagine in a place like this they're vast, and they hold what we call the dinosaur collection!"

"Dinosaur collection?" Sarah feigned ignorance.

"Historical records, they go back decades. Morton Manor heads a group which is the biggest in the whole field of assisted reproduction and it got that way by buying up much smaller clinics – we inherited their records."

"Oh I see, hence the dinosaur collection."

"I'll go and get the key from Janice," Shirley said.

"Can I come and have a look?" Sarah asked innocently. " I could do with a break, my eyes are going."

"Yeah, come on," Shirley replied. "Stretch your legs, eh?"

They set off down the carpeted corridor for Janice's office. The door was open but the room was empty.

"I'll leave her a note," Shirley announced. 'Got the dino keys, S', she scribbled.

So it was as simple as that, Sarah realised. Shirley lifted a bunch of keys from a grey metal key-box, which were tied together with nothing more than a piece of string, and off they set, out of the office, through the double doors and on down the staircase. On the ground floor near the laboratories Shirley took out the bunch of keys and opened a side door. It was dark. She found the light switch and went in. Sarah followed. There were stone stairs, very old and worn down by the years of traffic, no doubt from servants who in the past would have used them daily, fetching and carrying for the big house.

The air was cool, a relief from the summer heatwave taking place above ground, but the smell was musty.

"These can't be ideal conditions for storing paper records. What if there were a flood or a burst pipe?" Sarah asked.

"At one time Janice was told that we were each to spend two hours a week transferring them onto disk and then to the attic, but that idea died a death in no time. I don't think anyone really cares.

In the four years I've worked here this is only the third time I've needed to check a file. They're really just ancient history. They'll never see the light of day. I can't see the point myself."

Sarah bit her lip and asked a more useful question: "So, if they come from so many different sources, how are they collated?"

"By clinic name, which is often just a doctor and location. Then alphabetically and by date, depending on what they are: donor notes, semen batches and patient records. Look, here."

The floor of the cellar was littered with countless large boxes.

"Goodness, there are a lot!" Sarah was surprised. Her eyes darted around the room. The boxes were stacked up to four high. She wasn't certain how the clinic Marion had used would be labelled, but thought it was likely it would be in the name of the original owners: the Doctors Temple, or Dean Heath Clinic.

She wandered between the boxes feigning interest where she had none, running a finger over the labels. Suddenly she saw it: 'Temple/ Dean Heath Clinic' written in thick black felt-tip pen. She felt shaky with excitement. She moved closer and, as casually as she could, lifted the lid and drew out a file at random. 'Curtis' read the name at the top.

Shirley found what she was looking for.

"Here it is," she called.

Sarah jumped slightly and replaced the Curtis file in the box. She tried to appear casual and unhurried, walking over to Shirley.

"And the donors' details, are they here too?" she inquired innocently.

"Yeah, somewhere in this lot. Now I'll just pop these in their slot. Let's get out of here, this place gives me the creeps! When I've been here on my own I've always worried somehow I'll get locked in overnight. I don't fancy it."

*

In Wynshore, Julia was pottering in the garden. It was a beautiful day and she was staking up the acanthus that was falling onto the garden path. The very sharp spikes on the tall flower heads were in danger of scratching the children as they ran past. She was thinking how lovely it would be if only the kitchen opened out onto the garden. She wasn't going to give up. She was a determined woman and calculated that, with a little imaginative manipulation, she could achieve this ambition. She felt sure that charm, coupled with the helpful persuasion of their good friends, would do the trick. It was Breeda's turn to host the Sunday lunch in a fortnight and that would be the perfect opportunity to gang up on Michael in the nicest possible way, and effect a change of heart. After all, if Michael maintained the cost was too great then this would prompt derision and gales of laughter from Finn, at the very least, and even Andrew and Moya would find that excuse a bit thin. Michael was a proud man and he wouldn't want their friends to think he was being a skinflint. Julia stood back from the tidy herbaceous border and looked with growing satisfaction at a job well done.

*

Giles Strumpshaw was admitted to the Minister's office at twelve fifteen exactly. The Minister was unfortunately too busy for lunch but could give him fifteen minutes of his valuable time.

"Giles." Michael made an attempt at greeting him warmly. "Do come in, I am sorry this has to be so short but my schedule doesn't allow for long lunches" He gestured towards a chair. "Shall we sit over here. Sylvia, some coffee, if you wouldn't mind."

They sat by the window of the modern ministerial office. The department overlooked a square that could easily have doubled as a nineteen seventies shopping precinct with a hideous modern sculpture situated to one side. It looked for all the world like a child's cot mobile.

"Lord, Michael, can't you do something about the view?" Giles commented.

"Afraid not, this isn't a cabinet post. They're the ones in the attractive historic buildings," Michael told him.

"Ah, but you are nevertheless a man of influence," Giles remarked, alluding to the topic for the first time. Sylvia arrived with a tray of coffee and placed it on the modern glass coffee table between them and reminded Michael that the taxi taking him to his next appointment would be ready in twenty minutes. Giles, who was perfectly aware that this announcement was entirely for his benefit, smiled and said:

"We'd better cut to the chase then, hadn't we, dear boy?"

Michael eyed Giles with disdain. He had disliked him at university and regretted ever having turned to him for help. Michael had principles, and if Giles had ever taken the slightest interest in his career then he would know that he had a reputation as his own man and was no puppet. Goodness knows, his independence had got him into trouble enough times with James Logan.

"I have to say, Giles, that I am of course more than willing to consider a well advanced argument. But my votes in the house are just that, mine, particularly as this is a vote of conscience. Persuade me of the rightness of your cause by all means, but I'll make up my own mind. All right?" Michael was steadfast.

"Of course you will, Michael. You always were a very moral man." Giles twisted the signet ring on his fat little finger and made a show of examining his fingernails before eyeing Michael with what could only be described as menace. "That's why I feel sure that when you read the documents I have brought from 'StemShaw' you will see the possibilities and the enormous humanitarian benefit that therapeutic and chimerical combining will create for mankind. Truly, it's the medical nirvana that we've all been looking for. Imagine if we can programme cells to make livers, hearts, regenerate spinal cord and nerves. It will mean an unlimited supply of transplant material with none of the problems of rejection. And without any need for patients to take a cocktail of anti-rejection drugs, with all the attendant side effects, for the rest of their lives. We in Britain are leading the world in this field. Without this change in the law it will be impossible to develop the work. It will be disastrous not only for the bio-tech industry, but also for mankind. I can make no stronger case than that.

You're a medical man, Michael; you know what this means to those good people who've walked through your surgery door with dreadful and incurable diseases, Parkinson's, Alzheimer's and even cancer. All that would change. We need this passed. I want your vote. It's vitally important. We mustn't fail in this huge scientific leap forward."

Michael had picked up and was leafing through some of the glossy literature Giles had provided. He paused and then said:

"Giles, we already have the most liberal laws on therapeutic cloning. I see no reason to go further. While there may be incalculable benefits to society, and your industry, I have to consider this very carefully. There are those who maintain the embryo is a human individual – especially after the primitive streak – and that human life should be protected from conception to death and that, morally, the sanction of this technique is the killing of a human being, which is wrong. It's said that this proposal amounts to technological cannibalism! The public express revulsion at the thought of animal-human hybrids. People rightly fear genetic meddling – look at genetic crops. You see, it's opinions such as these that I, and the other Members of Parliament, will have to weigh up carefully before reaching any decision on which way to vote. I will have to take note of my post bag."

He looked up at Giles who, having taken a sip of his coffee, was fumbling in his waistcoat.

"And," Michael added, "there is the very real concern that therapeutic cloning is simply the thin end of the wedge and will be the bridge across which the cloning of full human beings will pass. That is what influenced me to vote against last time. I will not sanction cloning. Or chimeric hybrids, who knows where it would end."

From his waistcoat pocket Giles produced a small black notebook and opened it randomly, turning the page to face Michael.

"Remember this?"

Michael stared fixedly at the book.

"All my darling wives have complained that I am such a hoarder, but you see how helpful it can be to hang on to little mementos from one's past. There's just no telling when they will come in useful."

"I fail to see how this…" Michael began.

"Don't you? Then let me elucidate. You remember this little book, don't you, Michael? I was always a bit of a scribbler, wasn't I? I keep a tally of all sorts of little conquests, of any number of 'friends', small indiscretions, picking up young boys… very young boys!"

"I've never… *in my life!*"

"No, no, no, not you, dear boy; that was Stebbings, remember him? Now a leading member of the Royal College of Surgeons, and on countless boards and committees. Not much use in this case, but one just never knows when such intimate detail may come in handy"

The door opened and Sylvia came in to announce that the taxi was waiting downstairs.

"Tell it to wait, Sylvia," Michael commanded fiercely.

"And then we come to you, dear boy: gambling debts, though nothing so very harmful in that. Do tell me, Michael, why, when you were so very bad at poker did you go on playing? I think you rather liked the heady atmosphere in those Maltese clip joints I took you to. Go on, admit it, you enjoyed slipping behind those red velvet drapes at the back of that greasy spoon café, into the back room. The Camden Road was a favourite I seem to recall, and that place round the back of Kings Cross, now that really was a dive, full of tarts and pimps!" Giles' full pink lips were salivating, he hadn't had so much fun in years. "Remember that Serbian hood with the missing finger and an eye that wandered off? Funny, isn't it, the things that are etched in one's memory. Your Papa would have been none too pleased had he got to hear, and you could have been sent down; they took rather a dim view of getting yourself into that sort of mess back then. Not so these days, now they graduate with state sponsored debt. Yet the solution was so simple and I was delighted that it was to me that you turned for help, because I could help, easy…all those clinics, all those thoughtful, selfless donations. And now all those countless young Bartons out there, hundreds I should think. There was no limit on the number of births then, was there? Clinics weren't too bothered so long as they got their supplies."

"I fail to see, Giles, what bearing my having been a sperm donor as a student, for whatever reason, has on this vote. I've done nothing illegal or dishonest. So if you think you can threaten me then you are very much mistaken."

Giles threw back his head and rocked with laughter, his fat legs spread wide and his hands planted firmly on his knees.

"Come now, Michael! An intelligent chap like you! Let me paint you a pretty picture, shall we say one worthy of a tabloid newspaper. 'Minister's Moral Maze' or 'Minister's Handy-work'-that's really rather good, don't you think? I like that. Or 'Michael Barton, Minister for the Family, was today explaining to his lovely wife Julia and daughters, Tess and Katherine, that he has children scattered the length and breadth of the country. For Michael paid off his student gambling debts through persistent and widespread sperm donation. Such was his need for filthy lucre, that he was known to have made multiple 'donations' all over London and the Home Counties in the early nineteen-seventies, whilst his penchant for Maltese clubs and a hand or five at poker was legendary. Can this be the same minister who with grave concern for embryonic life voted against the therapeutic cloning of embryos? The same minister who recently called certain IVF techniques repugnant! A man who has spread his seed far afield – indeed practically made a career out of it purely for financial gain. Need I go on?"

Michael shifted uncomfortably in his seat.

"It's a tricky one this, isn't it, Michael? Not sleaze in quite the way the tabloids have come to love – no tarts, but sleazy none the less and with a truly twenty-first century angle. To have been a sperm donor could be seen as noble, worthy even. Yet your obvious enthusiasm for the fiscal aspects – so well documented here – and the reason, well, it's a little tawdry, don't you agree?" Giles waved the book in the air.

Michael had heard enough.

"GET OUT!" he bellowed.

Outside Sylvia looked up, startled. She had never heard the Minister shout.

"Messy, Michael, very messy. Public sensibilities involved. And imagine, up and down the country all the those young lads and lasses who think they share a passing resemblance to you will demand DNA tests, want their University fees paid and expect to be welcomed into the bosom of your family. Your cover will be blown. I wonder what Julia and the girls will make of it all? She's a devout Catholic, I understand." Slowly and deliberately Giles rose from the seat. "I can quite see that there is a lot for you to consider. I'll be in touch soon to see what conclusion you have come to. I'll give you a call, when you've had time to think it over."

Michael held open the door.

"Until we meet again, Michael."

The Minister slammed the door.

*

The plan that Nigel had hatched was a simple one. Sarah would start late that day, the excuse being a routine doctor's appointment and make up the work by staying on and taking the keys from Janice's office. If she were found in the building she would simply say that she got locked in. They would return to Maidenhead and Sarah McFadden would simply vanish.

Sarah arrived in the office at eleven fifteen.

"Thank goodness," said Angela.

"Doctors appointment. I've told Janice I'll make up the time this evening."

"Now that's dedication for you."

The day dragged on. Sarah could barely believe it when she looked at the clock repeatedly and the hands appeared not to have moved. Finally it was five thirty and the other girls closed down their computers, collected their belongings and bid farewell for the night.

"Now don't overdo it," Angela said as she skipped out of the door. Sarah could hear Janice tapping away at her keyboard. She had to think of a plan fast. If Janice were to leave for the night, she would lock her office door with the keys inside it. She heard the telephone ring and Janice answered it.

A moment later:

"I've got to pop along to the Scientific Director's office, Sarah. Tell anyone who wants me, would you, I won't be long."

"Of course," Sarah replied. And then said: "Thank you, God," as soon as Janice was a safe distance away on the other side of the double doors. Without hesitation she got up from her desk and slipped into the other office. The metal key box was slightly ajar. Sarah pulled it open and lifted out the keys for the cellar. She popped them into her jacket pocket. With luck, if Janice left in a hurry, she would just shut the box and not check the contents. Later, Sarah would leave them tucked under some files on Shirley's desk, and Janice would simply tick her off for having left them lying around.

At six fifteen, Janice locked her office and coming in to Sarah's room said, "It is good of you to make up the time. The others wouldn't, you know."

"Well, there's a lot to do," Sarah said amiably, gesturing to the pile of files on the desk by the window. "And it takes my mind off things. My mother isn't very well, you see."

"Oh dear, I am sorry. Well, thank you anyway. I don't know what we would do without you. Seriously, if you wanted to become permanent, I could arrange it. Give it some thought. Goodnight. See you in the morning."

"'Night," Sarah called.

She continued working until about half past seven. There were still staff bustling about but by quarter to eight a stillness fell over the building.

It was now or never.

13

Gene Genie

Sarah picked up the bunch of keys and, with some files to give her mission some authenticity, set off down the stairs towards the cellar. When she put the key in the lock she was shaking and struggled to open it. A passing lab technician, a young man with ginger hair, stopped and said:

"Having trouble? Here, let me."

Sarah's heart was beating so strongly that she felt sure he would hear it. She smiled weakly. Having thanked him, she went in and shut the door behind her. Her legs were trembling so much as she descended the treacherous steps that she was afraid she might fall and then be trapped in this dank cellar all night. She shivered at the thought as she watched a spider making its way quickly across the ceiling to a hole in the crumbling brickwork. At last she stood before the boxes labelled 'Temple/Dean Heath House'. She set about her task with her methodical attention to detail. She couldn't be sure until she opened the boxes that they were complete or even in alphabetical order. She would have to check very carefully so that she didn't miss anything.

But she was in luck. The doctors Temple had been meticulous in their record keeping and quite quickly she found Marion Laing's notes with her date of birth and the Brentwood address marked clearly at the top. Then she looked down at the treatment records. They matched those that Nigel had copied at Doctor Leatham's clinic in Wimpole Street. The code for the final successful treatment programme was identical. She had to check a further three boxes until she found the file of donor records as these were not as carefully collated and the box was brimming over. Sarah removed the files in batches of ten and began to check the codes one by one. At one point she became excited before realising that one digit was transposed. After about half an hour she had settled into a comfortable rhythm, checking and discarding. Then she found it:

the corresponding code.

For a moment she sat in the gloom staring down at the folder. Here in her hands was the real name of Nigel's father and the grandfather of her baby. Sarah closed her eyes briefly, took a very deep breath in and opened the file. 'Michael Barton' was clearly written at the top in a neat hand.

"Michael Barton," Sarah repeated. Next to the name in faded pencil was written 'Lanky' as if it were a nickname. "So I am Mrs Barton, not Mrs Laing. And you are young baby Barton," she said, putting her hand on her stomach.

"Well, Mr Michael Barton, what can you tell me?" Quickly she noted down his date of birth and the address he had given. Under occupation was written 'Medical student, Barts.' It listed the colour of his eyes as blue, his hair light brown/slightly curly, and his height as six foot three. It could have been a thumbnail sketch of Nigel. Under interests, it simply stated 'Music'. Like father, like son! But apart from a consent form and a long list of the frequency of donations, and there were a lot of those, there was no medical history. Sarah searched the files either side of Michael Barton's: nothing. She also looked through other boxes: nothing.

Sarah checked the time on her watch and found it was eight thirty. She had to leave with the file – it was the only concrete evidence that this was, in fact, the name of Nigel's father. She wrote down the information separately just in case she were caught and the file taken from her. Then she stuffed the battered folder into the bottom of her bag and left.

*

Nigel had written and then screwed up the letter so often that he had lost count. How do you tell someone who, in all probability, had never in his wildest dreams imagined your existence, that you are his son? At first Nigel wrote on the computer, but Sarah suggested that it might be better handwritten. She was right and so Nigel started again in his best hand. They spent hours discussing the content of the letter. Eventually Nigel realised there was no easy way to break such news.

"What precisely is the aim of this letter? Exactly what response do you want?" Sarah asked. A look of deep concentration came over her pretty face.

"I want to meet him. I want to know why he became a sperm donor and I want to know about the family history and background. I want to see if I'm like him and I want to see if he's a nice person, someone I would have liked as a father."

A lot of room for disappointment there, Sarah thought.

"I think that your best bet is to go for the family history stuff first, you can use the fact that you married recently and that we're expecting a baby. It sounds reasonable. Make it clear that you don't want to disrupt his family life or embarrass him. And then tell him a bit about yourself, your achievements and ambitions."

How could so few lines pose such difficulty? Nigel wondered. He had spent two nights scrunching up sheets of paper and starting again until nearly three in the morning. When finally, he felt he had a form of words that would do, he went to bed and decided to look at the letter again in a few days time before sending it. It was Sarah who suggested the photographs. He put two in. One of himself in a buggy, holding a Superman toy, where Marion's legs and hands were visible, but not her face. Nigel felt curiously protective and uncomfortable showing an image of his mother, as if it were indecent somehow to expose her to the gaze of the stranger who had fathered her son. And the other was a professional photograph taken for the school prospectus of Nigel rehearsing the string group in the hall at school.

He placed the envelope in his school bag with the intention of posting it on his way to school. But when it came to it, he couldn't do it. He stood by the box with the envelope in his hand. He looked hard at the collection times. If he posted it now, it would reach Wynshore on Tuesday morning.

"Excuse me," someone said behind him.

"Sorry," Nigel said and moved aside. He replaced the letter in his bag and set off for the bus stop.

That evening, as he returned home past the same post box, he took out the letter for the second time and again found himself staring at the neat envelope. Suddenly a Royal Mail van pulled up and next moment the postman was bending down inserting his keys, clattering and clanking on their chain, into the lock of the post box.

"I'll take that for you, shall I, mate?" he said and without a moment's hesitation he took the letter out of Nigel's hand and deposited it into the sack with all the others. He banged the box shut, locked it and was in his van and away in what seemed like seconds.

"Thank you," Nigel said softly under his breath and turned and walked slowly up the street. His sleep that night was fitful, disturbed by strange and fragmented dreams.

*

The buff A3 envelope that landed on the mat was indistinguishable from any other piece of mail that arrived at the home of Michael Barton MP. It was addressed to Doctor Michael Barton, marked 'Private and Confidential' with 'Please Do Not Bend' printed in a neat hand on the top left hand corner. Of course, by rights all the mail should go to the local party office where the staff would open it and take whatever action was necessary. But his constituents and some ex-patients knew Michael and where he lived, so there was often a pile of mail that Julia put to one side in readiness for when he returned to the constituency each Thursday night.

"It can wait," he said. "I'd rather play a game with the girls."

Sometimes he would bundle all the post up and take it into the constituency office and open it there, but often it lay on the hall table until he got round to looking through it. Saturday mornings were blighted by the red ministerial box, countless papers and tedious draft documents had to be read, signed or marked for some later action. Invariably, it was Sunday before he opened any of his domestic post.

So there it sat, this bombshell, on the highly polished hall table, between the telephone and the diary.

Michael and Julia had made love, as they usually did, on a Sunday morning. It was with this in mind that they let the girls go straight down in their pyjamas and watch children's television, enabling them to have this precious time alone together. Julia wondered how MPs ever added to their families. Not surprisingly, the majority of MPs' offspring were conceived on holiday. The summer recess affording the only opportunity for a bit of coupling that wasn't restricted to the weekend. Julia lay watching the sunlight dance and jump on the ceiling. They could have a leisurely brunch and then potter in the garden before Mass and lunch at Breeda's. Michael was taking a shower. Julia made a supreme effort and got out of bed. They hadn't discussed a summer holiday yet and she hoped to forgo one in favour of the renovations.

"I'll go and put the kettle on," she called to Michael who didn't hear.

Later, the buff envelope that would shortly alter his life and that of his family's forever, lay innocently on the pine table in the kitchen next to Michael's scrambled eggs. It was sandwiched between a request for Michael to open a local music festival and a complaint from a constituent about the council's overzealous building inspectors. His good intentions to clear all his work, so that Sunday remained exclusively a family day, had typically failed. He would just confine himself to opening and sorting his post into the various categories of required response. By the time Michael reached it he was just finishing the plate of scrambled eggs and looking forward to his chocolate croissant. Tess, who had bolted down her food and then rushed back to a favourite television programme, came up behind Michael and threw her arms around his neck.

"Daddy, if there's a spare croissant, can I have it please?" she asked, coquettishly planting a kiss on his cheek.

Michael slit the envelope and took out the letter.

"You'll have to share it with Katherine, darling, there's only one left." He took out the slim, neatly scripted paper and began to read it.

"Oh pooh!" Tess complained at the injustice of sharing. "She won't know if you don't tell her, Daddy."

Michael read Nigel's letter and then he read it a second time. The colour drained from his face.

"Daddy? Can I? Daddy!" Tess persisted.

"Answer her, Michael," Julia instructed mildly from the other side of the kitchen where she was loading the dishwasher. As she turned, Julia could see that something was very wrong.

"Michael, are you all right? Whatever is it?"

One of the photographs slid through his fingers and slipped onto the floor. Tess swooped down and picked it up.

She turned it over, and flashing it at Julia, said:

"Look! It's a picture of Daddy when he was a little boy with a Superman toy!"

Michael snatched the photograph out of her hand and stood up hurriedly, nearly knocking the chair flying. Then he left the room.

"Daddy!" Tess wailed after him. "He's always telling me not to snatch," she protested to her mother.

Julia looked on, utterly astonished, peering towards the empty doorway.

"Goodness! I wonder what on earth that was all about?" She remarked, completely perplexed.

"So can I have it, Mummy?"

Julia looked at Tess, confused by her question. Tess held up the pastry.

"Yes, but don't make any mess."

Tess bounced out of the room, the croissant stuffed into her mouth.

Julia went over and picked up the envelope. She looked at the postmark: Maidenhead. It meant nothing to her.

*

Sarah had done her best to keep Nigel occupied over the last few days, but it wasn't easy. She had even tried to interest him in some of the baby and childcare books but she recognised that he was only going through the motions to please her and she tried very hard not to feel hurt and resentful. Nigel wasn't sleeping well either. Usually they slept entwined, their bodies encircling one another, now they were out of rhythm. He was extremely agitated too, jumping up whenever the phone rang expecting the call to be from his father.

"I should imagine he'll write," Sarah suggested when the last phone call turned out to be her mother.

"It isn't like adoption, is it? Where for years parent and child have wondered about the other. I doubt he has ever given it a second thought," Nigel said forlornly.

"No. No, it isn't." Sarah was standing behind Nigel who was seated at the kitchen table and she wrapped her arms around his back, nuzzled into his neck and kissed him. "Give him time."

*

Michael sat in his study with the letter and the two photographs in front of him on the desk. Tess had been quite right: the child in the photograph, who appeared to be about four, could easily have been himself, and the picture of the young man teaching a string group was also remarkably similar in build and looks to a much younger Michael. So similar in fact, that if he had chosen to open one of the many photograph albums lining the walls of his drawing room, he would have been hard pressed indeed to tell them apart. He sat continuing to stare, barely comprehending that this was, in fact, his son. He turned the letter over again to re-read it. It was carefully written. He must have taken a long time to write this, Michael thought. Hearing Julia's footsteps coming towards the study, he quickly put the photographs into the desk drawer, turned the key in the lock and then slid the letter and the key into his trouser pocket. He would have to make some excuse to slip out of the house to read it again.

Julia put her head round the door.

"Is everything all right, Michael?"

"Yes, fine," Michael replied with forced gaiety. "I'd just forgotten that I must pop into the office this morning. Something Tim asked me to deal with that had slipped my mind."

"Oh, I see. And the photograph?" Julia queried.

"Uncle Francis sent it, found it when he was turning out a cupboard, apparently."

Julia stared hard at Michael. She knew he was lying, but she could think of no reason for it. He looked like a small boy who was attempting, rather badly, to cover his tracks.

"Oh? May I see it?"

"He thought I might like it," Michael said, pulling on a lightweight jacket and ignoring her request. "I shan't be long."

"Long?" Julia questioned.

"At the office," Michael explained as he opened the front door, and then added, "It's a lovely day, we could all go for a walk by the river later."

"But we're due at Breeda's for lunch after Mass," Julia called. Puzzled, she returned to the kitchen.

The constituency office wasn't far from the house, a brisk walk that was all, ten minutes at most. Michael sat at his desk staring out of the window.

Could Strumpshaw be behind this letter? Had he put this young man up to it to bring pressure to bear on Michael? No, that was ridiculous! Where would Strumpshaw find a young chap who looked so like Michael at that age? Sperm donations were anonymous; all the information was strictly controlled and even someone as wily as Strumpshaw wouldn't be able to get his hands on it. The timing, he concluded, must be purely coincidental. So how had he been traced? This simply wasn't possible! This boy couldn't know for sure that he was his biological son. Perhaps he'd just seen Michael on television and decided that there was a strong likeness.

What if it got out? How could he explain the presence of this boy – no, man – to Julia? And what about Tess and Katherine? Whatever would they make of suddenly being presented with a half-brother of nearly thirty? Michael felt sick.

And the tabloid headlines? Strumpshaw had been right about that, the press would have a field day with it. It was a nightmare. Michael drew his hands across his face and slowly massaged his temples. Then he sat back, took in a deep breath and withdrew the letter from his pocket. Placing it gently down on the desk in front of him, he smoothed out the creases. What, exactly did this young man want from him?

What would it take to make him go away?

A clinic, London, thirty years ago.

"*I see Lanky's back again,*" *Nurse Carol Roberts commented to her friend Mandy.*

"*Never misses. Just imagine in twenty or so years time there could be hundreds of 'Lankys' dotted around the country.*"

"*Makes you wonder, doesn't it?*" *Carol replied, popping another slide under the microscope.*

14

Offspring

When Michael didn't return home Julia rang the office and, receiving no reply other than the answer-phone, she hung up. Next she tried his mobile only to hear it ringing in the living room. With a heavy sigh she called up to the stairs to Tess and Katherine.

"Come on, you two, the Mass will have started."

"Coming," they called back down the stairs in unison. They arrived in the hall, Tess with a hairbrush still hanging out of her hair and Katherine with a shoe undone. Tess asked:

"Where's Daddy?"

"Oh, he's had to pop into the office. I'll leave a note on the door to remind him that we're at Breeda and Finn's for lunch. He can catch us up later."

*

"What if he's just chucked it in the bin?" Nigel said disconsolately.

Nigel and Sarah were treating themselves to a pub lunch by the Thames near Maidenhead. It was a beautiful day and there were ducks on the grass bank looking for scraps. Sarah had thought this little outing might cheer Nigel up. He had been morose since the letter had been posted. Preparing himself, she supposed, for a dreadful disappointment.

"I don't think that's likely," Sarah stated firmly. She took the crust off her steak and kidney pie to let some of the steam out. "But he could be away on holiday, and so he might not get to open your letter for a while. And let's face it, this isn't something you dash off a reply to, is it? It will be a shock. We'll just have to give it time."

"And if he doesn't reply?"

"Then we'll have to consider what to do. Perhaps ring. But until then I really think there is no point second-guessing his every move.

You'll just tie yourself in knots and probably make yourself ill into the bargain. You only posted it on Tuesday." Sarah placed her hand tenderly on Nigel's arm.

Nigel picked up his fork and stabbed at a piece of scampi.

"It feels like a year," he said.

*

Breeda saw Julia and the girls out of the corner of her eye on her way back from Holy Communion. Julia didn't notice her. She was lost in thought, which was curious because Tess and Katherine were messing about with the hymn book, throwing it and snatching it from one another, and that wasn't the sort of behaviour Julia usually tolerated. And no Michael – so far as Breeda could see. Not that he always came to church, but it was on the way to their house and convenient for lunch afterwards.

When Michael finally arrived in the garden the meat was already on the barbecue, the wine had been poured and Andrew was helping Finn carry the large dining table out onto the lawn. Breeda observed that not one word had passed between Julia and Michael. During the meal, the conversation, like the day itself, was lazy, drifting from nothing more exciting than the children's forthcoming sports and speech days to Finn's plans to extend his vegetable patch.

"Ah, don't you just love the summer! I'd never want to leave if we could only guarantee the weather in England," Breeda commented.

"We never do leave!" Finn retorted. "Much as I love Devon and Cornwall it would be nice to go somewhere foreign just for a change. A bit of foreign food and sun, different sights, sounds and faces, ah…" he sighed wistfully.

And turning to Julia, Moya asked: "Is it Portugal again this year?"

"We've nothing booked. I was thinking that we might not go away this year. We could get on with the alterations to the house instead."

Michael, who had been chatting to Andrew about the Test Match, stopped and stared hard at Julia.

"Ah, she's made marvellous plans for this extension. Moya, have you seen them?" Breeda asked.

"Not go away!" Michael's voice was already too loud. "Haven't you booked anywhere yet?" The others fell silent. "You usually book before Easter."

"No. No, I haven't. Things are rather up in the air, with the building work to consider. The builders thought they might be able to start work in the middle of August but they haven't got back to me yet," Julia said, turning to the group of friends and adding: "It's a relatively small job for them and they're hoping to fit us in. I even thought you might like to go away with the girls, Michael, and I could stay and manage the builders. Silly for us all to be here, putting up with the mess and getting in the way."

"What builders?" Michael bellowed. "I made it quite clear weeks ago, Julia, that we cannot afford this extension. The answer was no then and it remains no now. And as for my going on holiday alone with the girls, our family arrangements are quite idiosyncratic enough already!" Michael was on his feet. Having wiped his face with his napkin he threw it down onto the table. "If you'll excuse me, everyone, I have some work to do at the office. Thank you for the meal, Breeda." Michael turned and strode angrily out of the garden.

In the awkward silence that followed Breeda realised she had never before heard Julia and Michael have anything approximating a full blown row. And Moya wondered why a minister of Michael's rank should suddenly feel so impoverished; it didn't make sense. It was Finn who noticed that Julia's eyes had welled up with tears and so gave her a hug and a fresh glass of wine.

"Silly old sod," he said. "Who's rattled his cage then?"

"I don't think our family life is 'idiosyncratic'. And if it is, it's because Michael's hardly ever home," Julia sniffed.

"I think it's really quite straightforward for a politician's," Finn commented.

"Finn!" Breeda called sharply in the manner of a woman used to keeping her husband in check.

"Only a joke," Finn cried, palms up and looking all innocence.

"Maybe," Andrew suggested, "it's his work. We all tease Michael and complain about whatever the government's doing wrong, but he does work under the most enormous pressures and we're not very supportive as friends, are we? Mostly we take the piss."

"They're fair game though, aren't they, politicians?" Finn said. Breeda scowled at him.

"Andrew's right." Moya supported her husband's view. "Michael's our friend and half the time we treat him like a government spokesman. We didn't when he was a GP, he was just one of us then."

"That's because he is a government spokesman," Finn countered.

"Yes. But Finn, you don't expect me to agree with everything the Law Society or the Lord Chancellor's office does, and we don't hold you responsible for every computer glitch!"

"Oh, I don't know," said Breeda with a grin.

"Michael is our friend. We should remember that and be a bit more supportive," Moya insisted. "You should go out for a drink with him, Andrew, let him unburden himself – you used to meet up regularly."

Breeda knew she was right but didn't warm to Moya's head girl manner.

"What do you think, Julia?" she asked.

Julia had been miles away throughout the entire exchange.

"Oh, I don't know. I'd better go home." And with a weary smile she went to the French windows and called for Tess and Katherine.

In the weeks just before the summer recess the atmosphere in the Palace of Westminster is not dissimilar to that of public school before the summer holidays. Not a lot gets done and nobody much cares, the atmosphere is light-hearted, and occasionally people play silly pranks.

Michael plodded round the maze of corridors, hunched and despondent. Strumpshaw had rung him a week after their meeting, giving him until return of Parliament to come to his decision and hinting at exposure in the press. He did not mention Nigel – this Michael considered a good sign. He concluded with relief that the pair were unconnected. But as yet he had not replied to Nigel's letter. Michael was torn between the indignation of a righteous man falsely accused, and the fear that this would somehow all end up in the public domain and his career, reputation and family would be ruined. He found himself thinking obsessively, turning over and over in his mind what, if anything, he should do for the best. How would it look if he voted for this extension, when he had previously voted against fourteen days? Of course nature herself created embryos and discarded them, this was hardly the same as giving scientists the right to create life purely for spare parts, or worse, altering the species and creating hybids with unforeseeable consequences. Could the medical advantages outweigh the ethical and moral considerations? And, if known, would his earlier sperm donations be seen as prejudicing any decision he might come to? Because, it could be argued, he was a man who didn't much care about the value of life anyway given that to pay off gambling debts he had happily spread his seed far and wide without a moment's thought for his future progeny. His donations would hardly be viewed as selfless in these circumstances. Could he honestly let this get out and keep his reputation? Whatever would the Prime Minister say? Would he back him or ask for his immediate resignation? And where would it end if Strumpshaw believed that he had him in his pocket? And, hardest of all to predict – how on earth would Julia react?

Strolling through the lobbies and turning this over in his mind, Michael passed the wooden message board with its named pigeonholes. The light above his name was on, signalling a message waiting for him. He took out the slip of paper. Written on it was: 'Happy Holidays! En famille! Keep in touch, Giles'.

A hand clapped him on the back.

"Come on, old chap, cheer up – it's nearly the end of term!" It was Alan Enderby, Shadow Minister for Trade and Industry and a good friend. He was a genial man and Michael liked him, he had more in common with Alan than a lot of his own party members. They exchanged pleasantries and Michael screwed Strumpshaw's message into the smallest ball of paper and flicked it into a bin.

*

Frank Smite was in the Muck and Rake having lunch when Stanton breezed in. Smite always thought Stanton a flash bastard in his brightly coloured shirts and Paul Smith ties – like one of those young 'city boy' types. Weren't these lobbyists all fairly smarmy? After all, it was how they made their living, sucking up to people, ingratiating themselves. Smite was in the mood to trade: he had a tasty bit of information on Amery, the disgraced Mayor, implicating another MP from whom Stanton might need a favour. It was these little snippets of information that kept the world turning.

"Stanton, let me buy you drink!" Smite called as Stanton hopped onto a bar stool next to him.

*

Julia was vacuuming the hall. She and Michael had barely spoken a word since the incident at Breeda and Finn's. That night Michael had slept turned away from her and any attempts on Julia's part to raise the subject were met with a stubborn silence. Usually they spoke on the telephone every day but now it was Wednesday and they hadn't spoken since he left at dawn that Monday morning. And even then you could hardly call it speaking, more going through the motions. And Both Tess and Katherine were well aware that Mummy and Daddy had had a row.

The telephone rang. Julia turned the vacuum cleaner off and went to answer it. There was no one there.

"Hello, hello…" Finally she replaced the receiver. Half an hour later, as she was dusting the living room, it happened again. This time she said:

"Michael, is that you?"

Julia replaced the receiver and then dialled one four seven one. The usual voice told her that the caller had withheld their number. She dialled Michael's mobile; it was taking messages.

"Michael, if you're going to ring me, fine, but at least talk to me. Once, and I can accept that you've been cut off or interrupted – twice is just plain silly. Ring me when you can and next time, speak." She hung up and returned to the housework.

Half an hour later the telephone rang again.

132

"You've rung one four seven one?" Michael's voice sounded urgent.

"Of course. But it was caller withheld, which is why I assumed it was you on a department phone." Julia caught a trace of something in Michael's voice, something she'd heard only once before, on the dreadful night Katherine was born. It was fear.

"What is it, Michael. Whatever's the matter?"

Michael's changed his tone of voice. Julia knew then that he was edgy and yes, afraid. He tried to chat casually as if nothing was worrying him, but then ended by saying:

"If it happens again, unplug the phone. You don't want to be bothered by some crank."

"Am I likely to be bothered by some crank?" Julia asked.

"Just unplug the phone, Julia," Michael ordered and rang off.

Julia sank down onto the chair next to the telephone table.

Thinking back to the events of the weekend she could see that Michael hadn't been himself. Even on Thursday when he arrived home, he was later than usual and preoccupied. And although he'd played with the girls he was inattentive and his heart wasn't in it. Generally, Michael was good at setting to one side any problems from the week before, 'Ring-fencing' he called it. His time with the family was precious. "There are some people," he had said, "who would have you believe that there is a crisis worthy of my full attention every weekend."

Then there was the mysterious letter with the photograph in it, Michael's odd behaviour rushing off to the constituency office that afternoon. Perhaps he was in some kind of trouble – but what? Whatever it was, it must be serious.

"Poor Michael, and there was I going on about blessed builders," she said out loud. Possessed with a new urgency she got up, walked up the hall and opened the study door. Systematically she turned over the various papers on the desk and sorted through each pile. Of the letter there was no sign. She tried the drawers at the left hand side of the battered mahogany desk but they contained an assortment of paper, post-it notes and staples. Julia slipped into the captain's chair, the old one from Michael's days as a GP, which swung perilously on its base. She pulled at the centre drawer. It was locked. Julia gave it another hard tug to make certain that she was not mistaken but no, it was quite definitely locked. This in itself was unusual. She looked for the key but it was not in its usual place. Finally she remembered there was a spare in a pot on the mantelpiece.

Julia didn't have to look very far to find the photographs. They were face down at the front of the drawer. She hesitated for a moment, wondering what exactly she was about to see. She already knew that one of these photographs was of Michael as a child. But the other? However unlikely she considered it, Julia was afraid Michael had done something foolish and compromising.

So it was a relief when, on turning over the first photograph, she found a picture of a much younger Michael rehearsing a string group. She took out the other then and placed them side-by-side. What a sweet boy Michael had been, she thought, as she looked at the small face on the faded colour print. He had had a mop of curly hair, still blond at that age, and a lovely wide smile. It was thoughtful of his Uncle Francis to send these photographs especially as, owing to a dreadful house fire some years ago, there were now only a few precious photographs left of Michael as a child. Julia was about to turn them over and place them back in the drawer just as she had found them when something struck her. She looked again. Yes, she was right!

The buggy... It was a MacLaren buggy, the umbrella sort that fold away. She had had one for Tess; it made it far easier to hop on and off buses. But the child in this picture was only three or four and Michael would have been that age when? Nineteen fifty-six? And he was holding a plastic Superman figure which didn't seem quite right either. Julia looked once again at the black and white photograph of the young man conducting the string group. In the background there was a poster and she peered hard at the fuzzy image; it was advertising a forthcoming music festival.

Julia scrutinised the face of the boy.

"My God! Who *are* you?"

15

Smoke and Mirrors

By Thursday Julia was worn out. She had gone to bed with a headache and woken up with the same headache; painkillers had made no difference. She felt she would burst with the frustration and anxiety of it all. She sat at the kitchen table nursing a comforting cup of tea. On the telephone Michael remained remote and cool. He said that this coming weekend he was considering staying in London at the flat. His excuse was pressure of work, matters that he wanted to tie up before the summer recess. He rang off abruptly.

Julia didn't believe him. And at that moment she didn't trust him either. Worst of all, she didn't know what to do. Knowing that Michael was suffering in some way didn't help because he clearly wouldn't, or couldn't, confide in her – and there had to be a reason for that. Whatever was going on, Michael wanted to keep it from her, so it wasn't a great leap for Julia to realise that this was something that Michael was afraid to tell his wife. And Julia knew exactly what types of shameful behaviour warranted men hiding details from their wives.

Perhaps Finn's tactless comment about a politician's family life had hit the nail on the head. Why then had Julia believed that her marriage could never be rocked by the sorts of scandals that were often the lot of Members of Parliament? She knew full well that the corridors of power were full of attractive researchers, secretaries and lobbyists and that to a certain type of woman powerful men had an irresistible charisma. For a man away from home the loneliness and the temptations were an ever-present threat. And Michael was a very attractive man, there was no doubt about it. How smug then, to think that she and Michael had something so special that nobody could ever make him stray. Snatching the car keys from the table, set off to Breeda's house.

*

Michael had read and re-read the letter and it was clear that this young man didn't know that he was a member of the government. He had addressed him as a doctor and posted the letter to his home address, probably tracing Michael through the Red book, the register of all licensed medical practitioners. This needed to be settled – and urgently. He wrote the briefest of notes, telling the young man that his sperm donations had been anonymous and that however he had obtained Michael's details, it was illegal. He went on to say that so far as he was aware there was no history in his family of any inherited medical conditions, and that Michael's children, both girls, were born fit and well. But, he pointed out, there was no definite confirmation that he was in fact his father. He ended by saying that he hoped that Nigel and his wife would accept a small gift to help them with any extra expenses for the baby, and added that no further sums would be forthcoming. He wrote out a cheque for a thousand pounds, tucked it inside the letter, sealed and stamped it and popped it into the post box that evening on his way back to the flat, satisfied that he had dealt with this delicate matter generously.

*

Julia found herself greeted by Breeda carrying a life-sized, flesh pink, plaster-of-paris hand and a trowel covered in Polyfilla. She decided not to comment.

"It's the Blessed Virgin," Breeda explained. "Her hand dropped off – I'm sure it's a sign – an ill omen! Come in, you can hold it on while I do some handiwork with the trowel." They both looked a ridiculous sight kneeling at the feet of Mary alongside the adoring Enid Blyton-style children."Here, you push her hand onto the metal rod and I'll fill up the join. Then with a bit of careful paintwork, she'll be as good as new."

Julia slotted the hand onto the post, wriggling it from side to side.

"No, it needs to be the other way around – palm up – otherwise she's limp wristed and it gives quite the wrong impression!" Breeda laughed.

"Oh yes, I see what you mean!" Julia acknowledged, seeing the funny side of something for the first time in days.

"There! That's better, now shall we have a cup of coffee?"

Julia followed Breeda downstairs and into the kitchen.

"So how are things?" Breeda enquired cautiously, leaning on the kitchen units waiting for the kettle to boil. "I didn't ring," she added "I thought it best to let you and Michael sort it out between you."

"Something's wrong but I don't know what. Michael just isn't himself." Julia sat down on a battered chair covered in yellow brocade fabric with the stuffing hanging out; it was Breeda's next upholstery project. The chair was beside a gothic brass offertory box, decked out with beeswax candles, situated underneath a rather unnerving painting of the martyrdom of Saint Sebastian. Breeda had a habit of saying to the children when they refused some food on a whim, "Just look at poor Saint Sebastian, I don't imagine he'd turn down a helping of shepherd's pie."

"Michael's probably tired, he works very hard," Breeda suggested reasonably. "And needs a break like Andrew said. We should all take care of him a bit more. Finn and I do give him a bit of stick, you know, and never a thought for his feelings."

Julia produced the pictures from her bag.

"And then these photographs came at the weekend. There was a letter with them too, but Michael has it."

Breeda took the photographs hesitantly, praying that what she was imagining was wrong. When she turned them over she smiled and looked up at Julia and said:

"He was a good looking lad."

"These pictures aren't of Michael," Julia stated. Breeda looked doubtful. "No really. Take another look at the buggy and the poster on the wall behind the cellist. Michael told me they were of him and that his uncle had sent them but it's a lie."

"Well, if they're not Michael then they must be at the least be a brother or cousin." Julia shook her head. "Or his…" Breeda's voice trailed away to nothing. She dropped down onto an old pine chair, staring intently at the photographs.

"*Say* it, Breeda, I want to hear someone say it, because this has been going round and around in my head all week until it has

137

practically burst and I just can't believe what I'm thinking."

"Or his child…Michael's son." And then quickly Breeda added, "But it couldn't be. He'd have told you if he already had a son! It's years ago…must be! Unless of course he didn't know. But this picture of the young man," Breeda held up the photograph. "He's in his late twenties at least. So it would be a relationship from almost thirty years ago, perhaps when Michael was a student."

"Of course! How can I have been so stupid? Why didn't I work this out?" Julia threw back her head, laughing at herself. There was a hysterical edge to the laughter that alarmed Breeda. "I thought… no…I haven't been thinking straight at all. I imagined that these photographs meant that Michael has been having an affair! But of course this boy – is a man." Julia took up the picture of the child in the buggy. "This is years ago! No wonder Michael's been behaving so strangely. If he didn't even know of the child's existence! Oh God, poor Michael – the things I've been thinking. He must be utterly bewildered, especially as he didn't know! He's staying at the flat – the excuse is work – but really it's to avoid any discussion with me about this child," Julia rattled on with excited relief. "Please, could you have the girls overnight? I'll go up to town and meet Michael, we can go out to dinner and talk." She was standing up now, seizing the photographs from Breeda's hand and about to head for the door.

"Julia… Julia," Breeda called sharply. She looked at her friend, dear Julia, who was about to rush off to London like an excited schoolgirl. "Of course I would have the girls if you need me to, but mightn't it be best to give Michael a bit of time? He's had a shock and maybe a bit of time on his own in London will give him a chance to sort out his own feelings about this boy. He might just need some space. I think I would – if it were me."

"Do you really think so?"

"I do," Breeda said kindly. "And I think we can now see why Michael's so in need of a break, a proper holiday."

"Yes." Julia sat down again. "Yes, perhaps you're right."

"Also," Breeda continued, "he may be staying on in London in order to meet this young man, and perhaps see if it would be appropriate to introduce him to the rest of the family." Breeda couldn't possibly know just how far from Michael's intentions were the views she was ascribing to him.

"I hadn't thought of that. There's so much…If only Michael would talk to me," Julia said plaintively.

"He will. Just give him time. It's that cave thing, you know – men are from Mars, and all that," Breeda told her with authority.

"You know Michael always wanted a son," Julia said wistfully.

"Well then, that makes it all the more poignant and explains his confusion, doesn't it?

*

Frank Smite was doing his very best to get Stanton drunk and was having considerable success. They had moved from their precarious location perched on bar stools, to a table tucked away behind the pub door that led out onto the street. The sunlight streamed in through mullioned windows catching the fug of cigarette smoke dancing in its rays. They had already had two pints at the bar and now they were setting about a second bottle of red wine. The remnants of the pie and mash they had both just eaten lay next to them on the table, waiting for the hard-pressed barmaid to clear. Smite stubbed out his cigarette in the mashed potato. He knew he could keep his head; it took a lot to get him drunk, his body had the high tolerance for alcohol that goes with years of heavy regular boozing. Not so Stanton; he was well on the way to a drunken stupor and all the while his tongue was loosening. Another glass, thought Smite, and I'll have him.

Sure enough, by the time the cork was eased from a third bottle, a rather good Pinotage, Smite had introduced Giles Strumpshaw's name and that of his company, 'StemShaw', into the conversation. As he poured the last drops of wine into Stanton's glass he was listening to the very funny story of a prominent politician who had once resorted to selling his sperm for some badly needed cash. Drunk though he was, Stanton wasn't so indiscreet as to mention the politician's name – but then he didn't need to – because Frank already knew exactly to whom Stanton was referring. Now he knew what Barton had to hide and precisely how it could be used against him at just the right moment. Smug, moralising governments could do with a kick up the arse. Already he could see the headlines.

*

Breeda dropped in to Moya's house with the excuse that she happened to be passing and wondered if Tom would mind lending Seamus his old hockey stick. As soon as Moya invited her in for a cup a coffee she realised that Breeda had something to disclose – some tantalising snippet of information that made her feel important. She knew at once that this would be one of those occasions when Breeda's good points, whatever they were, would remain well hidden. It was the irritating way that Breeda wandered into the living room with a smug air of satisfaction. The clean modernistic interior usually put her on edge but not today, today she just threw herself down onto the cream leather sofa and hugged a grey felted cushion to her chest.

When Moya returned to the living room with the coffee on a tray she found Breeda was flicking through a copy of 'Interiors' magazine. Over coffee Breeda casually mentioned Julia's sudden visit to her house and intimated darkly that a long buried family secret lay behind Michael's recent uncharacteristic behaviour. She was always especially pleased when she obtained some private snippet of information ahead of Moya, although she knew it was just a silly piece of one-upmanship. Each considered herself Julia's closest friend.

Moya did her best not to react. "Really?"

"I don't know when Michael had intended to tell Julia and the girls, but that dilemma must have been what he was struggling with at the weekend," Breeda stated with the confident air of a friend with privileged information. "It was obvious. As soon as I saw the photographs I realised – the likeness was uncanny." Breeda sipped her coffee and replaced the cup on the minimalist Portland-stone coffee table in front of her. She returned to the magazine that Moya knew she couldn't possibly be interested in.

"Likeness?" Moya enquired.

"To Michael."

"I'm sorry, Breeda, but I seem to be missing something here – who exactly has a likeness to Michael?"

"His son, apparently. A son from a previous relationship."

Breeda enjoyed the satisfaction of watching Moya's jaw drop.

*

Rosalind announced her impending and unfortunately timed arrival with her customary short notice.

"I'll be with you by lunchtime on Saturday, darling," she declared to Julia over the telephone. "I had no idea that replacing a bathroom suite could be so dirty and destructive, my nerves are simply shot to pieces. You're not away, are you?"

"No…no we're here, it's just that Michael's rather tired at the moment."

"Well then, it will be an ideal opportunity for you and I to take the girls out somewhere and give the dear man some peace."

"How long are you planning to stay?" Julia asked.

"Oh, just the week," Rosalind replied brightly.

*

Never had an envelope been subject to such close scrutiny as the one Nigel now held. The address was written in black ink, the hand sprawling and untidy. Just like a doctor, he thought. He sat opposite Sarah at the small pine breakfast table tucked at the end of the kitchen/diner just off the living room. His hands were shaking and he was a deathly colour. He looked up at Sarah who was finishing the last of her orange juice.

"This is it. This letter is from Wynshore," he said shakily.

"Would you like to open it alone? Do you want me to go?" she offered.

"God no!"

"Then would you like me to open it for you?"

"No. No, it's fine."

He took out the folded page and, as he did, a slip of paper fell out and fluttered down onto the floor. It was the cheque. The letter was short and dismissive.

"He's sent money. I don't want money!"

"Let me see." Sarah took the letter from his hand.

Nigel picked up the cheque and turned it over.

"A thousand pounds…a thousand bloody pounds! Oh, that discharges his responsibility nicely, doesn't it? Cheap at the price." He exploded out of the chair as Sarah read and re-read the contents of the letter looking for any clues to the man's feelings.

"Nigel. Nigel, he has a family. And from the tone of this letter, I feel sure they don't know. He probably just wants to protect them. Imagine the shock – decades ago he was an anonymous donor – it must be a terrible dilemma. How's he going to explain you, and any others, to his daughters?" Sarah looked up to see tears in Nigel's eyes. He was distraught. He had waited for this moment, imagining that his father would at least want to meet him and that being a professional man – a doctor – he would share some pride in Nigel's achievements and, perhaps, his passion for music. Sarah had tried not to encourage this fantasising.

"I half expected this," she said cautiously.

"I thought he'd be curious, that he'd want to know how his son had turned out." He buried his head in the nape of her neck. "And he'd want to meet me… just once. I could never imagine doing this to my child. Just one meeting… That's all I want."

16

Summer Recess

Michael was more elusive than ever during his mother-in-law's visit. He took to retiring to bed early, so that by the time Julia had finished clearing up, set out the table for breakfast and had slipped under the duvet herself, he was fast asleep.

Their holiday in Corsica was a dull affair. Michael spent much of his time either with his head in a book or asleep, occasionally strolling into Calvi to look at the medieval citadel and then wandering the narrow winding streets, stopping now and again for a glass of wine or a coffee in one of the many cafés that lined the harbour. Julia spent her time keeping an eye on the girls at the beach and wondering just when it would be the right moment to bring up the delicate matter of the photographs of Michael's love child. The days drifted by and soon it was their second week away. Yet there was never quite the right moment for Julia to make the little speech that she had practised in her head, referring to the photographs and asking Michael, very gently, if there was anything he wanted to tell her. Julia's one attempt at getting Michael to talk failed miserably. She had taken the opportunity on an evening when, exhausted from their day at the beach, the girls had fallen happily into bed and slept soundly. Julia prepared some local fish and set out the table on the balcony of the villa, so that they might enjoy the sunset over Calvi.

"Michael, we really need to talk."

"Oh not now, Julia, not here. Don't spoil it, darling." And he lightly touched her hand.

Reluctantly, Julia settled for putting off the whole topic until they were back home in Wynshore.

*

Sarah seriously considered seeking some sort of counselling for Nigel. After all, she reasoned, if he were adopted and making contact with a birth parent for the first time, he wouldn't undertake that alone. There were support services for just such a situation. But, so far as Sarah knew, Nigel's predicament was unique. His fragile state of mind finally decided the matter; Sarah was going to confront Michael Barton and beg him to meet his son – just once. He owed Nigel that much.

The house was much as she had expected it to be. It was a substantial detached Victorian villa. Double fronted, it was expensively curtained with pleats and swags. The house gave off an air of authority and tradition. It was an ideal and fitting home for a doctor and his family. The front door was freshly painted in navy gloss, which set off the brass fittings beautifully. The gravel drive was neat pea shingle, whilst the low laurel hedge was beautifully trimmed. There was an almond tree and a magnolia.

Sarah got out of her car and approached the house. Although nervous, her overriding feeling was one of determination. She wanted the subject of Nigel's paternity over and done with, she had had enough of this awful business, it was blighting both her marriage and her pregnancy. Inside her their child was growing daily and, now reconciled to the reality of their baby, she was resolved to settle this matter once and for all. Sarah raised the heavy door-knocker and rapped confidently. She took in a deep breath of summer evening air, fully expecting to hear the sound of approaching footsteps at any moment. When none came she lifted the knocker and rapped again. Still nothing. She knocked just once more but without much expectation; there was no one at home. Disappointed, she turned to leave and then having taken just a few steps, she retraced her path and set off around the side of the house to peer in the windows.

In the late evening sunlight she could see into the living room, which was painted a soft yellow. Comfortably and traditionally furnished, the room had one wall lined with books, and to her surprise at the far end stood a marvellous grand piano. There was sheet music arranged on it.

"Someone plays it!" Sarah said out loud.

"Hrmm." Sarah spun around at the sound of someone clearing his throat. Behind her in the next door garden stood a man staring at her; just how long he had been standing there she didn't know nor did she wait to find out. She turned on her heels, ran back to the car, crashed into gear and sped away.

*

Breeda had been popping in to Julia and Michael's on and off throughout their absence to water the plants, gather together the post and generally make the place look inhabited. It was with some alarm that she received a warning from Julia's neighbour, a retired university lecturer, that a young woman had been observed watching the house and skulking about in the shrubbery.

Breeda rang Moya.

"Should I move in?" she asked.

"I'm not sure Michael would like that, and anyway you shouldn't be on your own there, not if there's a prowler about."

"Well, I can't just do nothing," Breeda stated.

"Inform the police and they can keep an eye out – after all, he is a Minister and must be entitled to some extra protection. And if you catch sight of this woman, challenge her, ask her what exactly she's up to."

"I was wondering if it might be connected to this other business."

"A woman? I wouldn't think so," Moya said, then adding. " No, I think that's most unlikely. When are they back?"

"Saturday sometime. I'm to leave some milk and basics and return the rabbits, Tate and Lyle. We've been looking after them for the girls."

"Well then, it's only a couple of days," Moya said reassuringly. "Don't worry, it must just be a friend or a visitor who wanted to surprise them and didn't realize they would be away."

"Maybe," Breeda acknowledged. But she couldn't shake off her curious unease.

*

The Barton family were back home by two o'clock that Saturday afternoon as planned. And in the disarray which follows any family holiday, the note from Breeda, warning them that a young woman with dark hair and driving a rather battered Mini had been seen by their neighbour peering in the windows, was accidentally brushed from the kitchen table. It floated down to the floor, finally settling under the telephone table in the hall, where Julia came upon it two days later.

It was the final straw.

She marched into the living room, turned off the Schubert Michael was listening to and said:

"Michael, is there anything you think you should tell me?" In front of him she placed the note from Breeda. She hadn't quite abandoned the notion that Michael was having an affair.

"It seems we had a visitor who discovered that we were away. I really can't find any reason for the sinister interpretation that Breeda places on this; it was probably a disgruntled constituent, you know how persistent they can be. Whatever has got into you, Julia?"

"And these?" Julia seized the photographs from her hiding place in the cookery section on the bookshelves and threw them down onto Michael's lap. "I don't think you can explain these photographs away quite so readily. After all, when you first saw them you behaved very oddly and you've gone to a great deal of trouble to keep them from me."

Michael fell completely silent. Then he stood up and closed the living room door. If the girls were still awake he didn't want them to hear any of this exchange. He wasn't sure how it would go.

"Sit down, Julia." His request was quiet but firm. Julia dropped into a chair with a terrible feeling of dread. "I should have spoken to you about this weeks ago and for that I apologise. But then, I didn't know that you had taken these," gesturing to the photographs, "from my desk."

"You didn't leave me much choice. Each time I tried to talk to you about this young man you made some excuse or just walked away."

"I'm sorry," he said with very little feeling. "I've had a letter from someone who believes that I'm his father and these are the photographs that came with it. He has absolutely no evidence to substantiate this ludicrous claim and I can categorically state that

I have never even *met* his mother." That part at least was true. "I believe him to be a crank, or worse."

"What's his name?"

"Nigel someone. I don't recall the surname."

"But he looks so like you!" Julia cried.

"Yes. Yes he does. Which is why these pictures took my breath away. It's quite a clever trick really, isn't it?"

"A trick?" Julia asked, confused.

"Yes. Find a public figure that you look just like and who is old enough to be your father, and then send him some photos and a begging letter."

"He asked for money? Did you give him any?" Julia asked anxiously.

"Good Lord, no!" Michael declared. "I bet a lot of men would fall for it, especially if they had been particularly promiscuous which, thankfully, I wasn't. And there is nothing wrong with my memory." He laughed lightly and then continued, "I'm really sorry, darling, if I've been out of sorts and given you a fright. I haven't meant to be unkind. But I've been under a lot of pressure this session. Everyone expects so much of me – I think I've just been utterly worn down. And I apologise unreservedly about the building work too, I know how much you wanted to go ahead this summer and we will have this work done – but next year, please. I just couldn't take it at the moment, I'm sorry." Michael held out his hand to Julia and pulled her towards him, drawing her into his arms and nuzzling the pretty nape of her neck and then kissing her passionately on the mouth. Relieved, Julia kissed him back.

"Come on," Michael murmured. "Let me take you to bed."

Breeda was in the middle of packing for the annual family camping holiday in Cornwall when Julia, looking relaxed, still tanned and more beautiful than ever, dropped by to share her news about the photographs of the boy. There were sleeping bags, groundsheets and a camping stove spread out all over the kitchen floor and, in the garden, the older children were erecting the tent to check that it was in working order and had a full complement of ropes and pegs.

So they had only the briefest of conversations, necessarily coded, as all the children were in attendance. Breeda's two casual throwaway remarks, "Oh, really?" said in a doubtful tone, and, " I suppose he has informed the police?" left Julia feeling slightly defensive and somewhat unnerved. Later when she put it to Michael that he might do just that, he laughed at her with amused indulgence.

"Oh, sweetheart, I think that would be overkill. It's all done and dusted. Please don't worry any more about it."

Julia buried deep within herself the small uncomfortable feeling that this wasn't the end of the matter, deciding instead to concentrate on enjoying what was left of the summer with Michael and the girls before the political party conference season began in earnest.

17

Off Message

Julia usually enjoyed the late summer. Although the sun was losing its warmth, it shone more reliably than ever it did in June or July. In fact, in the last two years June had been terribly wet – it had poured and poured – and as a consequence the garden wasn't as tidy as Julia would wish. Being prevented from gardening at the height of the season last year had a knock-on effect – slugs, snails and aphids got a grip and ravaged the plants – and Julia had never quite caught up. But the girls were more rested and relaxed than ever by the end of August and the pace and rhythm of family life gently resumed. Michael also returned home every evening and that was what made the real difference – they all ate together just like any other family. Some dull, although necessary, administrative and household tasks were completed and, along with working in the garden, Julia made preparations for the new school year, buying shoes and trainers and labelling clothes.

Michael went to work daily in the constituency office, where he was still kept busy, and occasionally he would give a radio interview or write a piece for the local paper. There was a sort of roster to cover for MPs who were abroad on holiday and so from time to time he was called upon to speak on subjects about which he knew very little and even to fill in gaps in what was otherwise a period of 'no news'. Andrew called in at the constituency office one evening and, keeping his promise to Moya, he took Michael out for an early evening drink at a pub by the river. Gingerly he brought up the subject of Julia's restlessness.

"Does Julia plan to resume a career now that the girls are older?" he asked as soon as they found a table by the river's edge.

Michael gave a small irritated laugh.

"Do I detect the voice of Breeda in this line of questioning?" he asked.

"Breeda isn't alone, Michael. Both Moya and I would agree that

Julia seems a bit lost, at a loose end. For an intelligent woman with no adult company in the evenings, it really must be quite lonely."

"Actually I've relented on the house extension. That was the cause of the disharmony. I hadn't appreciated just how much Julia had set her heart on it. But it'll have to be next year – I'm stretched to my limit as it is." Michael sipped his beer. "I'm not a heartless bastard, Andrew, I love Julia deeply and I worry about her too," he added in his defence.

"Moya thought Julia might work for you at the constituency office," Andrew told him.

Michael threw back his head and laughed.

"Haven't Moya and Breeda noticed that Julia, very sensibly in my opinion, keeps well out of politics? And that is entirely her choice. And she's not computer literate either so I think that's a non-starter."

"There are plenty of courses, Michael. She could retrain, it doesn't take long."

Michael smiled benevolently at Andrew, he knew he meant well. Michael was used to giving advice, receiving it was another matter – he changed the subject and asked after Tom. Andrew, who knew not to press his old friend any further, slipped easily into a discussion about his son's recent success in the school cricket team.

"It must be nice, having a son." Michael said. "It's a pity Julia and I couldn't have any more children."

"I'd have liked more, but Moya wanted her career back, which I understand. More than one child and it's a whole different ball game."

"A friend of mine has just had a long lost son turn up in his life…from a relationship years ago. He had no idea the boy existed," Michael began tentatively.

"Didn't he?"

"He doesn't know how to break it to his family," Michael went on edgily.

"It's hardly the end of the world," Andrew remarked. "Quite exciting really."

"You think so? It could affect his career." It was on the tip of Michael's tongue to tell Andrew about Nigel and Strumpshaw but he couldn't quite bring himself to do so.

Andrew was puzzled. "What is he? A bishop? I can't see who else would give a damn. It certainly wouldn't bother me. It happened to that journalist, didn't it, the one that does the election coverage – he had a son turn up out of the blue, welcomed him into the bosom of the family. Quite right too. His wife and children seemed to take it all in their stride as I remember."

"So they did," Michael agreed and offered to get the next round. Andrew observed Michael with concern as he strode towards the bar with the empty glasses – something wasn't quite right. Michael seemed a troubled man. When he returned with the beers Andrew asked:

"Everything is all right, isn't it, Michael? Only… You know, or I hope you do, that you can always talk to me. Anytime."

Michael gave a small quick sigh as if he were about to begin but simply said:

"Thanks Andrew, you're a good friend. I appreciate it."

*

The peace of those last summer days was soon to be shattered by a crisis that caught everyone, including the Prime Minister, unawares. Michael was completely unprepared for the sudden eruption of a popular national revolt, prompted mainly by the council tax revaluation. The nation was held to ransom with the apparent willing and widespread support of the general public. Ports and airports were blockaded, government offices seized, civil disobedience spread from students to pensioners.

"What will this mean from the work angle?" Julia inquired.

"All leave cancelled," Michael replied. "Pack a few things for me, would you please, I shall have to go to up to town and do some of the television interviews. Half the Cabinet is abroad and Parliament might be recalled."

"Oh. Bad as that?"

"Or worse!" he replied. She did not ask Michael to define exactly what 'Or worse' might mean. One of Julia's strengths was that she took such dramas in her stride and could be relied upon in a crisis.

Breeda was on the phone straight away.

"I've plenty of bread flour if you need it – it's the perishables that will go first," she told Julia with the confidence of a woman experienced in the phenomenon of shortages. "It's just like the war, isn't it?"

"Thankfully, Breeda, we're both far too young to remember the war. Even Michael doesn't remember rationing. Don't worry," Julia remarked confidently, "the Prime Minister says it will be all over in twenty-four hours."

"And you believe him?" Breeda demanded sceptically.

By Tuesday the government had invoked emergency powers and the country had run dry of everything from milk to petrol. Breeda was on the telephone again.

"Of course they have a point you know." She then proceeded to lecture Julia on the merits of the cause, and the unfairness of the tax system. Julia listened with suppressed irritation and resignation. This was one of the penalties of being a minister's wife.

"I thought you of all people would be on the side of the planet. You can't have it all ways, cheap petrol, an undamaged ozone layer, a brilliant health service and an education system without paying for it," Julia countered in an exasperated tone and then said, almost to herself, "And just as things were getting back to normal."

Breeda made no reply other than to offer car-sharing to the supermarket.

The telephone rang incessantly over the whole crisis-ridden week. Rosalind wanted to know how Julia was managing the school run. Andrew wanted to apprise Michael of the deepening crisis in the Health Service. And a number of constituents, who somehow had access to Michael's home number and weren't prepared to talk to Tim or Geraldine at the local constituency office, also rang repeatedly. Julia calmly gave them a number for the department in London.

Across the country schools closed, staff at hospitals couldn't get to work and the NHS was put on red alert. The government was accused of 'disgraceful spin' and talking the crisis up, while up and down the country routine surgery was cancelled, the postal service was in disarray and supermarkets were reporting panic buying.

The Prime Minister, speaking at a press conference, looked drawn, exasperated and ten years older.

Julia, having forgotten to put the answer-phone on that morning, was checking the contents of the freezer and the larder when she was interrupted yet again by the ringing of the telephone. She put down the tin of sardines she had just discovered well past its sell-by date and went into the hall to answer it.

"Hello, can I help you?"

There was a significant pause.

"Hello..." The caller, a hesitant, softly spoken woman, seemed taken off-guard, as if she had been expecting to reach someone else or maybe an answer-phone. "Is that the home of Doctor Michael Barton?" Her voice sounded young.

"Yes. Mrs Julia Barton speaking," Julia answered cautiously. She imagined the caller could be a cub reporter from the local paper.

"My name is Sarah. Sarah Laing."

The name meant nothing to Julia. "Yes?"

"My husband Nigel... I'm sorry, this is really very difficult. I don't quite know where to begin."

Julia sank down slowly onto the stairs.

"Did you say Nigel?"

"Yes," Sarah replied, realising that the woman at the other end of the telephone had some notion of what she was about to tell her. "We believe that your husband, Doctor Barton, is Nigel's father." She paused.

"Go on," Julia said.

"Nigel contacted Doctor Barton a little while ago. We don't need the money, it wasn't what we wanted at all and I've returned the cheque today." She cleared her throat. "Meeting his father would mean more to Nigel than anything – even it were just once. That's why I've taken the step of ringing. To appeal to you, because I thought you might understand as you have two daughters. I'm expecting a baby, you see, Doctor Barton's grandchild."

Julia sat completely still. Finally she said:

"You came here, didn't you, to the house, while we were away."

"Yes. I'm so sorry, this must be a terrible shock but I'm quite desperate. Nigel only found out that Gerald wasn't his father when his mother died of cancer in the spring. It's turned our world completely upside down."

And now you're doing just the same to mine, thought Julia.

"But my husband tells me he has never even met Nigel's mother," she countered, beginning to feel irritation rising in her.

"Yes, of course that's true. Because Nigel was born as the result of his mother's fertility treatment. Nigel is the consequence of your husband's donations."

"Donations?" Julia repeated, bewildered.

"Sperm donations," Sarah replied in her pleasant voice.

Julia remained sitting on the stairs long after Sarah had rung off, the telephone still in her hand. It seemed to her like a few minutes, but turned out to be three quarters of an hour. Outside it had begun to pour down with steady rain and she finally came to consciousness as an upstairs window that she had left open to air Tess's bedroom clattered and rattled against the increasing gale. Slowly she returned the handset to its base on the hall table. She unclenched her fingers and stared at the small scrap of paper on which she had copied down Nigel and Sarah Laing's telephone number. The paper was wet from the cold sweat on her palm, but the number remained visible, written carefully in biro, the code in brackets. Below it she had copied down the Laings' address in Maidenhead.

Julia stood up shakily and went back to the kitchen where she put on the kettle. Sitting down at the pine table and placing the scrap of paper with care directly in front of her, she looked up and stared hard into the slanting rain streaking the window. She felt cold and periodically she shivered. Wrapping her hands around the mug of tea for warmth, she thought back to the conversation with Sarah.

Julia had spoken to her for almost half an hour. The young woman and Nigel had married only last May and the pregnancy was a surprise, not at all what they had intended. She was an intelligent girl – working towards a PhD – and Nigel, according to his wife, was a talented musician who, having first trained at the Guildhall School of Music, had gone on to become at a very young age the head of music at an independent boys' school near Maidenhead.

Sarah feared that the search for his biological father was affecting her husband's work badly and that if only he and Michael could meet, just once, it would help him immeasurably. Increasingly he had suffered a terrible loss of confidence and purpose in life and he was displaying signs of clinical depression. A complete loss of self and identity, was how she described it. In short, she was desperate.

The pregnancy had made Nigel's search all the more urgent and she was extremely anxious for her husband. She came across as genuine and supportive, explaining to Julia how it had affected him. For his entire life Nigel had felt a stranger in his family. His father Gerald had always been distant. On the other hand his mother had fussed unnecessarily over him. At first when Gerald told him the truth, Nigel felt betrayed both by his mother Marion, and Gerald himself. But now he had come to understand his mother's desperation and that events had really run away with his parents. The deception hadn't been deliberate; somehow they could just never tell him, nor explain to their friends and family because of an abiding and deep sense of shame and guilt.

She then went on to explain that throughout his life Nigel had felt he might be adopted but never this.

"But how can you possibly know that my husband is Nigel's father?" Julia had asked. Without any hesitation Sarah had explained how she and Nigel together had followed a trail that led them to the notes and how Sarah had posed as a data input clerk and had stolen the documents that had proved Nigel's paternity beyond doubt. Sarah admitted to this illegal act but explained that it had been undertaken out of desperation.

"I have them, the notes," she told Julia. "I'll send you photocopies."

"And how much was the cheque for?" Julia had asked as lightly as possible.

"A thousand pounds. It was for the baby. For his grandchild."

'His grandchild.' The word caught in Julia's throat as a tear rolled rapidly down her cheek. The first grandchild: Julia's and Michael's – a thrilling event that Julia had always looked forward to and felt sure they would share together in time. An image of them both joyfully peering into a cot on the maternity ward, as Tess or Katherine glowed with pride at the new arrival, had been an indelible part of her texture and pattern of family life; something to look forward to when the stresses of the teenage years, university and careers had been successfully overcome. Now already a child was growing in Sarah – Michael's grandchild. Not theirs, but his. And Tess and Katherine had a half-bother, a sister-in-law and would shortly become aunts.

Julia's head throbbed. Michael had lied to her. Why? This son had only ever wanted to meet his biological father. Surely this was understandable? So why then had Michael denied him, and then gone on to accuse this couple of a cruel deceit?

Unless?

Could these documents be fabricated or forged? Was this really just a clever plot to blackmail Michael as he had said, to blacken his character because he was a public figure? But Julia had formed the impression that Sarah and Nigel Laing didn't know who Michael was and were ignorant of his public role. Why on earth had he sent a cheque? If there were any truth in this story then sending the cheque would prove that Michael had something to hide. So why had he lied to Julia about the money? Worse, why had he never told her that he had donated his sperm? Julia knew why. The technology, brilliant though it was, went against everything that she had been taught, that God alone is and can be the creator of life. Michael must have believed she would never find out.

By now her head was spinning. Sarah Laing was convincing, and yet…? Julia was thoroughly confused and frightened. Her life, her family, were vulnerable. She must confront Michael. She got up, went to the kitchen sink and splashed her face with cold water. She rang his mobile, it was taking messages. Next she rang the department where his secretary told her that Michael was involved in a series of emergency meetings which were likely to go on well into the night. She would pass on a message, she said, but it was unlikely that he would have an opportunity to ring until later. The national crisis meant that every department and every available minister was at full stretch and with the media baying and pressing for interviews, it was as she put it, 'All hands on deck and likely to stay that way until the crisis passes'. Julia knew that this meant stay home, field the press and tend to your family. Above all, don't do or say anything to make matters worse. In normal circumstances this is precisely what she would have done. But then these weren't normal circumstances, were they?

*

Michael was walking beside the Thames with Alan Enderby, when he had the misfortune to bump into Giles Strumpshaw striding along Millbank.

"Ah, the very chap," Giles boomed, grinning from ear to ear and hailing Michael as a long lost friend. "Good summer, old boy?"

Michael managed to raise a diffident smile and make a comment about the current crisis ruining his holiday. Making his excuses, he attempted to side step Strumpshaw and get away.

"Power to the people hey – bloody marvellous! Middle England is bringing this government to its knees. Puts you lot in your place, shows you who's boss, eh!"

"My goodness, Giles, I didn't have you down for an anarchist. You'll be telling me next you were on the picket line with the miners."

Enderby grinned.

"Ha ha! Still got your sense of humour then, despite other pressing family matters," Giles remarked nastily. "Of course, I shall be popping along to your department in a couple of weeks to convince you, should it be needed, of the merits of our cause. Not that I imagine," he paused for effect, "you will need any persuading. I feel sure that you've had time to reflect during a delightful summer with your family. I'm up for the Bio Science conference; you should pop in old man, catch up on all the human genome and genetics wizardry. Right up your street," he said, nudging Michael in the ribs.

"I must be going, Giles, things are rather hectic." Michael wanted to put an end to this exchange. "I'll see you in due course." Then as an afterthought he asked: "Does the name Nigel Laing mean anything to you?"

"Nope," Giles replied. "Was he a med school bod?"

"No. No, a music teacher I believe. It's nothing. We must get on." And with that Michael strode off purposefully along the river towards the department.

"A friend?" Enderby enquired, one bushy eyebrow raised.

"No, never that," Michael replied.

*

Sarah hadn't told Nigel of her conversation with Julia Barton, and until a meeting was agreed she intended to keep the entire episode to herself. Nigel had returned to school with depressed resignation.

Slowly, Sarah was starting to feel well again as the nausea and tiredness were subsiding and her anxieties were lessening as the baby grew. Occasionally she thought she could feel small flutterings; at first she dismissed these as imagined but increasingly it was clear that there truly was a small life growing inside her and it wanted to make its presence felt. She was relieved to know that Michael Barton had two healthy daughters and there was no doubtful medical history. The baby was due at the beginning of March, a good time of year everyone agreed, the beginning of spring.

"The worst of the colds and flu will be over," her mother had reassured her, "and by May you'll be able to pop the baby out in the garden." Sarah didn't remind her that they didn't have a garden. In fact, there was hardly room for the two of them in the flat, let alone a baby. But no one seemed to be giving the practicalities of this new arrival any thought except Sarah. When she could she indulged in trips to mother and baby shops, where she would finger tiny baby-grows in wonder and anticipation.

*

The train journey to London took hours. Numerous trains had been cancelled and people were packed together. The protests gave the impression that the whole country was coming apart at the seams. Everywhere there was an overwhelming sense of crisis and the frisson of excitement that went with it. The British temperament was coming to the fore, the spirit of the Blitz being commented on more than once in the press. For the government this spelt serious trouble: up and down the country camera crews were lurking at hospitals, stations and airports, in the hope of finding someone with a bad word to say for the blockade only to be met with stoicism and words of support at every turn. Meanwhile the country ran short of all basic supplies and the roads took on the appearance of an earlier age as they emptied of traffic.

It was ten to seven and the light was fading as Julia put her key into the downstairs front door leading to the lobby of the mansion block. They had bought the flat just after Michael had been elected when, fortunately, London property prices were depressed. It was a typically Edwardian building, red bricked and with tiny balconies just large enough for some pot plants. Once inside the gloomy hallway Julia headed for the lift. It sat in the centre well of the stairs with a concertina gate, difficult to open, snapping shut suddenly with great force. Their flat, number twenty-three, was on the second floor. She found it had the musty air of somewhere shut up for months. She went straight to the fridge. Thankfully it contained two pints of milk, some cheese, wine and ham; nearby there was a packet of open cereal, the dirty bowl and spoon dumped in the sink. Julia set about filling the kettle and switched it on, then threw her coat over a kitchen chair and reviewed the scene.

The apartment was generously proportioned and it was relatively safe from burglary; also the managing agents organised the maintenance, both factors making it ideal for periodic use. It had a small but adequate kitchen with just enough room for a table and two chairs, two bedrooms and a living room with three large windows that ran almost full-length floor to ceiling and afforded the flat excellent natural light. By one of these windows stood a modern dining table that extended for entertaining, and two comfortable plum coloured sofas, facing one another over a coffee table. Julia and Michael had furnished the flat in a hurry with bits and pieces picked up from local street markets and an auction.

Julia took her bag through to the bedroom and hung up a dress she had brought with her. Michael had left some loose change and a

159

packet of razor blades on the bedside table. She picked up the razor blades and took them through to the bathroom where she gave the hand basin a quick clean. Next she made herself a pot of coffee and, settling down onto one of the sofas, turned on Channel Four news. A regional health officer was pleading with some of the protestors outside an oil refinery – they appeared to be unmoved. Gradually, lulled by the television, Julia drifted off to sleep. She roused only after Michael had arrived home and was standing over her.

"Julia!" He touched her shoulder.

In the half-light from the flickering television Julia slowly stirred and, with only a hazy recollection of where she was, she asked Michael what the time was. It was nearly eleven and on Channel Four a bizarre nineteen-seventies cult film was showing. Michael went and turned on the nearby lamp. Julia shielded her eyes and went to take a sip of the now cold coffee. She winced at the unpleasant taste.

"Here," he said, taking the cup from her hand, "I'll make a fresh pot."

He gathered up the coffee pot and went to the kitchen. A moment later he was back leaning in the doorway. Julia looked at him in a detached way. He remained well built, handsome and confident. He didn't look like a man who had something to hide, and she had never imagined he would be an accomplished liar. She was suddenly conscious of the fact that he hadn't asked her why she was there.

"How's the PM coping?" she asked.

"Fraught and, underneath, pretty angry. The country has just had the highest growth figures together with the lowest unemployment figures in years, low inflation and interest rates – and yet it's being brought to its knees by teachers, students, truckers and pensioners. It was supposed to be Good News Week! "

"It was the council tax revaluation that set it off," Julia said. "So what's going to happen?"

"God knows! They're all in cahoots. The drivers who are blockading won't budge and the police, who thought nothing of bashing up the miners, are sharing cups of tea with middle England and middle England is liaising with tree huggers, hunters, hippies, pensioners and students. An unprecedented alliance of the pissed-off. Logan's running round like a chicken with its head cut off. The official stance is 'We understand, we're listening, but this is no way to behave and we don't make policy while the country is held to ransom'. The uncut version is 'These ungrateful bastards, who've never before enjoyed such economic stability and had money poured into education and health, can f... off'. But as you can imagine there's a strict embargo on what we can say publicly. We're all to behave and not inflame the situation any further.

"The public seem to love it," Julia remarked. "It's all that 'Return to the Dunkirk spirit'. And for some reason rationing is always very appealing to the British people. Breeda's enjoying every minute."

"That doesn't surprise me."

Julia wondered just how long they could go on having this conversation, skirting around the reason for her visit. Michael was clearly uneasy although making a good pretence of being relaxed.

"Where are the children?" he asked.

"I've left them with Breeda."

The kettle had now boiled and Michael disappeared for a few minutes to make a fresh pot of coffee. On his return he put the tray between them on the coffee table and sat down opposite Julia. Without speaking he handed her a mug. The silence was tangible, the discomfort intense.

"I've had a phone call," Julia began. Michael's head jolted up and his eyes met her gaze only fleetingly before he began examining the back of his hands with studied detachment. "From a young woman called Sarah Laing. She's the wife of Nigel Laing." Michael remained silent.

"Not talking to me about this isn't going to make it go away!"

Michael leant right back into the sofa and shut his eyes briefly. Then, apparently exasperated, he replied:

"Julia, I've said everything I ever intend to say on this matter. It's a scam – blackmail if you like. I've dealt with it and so far as I'm concerned the whole thing is over and done with."

"It's no good, Michael. You see she's returning your cheque – you remember the one you didn't send? I want to know what other lies you've told me."

Michael lent forward and drew his face through his hands. He looked very tired suddenly.

"I haven't wanted to lie to you. You just won't leave it, will you?" He jumped up and began shouting. "It's in the past, done with, finished. It has nothing to do with us."

"Nothing to do with us?" Julia shouted back. "She's having your grandchild. Now forgive me, Michael, but I rather thought that having married you and borne you two daughters, I might just be related to your first grandchild. Instead, I now find that the girls have a half-brother they know nothing about and by next spring they will have become aunts!" Julia's voice became uncharacteristically shrill. "And you have a son, a son you've rejected and denied – bought off. I cannot believe that the man I know would do that. It's simply despicable. I shall never forget your statement: 'Fortunately I was never promiscuous and can categorically state that I have never even *met* his mother.' Oh very clever, Michael! A real politician's reply, conveniently omitting that you were her sperm donor."

Tears of fury suddenly ran down her cheeks. Michael moved closer and tried to take her by the arm but Julia pulled away sharply and fell back angry and distraught onto the sofa. This wasn't what she had planned at all. Until now she hadn't realised just how enraged and distressed she was by this whole ghastly mess. The implications for her family were limitless.

Michael had retreated to the window where he stood staring blankly into the London night.

"I'm sorry," he said weakly.

"It's not enough," Julia replied, wiping the tears from her eyes. "You're hurting the people who love you. I trusted you and now I don't know whether I can. Worse, you made me feel that I was paranoid. I even imagined you were having an affair. You've patronised me and you've also denied this boy the right to know his own father."

Michael turned and looked at Julia in despair. It was true that he hadn't been himself ever since this whole business with Giles Strumpshaw. He'd been on edge and remote. And then when the boy made contact it was all too much. He had withdrawn even more from Julia and the girls. His behaviour was, he now realised, a mistake; had he let her get on with the construction work on the

162

house, she wouldn't even have noticed his altered behaviour. But he'd made so many damned mistakes.

He had to decide how he was going to explain his actions, and how much – even now – he should tell Julia. Reasoning that the whole truth really might not put him in a good light, and that Julia would look with genuine horror upon the fact that he had sold his sperm to pay a gambling debt, he thought it better by far to allow her to believe that it was an altruistic act on his part. Saying more would only serve to complicate matters.

"Let me explain," he began. "I was generally hard up, medicine is a long haul. This time I was flat broke. A friend of mine suggested that this was an easy way to supplement my grant. Even then it was fifteen pounds and that was quite a lot of money thirty years ago. I thought I was helping infertile couples. And anonymity was guaranteed. I was young, Julia, and never, in my wildest dreams, did I expect to have a grown man claiming to be my son and demanding that I meet him. What he and his wife have done is wrong. It's illegal. And for a very good reason: the distress it would cause donors' families. I don't know how he got this information and you must realise that he may not even be my son. Record keeping in those days was often unbelievably lax."

"That's easily proved – you can both take a DNA test," Julia suggested.

"No, absolutely not."

"Why not? It would settle the matter once and for all. And when we all get used to the idea of your having a son we can introduce him to the girls." Julia considered her offer both mature and generous.

"Introduce him to the girls!" Michael repeated, horrified. "He is not a member of our family. He never can be; he has parents who brought him up and no doubt love him. He isn't my son in that sense, Julia. Don't you see, he already has a father. He has his own family, his own life."

"Michael, he's your flesh and blood! And actually his mother died this spring, which is when he found out. And his father has always been distant. I understand he has never felt that he fitted in at all. You know he's a very talented musician, he's probably inherited that from you. Surely at the very least you'd be curious enough to want to meet him. It's all he's asking for, one meeting."

"Oh come on, it wouldn't end there. They're young and broke and before you know they'd be putting their hands out. He could even mount a legal claim."

"You must accept you have some moral responsibility towards him. He's your only son!" Julia argued. "I may not approve of what you've done and I am so angry with you – but he's here now. Like it or not he exists in the flesh and he's part of our lives."

Michael sighed despairingly.

"There is something I don't think you appreciate, Julia." He paused and rubbed his temple, wondering how on earth to put it. He had hoped to spare her this. "Nigel Laing is probably not my only son and he most certainly won't be my only child."

"What do you mean?"

"In the early days these clinics were basically unregulated and they followed their own code of conduct. My donations will have been used for numerous pregnancies. Today, there is a limit – ten live births per donor. Back then there was none."

"None?" Julia repeated. The full implication of what Michael was telling her was just beginning to dawn. "So there will be others?" Michael nodded. "How many? Dozens?

"More, I would imagine," came Michael's evasive reply.

"How many more?" Julia asked, alarmed. "How many more, Michael?"

"Perhaps hundreds."

"*Hundreds?*"

18

On Message

Michael slept alone in the main bedroom of the flat, Julia finally having retired at one in the morning to the spare room that the children used on the rare occasions they visited. Through the wall he could hear her rhythmic sobbing. The only other occasion Michael could recall Julia crying so pitifully was the day she was told she could never have any more children soon after Katherine's dramatic delivery.

It was three in the morning, still dark – glowing city dark – and apart from the occasional wail of a siren, London had that eerily quiet quality that he knew would be broken soon enough by the clatter of refuse lorries and the first essential workers making their way to tube stations, hospitals and bus depots. Michael hadn't slept at all. Over and over in his mind the thoughts turned and twisted in a jumbled mass. The palpable shock on Julia's face had jolted Michael out of his self-obsessed complacency. He had wanted to protect her of course; but in reality his main concern had been keeping this story out of the press at all costs and preserving his career and status.

Dear Julia, who was kindness itself and would do anything for anyone, had typically wanted to extend her warmth and love to a lost family member. Yet she was now faced with the extraordinary and horrible truth that they couldn't share such intimacy with dozens, possibly hundreds, of other siblings. Already it was likely that somewhere out there Michael had several grandchildren. Michael had told so many small lies and taken so many evasions recently. He lay shivering in the chill of an autumn dawn. He didn't like himself very much at that moment.

*

As dawn broke Frank Smite was wrapping his hands around a

mug of strong tea and sharing a joke or two with a law student and a sheep farmer. The power station, just outside Mere Port, had seen nothing come in or out in seventy-two hours, during which time a cheerful camaraderie had developed between the protestors, the press and the police. It was the most jovial, aggro-free protest that Smite could ever recall; and the most successful. A group roped together had climbed up on to the roof of the power station; the rest had set up a cordon around the perimeter fence.

In its day of course, Greenham Common had been quite jolly, a lot of singing and dancing and not too much violence. And then there were the eco warriors, the youngsters who suspended themselves from trees and lived in tunnels, they were very inventive. Yet nothing had ever crippled the country so simply, quickly and effectively as this. Who'd have thought that a mixed bunch of home counties types, students, teachers and farmers with mobile phones could bring the world's fourth largest economy to its knees? Of course, having the police on your side helped!

*

At Breeda's house, with the military precision of a well-rehearsed campaign, breakfast for nine was under way. There was no choice, it was always the same: cornflakes, toast and a boiled egg each, with a glass of orange juice. Feeding a large brood required nutrition, simplicity and economy in equal measure and Breeda brooked no dissent; you either liked it or went hungry. Both Tess and Katherine understood the house rules. The complaining and whining, which might have achieved a change of heart at home, would not work in this household, so without fuss they ate up.

"Are we staying tonight and tomorrow as well?" Tess inquired.

"Your Mummy didn't say. I expect she'll ring me later," Breeda replied, while spooning the hot eggs into an eclectic mix of eggcups. "I imagine she may stay in London until the weekend to look after Daddy, he's so busy with this crisis you see. Come on now everyone, eat up, we have to leave earlier now we're on a walking bus."

Breeda's contribution to alleviating the fuel crisis was a supervised crocodile of children with different stops along the route to collect and deliver more schoolchildren and supervising parents. They had trolleys for games kit and musical instruments and Breeda and the children had featured in the local paper's roundup of 'Beat the Crisis' initiatives. There was talk of the walking bus becoming a regular feature in Wynshore.

*

Logan had snatched just three hours sleep on a sofa in the ante-room and now he was back at his press office desk at Number Ten. He was preparing the schedule of ministers, spokesmen and women to satisfy the requests from the world's press for interviews. He was having to rope in anyone and everyone and they were all under strict instructions to adhere to the official line: 'The government is listening and understands your problems. But the country is suffering. You've made your point, now pack up and go home before lives are lost'. So far he had managed to keep everyone on message. He had threatened pain of death, or worse – being cast out into the oblivion of parliamentary darkness – and he'd also called in a lot of favours, even resorting to a few veiled threats.

*

Finally Julia stopped crying and fell into an exhausted sleep, where she dreamt of a frantic search for a lost kitten whose plaintive mewing came from underneath the kitchen floor. Each time she pulled up a floorboard the kitten had moved to some other hidden corner.

At seven Michael appeared with a cup of tea and having put it on the bedside table, he retreated to the end of the bed where he sat meekly, taking on the appearance of a small contrite boy.

"I'm truly sorry, Julia. I just wish I could turn the clock back and undo this mess."

Julia, despite being worn out from lack of sleep and worry, observed Michael in a curiously cool and detached manner.

"None of us can do that, Michael," she said reprovingly. "What we can do is conduct ourselves in a way that is honest and decent and does no harm. As a doctor you of all people should know that. 'First do no harm' is part of the Hippocratic oath after all."

"I was thinking of you and the girls."

"No, you were not, Michael, you were thinking of yourself and your career. How could you do this to us?" Michael looked like a guilty child. "It's true that whereas I could easily introduce one brother to Tess, Katherine and our family and friends, hundreds would be altogether another matter!"

"What are you going to do?" Michael asked weakly. Julia picked up the tea and took a sip. She looked pale and exhausted.

"I don't know. Go home I suppose, find a way to save the family from any more trauma; 'damage limitation', your spin doctors would call it, wouldn't they?" she said wearily.

"I'm sorry, Julia, truly sorry."

"Yes. I hope that you are. But your apologising doesn't make me feel any better. I'm nowhere near ready to forgive you yet and I don't know when I will be. What I actually feel is a terrible loss...almost bereaved." Julia looked sorrowful and then pulling herself together said, "Which doesn't solve the problem of Nigel Laing and your grandchild. It isn't going to go away." Julia stared hard at Michael and she wasn't at all sure that he understood her angry and confused feelings. She had never been able to provide Michael with the son he wanted and couldn't understand why he was determined to reject Nigel Laing.

"It might interest you to know that for the time being I don't think they've put two and two together – they don't know what you are – but that can't last. Sarah Laing is an intelligent woman and it's only a question of time before they both see you on television and if they're feeling as hurt and rejected as your letter and cheque undoubtedly made them, then who knows, they could sell their story to the tabloids." She plucked at the bedcover, picking off the small balls of fabric. "You must meet him. You owe it to him. Better by far to diffuse this before it blows up in your face." In all her anger and distress Julia couldn't quite relinquish her role as Michael's capable confidante and adviser.

"And the countless others?" Michael said very quietly.

"Let's try to live in the present, Michael, that's what I'm trying to do," she said crisply. "Anyway, how many of them even know? This boy... man... this Nigel, only discovered the truth because his mother died. And not everyone is as determined and tenacious as he seems to be. Undoubtedly they broke the law in seeking you out and that, at least, is in our favour if things get tricky. It's a risk you'll just have to take. If this gets out and you are accused of turning your back on your son, as well as trying to buy him off, then it will get far worse. For pity's sake, you're the Minister for the Family! Use your imagination."

"What do I do?" Michael asked with weary resignation.

"I'll ring Sarah Laing and arrange a meeting. The sooner the better."

"Thank you," Michael moved to take Julia's hand but she pulled away. "Julia, I never wanted to hurt you or the girls."

"Why on earth did you do it?" Julia asked sorrowfully. "However do you think Tess and Katherine are going to feel if they find out? They've been brought up to believe that they are unique, special, not just some of the hundreds of other children out there somewhere, children you spawned for easy money. This is really going make them feel valued. Good God, they could even fall in love with a half-sibling without knowing!" Julia swung her feet out of the bed and stood up, taking her pink cashmere cardigan from the back of the chair and slipping it over her shoulders.

"If you are born by donor you can check with the HFEA if you are about to marry, to make certain you're not related. Perhaps the girls would be allowed to as well," Michael said, delighted that his quick thinking had provided such an obvious solution.

Without hesitation Julia slapped Michael hard across the face.

"That will be a great comfort to Tess and Katherine. Because they don't have the right to check if every man they're dating is related to them through you."

Julia left Michael clutching his stinging cheek, marched out of the bedroom and locked herself in the bathroom where she let the shower run over her tear stained face. By the time she came out Michael had dressed and gone. He left a note in the kitchen propped up on the kettle:

'Julia, I know I've acted stupidly and I've hurt you very much. But I love you and the girls more than anything in the world. I hope that in time you will feel able to forgive me. Love always, M.'

Julia sat with a mug of tea, reading and re-reading the note. Insulated from the sounds of London by the double-glazing, she looked down to the street below and observed the people rushing about madly – like worker ants – constantly busy, on the move. From her vantage point two floors up, she felt remote from the hustle and bustle of the daily grind. It had been so long since she had been a participant in the economic world that she was able to look at the frantic scurrying back and forth of people, cars, buses and taxis, as a social anthropologist might. It all seemed faintly absurd, a quite unnecessary level of activity. An elegant woman about Julia's age in a camel-coloured suit, perfectly groomed in the way that Italians often were, suddenly stepped off the pavement opposite and then had to jump back as a thoughtless taxi driver sped towards her. She appeared to Julia the epitome of a well-ordered, supremely capable executive working perhaps for a perfumery or bespoke luggage company: definitely not a lawyer, something more glamorous, the world of designer labels or classic cars. Did she love her husband? Did he love her? Was she cherished?

It seemed extraordinary to Julia that down there in the real world other people were having quite ordinary days, going to meetings, drinking cappuccinos with friends in small cafés. And here she was considering whether she could learn to love and trust her husband ever again, a man whom she had always considered had the highest morals and faultless ethical standards. A man who had thoughtlessly sold his life-giving sperm for cash and who couldn't really see why anyone would have a problem with this; and a man who tried to buy off his son and accuse him of blackmail.

Julia sighed heavily. The road back from here would be a long one and she wasn't certain that she had the strength or the inclination to make the journey.

She put her cup down and stood up painfully slowly, every part of her body aching. Relentless crying had both exhausted her mentally and physically. She fetched her small overnight bag from the spare room and went into the bathroom to collect her lotions and toothbrush. In the mirror looking back at her was the face of a woman far older than her thirty-eight years. The sudden death of her father when she was just sixteen was the last time she could remember feeling so emotionally drained. How could she explain this situation to anyone? Underlying her shock and anger was an inexplicable sense of shame and disgust.

Once on the train to Wynshore Julia stared out of the window as the East End gave way, first to suburbs and then to patches of countryside. She was still thinking about Michael. He had changed. Politics had hardened in him in a way that years as a frontline doctor had failed to do. It seemed to Julia that he had lost the strong moral convictions that had impressed her, and once meant so much to Michael himself. How could he be so callous and calculating? Paying the boy off! His son. And worst of all casually dismissing the consequences of his actions for Tess and Katherine. Six months ago Julia could have argued with conviction to anyone who dared to suggest it, that Michael was not the sort of politician who would betray his family, lie, omit, or 'spin'. Rather the reverse: all too frequently he and the party machine collided owing to Michael's stubborn refusal to dissemble. Some even considered his appointment as a minister a bit risky.

She rested her head on the window and wondered what the future held.

*

Michael couldn't keep his mind on the job. So much so that, when interviewed on the 'Today' radio programme, he was prompted for a reply on three occasions. Logan, who was monitoring all broadcasts throughout the crisis, rang him for an explanation.

"What's the problem, Michael? That performance wasn't one of your best. Clearly your mind was somewhere else. You know how important it is to bring about a swift resolution to this fiasco."

"Yes, I know and I'm very sorry." Michael was well aware that he had just given the worst interview of his career to date. He had to think of an excuse and quickly. "It's a family problem. Julia isn't very well and I'm worried about her." Better keep it vague, he thought to himself, and not too dramatic or he could be seen as a weak link and might be bounced out in the next reshuffle. He knew Logan would like to see the back of him.

"Oh dear, I see. I'm very sorry to hear that, Michael. Nothing too serious, I hope?" Logan became conciliatory.

"It's a woman's thing. You know, probably needs an op. It's always worse when you're a doctor, you see, knowing all the ins and outs." There, that dealt with it nicely: serious but not life threatening. That was the good thing about the mystery of the womb, it was ideal for this sort of fix. Michael had never known a man to enquire any further, especially not of him. After all, he might just give all the gory medical details.

Logan's response was predictable.

"Well, you'd better get back to Wynshore, at least for the weekend. I'm sure we can manage without you. Crawley could step in, he's flying back from Tuscany tomorrow. Could you possibly hang on until then, just in case you're needed?"

"Of course. And I am sorry about…"

Logan didn't even give him time to complete the sentence.

"No. No, of course, totally understandable. I'll speak to you soon and all the best to Julia."

The line clicked and Logan was gone.

*

Outside the power station Frank Smite had listened with rapt interest to the broadcast. The men on the blockade considered the interviewer had Michael Barton on the rack. But Frank Smite thought he detected something else in the Minister's lacklustre performance. It wasn't that Barton didn't know what to say or that he was rattled; no, more that his mind was not on the job, something was bothering him. Something else.

"Now, isn't that interesting?" Smite remarked aloud to no one in particular.

*

At home in Wynshore, Julia spent an hour soaking in a hot bath, washing away the grime of London and the memory of her confrontation with Michael. Now dressed, but still feeling dreadful, she pottered in the kitchen carefully gathering her thoughts. She was determined to pull herself together for Tess and Katherine's sake, if nothing else.

As promised, a letter from Sarah Laing lay on the doormat. It contained Michael's cheque and the photocopies of Marion's and Michael's attendance records and the code that connected them. Julia read them with a sinking heart. At this clinic alone Michael had been giving donations three times a week, so frequently that they even had a nickname for him. In the top right hand corner the word 'LANKY' was scrawled in capital letters.

Julia couldn't bear to look at them any longer, so she marched into the study and dumped them on Michael's desk.

19

Testing Times

"Insist he takes a DNA test and get him to sign this." Tim Nash, sitting at his desk in the constituency office, handed Michael the brief document. "It gags him. And he can't come after you for any money."

"Right." Michael quickly read the paper and folded it back into the vellum envelope. "I really appreciate this, Tim."

"Apart from Julia, who else knows about this boy?" Tim demanded.

"No one, except Laing's wife."

"Good. Let's keep it that way. When do you meet him?"

"Saturday at three – that country club near Wrensham-Morely."

"Ring me afterwards, once it's settled. And Julia? How is she taking this?" Tim enquired.

"Shocked. Very angry with me, of course. But you know Julia, she's dependable," Michael replied.

"Good. With an election due next year the last thing we need is something like this blowing up in our faces – not after this protest fiasco."

"No. And thank you, Tim, for sorting this." Michael waved the envelope and gave him a comradely pat on the back.

*

Sarah drove the hire car because Nigel was far too nervous. He had hardly slept the night before. In the end, in order to let Sarah get some rest, he had crept out and settled on the sofa. Usually his large body gently enfolded Sarah's, his large square hand resting on the soft bump that was their baby. They would turn over together in unison, Sarah changing position to nestle against his back. By contrast, even without him, Sarah slept well. Although nervous, she was pleasantly excited, and happy in the knowledge that the meeting between Nigel and his natural father would put an end at last to the emotional roller-coaster that had marred the beginning of their married life.

They completed the journey in near silence. As the sign for Wrensham-Morely came into view, Sarah stopped the car, put her hand on Nigel's and said:

"Well, this is it. Ready?"

*

Julia had decided to wear a simple, sleeveless dress in pale pink with a yellow cashmere cardigan; it showed off her tan. Michael, in common with most men of his generation, saw no reason to give any consideration to what he wore and was in his usual weekend attire of battered trousers and casual shirt.

"You'd better put on a jacket and tie," Julia called from the bathroom where she was attaching a discreet string of pearls. "I'm not sure of the dress code there; it is a country club."

"It's only the tearoom," Michael complained.

"Nevertheless, you don't want to be turned away, or draw attention to yourself," Julia countered. She was right of course. Michael didn't want to draw attention to himself; Julia had picked this venue because it was well outside the constituency. All the same, it would be just his luck to have a local worthy descend on him, pressing some cause.

"The Laings mustn't know who I am either, remember," Michael warned her.

"You might get away with it," Julia said. "It's not as if you're always on the six o'clock news like the high-profile Ministers – Health, Defence or Education. Your department only ever seems to get a couple of column inches on the inside page, and it's ages since you were on anything but the radio."

"Will this do?" Michael held up a light-weight summer suit.

"Yes."

There had been precious little discussion between them about the meeting with Nigel Laing and his wife. Michael had returned to the constituency to find that Julia had made all the arrangements for the meeting. On several occasions he had attempted to broach the subject, but she had simply said:

"I've nothing else to say, Michael, until we have met your 'son'."

He found the Laings' correspondence and photographs dumped on his desk. It was unnerving. He had told Tim that Julia could be relied upon but in fact he wasn't sure. She continued to be the same thoughtful and loving mother to the children and, to an outsider, it appeared as if nothing was amiss. Even Breeda, whose antennae were acute, was taken in. However, Michael knew she was play-acting.

The vote on the Scientific Research Bill was likely to be taken in the autumn session. Soundings amongst his MP colleagues had yielded strongly held views. Parliament was struggling to keep up with the science. There was a good deal of ethical queasiness, especially about the chimeric experiments, and the arguments raged back and forth. For Michael the arrival of his 'son' on the scene clinched it. He knew he had no choice. MPs of all persuasions were being lobbied by the bio-tech industry and he was no exception. Given that he was the Minister for the Family, it was entirely fitting that he should take an interest and be fully informed about both sides of the debate. He decided that he would listen attentively to Strumpshaw, explaining his need to take note of his constituents' views, and then later advise him of his decision to vote *for* the bill. A decision that was, of course, entirely his and his alone – he would be very clear indeed on that point. It wouldn't do for Strumpshaw to come away with the idea that his attempt at blackmail had been successful.

*

The tearoom at the country club was elegantly and even opulently furnished. The windows were heavily draped with maroon and gold silk brocade, edged with tasselled trimmings and tied back with ornate swags. The carpet was monogrammed and the high gothic ceiling was studded with golden stars. Julia and Michael settled into a plush sofa in the darkest and most private corner, which commanded a clear view of the entrance.

"We could go out onto the terrace. It's such a lovely day," Julia suggested.

"Too public," Michael stated flatly.

"Yes, you're probably right," she agreed. The waiter came over and they ordered a pot of Earl Grey tea. A family came through from the terrace, the children, a boy and a girl, chasing one another around the sofas until they were reprimanded, and the wife lending her arm to an unsteady elderly relative. The tea arrived and Julia poured.

After a time Michael said:

"I take it we're early."

"Yes."

Michael placed his large square hands on the table and began tapping his fingers up and down rhythmically.

"It's a long journey for them." Julia placed her hand gently over Michael's to halt the incessant drumming. It was the first physical act of tenderness that he had received from her since his revelation. He gave a weak, grateful smile. Quite suddenly, in the doorway to the terrace, two people appeared and then halted, a very tall young man and a petite woman. They stood on the threshold with the strong sunlight behind them, momentarily casting them in deep shadow and hiding their faces. Julia rose to her feet and whispered:

"They're here."

It was all she could do to stifle a gasp. Advancing towards her was a tall young man walking with a slight stoop to disguise his full height. His jacket sagged slightly at the elbows. He had a square jaw with a wide mouth, a broad forehead and large nose. It was a kindly face, the eyes soft and the hair still displaying boyish curls like the ones Michael had once had. In fact, he was the exact image of Michael at that age. He extended his hand:

"Hello," he said, "I'm Nigel Laing and this is my wife, Sarah."

Julia hesitated; there was an appreciable silence before she regained her composure. Finally she said:

"I'm Julia. And this is Michael."

The two men stared intently at one another. Sarah tore her eyes away from Michael and Nigel only briefly, to shake Julia's hand and say hello. The greetings over, no one made a move to sit down.

"Shall we sit?" Julia suggested. She observed Sarah's neat rounded stomach. "I'll order more tea. Would you like tea?" Sarah and Nigel nodded. Julia got up and went up to the bar to place the order. From a distance she could observe the nervousness of both the Laings and Michael. Julia decided it would be up to her to break the ice.

"How was your journey?" she enquired on returning to her seat and glancing at Michael, who appeared awkward and uncomfortable.

"Fine. We got here quite early and walked in the grounds," Sarah replied.

Suddenly, they all began to talk at once; Julia to say something cheery about the ending of the blockades, Michael to establish the ground rules as if he were chairing a departmental meeting and Nigel apologising for any shock or distress his sudden appearance had caused.

Michael took the lead.

"So where do we start?"

"At the beginning. What made you become a donor?" Nigel asked.

Michael began by explaining that he had been a hard up medical student. Donating sperm, he told Nigel and Sarah, seemed to do some good, helping childless couples – and it had helped him pay his way through medical school. And no, he hadn't thought very much about the consequences: after all, he was a young man. Michael pointed out that, back then, environment was considered the overriding factor in the upbringing of children. Genetics, it was considered, had very little bearing on personality and were really only thought to be influential in determining looks, the colour of eyes, hair, that sort of thing. It all sounded very reasonable. When Nigel asked whether Michael had given any thought about all the children he had out there in the world, Michael replied that no, he had never given it a moment's thought. He didn't really consider them as his children and that he had almost forgotten that he had ever been a donor – until that is, Nigel turned up.

Julia observed her husband being urbane, charming and persuasive. She gave a small and imperceptible shudder. How easy it had been to father hundreds of children almost without thinking, and Michael made it sound so normal, simply the logical solution to a pressing financial difficulty. Julia looked hard at Nigel and Sarah; whatever must they think? Perhaps Nigel was so grateful to meet his father that he didn't register the callous indifference of the transaction that has brought him to life nearly thirty years ago.

"I'm sorry if things didn't work out too well for you, with your family," Michael added.

"A lie of this magnitude, in any family, causes damage. My parents were good people who did their best. This is not their fault."

"Nor mine," Michael stated firmly. Nigel dropped his head and ran his hands over his face; it was the mirror image of a frequent gesture of Michael's.

"Does your father know that you've found us... found your donor father?" Julia asked falteringly.

"No, not yet. Gerald would agree that he has never really felt like my father; his way of dealing with it was to detach himself and leave me to my mother. And my mother, Marion, who as you know died earlier this year, couldn't let me out of her sight. I was smothered by her. But again it was not her fault." He paused and took in a deep breath. "But it leaves me feeling so angry, dispossessed... and enraged. Apparently no one is to blame. My aunts and uncles aren't my relatives; my paternal grandparents, who incidentally, adored me, aren't my grandparents; my father is not my father! And the records which can tell me who I am and where I come from are kept secret from me, the one person who really needs to know, who has the right to know the truth."

Nigel drummed the table with his fingers. Julia was mesmerised. Nigel's every gesture was so like Michael's. He was exactly like Michael had been when they had first met all those years ago at the hospital.

"Adopted children have more rights to information about their past than I do," Nigel continued.

Julia shifted uncomfortably. Michael said:

"There has been a change in the law. I voted for it actually."

"It's not retrospective though, so how does that help me?" Nigel demanded. "Or anyone like me."

"What do you need to know?" Julia enquired gently. Nigel took a steadying breath.

"Everything. I want to know what part of the country my family comes from, I want to know about my grandparents, other relatives, health, education, talents. Sarah thought you might be musical, and you have two daughters, my half-sisters. I was raised as an only child. I want... No. I need to know anything and everything, as much as you are prepared to share with me."

"Look," Julia broke in. "Why don't you and Michael go for a long walk in the grounds and talk, and Sarah and I can stay here and get to know one another better."

Michael looked grave but made no protest. It would afford him the opportunity to broach the subject of the DNA test and the signature that would guarantee Nigel Laing's silence and the safety of his own political career.

Sarah popped into the toilet: her condition necessitated many such trips. She splashed her face with cold water from the ornate scallop-shaped sink. She liked Julia Barton and had warmed to her at once, although she was unsure of Michael.There was a slight defensive edge to the man and a certain lack of empathy, both of which she considered rather unusual in a doctor. Perhaps she was misjudging him after all, she reasoned; this was a very peculiar situation and one that he clearly had never anticipated.

When she got back to her seat she asked Julia where Doctor Barton worked because, so far as she could establish, he was not in general practice in the area. Julia quickly explained that he now worked on some obscure medical committee. She changed the subject by asking how Sarah's pregnancy was progressing, and how it affected her work. Sarah explained that she was a PhD research scientist and had arranged to take a year off.

Michael and Nigel were walking towards the lake.

"We want to avoid the golf course, don't want to get knocked out by a stray ball!" Michael advised. They fell into the same stride. Even a stranger couldn't fail to notice that they were father and son.

"Julia tells me that you teach music in a boy's prep school," Michael began amiably.

"Yes, Saint Edmunds. I trained at the Guildhall."

"Oh, I envy you," Michael remarked. "How I should have loved to study music professionally,"

"Why didn't you then?"

"My father had other ideas; law, medicine or engineering."

"Are my grandparents still alive?" Nigel enquired.

"Yes. My father was also a doctor and my mother was a nurse. They live in Sussex." Michael quickly added, "Please don't try and contact them yet, they're old and the shock would probably kill them."

"No, of course not," Nigel agreed, and then asked, "Are you an only child?"

"No, I've a younger brother, Jonathan, an engineer. He's working in Canada for a couple of years; he's divorced – no children. He's the rebel of the family."

They came to a bench overlooking the lake. Michael sat on it and made room for Nigel to join him. He said:

"You must understand that this isn't easy for any of us. I simply don't know how much contact you expect and, if I'm honest, this is already more than I was willing to do. I'm uncomfortable with your presence in my life. The donations were anonymous and part of me is quite angry that you've put my family in this position. Julia knew nothing of my donations and it goes against all her beliefs. It's been a terrible shock for her and I must admit it has put our marriage under some strain. Julia also anticipated that she would have a role in bringing up our first grandchild and now that's been taken from her."

Nigel said nothing.

"And, of course, you realise you have broken the law? I have quite a high profile locally, charity work that sort of thing. And then there's Julia and our children to consider. So if we are to get to know one another better, then I will need you to sign this." From his jacket pocket Michael produced the envelope containing the agreement, which he handed to Nigel. Nigel scanned the brief document quickly with rising anger. Michael Barton appeared to have no comprehension of the impact he had made on Nigel's life. He wasn't an understanding man at all.

"You want me to sign this? Why?"

"I want to keep my private life just that, private," Michael stated firmly.

"But I have no intention..." Nigel protested.

"No, I'm sure you haven't." Michael put a reassuring hand on Nigel's arm, at the same time deftly producing a pen. "But, I have to protect my family. Whatever our relationship, they will always come first."

"Do you always expect the worst from people?" Nigel asked coldly.

"Some aspects of my work are controversial. I'd rather leave it at that," Michael replied.

Nigel didn't want to risk losing contact with his father.

"Very well." He took the pen and signed and, returning the document to its envelope, held it out to Michael.

Michael slipped envelope and pen back into his inside jacket pocket. The sense of relief was overwhelming.

"I'll put you in touch with a centre local to you for the DNA test. I'll pay for it, naturally."

"A DNA test? You really think that's necessary? Just look at us."

"I must be certain beyond any doubt," Michael stated.

"Very well." Perhaps he might begin to like me, Nigel thought, when he finally accepts the truth.

"Now." Michael flashed one of his most endearing smiles, "Tell me all about yourself. Apart from music and teaching, what are your interests – current affairs? Politics?"

Nigel smiled. So his father was curious after all.

"I'm afraid I'm woefully ignorant in that department. We go to exhibitions quite a lot and I play in a jazz band and coach rugby."

Thank goodness for that, thought Michael.

"I was a keen player in my day," Michael replied genially.

They continued their walk.

"I think that went smoothly, don't you?" Julia asked as they drove back home to Wynshore. Michael was lost in thought.

"Yes, thank God. Now we can all get back to normal," he replied, sounding both dismissive and relieved. Julia wondered what 'normal' might be and certainly didn't see turning the clock back as an option.

"I think we have to move forward from this, everything has changed; you have a son, and soon a grandchild. Tess and Katherine have a half-brother. It will take some adjustment, for everyone," she replied coolly.

"Let's just take this one step at a time, Julia. I've met him, which is what you wanted, raked over my childhood for his benefit…it's more than many men would do in my position. I could have called in the police if I hadn't been obliged to consider how the publicity would affect you and the girls."

Julia stared hard at Michael's profile as he slowed the car and approached a traffic junction and said:

"If you would do that to your own son, I simply don't understand you any more."

*

"You're so alike! Even your mannerisms." Sarah had talked excitedly on and off for most of the journey. How kind Julia Barton was and so easy to talk to and very interested in the pregnancy and her career. How uncannily similar Nigel and his father were – even the gestures. Had they made plans to meet again? What about his daughters, Tess and Katherine, when would they be told about their half-brother? Did Nigel think they would be introduced to the rest of the family, his grandparents perhaps?

"I know this has been very stressful and I wouldn't wish this situation on anyone, but it's rather exciting too, there's a whole new side to your life that never existed before, don't you think?" As an afterthought she added, "He's a very good looking man, your father, and oddly familiar. But I suppose that's just the likeness to you." And not in the least like dear dull Gerald – although Sarah tactfully kept that thought to herself.

Nigel joined in only briefly but Sarah was so animated that she barely noticed his withdrawal. After the car drew up outside their flat, he put on the handbrake and said:

"He's arranging for a DNA test for us both."

Sarah looked surprised.

" Oh… a test." She took in a large breath. "I suppose he needs to be sure," she concluded uncertainly. "Perhaps that's a good sign. It means he expects more contact. This wasn't a one-off."

"And he made me sign something, a sort of gagging order."

"Sign what?"

"In case I decide to sell my story to the tabloids or something ridiculous like that. To protect his family's privacy," Nigel added.

"How peculiar!"

"He told me some areas of his work were controversial. I don't know what he meant. I didn't think to ask why."

"It hardly matters anyway, it's clear to me that Michael Barton is your father. He's probably just feeling panicky and scared. This has turned his world upside down too."

"He says that their relationship has suffered, his and Julia's, so I expect you're right. I like her. She's compassionate. I think she appreciates how I feel far better than he does. He's defensive but maybe in time that will change. Come on, I'd better phone Gerald and tell him, I can't keep putting it off." Nigel squeezed Sarah's hand and then leant over and gave her a gentle kiss on the cheek.

*

Gerald had just got out of the shower when the telephone rang. He had been enjoying an afternoon of surprisingly vigorous sex with Barbara, a lively red-headed divorcée he'd met at his cookery class. Their chocolate soufflés had shared the same oven; mysteriously Barbara's had risen successfully, whilst Gerald's had immediately deflated. There had ensued much good humoured banter during which Barbara suggested that, given the right inducements, she was available to pump up his 'pudding' anytime he felt the need!

"How did he take it?" Sarah enquired after Nigel had come off the phone.

"Very well indeed. Gerald is extremely happy for me. He was remarkably upbeat and big hearted. He said he always felt sure my father was a decent sort of chap because of the way I'd turned out." Nigel nestled down next to Sarah on the sofa and put his arm around her. "Which I think is a remarkably generous statement. I imagined he might feel jealous. It's curious, how you can sometimes see quite another side of someone. I actually feel rather proud of the way Gerald has handled all this. It can't have been easy bringing up someone else's child. He did his best. Mother too, I suppose, in her own way. Poor Marion, perhaps she would have been a very different mother without this secret," he added. "It all fits into place now. The jigsaw puzzle that is me is finally complete." Nigel smiled and planted an affectionate kiss on Sarah's cheek. "Whatever happens next, I feel so much better. It's as if I've had someone standing on my chest for months, pressing down on me, and finally I can breathe freely again." Sarah snuggled close, feeling satisfied and content for the first time in months. She had her Nigel back. It was all going to be fine now.

20

Visitation

The Minister for the Family's postbag was full to bursting. A letter writing campaign, set up by the pro-life lobby and various religious groups, was responsible for most of it. Geraldine, Michael's able constituency secretary, dealt with the correspondence, with Michael only dictating a personal reply to the Bishop, church elders and other important dignitaries and leaders. Breeda's letter merited no special attention and much to her annoyance she received only the standard reply. She cornered Julia outside the school gate.

"I'm no nearer knowing how Michael intends to vote now than I was before," she protested and then, waving the letter at her, read it out: "'Parliament will debate the Bill thoroughly, and carefully weigh up the arguments both for and against...the Minister understands your concerns and deeply held convictions...and he thanks you for bringing your views to his attention.' Pah!"

Julia gestured for her to stop.

"I just don't want to go down this road, Breeda. I won't discuss it. It's a vote of conscience and I have to trust Michael to make the right decision. You've known him long enough and I hope you'll do the same."

"You do realise that, if this bill is passed, before you know it they'll be cloning babies for spare parts and dressing it up as life saving! It's cannibalism! These scientists are undermining our species, there is even talk of a humanzee. Cross breeding the... "

"Breeda, enough," Julia snapped uncharacteristically, and slamming the car door she drove off at speed, leaving the indignant Breeda on the pavement.

Julia and Michael had barely discussed the issue, Julia just once asking how he intended to vote, and Michael replying that as yet he was undecided. She had left it at that. Once she would have known how her husband would act in any given situation. Not any more.

*

Michael was attending a lecture on new treatments for degenerative diseases that was being held in a hall opposite the Palace of Westminster. His diary secretary had scheduled a brief visit. Michael was a key-figure on the all-party group on degenerative diseases and he had a special interest in Alzheimer's, motor neurone disease and multiple sclerosis because as a general practitioner he had witnessed the relentless destruction of his patients' lives and personalities. Undoubtedly, new treatments arising from stem cell therapy held the best hope of a cure. The Minister for Health was on the platform, looking faintly bored and inattentive. The audience was a mixture of specialists, health professionals, patient groups and pharmaceutical industry giants. Amongst them, unknown to Michael, was Giles Strumpshaw, and when the group broke for drinks and a buffet lunch Giles spied Michael and set off after his quarry.

"Dear boy! How wonderful to see you again and looking rested. I should say the holiday has done you a power of good." Strumpshaw clapped him on the back and shook his hand enthusiastically. Somewhere off to the side flashbulbs flared. Skilfully Michael manoeuvred Giles away from the throng.

"Giles, I'm glad I've run into you," he began softly. "You will want to know that having very carefully weighed up all the arguments, I am going to vote for the Scientific Research Bill." Giles beamed. "It's an important matter and it was necessary to take soundings from my constituents and various other bodies," Michael continued. "We have all had a very large postbag, much of it..."

"Splendid, old chap," Giles broke in. "Now, I knew you'd see sense, don't want a whole lot of nasty rumour and innuendo. I must let Stanton know – he's about somewhere."

Michael took Strumpshaw by the elbow.

"Giles, I must make this absolutely crystal clear: this was a decision made solely on the scientific and medical evidence and was in no way influenced by any other party, yourself and your lobbyist included."

"Of course, my dear fellow, if that's the way you want to play it." Giles tapped the side of his nose with his finger in a gesture suggesting secrecy and skulduggery. "Your little secret's safe with me."

"I don't believe you're hearing me, Giles." Michael was becoming agitated.

"Ah yes, dear boy. You're the squeaky clean lot, isn't that so? 'Sustaining the highest ethical and moral standards in public life' and all that tosh." Strumpshaw, his lips glistening, threw back his head and roared with laughter. He seized a glass of red wine from a passing waiter and disappeared into the throng, calling over his shoulder: "Now mind you don't get into any other mischief, old boy."

*

The results of the DNA test merely proved what they all knew anyway: Nigel was Michael's son. He was also a very pleasant young man, with a lovely wife, and he was Tess and Katherine's half-brother. And while Julia wasn't yet ready to explain Nigel's parentage to her daughters, family and friends, she had decided that the only Christian thing to do was to embrace Nigel and include him in the Barton family. Julia had a very clear sense of right and wrong. The DNA result gave her permission, or so she thought, to invite Nigel and Sarah to come and stay with them for a couple of days during the forthcoming half-term, a plan that she only confided to Michael when the arrangements had already been made.

"Just un-arrange it at once!" Michael had bellowed down the telephone. "I've done more than my duty already and I have no... let me repeat...no intention of letting Nigel Laing and his wife insinuate their way into our lives."

Julia mustered all her calm authority and replied:

"Whether you are present or not, Michael, is entirely up to you. But so far as I'm concerned, the invitation stands. I want the girls to meet their half-brother. I hope that you will explain his connection to them. Nigel doesn't have to 'insinuate' himself into our lives, he's your son and as such very much a part of this family, more so, as your first grandchild will be born this spring. The suppression of these facts has caused quite enough pain already." With untypical cruelty, she added, "I suppose you could always take the coward's way out and hole up in the London flat."

While Julia found it a simple task to forgive Nigel his untimely arrival, she found that forgiveness of her husband was proving altogether more difficult, if not impossible. She tried hard to resurrect her affection for Michael but she was furious with him. Julia had understood completely when Nigel had described the feelings of impotent rage that had engulfed him. She had taken to wandering into the empty church and sitting quietly reviewing her life. She found the chill silence of the nave comforting and it was the only place where occasionally her anger diminished and she found solace. Julia didn't pray, not in the accepted sense; she was having trouble with her God – with her faith. "If this is a test," she murmured wretchedly, staring hard at the Tabernacle, "I'm failing miserably. Tell me then, how I can stop hating Michael? Just tell me," she begged.

Father Frank had observed Julia several times recently. She appeared troubled.

"Julia," he called gently as he slipped into the pew beside her and rested his old veined hand on hers. "I'm here to listen, if you think it might help."

"Oh Father, I don't know if I can begin to..." Julia's voice trailed away. "I'm struggling with anger and the impossibility of forgiveness."

Father Frank nodded. "Anger has a destructive nature, as I'm sure you know. It can be corrosive and often as harmful to you as to the person you are angry with. Healing cannot begin until you let it go."

"I understand that, I do, but this is..." Her voice broke. "This is so hard, this struggle. What do you do, Father, when you find someone you love has committed an act that goes against everything you believe in and continues to cause so much pain to so many people... and they can't see it? Won't see it."

"Talk to them, don't put up barriers. And ultimately it's Time that's the greatest healer of all." Julia looked unconvinced. "If you have reached such a great impasse well then, sometimes you might need the wise counsel of a third party," he suggested. "You could also reflect on the time when loving was easy – it helps, you know, reminding yourself of the qualities that once existed; rekindling such feelings can be a path to reconciliation."

"I hope you're right," Julia replied.

"You know, Julia, being the wife of a public figure can be very isolating. It can be hard to know where to turn." He held her hand a little tighter. "You know where to find me."

"Thank you, Father."

"God bless you, Julia." The priest rose from the pew, genuflected, crossed himself and slipped quietly into the darkness of the transept.

*

Nigel and Sarah arrived by car in Wynshore at four o'clock on the Sunday afternoon – at the same time Michael's train was pulling out of Wynshore railway station for London. Even though the crisis had passed and the country was slowly returning to normal, he had set off for The House a day earlier than usual.

Julia, Tess and Katherine provided a warm welcome, despite Julia giving in to some unexpected nerves.

"How do you know them?" Tess had enquired innocently.

"Oh, Sarah's mother is an old friend of…" Julia hesitated and then added hastily, "…the family." Whilst this explanation sounded unconvincing, Tess appeared to accept it readily.

"I'm so sorry Michael isn't here, he has to be in London this week. What with the trains still unreliable and now floods and another storm forecast for tomorrow…" Julia stood by the kettle waiting for it to boil. "Anyway, he'll be here another time." Filling the teapot, she asked brightly, "How was your journey? How were the roads?"

Nigel smiled warmly at Julia, recognising her discomfort and the lame excuse for Michael's absence.

"I'm sorry," Julia said, looking over at Nigel.

"Don't be," he replied reassuringly. "It's an unusual situation." And then crossing the kitchen, he took a mug of steaming tea from Julia's hand.

"Unique," Julia commented. "I'm sorry, I shouldn't keep staring. It's just that you're so like Michael it's eerie. It brings him back, conjures him up as he was." Julia stopped herself. "Oh dear, I'm making an utter mess of this, you must think me a complete fool."

"I don't think that at all. In fact, I think you're very brave," Nigel replied, looking at Julia with genuine compassion.

Julia was afraid she might cry. She cried so easily now. It felt so long since anyone had given her credit for anything, least of all being brave.

"He didn't want to be here, did he?"

"No, I suppose he didn't. Originally he agreed to have dinner with you this evening – he usually catches the dawn train – but the weather and the trains gave him the perfect excuse to escape."

"It's a shame. But then I've been living with the knowledge of his existence for six months. Poor Michael's never expected me to turn up in his life. And although I'm disappointed, I'm meeting my half-sisters for the first time and that's a bonus." Then changing the subject, Nigel enquired, "Does he work in London often? You said he usually catches the dawn train?"

Julia shifted uncomfortably.

"Meetings, conferences. Yes, quite often. Let's take this tea through to Sarah before it gets cold." Julia gathered the mugs, biscuits and sugar onto a tray and set off with Nigel for the living room where Sarah had been press-ganged into a game of Monopoly with Tess and Katherine. As usual Tess was cheating and Katherine was protesting loudly.

*

At *The Daily Record* Frank Smite scrolled through a batch of photographs. His eye was caught by the image of several familiar faces in the background of a line-up.

"Well, well, well...and Stanton too!" Smite grinned and then gave a long satisfied sniff. The snapper had kept his finger on the button with the result that each frame showed Strumpshaw, Barton and Stanton, as if they were movie stills.

"Archie!" Smite called excitedly across the pressroom to where the picture editor was standing chatting with a colleague. "Got a minute? You using these?"

Returning to the desk Archie took a look at the screen.

"Nope. Dull little conference. Why the interest, Frank? You onto something?"

"Now that would be telling, Archie old boy, wouldn't it." Smite winked. "Just watch this space." And, crossing the floor to his desk, he added, "When the time comes, the drinks are on me!"

Curious, Archie took a closer look. There appeared to be nothing of interest in the images before him. Still, Frank had a nose for a good story – he'd better save them.

*

The overnight storm hadn't hit Wynshore with quite the same ferocity that the rest of the England had suffered, nevertheless the roads were littered with stray branches and, in some cases, whole trees. Several mainline railway stations were closed, including Liverpool Street, and flooding on the underground network had brought London to a near standstill.

Julia had spent a fitful night haunted by curious and disturbing dreams; she had woken with a start on several occasions in the small hours. Once again she thought she had heard the plaintive mewing of a tiny lost kitten which seemed to come from under the floorboards in the kitchen. She set about pulling them up. The sense of urgency was overwhelming and yet when she asked Michael for help, he had just sat at the table reading some papers from his red ministerial box. Feverishly she went on ripping up the boards with a crowbar, her anxiety growing by the minute but finally she rescued the frightened creature and placed it in Michael's red box.

"What am I supposed to do with this?" he had said disdainfully, handing it back. Julia held it on her lap, only to find that the mewing, far from stopping, grew increasingly intense and desperate. She then discovered other tiny kittens, brothers and sisters, each with different markings and colouring, were also trapped under the floor, in corners and behind pipe-work, and that she had to unearth each one of them in turn and without help. She woke with a start, covered with a thin film of sweat.

All around the house the wind was howling and you could hear pieces of fencing and shed roofs flying through the air, battering and flapping in the gales. At six she gave up all hope of sleep and crept downstairs and made a cup of tea. Half an hour later she was joined by Sarah.

"What a terrible night!" Sarah said, appearing at the kitchen door in her dressing gown.

"Yes, wasn't it. Part of the garden fence is down. Tea?" Julia offered. "Is Nigel asleep?"

"Yes. He can sleep through anything. He could fix that fence for you later."

"Thanks. Michael sleeps well too," Julia said, filling the kettle. "Men always seem able to switch off, nothing disturbs them."

"Well, this business has," Sarah replied doubtfully. "At one point sleeping for Nigel became a real problem. I think it was part of the depression associated with all this."

"Oh, dear. And now?"

"Oh, much better. In fact I was hoping to catch you alone to thank you. I do realise this is very difficult for you and your family. Asking us here was very generous and... brave" Then just like Nigel before her, she added. "This isn't easy for any one of us, is it?"

This was the second time in twenty-four hours that Julia had been called 'brave'.

"Thank you," she murmured. Pouring the tea, she added, "Perhaps in time we can explain to Tess and Katherine what Nigel's real relationship to them is but for now...well, it's going to take time, we're all going to have to make adjustments and that can be hard. Especially for Michael."

Sarah looked sympathetically at Julia.

"Especially for Michael," she repeated.

"Nigel seems very caring." Julia paused. "Michael was when I met him," she murmured wistfully.

Sarah had no idea what to say.

"Now," Julia began more brightly, regaining her composure. "The storm has blown away and the sun is breaking through, so I believe a tour of Wynshore is planned for today – although we may have to bribe the girls! They tend to get fed up with my guided tours for guests."

*

Breeda was gathering the wholemeal ingredients for fruit crumble into a bowl; roughage was never lacking in her baking. The doorbell rang and the children, scattered throughout the house, all chose to ignore it. After two further persistent rings, she dusted off her floured hands and set off to answer the door herself, shouting up the stairs as she went: "If this turns out to be for one of you lot, I'll say you're all out!" She pulled back the door to find an attractive blonde standing on the doorstep between two elegant pieces of matching luggage.

"Imogen!" Breeda cried. "How wonderful to see you! Come in, come in. Is there no one home at Julia's?" And without waiting for a reply she drew Imogen into the house and called up the stairs for Seamus to bring the suitcases into the hall.

"Not a soul! The place is as quiet as the grave. Not that she's expecting me," Imogen replied in her clear, calm tones that were so reminiscent of her sister's. "They're not away, are they?"

"Not so far as I know. Come and have some tea while I finish this crumble. I can always let you in, I've a key. You're looking very fine, Imogen, very fine. I heard about your promotion, congratulations. Now careful where you sit, you don't want to be getting something nasty on that fine suit of yours." Breeda handed Imogen a cloth to wipe the seat.

"Oh Breeda, don't tell me you still haven't moved that awful Saint Sebastian picture. It's gross! How can you sit down and eat in front of it? The children will be in therapy for years over this. As if it isn't enough of a short straw starting life as a Catholic!" Imogen, more a confirmed atheist than a lapsed Catholic, finished wiping down the chair and tucked herself neatly into the seat with her back firmly to the offending picture.

"Two feet in the door, only one sentence and already you've criticised my parenting, my decor and my faith! Just because you're an international executive, young woman, don't think you know it all!"

Imogen rather liked Breeda. She had got to know her when Julia and new-born Katherine were so ill and still in hospital when, without a murmur, Breeda had scooped Tess up and saved Imogen from missing an important interview. And she gave Michael a run for his money and, although Imogen liked her brother in law, she detected touches of vanity and pomposity that often required regulating. She could certainly always rely on Breeda and Finn to join in and gang up on Michael for some entertaining teasing.

"Drink this and behave yourself." Breeda put a cup of tea down in front of her. They were an unlikely pair, Breeda with her luxuriant auburn hair and curious and outmoded dress sense, Imogen petite and immaculate in a little woven suit with large buttons in the Jackie Kennedy style.

"So how is my big sister?" Imogen asked.

For a moment Breeda hesitated and then replied, "At a bit of a loose end. She's thinking of doing a course – resuming a career."

"Oh! And Michael?" Imogen enquired mischievously.

Breeda raised an eyebrow and smiled a knowing smile, at the same time adding the oats and bran to the crumble topping. "Ah well. Michael is Michael."

*

Julia, Nigel, Sarah and the girls had just enjoyed coffee and a selection of homemade cakes at Thackery's, one of Wynshore's favoured tearooms – its oak beams, crooked floor and thatch making it popular with tourists and locals alike. They were just debating whether to visit the cathedral or the castle when Julia was hailed by Moya, who was making her way towards the law courts.

"Julia! How are you? Hello girls, enjoying half-term?"

Her eye fell upon Nigel.

"I'm Julia's friend, Moya," she said and, transferring her briefcase across, she stretched out her right hand in anticipation of an introduction.

"Oh, I'm sorry, Moya. This is Sarah and Nigel, they're visiting from Maidenhead." The little group proceeded to indulge in a seemingly casual conversation regarding the visit. The only suggestion that this was anything other than an innocent meeting between friends was indicated by Julia's attempt to mask her discomfort by being especially light hearted, and by Moya's inability to take her eyes off Nigel. Finally, they parted and Moya continued on her way to the county court.

So Breeda was right! There was a son.

*

Breeda let Imogen into Julia's house by the back door. They had been in the kitchen just long enough to observe that the breakfast dishes hadn't been loaded into the washer and concluded that Julia couldn't have gone far, when the key turned in the front door lock. They moved out into the hall to greet her.

"Imogen!" Julia cried aghast, as Nigel, Sarah and the girls bundled in through the door behind her. "What on earth are you doing here?"

21

Revelation

"And a very warm welcome to you too, my darling Julia!" Imogen responded as she opened her arms to embrace her sister. "I've just landed in that ridiculous little airport of yours: Washington, Schiphol, Wynshore! Talk about coming down in the world, it's Toy Town!" She laughed as she hugged Julia to her. Over Imogen's shoulder Julia spied Breeda advancing up the hall from the kitchen. Oh my God! Not Breeda too!

"Honestly Julia, I've only been out of the country for eight weeks and it seems to have completely fallen apart, blockades, floods and crashes – what's the government doing about it? Whatever does Michael say?" Then releasing Julia from her embrace, Imogen looked up at Nigel and said:

"Oh, hello, who are you?"

Sarah, recognising the impossible situation in which Julia found herself, quickly introduced herself and Nigel to Imogen, and then asked Nigel to carry the purchases they had made that day upstairs to the spare room. Breeda, apparently awestruck, remained standing at the end of the hall by the kitchen door, only coming to life when Julia suggested she put the kettle on. In the meantime Julia seized Imogen by the elbow and hustled her into the study, simultaneously commanding the children to watch television – they would see their Aunt Imogen in a moment.

"Julia! What are you doing?" Imogen asked, wriggling free of her sister's hand.

Julia leant firmly against the study door, blocking the exit and took in a deep breath.

"Look, I can't tell you, not now. You must promise me this, whatever happens, you must not tell Nigel and Sarah what Michael does or who he is. This is serious, Imogen. Promise me."

"Good God, Julia! Whatever's going on? Who are Sarah and Nigel? Why so cloak and dagger?" Imogen was bewildered.

"Don't ask me that either. Please, Imogen, this is important. When I can, I'll tell you, but not now. Promise me."

"All right, all right, I promise. So what am I supposed to say Michael does?"

"I've kept it vague. They think he's just an ex GP. We've suggested he sits on some quango or other. Just keep it that way and if you can avoid answering any questions about Michael, then so much the better. Because they'll probably ask. Just talk about what you do, everybody's always interested in what you do, so it shouldn't be too difficult."

"Thank you very much, I am overwhelmed by the warmth of your sisterly welcome. Now may I go and speak to my nieces? Or are they under some sort of embargo as well?"

"Don't mock me, Imogen, this is very important. Oh my God! Breeda! I must get rid of her." And with that Julia shot out of the study and down the hall to the kitchen.

"I think I've just been scripted into an Ayckbourn farce," Imogen said to no one in particular, and then adding, "Let's see if the children are still sane."

Imogen had always been a big hit with Tess and Katherine. She was that rare breed of aunt who actually knew what girls of ten and twelve wanted. In their eyes she was modern, single and glamorous. She didn't wear dull grey or navy business suits like the other executive women that they saw in Wynshore. No, Aunt Imogen, whose figure was a perfect size ten, wore colour. Tess happily unpacked her suitcases for her, reverently fingering the beautiful garments and checking the labels as she did so; Agnès B, Maxmara, Chanel and Prada. And she had an exciting career, and went on frequent foreign trips, with the added thrill for Tess and Katherine of receiving remarkable gifts only found in the States or the Far East.

Imogen discovered the girls, with their legs tucked up under them on the sofa, watching Blue Peter.

"Is there room for me, girls?"

"'course," Tess replied and shuffled along.

"What's happened to that chatty girl who used to present it?" Imogen enquired.

"Oh, she went ages ago, and the one that did the gardening. It's all new people now," Tess informed her.

"That's a shame – I liked her," Imogen remarked.

"So did Katherine, she cried on her last show," Tess declared.

"I did not!" Katherine leaned across Imogen and hit Tess with a cushion.

"Hey, cut it out, you two, I've only just got off the plane and I'm still waiting for the warm welcome. Now tell me, how long have Nigel and Sarah been staying? And why do we know them?"

"Dunno," Tess said vaguely in an expression she would not have got away with in front of her father. He would have said; 'Let's have that again shall we, Tess, and as a whole sentence this time please.'

"Very helpful, Tess," Imogen commented.

Katherine leant out from her snug corner at the other end of the sofa. "They're friends of Mummy's."

"All Mummy said was, 'they're friends of the family'," Tess confirmed.

"Really," Imogen said.

"They come from Maidenhead. He's a teacher, she's a scientist. And they go home tomorrow afternoon. Oh, and Daddy was very cross with Mummy for inviting them. He went to the London flat last night."

"Ah! Now that is what I call information. Thank you, Katherine."

In the kitchen Breeda was lining up the mugs and preparing a tray of tea. She had put out a mug for herself, she was planning on staying.

"Thank you, Breeda, that's lovely," Julia said, taking over the task. "It was kind of you to drop Imogen off. I won't keep you, your children will be wanting their tea."

Breeda took no notice.

"That's him, isn't it? He's the image of Michael, younger of course but unmistakably Michael. Is he nice? Do you like him? What does Michael say – he's met him, of course? And the girls?" Breeda continued in a stage whisper. "Bit of a shock, Imogen turning up like this. Should I take her with me and put her up at our house?

No. I suppose that would look odd. Does she know? She doesn't know...there'd be no time to tell her."

"Breeda, Breeda!" Julia said sharply. "If you don't mind, could you please come around another time? We need to be on our own. This is an awkward situation, as I'm sure you realise."

"Oh. Oh, I see." Breeda was clearly offended.

"Why don't you drop by on Thursday morning? We could all have coffee," Julia suggested, implying that Nigel and Sarah would still be there while knowing full well that they would have already left. To emphasise her point, she held open the back door.

"Well, I'll leave you to your guests." Breeda's voice had a distinct edge to it.

"Thank you, Breeda, for being so understanding." Julia mustered a warm smile and, closing the door behind her friend, she sank back against the door and let out a long sigh.

Imogen found that Nigel had returned to the sitting room and was playing 'Don't Panic'. You had to beat the clock and name several items before the buzzer went off. They were all panicking and every so often the girls would roll on the floor squealing, all satin legs and tummy tops.

From her vantage point at the other end of the sitting room Imogen flicked through a magazine watching them. Nigel threw back his head and laughed at some antic of Katherine's and there was no mistaking it – he looked just like a younger Michael, same mannerisms, same laugh. This was no friend of the family; there was clearly a closer link. Nephew? Cousin?

A few moments later Sarah entered carrying the tea tray. They began a trivial conversation largely about work. When Imogen ran out of bland and uncontroversial questions to ask, she excused herself saying the tea was too strong and she needed to add some water to it. Slipping into the kitchen, she found Julia preparing a salad.

"What's going on, Julia? Who exactly is Nigel?"

"He's Michael's son," Julia stated.

"Ah!" Imogen didn't seem very surprised. "And so who is his mother?"

"Marion Laing. She died in the spring, which is when Nigel found out." Julia stopped chopping the lettuce and sat down at the table. Now off guard, she looked more weary and older than Imogen had ever seen her. "But Imogen, there's more. I haven't told a soul and you're not to either, promise me. Please."

"Of course. But does Breeda know?" Imogen asked.

"She knows there's a son and having just seen him, it's obvious it's Nigel. But she doesn't know the rest."

Imogen looked at her sister quizzically.

"Which is?"

"Nigel's father, Gerald, is infertile. His birth was the result of assisted reproduction. Michael was the sperm donor."

"My God!" Imogen stared at her sister in utter disbelief. "Did he know her? Was it a favour to a friend?"

Julia shook her head and tearfully replied:

"He did it for the money – he was broke at medical school." And then in barely a whisper, she added. "Twice or maybe three times a week…for months and months, in numerous clinics."

"Oh Julia, no. There must be others!"

Almost inaudibly, Julia said, "Dozens, possibly hundreds."

"Then why have you asked him here?"

"Because he's Michael's son and the girls' half-brother," Julia replied defensively. "He's part of our family – however that came about."

"Oh Julia. No wonder Michael's fled to London. It can only be a question of time before Nigel finds out who he is. The press will have a field day, especially the tabloids. I can quite see why Michael has refused to meet him. And he must have stolen some records – why on earth didn't you just call the police? Surely you could have passed him off as a sad crank or a stalker?"

"I think that would be worse. Luckily, Nigel and his wife are not very worldly; they're both obsessed with their work and not the slightest bit interested in politics. But anyway, things have already gone too far for that. Michael has met Nigel, we all had tea together at the country club. And I've already had to rescue Michael from his own foolishness. His first response was to send a cheque, which thankfully they returned and I destroyed. He sent a callous little note too, supposedly meant to reassure Nigel and Sarah that there are no known congenital defects in the family. Sarah is, as you probably noticed, pregnant." Julia's voice cracked on the word pregnant and tears began to course down her cheeks. "Michael's grandchild will be born this spring."

"My poor Julia." Imogen took a tissue from her pocket, wiped her sister's face and then put her arms round her.

"I thought if I could just make them feel part of the family before then we could put on united front. Michael got Nigel to sign some document to protect our privacy."

"Good grief! It doesn't get any better, does it!"

"No. No it doesn't," Julia replied sadly.

In the living room, sprawled on the carpet enjoying the game, Nigel had just managed to name six Latin American countries before the buzzer went off. Tess and Katherine worked as a team to try and even up the odds against them. Tess pulled a blue card from the pack and Nigel set the clock.

"Political figures," Tess read out the category from the card. The timer started to turn, the seconds ticked away.

"Winston Churchill," Katherine stated confidently.

"Abraham Lincoln," Tess added. Then there was a significant pause as the timer clicked on before Tess suggested: "The man who does the tax. Daddy doesn't like him, he never gives out enough money, what's his name...and ..." The arrow on the timer was already near the end and the buzzer was about to sound when Katherine cried:

"And Daddy! That makes three!" She sat back pleased with herself.

Nigel's head shot up and his eyes met Sarah's.

"Daddy?" Sarah queried.

"Daddy's an MP and a minister now. He works to improve life for families," Katherine said and then, sounding slightly put out, she added, "I thought everyone knew that."

22

Crossing the Rubicon

By the time Breeda arrived for coffee on Thursday, Nigel and Sarah had long gone. They had set off late on Wednesday morning, declining lunch and expressing some concern about the possible traffic delays given the paralysis of the railway network and the widespread flooding caused by the appalling weather.

Nigel and Sarah had kept Katherine's extraordinary revelation to themselves. Nigel felt he needed to investigate further. Having only just successfully tracked down his biological father, to then discover that he was an MP as well as a government minister was a shock. At the same time it explained Michael's curiously offhand behaviour and, for the moment, he couldn't decide whether his father's efforts to avoid a scandal made him like or dislike him more or less. However, it also explained why Michael Barton appeared familiar. Not only were he and Nigel similar in every way, but without doubt, Nigel must at some time have seen a picture of him in the paper. As soon as they were home he would get onto the Parliamentary website and see what he could find out about Michael Barton, MP and Minister.

He felt for Julia, it was no wonder she was so on edge. What an appalling predicament she was in, caught between her desire to welcome Nigel into the family, to do the right thing by him, and her instinct to protect her own children from unwarranted press and media intrusion. Clearly she was a woman who regarded it as her duty to extend a welcome to this lost member of the family, and yet his presence in her life represented a terrible risk to both her marriage and her children. Now, knowing the public office his father held, Nigel realised that Julia Barton was an extraordinarily good and courageous woman.

"No wonder Julia was so aghast to find her sister and friend at the house waiting for her," Sarah remarked. "Imogen can't have known."

" Julia's been remarkable," Nigel said. "I hope she won't regret it."

"This can't be doing her relationship with Michael any good," Sarah commented. "It not only explains his reluctance to meet you, but also that document he got you to sign." After a long pause, she asked: "Are you angry with him?"

"I don't know. I'm stunned, I don't know how I feel about having Michael Barton MP as my father."

Breeda was not at all amused to find that Michael's son and his pregnant wife had left the day before. And while it was put to her that this was entirely their decision and unexpected, Breeda suspected that the early departure had been engineered to keep her from meeting the young couple.

Imogen was at a loss to know what advice to give Julia regarding divulging Michael's public identity to Nigel and Sarah. Especially as, unrealistically, Michael wanted it kept secret.

"They will find out in time, Julia. Better by far that you tell them yourselves than leave it to chance. What happens if they see Michael on television? Because, let's face it, that's quite likely and must be avoided at all costs. In fact, Michael's been jolly lucky that they haven't discovered all this already. Surely he sees that?"

"Michael isn't actually speaking to me, Imogen. He doesn't see my invitation to them as an act of human charity but as insanity."

"He may have a point," Imogen conceded unhelpfully.

*

Frank Smite and Nigel Laing were both, for different reasons, accessing the House of Commons website, Smite to find out the date of the vote on the Scientific Research Bill, and Nigel to find out anything about the MP for Wynshore.

To Nigel the information offered was concise:

Barton Michael.
Min: Family. PUSS
Minister for the Family.
SEL: Health

SEL: Primary Care Public Health.
jvch – Cancer.
APG: Community Heath Councils.
Sec: Parliamentary and Scientific.
Sec: Motor Neurone Disease.

Listed under members' interests was:

Occasional fees from writing and broadcasting.
Occasional fees lecturing and speaking.
Two tickets to Wynshore City football club.

It was clear that his father took his public duties seriously and had made a strong commitment to using his medical knowledge for the public good. It was also clear that Michael Barton had a fine parliamentary career and reputation to protect.

Smite, however, was having less success. His query took him around the website in frustrating circles, only serving to confirm Frank's distrust and dislike of the infernal technology.

"For gawd's sake!" He just managed to restrain himself from chucking the thing out the window. "Where's Gideon this morning?" Smite called out to his colleagues in a tone that was clearly a cry for help.

Gideon Wentworth, the Parliamentary sketch writer, old Etonian with a taste in amusing bow ties – Wallace and Grommit, the Simpsons – was only occasionally to be found in the press room. More likely he would be reclining languidly in some bar or club favoured by parliamentary high-life or low-life depending on your point of view, but nevertheless picking up juicy titbits of gossip. Gideon was a savage and witty hack who frequently penned acerbic and biting critiques of the daily doings inside and outside the House.

"Why? What are you after, Frank?" The disembodied voice of Sam Denton, the medical correspondent, came from behind a terminal.

"The date of the vote on the Scientific Research Bill. I know it's sometime this session."

"The eighteenth of December," Sam called back. "I'm doing a piece on it."

"Oh are you. Interesting. What's the result going to be then?" Smite asked.

"My guess is, that a bit like last time, it'll get passed by the Commons but get a rough ride in the Lords – all those bishops and baronesses."

"Bit close to Christmas, innit? Won't they all have buggered off home to their constituencies?"

"Almost. The right-to-life lot are already complaining."

"So what are the arguments?"

Sam, who was a good twenty years younger than Smite, had clean-cut good looks in the preppy American style. Hang a stethoscope around his neck and he could easily be mistaken for a medic himself. He took the pencil, which he was intermittently chewing, out of his mouth and stuck it behind his ear.

"It's by no means in the bag. This Bill extends the remit of scientists beyond anything seen before. They're chipping away at the restraints previously set by parliament. They argue that to curtail this research condemns people to lifelong suffering which could be prevented. Like last time, there's been massive behind-the-scenes lobbying. Now it's more contentious. They point out the laws on embryo research are inconsistent given the limits on abortion. They've been creating hybrids for years, pigs that produce human blood, for example, all worthy stuff, the aim an uncontaminated blood supply. But now there's a lot of unease.

"The Minister and Lord Crawell are briefing MPs on the merits of the case – even writing to them individually. And there's a lot of pressure being applied – the bio-tech industry in this country is very powerful and parliament doesn't move quickly enough to keep up with the science, which is why we're back here again so soon. They need to use the differentiated cells – because they can be turned into livers, hearts etcetera. Any earlier and they become tumours, which, obviously, you don't want; and adult stem cells don't have the potential to turn into any organ."

"And these new treatments will be money spinners?" Smite queried.

"You bet. It's feasible that by 2040 they'll be able to build new organs. No more organ donors, and no lifetime on a cocktail of drugs. Interestingly, we've a number of our doctor MPs, as well as the PhDs, that are against. The real worry is still full cloning. There's a lot of mileage in the argument that this technology is the bridge across which full human cloning will cross. They'll get very skilled at this technique, so why stop at cloning livers and hearts when you can reproduce a complete human? More worrying are the chimeric experiments, you could end up with a 'humanzee'. And controversially some scientists argue that there should be no difference between the standards set for abortion and research, that they're inconsistent – some advocate the same time limit. The key decisions for legislators are, one, what don't we want to create, two, let's not prevent progress in medicine and three, how do we actually enable exciting research opportunities and scientific advances."

Smite gave his idiosyncratic sniff just as Sally-Anne Jenkins clipped by in her high heels.

"If excess mucus is the problem, Frank dear, I recommend you lay off dairy products and yeast, they're generally the cause." Sally-Anne edited the women's page, writing tedious articles about health and fitness, occasionally interviewing some celebrity and then bitching about them in her column. From time to time she would pen a sympathetic piece about some brave soul who had borne up well to a tragic loss, but this, Frank reckoned, was purely to show the readers that Sally-Anne had a heart and wasn't a complete cow – it didn't wash with him. On Smite's reckoning the women's page ranked just below the weather forecast for newsworthiness.

"Stupid cow," he muttered. "So what if an MP isn't clear about the process, or undecided about the ethics? How are they going to make up their mind?" he asked Sam.

"Some of them have written about it in their local rags and actively canvassed constituents, encouraging them to write in and express their viewpoint, and others have taken note of both sides of the argument. Also they listen to the moral, religious and ethical groups who are very vocal and persuasive. In the end, an undecided MP will weigh it all up and vote accordingly. That's why it can be hard to tell how this will go – some of the scientists are getting quite jittery. But we'll know soon enough. And the Lords will vote about a month later, in January."

Sam looked up at Smite. He was an odd character, he thought, scruffy and in many ways repellent. This was the longest conversation he had ever had with the man, and why Smite should want to know about embryo research was anyone's guess. He was a bit of a troglodyte in the modern newspaper world but he had a keen nose for a story and enviable contacts. If you needed a snout or a source, Smite was your man; he had mates in vice, the robbery squad, the criminal fraternity and any form of the city's low life. People talked to Smite. That said, in Sam's world of science and medicine, he had little need to call on him. They simply inhabited the same office.

"Thanks for that information, Sam, very useful." Smite gave his colleague a comradely pat on the shoulder with his nicotine-stained hand and set off for a pint at the Dog and Leg-it.

*

Michael was becoming an increasingly isolated and lonely figure at the House. His friends missed him in the bar and questioned his self-imposed punishing schedule.

"After a spot of promotion, I'd say," Harry Lambton commented.

Michael restricted himself to the public restaurants, stayed well clear of the member's bar and terrace and worked into the small hours at the department. It was all quite understandable. The country appeared to be going through a series of unrelated mishaps and disasters of Biblical proportions and, to all outside appearances, it simply seemed that the Minister for the Family was setting his own department in order and working extremely hard with a view to getting something big in the next reshuffle.

He was finding the limits of his department frustrating. In reality it had been set up to appease various factions who felt that the traditional family had been sidelined by successive governments, whether in policy, legislation, benefits or taxation. It looked good, raised the media profile and meant that a department with virtually no clout could make meaningless positive press statements that it never had to justify, nor back up with any action or funding.

In point of fact they were no nearer enjoying a consensus, either within the government or opposition, nor within the nation at large, as to what exactly constituted a family these days. The fact that there was a fledgling department, with 'Family' in the title, didn't help at all. The debate continued to rage back and forth even amongst department members. Michael had finally put a stop to it, documenting a family as any nuclear group that was responsible for the rearing of its children or the care of the elderly relatives. This seemed to satisfy most of the complainants and left him to get on with the real business of making a difference to ordinary people's lives. Although what he was left with was a department which spent most of its time monitoring bits of policy from other more weighty departments to see if they were 'family friendly'. And if they were not, which was often the case, it was up to the Ministry for the Family to amend them or make counter proposals. To Michael it smacked of consciousness-raising of the type that was so prevalent in women's groups in the nineteen-seventies and early eighties. He longed to get his hands on a real department with a serious budget that would make a difference to people's lives. He longed for the big job, Health.

At home, life with Julia remained strained and unhappy. Michael's new-found work ethic meant that he could side-step family confrontation. He remained dismissive of any suggestion from Julia that he should have further contact with Nigel Laing. He refused to be drawn. Appalled as he was by the half-term visit, he reasoned that if he remained silent and unforthcoming, in time Julia would give up her campaign to make this young man and his wife part of their family. He refused absolutely to countenance her suggestion that he should explain Nigel's conception and relationship to the girls, unaware that Julia had resolved to tell them herself.

Since their visit in October, Julia had apparently being speaking to both Nigel and Sarah on the telephone at quite regular intervals. Although this infuriated Michael, there was precious little he could do to stop her. Particularly irritating was the flying visit he had received from Imogen, who had strolled into the department as bold as brass and without even the courtesy of telephone call. She had demanded a lunchtime meeting on the terrace. Next she proceeded to lecture him about Julia's fragile mental condition, the state of his marriage and the likelihood of Nigel and Sarah Laing discovering Michael's government role.

"Nigel Laing has signed an agreement, Imogen. He cannot speak to the press and I don't consider him the type to sell his story for money. In common with a lot of under-thirties he has absolutely no interest in politics – half of them don't even know who the party leaders are let alone low profile ministers like me. Anyway, he's intelligent enough to know that should he go public, that would be the end of any further contact between our families."

"Really, Michael, sometimes I think you have an emotional screw loose. Hasn't it occurred to you that when he does find out exactly who you are, he might just feel lied to and betrayed all over again? And given that you aren't having any contact with him anyway, he has nothing to lose. You've left this whole parcel of shit to Julia. You haven't got her to sign your gagging order, have you?"

"Julia? Don't be ridiculous."

"No, Sarah Laing. There's nothing to prevent her going to the press with a touching story about how her baby's cruel grandfather wants nothing to do with them, despite being the Minister for the Family. My strong advice to you, Michael, is to start showing some respect, love and affection to my sister before it's too late, and come clean with Nigel and Sarah before this whole fiasco blows up and you lose any control at all!"

Michael conceded nothing, but he was worried by what she had said.

*

Tess had taken to sneaking out onto the landing and listening to her mother's late night telephone conversations. There were a growing number of these and she was curious. Something odd was going on. Perched in her clandestine hideaway by the linen cupboard, she gleaned two things; one, her parents had had a serious falling out, and two, there was something about Nigel and Sarah that made them more than just friends of the family.

"You know I favour openness, Imogen. It's Michael who doesn't want the girls told," she overheard her mother saying. "But as soon as I can be assured of Nigel and Sarah's co-operation with regard to Michael's career, then I'll tell them. And Mother too. But until Michael has been persuaded…"

Tess listened intently, her ear between the banisters.

*

Julia was caught up in the frantic round of responsibilities that is the lot of women at Christmas.

"I think Christmas is a hoax on women," Moya had declared when setting out the 'festive trimmings' stall at the church fayre. "I'm seriously considering mounting a strike next year," she added, as a gold fir cone separated itself from a red candle and fell from the table and rolled across the hall at speed.

"Ah, but don't you just love the excitement! It's so infectious. This is my favourite time of year," Breeda said cheerily.

Moya gave her a look of cynical resignation. You would, although Finn hates all your enforced festive jollity, she thought. What am I doing here with the earth mother set? Sighing, she set off across the hall to collect the offending fir cone.

*

The Scientific Research Bill put forward by the government was supported by a majority of one hundred and ninety two votes. Debate had raged on both sides of the argument with the diminutive Ms Gough urging members to vote for the proposal and arguing with conviction for the benefits to patients with life threatening and degenerative diseases. Equally powerful was the argument put forward by Godfrey Fenton, a prominent opposition Catholic: '…that science was poised to create a new cloned hybrid that, unless destroyed, would grow into a sub-species of human being.' And Dr Ivor Deveroux, MP, made clear his opposition to the rule change. Ms Gough insisted that human cloning would remain illegal. MPs of all persuasions, political allegiances and faiths made up their own minds, with the curious spectacle of devout Christians voting 'for', and some ex-doctor MPs voting 'against'. Michael's appearance, when the division bell sounded in the 'Yes' lobby, was of no special significance and went unremarked as he was counted through.

Gideon Wentworth's parliamentary sketch took vicious little swipes at the elfin Ms Gough, calling her speech 'mawkish' and nick-naming her 'Little Miss Goody Two Shoes'. And the statement by one member that 'tomorrow the world will wake up horrified by what we have done' appeared to be borne out by the article from the foreign service of 'The Daily Record': 'UK's Research Bill will undermine the species, say Germans'. And there were demands for European Union sanctions against Britain. The French premier and the Vatican were similarly, if more predictably, appalled.

In The Minister for the Family's office a case of finest malt whisky appeared, with a congratulatory note from Giles Strumpshaw serving as an unpleasant reminder.

"Send it straight back!" Michael snapped at his secretary, who raised an eyebrow at her colleague across the desk.

*

Frank Smite had had a few too many to drink – it was Christmas after all. He had his arm around the editor of a political satirical magazine, 'The Mole', and was whispering confidentially in his ear. Frank was telling tales. Not big, full-blown, unexpurgated tales – more like tempting snippets. Smite knew enough to hold on to the really juicy stuff, to drip-feed it out when the time was right and then break the story and watch the mighty fall and the smug surrender. A tasty little rumour to whet the palate never did any harm.

*

"Mummy," Tess began, adding the figure of Father Christmas to the top of the newly iced cake. "Will your friends Nigel and Sarah be coming for Christmas as well as Granny and Auntie Imogen?"

Julia considered her daughter carefully.

"No," Julia replied hesitantly. "Not for Christmas itself, but we might see them at sometime over the holiday. It depends on what else we have to do." Tess appeared quite absorbed in placing a small plastic tree at just the right angle. "Do you like them?" Julia inquired as innocently as she could.

"Well, they're nice. Nigel likes playing the same board games as we do." Then Tess added, as if she knew, "It's a shame you couldn't have any more babies – we could have had a brother."

Julia dropped the sticky palette knife on the floor, composing herself just in time to reply: "Yes, a brother would have been nice. Now, don't we have a reindeer somewhere?"

*

The donation, from Giles Strumpshaw, in the form of a cheque for two thousand pounds payable to the Wynshore Constituency party, was sent directly to the constituency office and processed by a young girl named Monica who had stepped into the breach whilst Geraldine was away. Banking was normally Geraldine's job and such an unusually large donation would have been drawn to the attention of both Tim Nash and Michael. There were rules about this sort of thing. Michael, too, would have taken personal charge of the letter of thanks. They rarely got anything above two hundred pounds. As it was, Geraldine was absent from the office nursing her elderly mother. And so Monica simply dispatched the standard letter of thanks that was housed in the computer along with the passable blue ink-effect reproduction of Michael Barton's signature which modern technology provided for large-scale mailings. She banked the cheque along with all the others between popping into the chemist for shampoo and buying a calorie-counted sandwich during her lunch break.

23

Familial Festivities

"So what do you make of him then, your new father?" Gerald was spooning the roast potatoes into the serving dish that Nigel was holding steady for him. Nigel and Sarah had joined Gerald and Barbara for Christmas lunch.

Barbara had been a bit of a surprise, having rather brassy hair and wearing a green velour dress with a festive corsage of sleigh bells and plastic holly pinned next to a portion of freckled cleavage.

"It's rather a peculiar situation. He is, and isn't, my father because you are, if that makes any sense? You brought me up, taught me right from wrong and in that way I can only ever be your son."

Gerald looked up at Nigel proudly.

"I didn't leave you too much to your mother then?" This thought had been bothering Gerald for a long time.

"Oh Dad, you did what you could. I won't pretend it was an ideal childhood but now I know why and I understand. Finding Michael Barton has helped me deal with a lot of the anger. For a time I was really confused."

Gerald met Nigel's steady gaze and gave a grateful smile.

"Sarah tells me you went to stay – met the family." Gerald went over to the cooker to pour out the gravy. With Barbara's help he was becoming an accomplished cook. "He's pleased to have you as his son then, not too much of a shock? Does he know about the baby?"

"It's early days Dad, I think he's coming round to the idea." Nigel sounded cautious.

They both set off for the dining room, Gerald with the gravy and sprouts and Nigel carrying the potatoes. Barbara and Sarah were chatting about babies and the forthcoming birth.

Gerald smiled happily. They all seemed to be getting along so well now. After Marion's death, when he had finally plucked up the courage to explain Nigel's conception, he fully expected the boy to reject him. It was a devastating piece of news to break, and Gerald prepared himself for the possibility that Nigel might never want to see or hear from him again. After all, the boy had been lied to all his life. A child was entitled to trust its parents to tell the truth, especially about something as important as this. And his upbringing had been peculiar. Even at close quarters Gerald could see that. He compared his stilted, distant, relationship with Nigel to Barbara's family: her two boys, now men, were entirely at ease with their mother, they knew one another's likes and preferences, shared jokes, looked out for each other and seemed a complete and normal family despite their parent's divorce.

"This makes a nice change," Nigel commented. "Duck."

"Yes, it was Barbara's idea. Barbara likes ringing the changes." Gerald gave a fulsome laugh and Barbara joined in – there was just a hint of sexual innuendo. Sarah and Nigel exchanged an embarrassed smile.

"Gerald tells me that you've met your real… I don't know what to call him? What's that word bio…?"

Nigel blanched. The casual cheeriness of Barbara's enquiry was somehow at odds with the delicate subject matter and he was surprised that Gerald had confided in her.

"I call him Michael," Nigel quickly interrupted to save Gerald any awkwardness. "Gerald is my father, always will be, won't you, Dad?"

Gerald beamed.

"Ah, that's nice. Isn't that lovely, Gerry," Barbara squeezed Gerald's hand. "So he's pleasant, is he, Michael? And his family?"

"Yes. They're a lovely family. Of course, for Michael this is still very difficult. It's not what he was expecting, a grown-up son to turn up on his doorstep. It'll take time. But Julia, his wife, has been very welcoming, which can't have been easy. And they have two lovely girls, Tess and Katherine."

"Julia's been marvellous to us," Sarah added. "It's not an easy situation for anyone, is it? And now there's the baby as well. Michael sent Nigel a cheque for a thousand pounds but we thought it best to return it; keeping it might have given the wrong impression."

Barbara and Gerald nodded their agreement.

"He's a doctor, I understand," Barbara said, failing to realise that this wasn't quite the time or the place for such a conversation.

"No. He was a GP, but not any more. Actually," Nigel took a deep breath, "Michael is the MP for Wynshore."

Gerald stood stock-still and withdrew the carving knife – he was half way through dismembering a wing.

"Then you're the son of an MP!" Barbara was clearly impressed.

"And a minister," Sarah interjected. "Michael Barton is, we've just discovered, also the Minister for the Family."

"Well, I never!" Gerald sank into his chair. "Minister for the *Family!*" he repeated incredulously.

"Ironic, isn't it," Nigel remarked drily.

*

Christmas in the Barton household was, to an outsider, its usual chaotic and entertaining fun. To Julia, however, it was an ordeal to be completed with as much good grace as she could muster. Michael had made countless excuses in order to remain in London at the flat until the very last moment. And even Rosalind had remarked upon his punishing schedule.

"Poor Michael, all this constituency work that he will have to deal with as well. He doesn't get much of a break. You must take care of him, darling. Such pressure on a man of a certain age can be dangerous, as I can testify – look what happened to your father." Julia, who was frantically shopping, cooking for the constituency workers' annual Christmas party, and preparing enough clean linen and bedding for her mother's and Imogen's stay, felt that realistically she was at far greater risk of physical and mental collapse than her husband. She said nothing, except for:

"Yes, poor Michael."

There were a number of functions and engagements that she would have to endure as the wife of the local parliamentary representative. Apart from hosting the local party workers' do,

Julia also had to attend three deadly drinks parties where she would be expected to make small talk and where the children would be on show suitably dressed in garments they loathed. On top of which, Breeda was throwing a potluck supper on New Year's Eve and the usual lunchtime group was expected to attend.

Julia was not looking forward to the party at all. She disliked New Year's Eve anyway, often finding it maudlin and depressing. Far from looking ahead with excitement and anticipation to the forthcoming year, Julia inevitably looked back on the year just passed. Just what had she accomplished? It was difficult to say. She felt so trapped by her husband's high profile career. This year, to add to her reservations, was a curious sense of foreboding in regard to her relationship with Michael. And Nigel's presence, with all its implications for her family, weighed heavily on her. When Julia had felt cherished and loved by Michael the daily sacrifices she made had seemed reasonable. Now she was aware that a bitterness and resentment was insidiously creeping in, eating away at her. Try as she might, she couldn't make any progress. Her contempt and anger for Michael was growing, not diminishing. He made no effort to meet her half way, he barely spoke and the very mention of the Laings' names guaranteed his absence. Perhaps Father Frank was right and they should get some outside help, counselling or something. But how could they of all people, the local MP and his wife, pop down to Relate? After all, Michael had opened the building and his name was even on the commemoration plaque!

On Christmas Eve Imogen and Rosalind arrived laden with beautifully wrapped parcels. Imogen was hardly over the threshold before she hissed:

"Well? Have you told Nigel and Sarah yet?" And when Julia declared that she hadn't, Imogen said exasperatedly:"For goodness sake, Julia, get on with it, because your stubborn husband won't."

"I think I ought to explain to the girls first," Julia replied.

"All right, then explain to the girls. Just do something and soon."

Julia had sent Nigel and Sarah boxed presentation wine and a Christmas card, which she signed for all of them. In return, Nigel and Sarah had sent presents for the children. These sat under the tree and were the source of much speculation by Tess and Katherine.

"So just why is he sending our children Christmas presents?" Michael had asked Julia as he opened a bottle of sherry in the kitchen.

"Because our children are Nigel's half-sisters," Julia said, trying hard to control the level of disdain in her reply.

Michael left the room.

Between Christmas and New Year, Michael went into the constituency office every day. Julia realised that this was a tactic to avoid her. Usually he allowed himself a complete break between the two holidays. He would read a great deal, take Tess and Katherine out for walks and stroll into the town and explore the bookshops. On the Thursday, Rosalind was driven back to her home in Hertfordshire by Imogen, who was on her way to Stansted airport from where she was flying to Austria to join friends on a skiing holiday.

"Don't wait any longer, tell them, the Laings and the girls. You must," she said to Julia before she left. "Dear Sis, just get on with it."

A few days later Julia went into the living room where Tess and Katherine were sprawled on the sofa watching an old Bette Davis film. She switched the television off.

"Oh" Katherine whined. "We were watching that."

"And you can watch it again later. But at the moment I've something I need to talk to you about." Julia looked at her young, innocent, daughters. In a moment she would explain the mechanics of sperm donation and introduce a newfound brother to them, certain that this knowledge would change their lives forever. Gone would be the notion that they were special. Gone too the belief that children were created solely through love, and also diminished would be the implicit trust that their parents wouldn't lie to them.

Julia sat down on the chair opposite. Tess and Katherine glanced at one another, perplexed.

"What is it, Mummy?" Tess asked in a small voice. She wondered if her parents were going to separate. They had been arguing or else not talking for what seemed to Tess an age and exactly that had happened to a friend of hers at school.

Julia took in a deep breath.

"You remember Nigel and Sarah who came to stay in October and sent you a Christmas present? Well, a long time ago… No, this won't do…" Julia stopped. Katherine had moved across the sofa closer to Tess, as if preparing herself for dreadful news. "I'm sorry, I'm finding this very difficult. Look, you both know the facts of life."

"Of course we do," Tess spoke for them both with the slight belittling tone used by more accomplished teenagers.

"Bear with me, Tess. Please."

"The film will be finished and we'll never know whether it was the good twin that drowned," Katherine complained.

"Shh…" Tess told her.

"Not everyone is lucky enough to be able to conceive children in the natural way. Sometimes one of them, the man or the woman,doesn't have enough healthy sperm or eggs, and so they use someone else's. Some person who very kindly donates her egg or his sperm, which is put into the mummy and that is how a baby is made."

"Aren't we yours, yours and Daddy's?" Katherine asked.

"Oh my goodness! Yes, you're ours, you are both our children. I can assure you of that, my egg – Daddy's sperm – you're ours. But a long time ago when Daddy was a very young man – a student doctor, in fact – he gave away some of his sperm to a clinic where they treat women whose husbands are infertile. Years before we met, or you two were even thought of! And it doesn't alter the love that we both have for both of you. Daddy has a son who has been searching for him and found him…and that son is Nigel. Nigel Laing. And so that makes Nigel your half-brother."

Julia looked at her two lovely daughters who were staring first at her and then at one another; Tess almost a teenager, Katherine, young for her age and still very much a child, Daddy's girl. Their faces mirrored their surprise.

"So we've got a brother?" Tess asked for both of them.

"You seemed to quite like him," Julia said tentatively.

"Yeah, Nigel's nice." Tess replied, distractedly picking a piece of fluff from her reindeer socks.

"Katherine?"

"So if Sarah, Nigel's wife, is having a baby, is that our quarter sister?"

"No. A sort of niece. You'll be aunts."

"Oh cool." Tess exclaimed. "I hope it's a boy."

It seemed to have gone better than Julia had imagined.

"Now the only thing is that Nigel still doesn't know what Daddy's job is, so for the moment I'd like to keep it that way until we've got to know them a bit better."

"Oh he does," Tess interrupted. "Katherine told him."

Julia was horrified.

"Don't blame me!" Katherine took a swipe at her sister. "It's not my fault!" she cried. "We were playing 'Don't Panic' and I had to name as many politicians as possible."

Julia composed herself and lightly touched Katherine's forearm to reassure her.

"Darling, it's all right – don't worry, we were going to tell them soon anyway. Nobody is blaming you. This whole situation is a grown-ups' problem. I don't want either of you to worry, all right?"

Katherine sniffed and both the girls nodded their agreement.

"Can we watch the rest of the film now?"

"Of course." Julia picked up the remote control. "And if you have any questions or worries, just ask me, will you?" They both nodded, but already their eyes had drifted past Julia and settled on the television screen. Apparently Tess and Katherine had accepted this story readily, but Julia realised that as the reality of their father's donations sank in, then she could expect closer questioning. She also knew from her own past work with sick children that often at the point of explanation they would appear understanding and compliant. Only later would the children display the anxiety that was often beneath the surface.

It was getting dark as Tess sat on the edge of her bed listening to music on her headphones, at the same time turning the pages of her photograph album. It contained the left-over photographs, the ones that Mummy didn't like enough to frame or send to Granny. The photos that Daddy had got in the post, the ones that looked so like him, must have been of Nigel when he was a little boy. Downstairs she could just hear the voices of her parents in the living room, the exact content of their conversation muffled by the music. Nevertheless the rhythm of their speech told Tess that, whatever they were discussing, they were certainly not in agreement. But these days it was common to hear them disagreeing. The rest of the time they didn't really talk to each other. They didn't seem like friends any more, and Daddy didn't like Nigel or Sarah coming to the house and got very cross if Mummy spoke to them on the telephone. Tess couldn't understand why Daddy would behave like that, not if Nigel was his son.

24

Should Old Acquaintance Be Forgot

"Champagne! How lovely," Breeda greeted them warmly. "Come in, come in. Trust it to pour down when we're all done up in our finery. Moya, Andrew and Tom are here already and we've a smattering of neigbours." Breeda, who wore a backless green velvet cat suit with a distinct nineteen-seventies flavour, drew the Barton family into the kitchen. Finn, the children, Moya and Andrew, were all standing around the kitchen table. At the other end of the room grouped on and around a battered sofa were a selection of neighbours and friends, along with Father Frank who was enjoying a drop of the Irish. Finn was opening the wine and their three-year-old twins, Niall and Shauna, were somewhat shakily taking around bowls of snacks and offering them to the guests in between popping handfuls in their own mouths. The other children had scattered themselves around the house and Tess and Katherine set off up the stairs to join them.

"Michael, good to see you. It's been an age," Finn called across Breeda's shoulder. "And the very beautiful Julia, you I will kiss." Finn slipped out from behind his wife and taking Julia's hand planted his lips on the back of it flamboyantly. Breeda rolled her eyes at the same time explaining:

"He's been tasting the mulled wine all afternoon, just checking it has the correct balance of spices and alcohol you understand!"

Julia laughed.

Michael thought Breeda looked lovely. Her hair was worn up, with strands of auburn breaking free and cascading provocatively down the nape of her shapely neck, and the halter-neck top revealed a very appealing back with elegant shoulders.

"I like the cat-suit, Breeda – very James Bond," Michael declared. "I mean the sort of outfit the fabulous girls wear," he explained.

"Why, thank you, Michael. It's vintage!" Michael looked puzzled. "It means antique," Breeda explained. "I got it in a little second hand shop in Swanton Acre. I thought hell, if Julia Roberts can wear a second-hand frock to the Oscars and call it vintage, then so can I."

Michael laughed warmly and gave her a friendly peck on the cheek. It looked like hostilities had been called off, at least for the evening.

Michael looked over at Julia, sizing her up in the way that any stray male at a party would. His wife certainly was a lovely looking woman. Her pale blonde hair was pulled back simply into an ornate oval hair slide and she wore an uncomplicated gold and cerise striped trouser suit made from silk. She had an air of understated elegance. He took a sip of wine. I can't wait to see the back of this year, he thought to himself. At least with the election due, life would be full – frantic even – but predictable. These past months had been a nightmare – never knowing what was around the next corner. Just as he survived one test or disaster, another crisis emerged to hit him full in the face. It was just the same for the government in general. How could you meet all your pledges when around every corner there was a new and completely unforeseen catastrophe waiting to happen? And perhaps the election would take Julia's mind off the Laings; she generally helped out with the campaign. But with an election due, it made it more likely that Nigel Laing would see him featured in the media. Michael was coming round to the idea that Nigel would have to be told. Perhaps he would take him out to a good lunch; that would do the trick. Then after a few such meetings things could cool down and gradually tail off, he could send a card at Christmas and birthdays and even have a meal once a year, then life would return to normal.

Moya looked across the room to where Julia was helping herself to another glass of wine. It wasn't like Julia to down alcohol at speed. Come to think of it, Julia didn't look at all relaxed – beautiful, yes, but then she always looked beautiful. This evening, though, there was a forced quality to her smile and she was clearly keeping her distance from Michael. Usually they either spent a social evening closely linked, Julia constantly at Michael's elbow or, if it was a political do where Michael might not get round to all the people who expected to talk to him, they would split up and work different sides of the room.

"How are you, Julia? I haven't seen you in ages," said Moya. "Not since I bumped into you outside Thackery's, with your houseguests. Nigel and Sarah, wasn't it?"

She knows, Julia thought to herself. Breeda's told her.

"That's right. Silly, isn't it, such a busy time of year – I don't know, there always seems so much to cram into these few weeks. This is our fourth party already! Anyway how are you and what's Tom up to?"

"Complaining bitterly because we made him come here with us – he and some unsuitable friends who thought he was going clubbing with them. We've just won the prize for being the most Victorian parents in Wynshore," Moya said.

"I rather thought Tom was quite bookish and would never give you any trouble."

"So did we, we were relying on it. It just shows how wrong you can be, and I admit to having been smug. Let it be a warning to you. If Tom, in a matter of weeks, can turn from a scientific bookworm into a testosterone-fuelled party animal, then no one is immune. There is absolutely no hope at all for you with Tess!"

"I never thought there was," Julia replied, with resigned good humour.

Upstairs in Seamus and Dominic's bedroom Tess was sprawled on a bed looking through the boys' CD collection whilst Katherine was using the Internet on the computer – something she wasn't permitted to do at home in case she should stray into a chat room. Tom had just joined them, and he was pissed off – being dragged to a cruddy party with his parents was no longer his idea of how best to spend New Year's Eve. Tess glanced casually and then took a second look. This was Tom? She hadn't seen him since the summer barbecue and he'd changed markedly, and for the better. He'd got taller and had filled out. He looked really fit.

"Hi Tom," Tess said coquettishly.

"Hi. All right?" Tom replied. It was the standard teenage greeting.

"Uh huh," Tess returned, sitting up and smoothing out the

creases in her lilac satin trousers. "It's dead boring here, though, with the wrinklies."

"Tell me about it!" Tom had developed a slight American twang to mask his public school accent. "What's new?"

"Not a lot."

"Except we've got a brother!" Katherine cut in from behind the computer monitor. She popped her head out, "A grown up one, with a pregnant wife and everything! We're going to be aunts!"

"How come?" Tom asked as casually as he could; being fifteen he didn't want to show too much interest in anything. Tess shifted uncomfortably on the bed. Not so Katherine who, recognising that she had something exciting to tell, got off the keyboard and came out from behind the desk and plonked herself down on a bean bag.

"Ages ago Daddy gave his sperm away to help invalid couples."

"*Infertile* couples," Tess corrected her in the condescending manner most usually associated with eldest children.

"Same difference," Katherine defended herself. "Anyway, Daddy helped this lady get pregnant with his sperm. She had Nigel and he fell in love with Sarah and they are having a baby in the spring and because Nigel is our half-brother we're going to be aunts. I can't wait. It's taken Nigel ages to find Daddy," Katherine added, wondering out loud: "Does it mean Daddy's going to be a granddad?

"Suppose it does," Tess agreed. "But Mummy won't be a grandma."

"Oh, poor Mummy, she'll feel left out," came Katherine's insightful response.

"They sell it, you know...sperm," Tom said. "And eggs. In the States you can get loads of money if you're clever or good looking. Students do it to pay for the tuition fees. And if your Dad sold it, there won't just be this Nigel bloke, there'd be others."

Katherine thought about this and then said:

"Oh no, I don't think Daddy would have sold it, he wouldn't need the money, he just helped the one lady." Katherine was sure on that point. Tess, however, wasn't.

"You should ask," Tom suggested helpfully.

"Come down, you guys. It's nearly midnight. Time for Auld Lang Syne," Finn called up the stairs.

They all linked arms and sang, the children more enthusiastically than anybody. From the other side of the circle, Julia observed Moya and Finn. Their hands were linked and for a moment their eyes connected and Finn gave Moya's hand an extra squeeze. This encounter was immediately broken up by the ever vigilant Breeda, who immediately instructed Andrew and Finn to open the various bottles of bubbly that guests had brought with them – and so with glasses charged they toasted the New Year.

Julia had been cornered by Father Frank, who having already put a serious dent in a bottle of whiskey, was now into his second glass of champagne and becoming increasingly incomprehensible. She took a discreet look at her watch, twenty past twelve. She wondered when they could realistically get away. Not before one, or they would seem such killjoys. The older neighbours hadn't even made it to the appointed hour and now, apart from the priest and the children, the usual lunch group were the only ones left. They could all have a lie-in tomorrow, no more parties, thank goodness. It was all over for another year and, more than ever, this was an enormous relief. Julia excused herself, leaving Father Frank settling into the sofa next to Moya, who was telling him about aspects of youth custody. Michael was perched on the arm listening. The old priest tipped his head to one side and adopted an expression of interest, having had years of practice in the confessional. Just for a moment he rested his eyes.

Julia set off for the bathroom.

Breeda had assembled all the children by the table. She had make a special chocolate cake for them covered in little edible silver balls and purple stars. It was lit with sparklers forming the numerals. Breeda called it a 'wish cake'. There was much oohing and aahing, especially from the little ones as they grouped around the table eagerly.

"Now, you all cut your own slice. I'll help the twins and when you cut you make a wish!"

Finn stood by with the camera, ready to take a photograph. They made a delightful picture, each face lit up by the sparklers and the excitement of the occasion. One by one the children cut a slice of cake and made their wish. Breeda advised them all to keep the wish a secret, or it wouldn't come true.

"I wonder what this New Year will bring?" she said to Finn and Andrew who were standing by the fireplace.

"More money," Finn said jokily.

"More qualified theatre staff? The eradication of super bugs?" Andrew suggested hopefully.

"We're going to be aunts!" Katherine declared, clearly thrilled.

Finn looked puzzled and Andrew gently explained:

"To become an aunt, Katherine, you'd have to have a brother or sister who is having a baby."

"Well, I have," she declared triumphantly.

Andrew and Finn shot one another a concerned glance and then both stared hard at young Tess' stomach. From the corner of the room Father Frank let out a colossal snore, finally subsiding back into a light slumber, his chin nodding onto his chest. Michael gently lifted the half-full champagne glass out of his hand and popped it safely on the mantelpiece.

"No, silly," Katherine said. "Nigel is Daddy's son. He's only just found us. You see his Daddy couldn't make any babies, his what's-it's-name wasn't any good, so Daddy gave him his. And now Nigel is married to Sarah and they are having a baby in April, so that means Nigel is our half-brother and that makes Tess and me aunts to Nigel's baby. Simple, you see."

At the far end of the room, hearing the name Nigel, Michael's head shot up – the expression on his face one of horror.

"Tom says Nigel might not be the only brother Daddy made," Katherine continued cheerfully. "Because the doctors sometimes help more than one lady have babies."

No one said a word.

Arriving in the doorway, Julia stood smoothing down her silk jacket ready to make her reappearance. As she walked in, smiling at the assembled company, she became aware of the oppressive silence. Father Frank stirred from his slumbers, opened his eyes briefly and exclaimed, "Five Hail Marys and two Our Fathers." Raising his hand he went on to enact holy absolution on an imagined supplicant and then fell back into the sofa, snoring louder than ever.

"Katherine, Tess, get your coats. You too, Julia. We're leaving."

Michael's voice was so commanding that they all obeyed instantly.

Tess and Katherine were sent immediately to their beds. Julia, meanwhile, was ordered into the sitting room. There was no dissent. Michael assumed a powerful position by the fireplace.

"Sit down, Julia."

"I prefer to stand."

"How dare you – how dare you tell the children!" he bellowed.

"Keep your voice down, Michael, the girls are upset enough as it is. Your shouting at me will just scare them."

"Are you trying to destroy me, Julia? Destroy us? Because you are certainly going the right way about it! There was absolutely no need for the girls ever to know. If it wasn't for your interference I could have met Laing for the occasional meal in town, and he would have been satisfied with that and no one would be any the wiser."

"You can't honestly believe that." Julia retorted. "You refused to meet him, remember – you even tried to buy him off."

"You know what I should have done; I should have called in the police in the first place – two years in gaol, that's what you get for this – they stole this information, so add breaking and entering on top of that."

Julia had never seen him so enraged. He was unrecognisable.

"They didn't break in. Sarah got a job there."

"Oh, sorry – my mistake." Michael said sarcastically. "Deception and fraud then. What they have done in tracing me is illegal because it wreaks havoc with the donor's family."

"Then, forgive me, Michael, but doesn't that tell you something? Doesn't it tell you that if the very existence of these donor children is so shameful that our society has chosen never to acknowledge how they were brought into being, if that's taboo, then the whole process is utterly and completely wrong! And so is pretending that children created in this way belong to someone else – and altering their birth certificates for God's sake, documents whose sole purpose is to represent a true record of maternity, paternity and heredity. It's lying to them about who they are, the fundamentals of their existence. It's absolutely appalling – even adopted children have more right to the truth. If what you had done was considered so decent and altruistic by society at large, then this revelation wouldn't have met with a room full of horrified faces. Our close friends, remember? Thank goodness Father Frank was asleep," she added.

"Damn Father Frank! Do you realise the whole of Wynshore will know by the start of the school term. Anyway, why should it bother you? You're the one enthusiastically embracing the Laings. It's you who insist on openness at every turn," Michael yelled. "All right, so years ago I made a silly mistake. I did something that, although it seemed harmless at the time, I now realize was a dreadful error. I regret it bitterly. I was young, for heaven's sake. But you're a grown woman. You took it upon yourself to invite Laing into our home and introduced him to our children. Surely you didn't think it would remain a secret once you had told Tess and Katherine? For pity's sake Julia, they're too young to understand that you simply don't blurt this sort of thing out. Imagine how they will be treated at school; the taunts and teasing, there'll be no end to it. It's a convent, isn't it? What on earth are they to make of this? And the girls have barely got to grips with the facts of life. Tess, especially, is at a very vulnerable age, this will be mortifying for her."

"You believe, Michael, that by ignoring Nigel this will go away, and we can all pretend that it never happened. Including the grotesque fact that you have hundreds of children out there somewhere. Well, we can't – I just can't. I try to live my life by a code of decency and honesty and I want my children to share those standards. Deceit plays no part in the values I want to share with my children and, besides, I want them to confront their problems – not sweep them under the carpet as if they didn't exist. Which is exactly what you're doing with Nigel Laing. You'd better realise that I have no intention in colluding in this – my support of you as your wife is not unconditional. You must understand that I have a set of beliefs and values that matter to me, they are my bedrock. And they're not so easily swept aside because it happens to be expedient."

"And just how far, Julia, will these sanctimonious values hold when the world's press is at the gate and daily life becomes unliveable?"

"The problem is, Michael, this isn't only about *you*, not everything has you at its centre. This involves the feelings and the lives of other people. For goodness' sake, your grandchild will be born in a few months time – don't you think it has been hard for me to come to terms with that? Frankly, I've heard enough about how this will affect your career. It's just as well I did talk to Tess and Katherine because, apparently, Katherine let slip to Nigel just what it is that you do for a living. She didn't mean to, it wasn't her fault. They were playing 'Don't Panic' and she got the card asking for a list of political figures and added your name. So you must explain everything to Nigel and Sarah and soon," Julia insisted.

Michael swung around and for a brief horrifying moment Julia thought he might strike her. Instead he threw his hands in the air.

"Do you have no imagination, Julia? Surely you've seen enough cretins crawling out of the woodwork and selling their sordid little stories to the press?"

"If you treat Nigel decently, it won't come to that," Julia retorted. "It's not too late. He only wants you to acknowledge him, to show some pride in his achievements and show him that you care."

"I only wish I had your confidence, Julia," Michael said angrily, and left the room, slamming the door behind him.

*

"If what Katherine says is true, it explains a lot," Moya said. "Julia has been looking very strained and she's been avoiding us. I thought this Nigel was just a love child, the product of some relationship in Michael's past. But I'm certain he would have corrected Katherine if it wasn't true – he wouldn't have left us with that impression nor stormed out."

The friends were grouped together around the kitchen table amid the debris of the party. Breeda had sent the children to bed and Tom was sleeping on a mattress on the floor in the boys' room. Finn had doled out yet more champagne and they were all sipping it at intervals, although now there was no hint of the earlier celebratory atmosphere, more a shocked disbelief.

"You mean you knew about this son? You didn't tell me." Andrew said.

"Yes, we met outside Thackery's. They were visiting, the son and his pregnant wife."

"And they were at the house when I dropped Imogen round," Breeda added. "He looks the image of Michael, there's no mistaking it."

"You're the gynae, Andrew. Could there be others?" Finn asked.

"If it was a commercial transaction at a clinic, which is likely, and he made regular donations, well then yes, there are bound to be. But Michael may just have donated his sperm as a favour to an infertile friend."

"If it were a favour to a friend he would have known of his son's existence. And I know for a fact that he knew nothing at all until he received a batch of photographs through the post. Julia showed them to me. At the time she was very confused and wrongly assumed Michael was having an affair." Breeda said.

"An affair would hardly have produced a grown-up son," Andrew commented.

"As I said, Julia was very confused and naturally upset, she really wasn't thinking straight."

"Donor anonymity was protected by law," Moya remarked.

" It was. It is. But the law's changing and in the future it won't be. I wonder how he found him. I expect Michael gave donations when he was at medical school – lots did," Andrew added. "They used to advertise for donors on the notice board."

"Not you though?" Moya asked, alarmed.

He placed a reassuring hand on her arm and said:

"No. Not me. Looking back I see that Michael was trying to ask my advice about this, last summer, when we went out for a drink. My comments can't have been particularly helpful."

From the far corner of the room Father Frank began murmuring the Sanctus in Latin.

"Lord have mercy on us! There's Father over there able to hear every word!" Breeda whispered.

Finn put a hand on her shoulder.

"My darling Breeda, Father has been with us only in body for some time now. The combination of Irish and champagne has rendered him quite insensible. However, this might be a good moment for Andrew and I to help him up to bed, and if you could find a large jug of water and one or two painkillers to put on the bedside table, I think it would be a kindness. I fear the good Father may not be his usual sprightly self in the morning."

Finn and Andrew lifted the corpulent frame of the priest from the sofa.

*

Tess crept into Katherine's room and snuggled into the bed next to her. She gave her little sister a cuddle. In fact Katherine was sobbing very softly, so that her parents wouldn't hear, although there was little chance of that given the raised voices downstairs.

"Don't cry, Katie. It's not your fault."

Katherine let out a little sob.

"Mummy never said it was a secret," she protested.

"No. And she didn't say that there might be others either," Tess said, her own disenchantment with her parents clear in her tone. "Grown-ups always mess things up," she added crossly and then more gently:

"Go to sleep, it won't be so bad in the morning." It was a phrase her mother often used along with, 'Like a shower it will pass,' although in this case Tess thought it unlikely. It had been raining forever and showed no sign of stopping. Hugging Katherine tightly to her and closing her eyes, Tess lay quietly on the first miserable morning of what was a brand new year.

25

Spermgate

It came as a great relief to the entire family when both school and parliament returned. Julia craved normality, but it was a faint hope. Michael had spent several nights sleeping on the sofa in the study, finally returning to the bedroom only two days before he was due to leave for the House. Conversation had been restricted to day-to-day housekeeping issues and administration. He had taken the girls out a couple of times, once to ten-pin bowling and another time to the cinema. He had spoken to them only briefly about Katherine's slip up at the party, and advised each of them to keep all information within the family from now on. Without Julia's knowledge or approval he had called in on both Moya and Andrew, Finn and Breeda, asking them to speak to their children in order to prevent any further revelations at school. This they had agreed to do, although with some misgivings.

"We will talk to them, Michael," Breeda had said . "But it will be for Julia's sake and Tess's and Katherine's. So long as you are aware of that."

"That is why I am asking this favour, Breeda, to protect my family," Michael had replied tersely.

"Isn't it a little bit late for that?"

Later she complained to Finn:

"It's a bit rich! Michael of all people – doesn't trust us to manage our own children. Just look at the mess that he's made!" His visit had cemented her latent aversion to Michael and, on this occasion, Finn was in complete agreement.

"I just hope he's cooled his temper. Poor little Katherine didn't know what on earth she'd done wrong," he commented.

When Andrew spoke to his son Tom, he was perplexed.

"What's the problem? I don't get it."

"Tom, please accept my word on this one. Michael's a politician, so maybe he's fair game but it's Julia and the girls we've got to think of. And take it from me, if this becomes public knowledge they'll have a really hard time. So, I want your guarantee that you will say nothing – not to a living soul."

"Okay, okay. Do want me to swear on oath?"

"No. I trust you. And thanks."

"I still can't see what the big deal is."

"Maybe not, Tom, but there is one." Andrew put a hand on Tom's shoulder. "Believe me, there is one."

*

On returning to London, Michael found his diary secretary had booked numerous public appearances in what was, after all, the run up to a probable spring election. He rang Julia.

"Look, I've been thinking," he began. "You have a point about Nigel and Sarah. Now they know who I am, it will need some further explanation. With an election due I can't really afford to take any chances. I'm sure to be photographed at the hustings and I'm booked for more TV and radio than usual. We've got this parenting initiative in April, it'll be big news, headline grabbing stuff. So perhaps some clarification is called for – clearly he'll wonder why we didn't say anything when we met. The thing is, Julia, I'm terribly busy, I was just wondering could you, would you, go over to Maidenhead for me and talk to him? It might even be better coming from you. You'll be better at explaining how upsetting it would be for you and the girls…press intrusion, all that. And you get on well with him. Julia? Julia, are you still there?"

"Yes. Yes, I'm still here," she answered. "So let me get this straight. Having spent months trying to suppress all knowledge of your son and arguing constantly that he should never be told who you are and what it is that you do, and having put me and the girls through the most hellish time, you now want me to explain your career and public life to Nigel and Sarah, at the same time as asking them to keep totally silent. Have I got that right, Michael?"

"Oh Julia, I'm sorry. I'll understand if you don't want to. And, really, I should go and take him out for lunch. I know that I've handled this badly." He paused and Julia softened. Michael sounded genuine for the first time in months. "I was thinking about you last night," he went on. "I couldn't sleep. I nearly rang you then, but it was past one in the morning and I didn't think you'd appreciate a call at that time. Let's go out for a meal at the weekend, get that sitter, what's-her-name. We could to the Auberge, we haven't been there for ages. It's my fault, events have just overtaken me, I feel as if everything is out of control."

"A meal out in return for seeing Nigel for you?" Julia asked.

"No, Julia, no, please don't take it that way, that isn't it at all."

Julia was not convinced.

"All right, I'll do it," she reluctantly conceded.

Later when the arrangements had all been finalised, Julia found that she felt inexplicably lighter, not happy exactly but as if some pressing weight had been lifted. She found the prospect of a trip away and a night in a hotel curiously pleasing. Also she was looking forward to meeting Nigel once again. She even found herself humming.

*

At the offices of *The Daily Record* Frank Smite was setting things up. He had dropped in to see his editor Matthew Lake to map out the bare bones of the scandal – potentially big – but he would need to do a bit more digging. In all a nasty shock for the government, pushing 'Cash for Questions' into the junior league, was how Smite put it. 'A Minister Blackmailed – a vote bought!'

Lake could smell it too, the whiff of imminent outrage.

"If you need anything, Frank, an extra hack or a snapper, just shout."

Frank knew more about the workings of the newspaper world than Lake ever would. He might not be a money man but Frank knew precisely how to drip-feed a story into the system, a word here, a nod there, when to run with it, when to let it take its course. Finally, when to strike. He wasn't about to tell all to the likes of Lake. He would keep some vital details to himself. After all, it wouldn't do to create a feeding frenzy too early. A story like this required a delicate touch.

*

"She's gone away for a couple of days, apparently." Moya had run into Breeda in the local supermarket,

"So who's looking after Tess and Katherine? They always stay with us."

"I saw them getting out of Anne Cassidy's car outside the school gate this morning. So I presume they're staying at the Cassidys'."

Breeda looked wounded.

"I was only saying to Finn, the other night that this could be grounds for an annulment. You see, if Michael was a sperm donor, then I'd be sure that in the eyes of the Church the marriage was never valid in the first place, not with Michael creating babies for other women all over the place."

Moya looked aghast.

"I strongly advise you to keep that view to yourself," she told her firmly.

"Hasn't it occurred to you, Moya, that Julia might be grateful to have a friend find her a way out of her hopeless marriage?"

"I wouldn't presume to know whether Julia's marriage were hopeless or not and nor should you. Michael and Julia have been very happy in the past and I feel sure that once they get this sorted out they will be again. Now, I must get on, I've a difficult case coming up in the morning." And turning her trolley, Moya strode off towards the aisle containing low fat yoghurts, leaving Breeda angrily wrestling with a giant pack of toilet rolls.

*

Sam Denton put his head up over the computer terminal and called over to Smite.

"Frank. Thought you'd want to know, the Lords passed it – the new Scientific Research Bill. It went through 214 to 90, a majority of 124."

"Blimey! Unexpectedly big, innit?" Smite commented.

"There are a lot of upset bishops this morning and the Chief Rabbi's none too happy either. Lord Thaxton was at his sanctimonious best. The Bishop of Chalford was impressive though – masterly. "

"Cheers Sam, useful stuff."

Julia unpacked her bag at the Boulters Lock Hotel. It was a very smart place with a slightly racy atmosphere. After hanging up a few clothes she pottered aimlessly about the room, inspecting the en-suite and the mini-bar. Julia had invited Nigel and Sarah to the hotel for a meal, but apparently Sarah couldn't join them, she was completing a series of urgent laboratory experiments essential to her PhD studies before she took maternity leave the following month. She would join them later for a drink at Smokey Joe's Roundhouse where Nigel and his jazz band, 'JustJazz', were playing a set. Julia was excited. Not since she was a student teacher had she frequented the sort of pub that was a showcase for live jazz, although at one time she had loved jazz, and somewhere in the attic she had a collection of LPs; Ronnie Laws, John Coltrane and Wilba Harding. Nigel had arranged to meet her in the hotel bar, where she would explain Michael's parliamentary career to him. In the meantime she went for a walk.

The river had only just subsided and a few weeks earlier a walk would have been out of the question. Then, the water had overflowed not only the paths, but also many of the roads in the surrounding area. The paths were still covered with a fine silt and before long Julia was freezing cold and it was growing dark and so, reaching a particularly boggy and impassable section, she decided to turn back and take a warming bath.

Later she sat at a table in a corner by the window with an unrivalled view of the river. She watched the lights reflecting on the water, dipping and elongating in the darkness with the dancing rhythm of the ripples. For a moment she was lost in thought. What a bizarre twist of fate had brought her here to Maidenhead, a place with which she had absolutely no connection and which, under normal circumstances, was likely to have remained a complete mystery to her. Now Julia Barton, thirty-nine, was about to go out to a jazz night with her husband's new-found son.

"Hello," a voice broke in. "I hope I haven't kept you waiting. I took rugby last lesson and the mud took some shifting."

"Nigel." Julia stood up. "Not at all. I went for a walk and I've been enjoying this view of the river. There's something so therapeutic about water, isn't there?"

Nigel smiled down at her. Julia Barton had such an easy grace and elegant charm, so unlike her husband.

"I was just thinking how curious this all is," Julia continued, "me here in Maidenhead. A year ago if anyone had suggested that I would be sitting in a hotel bar meeting my husband's son, it would have seemed absurd. Life's very strange, isn't it?

"And does it seem absurd now?" Nigel asked.

"No, not at all. It did, but now it seems entirely natural."

"Another drink. White wine?" Nigel offered.

"Thank you." Julia took the opportunity to observe Nigel as he stood at the bar. She watched as he engaged the barman in effortless conversation, sharing a joke. He was very easy to like, warm, amiable, uncomplicated. Would Michael ever realise how lucky he was to have such a son?

"Chardonnay. I hope that's okay, the barman will bring it over. I've ordered some olives and a plate of canapés. Running around the pitch shouting at the boys works up a terrific appetite." Nigel sat down.

"Lovely. How's Sarah?"

"Blooming. Actually Sarah needs to slow down. She's getting very tired and the bump seems to have just exploded into something gargantuan – kicks like crazy."

"How many weeks is she?"

"Thirty-four." Nigel laughed. "You didn't expect me to know did you?"

"Just testing," Julia returned, grinning. "You've passed. Seriously though, get her to rest because once the baby arrives, you'll both be shattered and the simplest things will take an age. It's an altogether different way of life."

"This warning is coming far too late, Julia. Nine months ago would have been better."

"And don't listen to any of those dreadful birthing stories. Because what everyone forgets to tell you about is the amazing joy as soon as you hold your baby in your arms."

"Mmm…" Nigel leaned back in his chair. His smile suddenly dimmed and was replaced by a pensive look.

"Oh, Nigel, I'm sorry, that was hardly tactful."

"Silly isn't it? Here I am a fully-grown man about to have a family of my own and yet it's still surprisingly raw. Odd things…when I least expect them. I think that all I'm hoping for from Michael is that, one day, he might look at me with a certain fatherly pride. That would do, you know."

"Nigel I'm sure that he will. He just needs time."

There was a silence. The waiter placed the little bowls and plates on the table. Julia took a sip of her wine and began:

"I found it a healing experience becoming a parent, having a family of my own."

"And why did you need healing?" Nigel asked curiously.

"When I was sixteen, quite without warning, my father dropped dead of a heart attack. And before that my younger brother died in infancy," Julia replied. Nigel looked at her intently. "On both occasions my mother's effort to both cope and grieve eclipsed my own misery. I didn't get the chance to say goodbye to either of them. On the day my father died I rushed off to school early, to show off something new to a friend – I don't remember what it was now. Anyway, instead of kissing my father goodbye, as I always did, on that day I just called up the stairs to him and I never saw him alive again." She paused to collect herself. "With Tom, my baby brother, he wasn't feeding and was very poorly and so my parents took him to the hospital and I was sent to a neighbour's house. He never came home. I wasn't allowed to go to the funeral…" Julia's throat constricted and her words were hoarse, barely audible. "These days my loss would have been acknowledged, but back then they did things differently. Having Tess and Katherine has eased a lot of the pain and I expect your baby will do the same for you, Nigel. You'll be shaping your own family. It's a chance to get things right, to put the past behind you." Julia took a deep breath in, sat back and smiled.

"I'm sorry Julia. I had no idea."

"Now," she said, composing herself. "I have something to tell you about Michael that might help you understand his behaviour towards you." She launched into her prepared speech.

"Although Michael remains a doctor and was a general practitioner

239

in Wynshore, Michael is Wynshore's Member of Parliament, and he's also the Minister for the Family. I believe Katherine may have mentioned something?"

"I looked him up on the House of Commons website when we got back from your house. He's had a distinguished career, my father."

"Yes, he's done very well," Julia said softly. For a moment neither of them spoke. "And he's frightened."

"Not of me?"

"Of the press. And what they might do to us – me, Tess, Katherine. And possibly even to you and Sarah."

"I don't quite see…" Nigel ran his hands through his hair.

"Michael is right about this. They would have a field day with it, the puns and the innuendo. Tess and Katherine would have to face a barrage of reporters and photographers each day on the school run. Our dustbins would be gone through, the milkman bribed. I'm sure you've seen other ministers' families go through it. And what's worse is that our children are still young. It wouldn't last long of course, some other more newsworthy story would soon take its place, but by then the damage would be done. And you and Sarah, your new baby, all your relatives in fact, would have to endure much the same treatment."

"And Michael believes I would sell this story to the press!" Nigel was indignant.

"No, neither of us do. Not now that we know you. But that's what he was frightened of, it's why he's been so…"

"Unfeeling?" Nigel suggested.

"I was going to say distant. He isn't really at all like that. Actually he's very like you. Or rather, you are very like him at the same age – not just in looks but character too. Oh, I know he's a politician now and that plays havoc with a man's sensibilities, but deep down Michael is still decent and principled and a rare politician because of that." Julia wondered just who she was trying to convince. She decided that she'd better draw the conversation to a close.

"This has all been explained to the girls and they are honestly thrilled to have you as their big brother. They like Sarah too, and they're especially delighted about your baby. You're going to have two persistent little aunts. When you visit you won't even get a chance to change a nappy."

"Michael told Tess and Katherine, did he?" Nigel asked.

"Well, no, I did."

"Does my father always get other people to do his…"

"I felt it was better coming from me," Julia lied quickly.

"I want to like my father, Julia, but it's proving to be rather a challenge."

"If it's any consolation, Nigel, Michael knows he's made a complete hash of this. Putting it right is proving harder than he thought."

"But he could have come here. He could have told me this. That would have been a start."

"Just give him time."

"It's been months now Julia, and it's you that makes contact every time."

"But now he knows that you represent no threat either to us or the girls, it'll be better. You'll see, I promise."

"Will I?" Nigel lifted his glass to finish his wine and stared out into the black, watery night. Turning back to Julia, he asked: "And are you all right?"

Shakily she replied:

"Only just."

*

Frank found the little snippet he had offered to the satirical magazine, 'The Mole', under a heading on page eight.

'WICKED WHISPERS

The vanity of politicians can never be overestimated. Which Government Minister has been putting in some, ahem, 'handiwork' on behalf of the nation's infertile couples? Can the infertile be that desperate for sperm? Whatever next? MPs cloning themselves! They've passed the bill – they have the technology!'

Perfect. The press and parliamentary rumour machine would now swing into action. Frank gave a delighted chuckle and, offering to buy Sam Denton and Gideon Wentworth a pint, he set off for the Dog and Leg-it with his two surprised colleagues in tow.

"Won the lottery have we, Frank?" Gideon enquired.

"I tell you, you'll enjoy this, Gideon. It involves a tasty bit of blackmail, skilfully done." Frank hit the sketch writer lightly on the shoulder with his furled up copy of the magazine as they headed for the lift.

"Really, Frank?" Gideon commented sceptically winking at Denton.

"One of those whiter-than-white, principled bastards too," Smite added.

"Oh jolly good." Gideon adjusted his Bart Simpson bow tie. "There's nothing I like more than seeing the holier-than-thou sods brought to their knees. That's my favourite sport."

*

When Michael returned to Wynshore on Thursday night he found the house deserted save for distant jazz music floating down the stairs from the attic. He wandered through the house calling for Tess and Katherine. No reply. So having dumped his case in the bedroom, he climbed the narrow stairs to the very top of the house where he fully expected to find the girls with a few friends messing about with the old record deck. Instead, to his surprise he found Julia dancing, wearing denim jeans and a polo neck. He stood and watched his wife who, oblivious to his presence, continued to move her hips and body seductively. Michael smiled – he hadn't seen Julia behaving so playfully for years. When the track ended he clapped slowly in appreciation.

"Oh! Michael! You made me jump," Julia cried.

"Having fun?"

"I went with Sarah and heard Nigel play the other night, and it got me thinking about these records. I never play them any more now everything's on CD, and I love jazz, always have."

"Is he any good?"

"Great! A brilliant saxophonist and the piano playing goes without saying. He even played a Ronnie Laws' piece brilliantly. I think I should get into jazz again. There's a festival here in Wynshore, so why do we never go?"

"The same reason we never do anything – my job."

"There's nothing to stop me going, is there?" Julia responded, dancing across the floor.

"No, nothing at all," he agreed. A change had come over her, he thought. She seemed brighter somehow. It was hard to put his finger on it but Michael was in no doubt that there was something different about his wife.

"How was Nigel? How did he take it?" he asked.

"Fine. Pissed off with you, of course, but then aren't we all?"

Michael was startled by Julia's uncharacteristic and casual use of a swear word.

"Where are the girls?" he asked.

"They're both out but will need collecting later, so I thought we could go and have supper in that pub by the river – they sometimes have live music. We can collect Tess and Katherine on the way home."

"Tonight? You mean go out tonight?"

"Yes, why not? Is that a problem?"

"No. Not if that's what you want."

"It is."

*

Logan dropped into Michael's office in a seemingly casual manner. A tray of coffee was carried in by his parliamentary secretary who, sitting down just behind Logan, took out his pen ready to make notes. Michael assumed the purpose of the visit was to firm up some electoral detail and to make certain Michael was fully appraised and not likely to go 'off message'. So he was surprised when, in the middle of discussing the launch of the parenting initiative, Logan began a quite different line of enquiry.

"Michael, I had a call yesterday from Matthew Lake." Logan paused for a moment. "The editor of *The Daily Record*."

"Yes," Michael acknowledged, assuming that they were still concerned with parenting courses. He took a sip of his coffee.

"They're running a piece tomorrow, silly little item really…how the good and the great paid their way through university, tips for debt ridden students, that sort of thing. You know, what odd jobs they did; waiter, bouncer, croupier." Michael blanched, although it was nothing compared to Logan's obvious discomfort as he continued: "They have you down as a sperm donor! I wonder just how they got hold of such an idea. And apparently there were a few words in 'The Mole' recently alluding to the same thing, no name though. Did you see it?"

Michael swallowed hard and then, recovering, said:

"No. No, I didn't. I was a medical student. Clinics advertised on the med school notice board." Looking at Logan, he quickly realised that he was unlikely to get away with that reply.

"And were you one of the students who made donations, Michael?"

"Yes, as a matter of fact I was. I've never hidden the fact that I'm in favour of helping infertile couples, although, as you know, from time to time my views have been misrepresented." This was a clever swipe at Logan's handling of the 'Question Time' débâcle. "There is nothing improper in my having been a sperm donor – it is rightly considered generous, bringing a good deal of happiness to the couples involved."

"No. No, of course not," Logan conceded. "But you were paid?"

"Expenses: ten or fifteen pounds a time. I believe the amount has barely changed in the intervening years," Michael added.

"Quite a lot thirty years ago," Logan suggested.

"It helped."

"I wonder how they got hold of this information?" Logan pondered, and then asked, "There's nothing in this, Michael, that could embarrass the Prime Minister or the government in any way, is there?"

"Nothing whatsoever," Michael stated emphatically.

"Good." Logan took a last sip of his coffee and put down the cup. Clearly the interview was over and, satisfied, he was ready to take his leave. "I wonder how they got hold of this story?" he reiterated and, rising out of his seat, walked towards the window.

"I do hope the knives aren't out," Michael said. "Mind you,

they're clearly scraping the bottom of the barrel if this is all they can come up with for a pre-election sleaze scam."

"I told the Prime Minister that's what it would be. Those bastards will try and pick off anyone vulnerable in order to taint the election and make us look as sleazy as the previous administration. We just don't want to give them any ammunition, now do we?"

"No, of course not. Does the Prime Minister know?"

"Oh yes, he's been kept informed. It's a private matter, as he rightly pointed out. He gives you his full backing. Don't worry, Michael. I'll handle it. What a truly hideous sculpture that is," and then, turning away from the rain lashed window, Logan walked with Michael towards the door.

"Oh, one more thing. Have you ever met up again with a fellow student of yours, a chap by the name of Giles Strumpshaw?" Logan looked hard at Michael who, despite the shock, managed to remain composed.

"Yes, as matter of fact I have. I ran into him in the tea-room. Apparently he's in the bio-tech industry now. He was there for a meeting with the Trade and Industry Secretary. There was a group of them lobbying about something or other. Tim was with me – you know, my agent, little fellow with the leg."

"Good. So just a very brief chat then?"

"Wives, children, that sort of thing," Michael confirmed and then asked, "Why?"

"Oh, it's nothing." Logan dismissed the question with a wave of his hand. "By the way, the Prime Minister asked me to thank you for letting him run with the parenting course initiative – he fully acknowledges that it was your baby – if you'll pardon the dreadful pun!" Logan's hand rested on Michael's shoulder and, after this unnaturally genial moment, the master of spin and his secretary were gone.

Michael, leaning back against the office door, let out a huge lungful of air. Christ! What the hell was going on? 'The Daily Record' could only have this information if someone had sold the story. It must have been Nigel or Sarah. His worst fears realised, Michael picked up the telephone to ring Julia but after a moment he replaced the handset. No, wait, he thought, Logan just might get the story spiked – do a trade.

The following day page four of *The Daily Record* contained the nasty little set piece – half a page, dressed up as a light-hearted look at undergraduates financing university. It focused on Michael Barton, although another minister or MP also slipped into the text occasionally to make it look like a legitimate editorial. Nevertheless, all the digs and innuendo were aimed squarely at Michael. 'Minister's Handiwork' was one subheading, followed by 'Minster for the Family in more ways than one! Michael Barton is taking his role as Minister for the family farther than anyone could have anticipated!' 'Farther' was just one of many plays on words scattered throughout the piece.

Michael could hear his staff grouped together in the outer office, poring over the detail. He detected the occasional snigger. It was Wednesday and time for Prime Minister's Questions in the House. He dreaded running the gauntlet of both the press pack and his parliamentary colleagues but there would be no escaping it, and the opposition would, no doubt, have a lot of fun at his expense.

Julia had rung him earlier.

"Just how did this get out?" she demanded.

"I don't know, Julia. You tell me," Michael barked back down the line.

"It definitely wasn't Nigel. I asked him when he rang earlier this morning. He read it over someone's shoulder on the bus to work."

"Oh really? Come off it, Julia! Who else could it be?"

That afternoon in the chamber of the House of Commons, the opposition leader was on biting form. He complimented the Prime Minister on choosing such a worthy 'member' as Minister for the Family and finished off by suggesting Michael Barton was, " 'a handy man' to have working 'hand in glove', whilst supporting families up and down the land." The House roared. The Prime Minister, with Logan sitting beside him, showed just the trace of an amused smile before moving on to more pressing matters.

As soon as he could, Michael left the chamber. A few friends clapped him on the back, making heartening comments as well as the odd jibe. In the lobbies, as he passed, groups of MPs stood chatting and joking, no doubt, Michael concluded, at his expense. His expression passive, he walked out of the Palace of Westminster to the relative safety of the department.

The following day Gideon Wentworth penned a hilarious critique of the parliamentary goings-on. This Michael scanned in minutes and binned within seconds. Julia also complained that the press were door-stepping her and the children, and that both Rosalind and Imogen had been on the telephone and Rosalind was utterly bemused. Worse, at the school gate she was being whispered about and Breeda had made a comment about her own family having kept their end of the bargain. Julia assumed Breeda meant that they had said nothing. Even so the usual offers of support from her friends had not been forthcoming. Julia felt increasingly uncomfortable and isolated.

"Make a statement," she urged.

"I've nothing to say," he snapped. And then, "Julia you know that any comment I make will only make matters worse. Logan thinks it's a pre-election tactic." He was surprised that, given Julia's support of Nigel, she appeared so rattled. Perhaps this was too personal and embarrassing and the reality was turning out to be far worse than she had ever anticipated.

"And when have you ever taken any notice of Loathsome Logan?" she retorted.

Before Michael could reply there was a click, and the line went dead.

Michael sat in the deepening gloom of the department as, one by one, his staff said their goodbyes and left for home. Outside the window the unrelenting rain coursed against the over-bright painted sculpture and the weary stream of London commuters took on the image of a Lowry painting, slanting against the wind and rain and fighting to keep control of their umbrellas. Michael felt his life falling into the same chaos that had recently enveloped the country. Somehow he was losing his grip, it was all slipping away.

Later that evening he rang Nigel from his office. He couldn't get the notion out of his head that it was Nigel who had informed on him. He remembered that, according to Julia, his aloofness toward his newfound son had given Nigel just cause.

"Hello, Michael," Nigel said. "This is a first!" It was clear Michael didn't understand, so Nigel added. "You, ringing me."

"Oh, I see, yes. I'm not very good at this, am I? This stuff in the press," Michael began. "I hope it doesn't bother you."

"No, Michael, the 'stuff'' in the press doesn't bother me."

"I understand from Julia that you're a great on the sax. You know, it's quite awakened her interest in jazz."

"That's good." Nigel decided he was not going to play this game. He knew that the only reason his father was ringing him was because Michael wanted to ascertain whether or not he had anything to do with today's press exposure.

"I'd like to come and see you play. Will you let me know when?" Michael asked. "And how's Sarah?"

"She's fine. Well, big and uncomfortable, but then that's to be expected."

"I hope this press business hasn't upset her. I don't know how they got hold of it although, luckily, they don't seem to know about you. So hopefully I can keep you both out of it."

"Someone would have to tell them about me. And neither Sarah nor I would want that, Michael. You see we value our privacy, too," Nigel said coolly.

"Yes, of course you do," Michael readily agreed. "If anyone from the press should try to contact you or your family, then I recommend that you make no comment. They'll soon go away when they get nothing."

"Michael, I can honestly say that it doesn't matter to me whether you believe this or not – but this article has absolutely nothing whatsoever to do with me or Sarah."

Michael could detect Nigel's rising anger.

"No, of course. I'm sorry. Now don't forget to let me know about that gig."

"Okay," Nigel agreed reluctantly.

*

At the offices of 'The Daily Record' Frank Smite was setting out his stall at a full meeting with Lake, Gideon and the political editor. Smite was enjoying every minute of it. It had been a while since he'd held such sway. They planned to continue to drip-feed the story, a tricky act to pull off because, if one of the weighty national Sundays decided to snoop around, then they could steal a march on them.. Smite wasn't having any of that. Lake was trying to hold off until the date of the election was announced, he wanted to time it for maximum impact.

"This'll wipe that smug grin off their faces," Lake contended. "So next, we introduce the gambling element, get a quote from Barton denying any involvement with this Strumpshaw character and then interview Strumpshaw. Later we can hit him with the blackmail scam. Frank, get a stringer, someone they won't be wary of, to snoop around the local constituency party offices – pretend it's for election coverage, check out funding, gifts, donations, that sort of thing."

They chuckled at the word 'donations', which was rapidly gaining a new connotation both in the offices of *The Daily Record* and in the corridors of power.

*

Barbara, Gerald's lady friend, was just slipping into her silk lilac wrap; it had the softest swansdown trim. Gerald had taken to treating Barbara to these feminine items of lingerie. Remarking how it gave her an hourglass figure in the style of Monroe, Gerald relished undoing the neat row of hooks-and-eyes that contained Barbara's ample bosom during their now frequent afternoon assignations. Barbara wondered just how a man with Gerald's robust tastes had remained married to such a mouse as Marion.

She began to leaf through *The Daily Record* that had been left on the bedside table.

"He's a handsome man, this Michael Barton," Barbara called to Gerald who had just finished in the shower. "And Nigel favours him."

Gerald emerged from the en-suite towelling down his large hairy belly. He'd put on weight since joining the cookery club.

"I used to think he was like Marion; just shows how wrong you can be. Mind you, I don't know that they've hit it off that well."

"No? Has Nigel said as much?"

"It's more what he doesn't say. Sarah told me that cheque he sent was to buy them off, not for the baby at all. Nigel returned it, he was very put out. Apparently it was only when the wife, Julia, got to know about Nigel that he got introduced to the family. Before that Barton just wanted rid of him. From what I can gather Michael Barton has only met Nigel the once."

"Well I never. Shame. Serves him right then." Barbara gestured to the newspaper article. "Fancy, denying your own son. That's these big-wigs all over, isn't it, Gerry?"

*

"You can run it, Matthew, but I have to tell you that your informant is quite wrong. The only meeting, if you can call it that, between the Minister and Giles Strumpshaw was when they ran into each other in the public tea-room. And Tim Nash, the constituency agent, confirms that he was party to the entire conversation, which I am told centred on catching up on family matters and old times."

"Really? Ha ha ha, nice try Logan." Matthew Lake replaced the receiver and rocked from side to side in his black leather executive chair, a broad smile settling across his face. This was going to be fun.

*

In the chamber of the House of Commons, Logan responded to a question by the pugnacious Sebastian Flint.

"Could he confirm whether the Minister for the Family had a meeting with one Mr Giles Strumpshaw, a director of 'StemShaw'?"

Logan bobbed up out of his seat. No, he reassured the House, Michael Barton neither met nor corresponded with Mr Strumpshaw in any official capacity. His response provoked some murmuring.

Logan was quickly on his feet again and at the dispatch box once more.

"Apart, that is, from when they ran into one another in the public tea-room There followed the briefest of conversations about old times."

Logan sat down again. There were some guffaws and the word 'handy' could be heard quite distinctly. The speaker then took control and moved on.

In an ante-room Michael stood watching the chamber on one of the television monitors set high up on an ornately papered wall. A hand clapped him on the back. It was his friend Alan Enderby.

"Don't let the buggers grind you down – it'll be some other sod's turn next week, you'll see. Come and have a drink in the bar, it doesn't do to go into hiding, makes them think they're onto something."

Michael gave a weary smile.

"It's Julia I'm worried about, and the girls. The innuendo is fairly unpleasant."

"It's always worse for the families, especially when we can't even be there to fend off the gentlemen of the press," Enderby agreed. "She'll cope. Julia is made of sterling stuff. Come on, I'm buying."

*

The Daily Record hit the news-stands just before dawn. The telephone at Michael's apartment rang at six thirty-five that morning. It was Julia and she was distraught. There was a press pack at the front door and Frank Smite had just pushed a copy of 'The Daily Record' through the letterbox.

"They're saying you've been blackmailed, Michael. You did it because you gambled your grant away. The headline is 'SPERMGATE!'"

In the background Michael could hear Smite calling through the letterbox demanding an interview, and the voice of a confused and frightened Katherine:

"What's happening, Mummy? Why won't they go away?"

26

In a Spin

"Michael." It was Logan – and he was necessarily brief. "Don't go into the department. You're to come straight to Number 10, the Prime Minister wishes to see you. I don't have to remind you to say nothing to the press. I'm sending a car and a policeman has been stationed outside your home, it was getting a bit out of hand there. Tim Nash will go round and keep an eye on things and brief Julia. Be ready in ten minutes."

Michael did as he was told. Outside a group of hacks were door-stepping any and everyone who came in or out of the apartment entrance. Michael ducked back behind the curtain and shuddered, feeling sick. On the breakfast television news a picture of Strumpshaw appeared: he was grinning and one arm was on Michael's shoulder, his hand was pumping Michael's. They looked like great friends.

When the telephone began ringing, Michael seized the plug and wrenched it out of the socket.

*

In her kitchen Julia was beside herself. The number of press at the gate far exceeded anything she had previously endured. Some of the photographers even had stepladders. Tess and Katherine were frightened. Julia had gamely attempted to run the gauntlet of the local and national press but, as she bundled the children into the car, a group of reporters had surged into the drive and surrounded them, blocking her way and forcing open the doors, pushing microphones right in their faces, all the time shouting a barrage of questions. As Julia edged the car forward one girl, Samantha, whom she recognised from the local paper, had tripped and practically ended up under the wheels. The girl was grazed and shaken and Julia dissolved into tears. Around her she could hear the whirring and clicking of what seemed like a hundred cameras. Julia rang Breeda from her mobile phone. Breeda then called the police and came around at once. And it was Breeda who shooed the press out of the drive and shepherded the terrified family back to the safety of the house.

"Holy Mary, Mother of God!" Breeda exclaimed once they had retired to the relative safety of the kitchen. "They're animals, that's what they are. Is it any wonder they call them the Press Pack."

"'Minister's wife runs down reporter' – that'll be the bloody headline!" Julia wailed, tearful and angry all at once. Actually Breeda thought it was more likely to read 'Disgraced Minister's wife runs down reporter', but she kept that to herself.

"I'll ring the school – you girls will not be going anywhere today," Breeda told them firmly. "If this keeps up, we'll have to find somewhere else for you to stay. It would be best, Julia, just until the hoo-ha dies down. Now a cup of tea before anything else, and then you girls go upstairs and play some music or something. Oh, and stay at the back of the house," She had assumed the authority of an army brigadier who was gamely manning command and control.

"Thankfully there's nothing about the boy, about Nigel," Breeda said.

"Oh no," Julia cried. "Nigel!"

*

Nigel had the morning off and the headmaster had kindly offered to cover his lessons. It was time for Sarah's scan, the last before the baby was due. They sat together in the crowded antenatal clinic, Sarah downing the copious glasses of water required for the procedure and Nigel reading the headline from the paper of another father-to-be opposite:

'SPERMGATE'.

Staring out at him from the page was a picture of his father, Michael Barton, and next to it was a photograph of a corpulent middle-aged man with obviously dyed hair getting into his Jaguar. Next to that was a picture of the fat man beaming and shaking his father's hand at some function.

The drive to Downing Street seemed interminable, the traffic was a nightmare. Apart from a formal, "Good morning, Minister," the driver, who was not familiar to Michael, said nothing. The car made its way to the back entrance. This was not good news and in all probability heralded Michael's sacking. On stepping out of the car he was escorted through the back entrance by an elegant middle-aged woman. She deposited him in a graceful ante-room, where he was instructed to wait, the Prime Minister would see him shortly. Coffee was offered. Michael, feeling like a condemned man, politely refused although his mouth was dry.

After twenty minutes he began to pace the floor. Perhaps this wait was a strategy to wear him down, make him put up less of a fight, go without a fuss. Ten minutes later he heard footsteps and the same woman came to escort him through a series of rooms to the Prime Minister. As he approached the door, a tall greying man he recognised as Sir Julius Pink, a senior civil servant, was just leaving. It was Pink who was charged with the task of alerting the Prime Minister to potential blackmail risks: misdeeds, peccadilloes, vices and the like. He gave Michael a look of imperious contempt and swept by without a word.

"Michael, do sit down." The Prime Minister was both courteous and genial although he did not offer Michael his hand. To his right sat Logan, stern and unyielding. He gave Michael the briefest nod of acknowledgement.

"I'm sure I don't have to tell you, Michael, that in a general election year, these were not the headlines we were looking for." Michael looked suitably chastened but made no reply. "Perhaps you'd like to fill me in on exactly what has, or has not, taken place between you and this man, Giles Strumpshaw."

So, at least he was to get a hearing. Michael, deciding that his only option was to come clean, set about explaining the whole ghastly sequence of events. The casual meeting in the tea-room, Strumpshaw inveigling himself into a meeting at the department, the threats. But, Michael insisted, he had already decided how he would vote in the Scientific Research Bill. And he'd made it absolutely clear to Strumpshaw that his arm-twisting had nothing whatsoever to do with that decision.

"He sent me a case of finest malt but I had it returned immediately."

The Prime Minister, his chin resting on his hands, listened intently but impassively. Logan was poker faced.

"Is that everything?" the Prime Minister enquired. Michael considered that there was some hope in that question, the die was not cast then. Not quite.

"No. No, it isn't." Michael began.

Logan lifted his eyes heavenward. The Prime Minister waited: "Go on."

"About six months ago I was contacted by a young man who believed that I was his biological father. His mother had recently died and he was then informed – by the man whom he had always believed to be his father – that in fact his birth was as the result of a cycle of sperm donation. This was a terrible shock, he was newly married and his wife was pregnant. They set about tracing the donor. Illegally, I might add. Over a period of months this resourceful couple tracked down the notes and stole them. I've met him, as has Julia, and the DNA tests prove that he is my son."

Logan looked worried.

"Their names?" he asked.

"Nigel and Sarah Laing. He's a music teacher, she's a PhD research scientist." There was a significant pause, then the Prime Minister asked:

"And these two approaches, Strumpshaw and Laing, were they simultaneous?"

"Practically," Michael replied. "Which is why I've made such a complete hash of the whole thing."

The Prime Minister sat back and looked over at Logan and then, turning back to Michael, said:

"Did you ever consider that Strumpshaw and Laing might be in it together?"

"Naturally; but I'm now as sure as I can be that they aren't connected. I haven't exactly embraced Nigel Laing as my long lost son. The way donor sperm was used back then there could quite literally be hundreds of other children claiming me for their father.

I don't deny the prospect is alarming."

The Prime Minister sat thoughtfully for a moment.

"The problem that I'm presented with here, Michael, is that my spokesman stood up in the House and categorically denied that any such meeting with Giles Strumpshaw took place. You see the position this leaves us in? It will be interpreted as lying to the House and lying to James here, who is understandably very angry." The Prime Minister gestured to Logan. "You will, I'm sure, appreciate that I am being asked for your head on a plate."

"Yes, Prime Minister, I fully understand. And I would like to take the opportunity to state that my vote has always belonged to my party and my conscience. I have never been persuaded to use it otherwise, nor would I. I should also like to apologise to you for any damage I have caused you or the Party." Michael let out a deep breath and waited to be formally sacked. But the Prime Minister pressed a small red button on the table next to him and the same middle-aged woman appeared at the door.

"I'm just going to take a few moments, Michael, to talk a number of things through with James here. If you wouldn't mind waiting."

To his surprise Michael was escorted back to the ante-room where a tray of coffee was produced. This time he drank it. It was forty minutes before he was called back in.

"The nice thing about this job, Michael, is that I am the boss," was the Prime Minister's cheery opening gambit. "And I've decided we're going to tough this out. You're a good minister and for the time being you can keep the job. However, I must stress that from this day forth everything and I mean everything you do, say, even think, goes through James here, who will in his own masterly way turn this story around. You will do exactly as he tells you, when he tells you. Is that clearly understood?"

"Yes, Prime Minister, and thank you." Michael was too stunned to show any hint of the delight or relief he was feeling.

"James will put together a damage limitation exercise; it transpires that there have been a few irregularities with licence applications at 'StemShaw' and some questionable scientific activities. Also Giles Strumpshaw has some curious links to the Opposition's

Central Office. So James will write the statement and you'll read it verbatim. Can we rely on Julia?"

"Oh, a hundred percent," Michael replied with touching faith in his wife.

"Good. And James will arrange a photo opportunity with the newfound son, on the green with Parliament in the background." Turning to Logan, he asked, "What is current policy on the right to knowledge of paternity for donor children?"

"It was altered: openness from now on and the first children will get their biological parents details in 2023. However the legislation wasn't retrospective. The Nigel Laings of this world will never legally be entitled to details of their biological parents," Logan replied.

"When asked, you're for openness, Michael. You will add your name to any voluntary register of donors and offspring, which the children could consult when they are eighteen. Rather like adoption...understand? Let's make sure all our statements tally, shall we? Good. Sort out the detail and keep me informed." The Prime Minister rose out of his seat, buttoned up his jacket and, giving Michael a brief handshake, strode off to his next engagement.

Logan spoke with quiet menace:

"Fart in the wrong place and I'll have you."

27

Homespun

Julia and the children were removed to her mother's house in Hertfordshire. It was considered by Tim Nash, amongst others, to afford the best opportunity for some much-needed time and privacy to work on Julia, who might have to be won round. What's more, Rosalind's house near Bishop's Stortford was set well back from the road behind a high wall and with some woodland for cover against prying eyes and lenses.

"I'm not saying I understand all this, Julia," Rosalind began, "but I really cannot see what exactly it is that Michael is supposed to have done wrong." Michael still remained an exemplary character in his mother-in-law's eyes; nothing could be said against him, and Rosalind simply refused to understand that Michael had been caught lying. "I mean lots of young men Michael's age got into scrapes at university – it's all part of leaving home. I can quite see that Michael thought it would bring a lot of happiness. It doesn't conflict with *his* beliefs and really it's the intention that matters, darling." A venial, and therefore forgivable sin in Rosalind's book. "Anyone would think he was a white slaver or peddling drugs the way the papers are laying into him. I think poker is considered a perfectly respectable game for a man, although your father and I always preferred bridge," she added. "And I think they're really making far too much of the Maltese clip-joint angle. I mean everyone knows that both the Maltese and the Chinese are very keen gamblers. And just look how good he is to you and the children. It's a measure of a man, you know, how he treats his family."

"Yes, Mother, it is, isn't it," Julia responded, the irony in her tone quite lost on Rosalind.

When Imogen turned up, Julia instructed her: "You're allowed just one conversation in which you say 'I told you so'. Is that absolutely clear?"

"Oh, Sis, what a mess!" Imogen hugged Julia to her. "God, he's been lying all over the place, hasn't he? Mind you, it's easy to see why. It puts all his shitty behaviour in context, doesn't it? He must have been trying to keep the lid on rather more than we realised."

"I thought he'd be sacked. So did he," Julia stated, adding wistfully, "In a way I wish he had been. I'll be back on parade as the dutiful wife. Tim Nash was here this morning working on me, they're planning some kind of photo opportunity."

"Will you do it?"

"Yes. But I'll play hard to get and impose some conditions of my own."

"Good for you."

*

Frank Smite was loving every minute of it.

The broadsheets were now also in full cry, 'Why did the Minister deny meeting Strumpshaw?' they asked, and went on to accuse Logan of 'struggling to kill this unhelpful story'. 'Was the Minister blackmailed into a yes vote?' ran the headline.

Smite could smell a resignation.

*

Nigel had been ringing the house in Wynshore constantly but kept getting the answer-phone. Suspecting Julia wasn't there, he left the briefest message, expressing his concern for her and the children, offering help and asking her to call him when she could.

*

Michael, who under normal circumstances refused the ministerial car, decided in the light of his current notoriety that it was his best bet for reaching Maidenhead undetected. He had already rung the Laings and reached Sarah who, though surprised, had informed Michael that Nigel was at a parents' evening and would be back later, and yes, they would be pleased to see him. It suited Michael to arrive late as he was keen to slip in and out of the flat unseen.

"It's time I explained to you both what all this press stuff is about and why I have been reluctant to…" he hesitated. "Why this is all such a mess."

The flat was upstairs in an Edwardian house that had been divided up. It was not very large and had a suburban feel to it, despite being close to a row of shops and the local thoroughfare. Michael told the driver to wait for him. He had no idea how long this would take, or whether Nigel would just throw him out – nothing would surprise him. It was Sarah who came down to the door to let him in. She looked tired and was breathless from the stairs. Michael felt awkward but he kissed her lightly on the cheek and said:

"My goodness, look at you! How much longer?"

"About four weeks," she said holding her painful back and waddling up the stairs clinging to the banister for much needed support. "Nigel won't be a minute. He's just popped out for some milk."

The flat reminded Michael of his early accommodation in London, small and makeshift.

"This is very nice," he said clumsily.

"Have a seat, Michael."

He took off his coat and laid it next to him on the sofa. He both felt and looked very uncomfortable. After a few more pleasantries they fell into a difficult silence. Nigel arrived shaking the rain from his hair and proffering a pint of milk. They shook hands. Nigel threw himself into the chair opposite in the way that proud and defensive young men do and asked:

"How's Julia? I've rung but I always get the machine."

"Pissed off with me, as everyone is," came Michael's self-deprecating reply. "Julia and the girls have been moved to her mother's. There's better security and the press can't get close. There was an incident at our house so it seemed sensible to move them until this all dies down."

Nigel glanced at Sarah, an eyebrow raised. This was a Michael Barton that they had not met before – an altogether humbler man.

"And will it die down?" Nigel asked somewhat sceptically.

"Who knows. Anyway, I owe you and Sarah an explanation. Which is why I'm here."

Sarah produced a tray of coffee and proceeded to hand each of them a cup.

"I imagine your role as an MP could often conflict with Julia's beliefs?" Nigel said to his father.

Michael took a sip, steadied himself and began to explain his actions:

"Yes, I think it does. But from the outset when I entered parliament we agreed that my role as an MP was quite separate. I represent my constituents, my party and my conscience and generally Julia and I don't even discuss such matters. She trusts me…" Michael's voice trailed away. "She trusted me."

Sarah glanced across at Nigel; she was feeling quite sorry for Michael. Poor man. He'd made a series of mistakes; in his marriage, in his relationship with Nigel, and certainly in his political career. He had taken the wrong decisions, although he couldn't have known that at the time. Now instead of seeing him as callous, in the course of this explanation Sarah was reinterpreting his actions as those of a confused man.

"So, I'm really sorry that I got all of this so badly wrong. I was hoping we could start again, that you would be generous enough to give me a second chance."

Nigel looked towards Sarah who signalled her ready agreement. His father was drawn, and looking a good deal older. Nigel gave a half smile and said:

"Where do we start?"

Michael visibly relaxed and said:

"Why don't you and Sarah have lunch with Julia and me at the House, as soon as it can be arranged? If we ever get any sunshine the terrace affords the most wonderful view of the Thames. I'd very much like to show you both round."

Sarah beamed. Was it possible that father and son were reconciled at last? It made the prospect of their first baby all the more exciting.

"And I should like us to issue a joint statement introducing you as my son."

Nigel nodded in agreement. His father was a likeable man after all.

"Also," Michael continued, "I don't know if this is jumping the gun a bit, but in discussion with the Prime Minister the voluntary register came up; it's just a suggestion, but as the legislation isn't retrospective, a voluntary register might be a way forward. Some donors might be happy to meet their children. I realise that it falls short of your desire to access your records by law, but your thoughts would be invaluable."

Nigel nodded again, delighted at last to have a father who owned up to the relationship and was prepared to publicly endorse it.

"I'd certainly share this experience if it would help others. I can see now that for donor families this can be very difficult. It's hardly cut and dried is it?"

Sarah found a bottle of champagne that they had been keeping for the baby. She handed it to Nigel with some glasses, even indulging in a small glass herself, which made her baby kick.

The conversation between father and son went on to embrace music in general, the classics as well as jazz; Nigel's hopes for his teaching career and Sarah's plans to take up the reins of her PhD when the baby was old enough. Finally Michael, realising just how long he had kept his driver waiting in the cold and wet, said regrettably that he must leave. On parting he and Nigel hugged. It proved impossible to hug Sarah, the baby prevented any close contact. They all laughed good-naturedly.

"You're going to need a bigger place," Michael commented.

"Impossible on one teacher's salary," Sarah stated lightly but with resignation.

"Perhaps I could help. A loan? Fathers being altogether cheaper than bank or building societies – no interest you see!" Nigel and Sarah turned to each other, surprised. "Think about it, I wouldn't want to push any noses out of joint. I've done enough of that already. I'll ring you about lunch. Don't come down, you'll get cold." And with that Michael hurried down the stairs and was gone.

"Oh, Nigel, I'm so pleased for you," Sarah said, giving him a kiss. "You see he is a decent man after all. Let's face it, any father of yours would have to be."

And she kissed him again.

*

The photo opportunity on the green, with the Houses of Parliament as a backdrop, took place the following week. The press was issued with an upbeat and carefully worded statement, introducing Nigel as the Minister's newfound son and accompanied by his pregnant wife. Logan allowed just three questions, all vetted from various branches of the BBC and ITV. But this didn't stop Smite from chipping in with:

"Would Mrs Barton like to comment on the prospect of hundreds more little Bartons pitching up?"

Julia, who had been instructed in exactly what to wear – an elegant suit – and exhorted to smile warmly, showing motherly concern for her pregnant daughter-in-law, did not respond. Instead, Michael replied:

"I believe I speak for us both when I say that any other children of mine will always be greeted with affection and welcomed into our family." He smiled warmly at Nigel.

"How have little Tess and Katherine taken to their new brother, Julia? And do you realise there could literally be hundreds more out there somewhere?"

Julia, who had refused to involve the girls in this charade, looked across to James Logan, her expression indicating that as far as she was concerned, the show was now over. Logan and his henchmen moved in and ushered the Minister and his family away from the press pack and back to the House.

"Gordon Bennett, the master of spin reckons he can transform that lying toad into a national hero! Breeding for the bleedin' nation!" Smite sneered to a fellow hack as they made their way across the thronging traffic to the nearest pub. Smite was enjoying the minor celebrity he'd achieved amongst his colleagues which had followed the breaking of one of the tastiest stories for months. "There's more," he assured them, tapping the side of his nose with his nicotine-stained finger. "I'll have that sanctimonious bastard." On the bar lined up for him were three pints, each with whisky chasers.

"Without Logan's life-support system Barton is doomed," Smite prophesied.

*

"This doesn't seem right to me, Gerry." Barbara was pouring over the colour spread of photographs in *The Daily Record.* "I mean it's not as if this Michael Barton welcomed Nigel into the family at all – it's his wife, Julia, who's done all the running. And now look – Nigel's his long lost son and he's looking forward to being a grandfather! When it suits, Gerry, when it suits."

Gerald was looking over Barbara's shoulder and feeling quite out of sorts. Gerald felt he had lost his son altogether now. His role as grandfather to Nigel and Sarah's baby had even been assumed by Barton.

"It's all wrong, there's no mention of you or Marion, you should get some credit for bringing the boy up as your own!" Barbara continued. "You're the one who's taught him right from wrong, made him what he is. Nigel even said as much."

"I think Nigel's being manipulated," Gerald suggested. "He's that desperate for his father to acknowledge him. That's what it is, Barbara. It's a publicity stunt – a put up job to get Barton out of that other trouble about that Strumpshaw fellow."

"You're so good with words, Gerry. 'Manipulated', that's just right. Poor Nigel and Sarah have been manipulated. I bet this Frank Smite would like to know the real truth behind what's gone on with Mr Michael Barton, and him Minister for the Family – trying to get rid of Nigel with that awful letter and then buying him off. He wouldn't look so smug then, would he, they'd soon see he's a – what do they call it? Hippo… something?"

"Hypocrite," Gerald replied.

*

It wasn't long after Julia arrived back home in Wynshore that Breeda came round.

"That was all very touching." Breeda made no effort to hide her

264

contempt for the publicity stunt she'd just witnessed in the national press and on the television news. "Given that at every turn Michael has denied his son, I don't know how you could go along with such a farcical manipulation of the truth, Julia, really I don't. And as for Michael, how does he think he's going to get re-elected with this fresh in everyone's mind."

"I'm just glad it's out in the open at last. Now Michael and Nigel can get to know one another properly. It's been fear of exposure that has prevented Michael spending time with Nigel as he should. I think that this will all be for the best in the end."

"I have been praying to Saint Severinus."

"Saint Severinus?" Julia queried.

"He stood for justice and standards in public life – something we are seeing precious little of currently. Don't laugh at me, Julia. You often laugh at me. I'm serious. Michael and I have always had our differences, but for me this has gone too far and, frankly, I am surprised at you." Julia could feel her blood rising. "I've given this a great deal of thought and although Moya says I shouldn't interfere, my conscience would not be well served by holding back. Michael's sperm donations give you the grounds you need to have this fraudulent marriage annulled – sure you might be thinking that this would render the girls illegitimate but I've looked into that and it just isn't so."

Julia stood incredulous, colour rising in her face with anger.

"How dare you! Just who do you think you are? You of all people to consider that you have any right to judge my marriage as fraudulent. Finn is hardly a model of fidelity and rectitude, he and Moya carrying on right under your nose these past two years. And you, you simply choosing to ignore it!"

The two friends stood stock-still opposite one another, the silence only broken when Breeda's hand met Julia's face, slapping it very hard.

"Liar!" Breeda screamed and fled the house, a shrill screech of tyres on gravel and the back door left banging back and forth the only evidence that she had ever been there.

"Oh, my God! What have I done?"

"Do come in, Mr Smite, Gerry's just through here in the living room," Barbara said opening the door and smiling broadly. Observing Smite's filthy mackintosh collar, Barbara was thankful as yet she hadn't removed Marion's antimacassars. Quaint though they were, they would serve some useful purpose after all.

*

The donation from Giles Strumpshaw to the local Wynshore Constituency Party came to light later that week. Michael received a telephone call from Matthew Lake.

"Would you like to comment, Minister?" Lake had enquired mischievously.

Michael was adamant: he knew of no such donation and, naturally, a gift of that amount would not only have been made known to him but would also been drawn to the attention of central office. There were regulations and Michael always adhered to them rigorously. And no, he could not explain how a letter of thanks reportedly signed by himself could possibly have been received by Giles Strumpshaw. Michael slammed down the receiver and then urgently rang Tim Nash. Too late.

The following day *The Daily Record* carried the headline 'CASH FOR VOTES: Minister denies all knowledge of generous gift from 'StemShaw' director'. Worse was to come. The centre spread was an interview with Gerald Laing and his 'friend' Barbara, a rather brassy looking redhead, with too much cleavage. The exposé suggested that far from welcoming his son, Nigel, into his family, Michael callously connived to rid himself of this troublesome son, his daughter-in-law Sarah and his forthcoming grandchild, by paying him off. A summary of the dismissive letter which Michael had sent was also referred to. Only Julia came out of the story with any credit.

Michael was immediately summoned to Number 10. He knew it was all over. This time he was doomed.

*

In Wynshore two extraordinary events were taking place at one and the same time. Julia Barton, having agreed to Tim Nash's appeal to make a statement supporting Michael, was inviting Sally-Anne Jenkins and a sharp looking photographer from 'The Daily Record' into the elegant drawing room for an exclusive interview.

Whilst only a few streets away Breeda, having smashed a gleaming plate glass window with a brick, gained entry to Moya's house. There she set about pouring copious amounts of indelible Indian ink over each and every clean white minimalist surface, paying particular attention to the cream leather sofa, the Portland stone coffee table and the cream, handcrafted designer rug. By the time Moya and the local police arrived it was too late. Moya's perfect house looked for all the world like a large Jackson Pollock painting, the more restrained areas inviting comparison with the work of Victor Passmore. Great gestural blobs, fine trails and dribbles set off by the occasional dark inky pool. There Moya, and the astonished young constable, were greeted by the vision that was Breeda, kneeling in the middle of the parquet floor, her ink stained hands clasped in prayer and tears coursing down her face.

28

Spun Dry

The article in *The Daily Record*' the following morning read: 'Michael Barton cut a lonely figure as he walked out of Number 10 to announce his resignation as Minister for the Family. During his emotional hour-long meeting with the Prime Minister at Downing Street, he continued to deny any wrongdoing. The Prime Minister's press spokesman, who had done his best to kill this unhelpful story using charm and menace to equal effect, was incandescent when he found Barton had lied to both the press and to him.

'A rattled Mr Barton made the following statement to the press, having just lost the job he loved and the prospect as a future Minister for Health. It now looks doubtful that he will hold on to his Wynshore seat, with this scandal fresh in the minds of the electorate. His constituency party is holding an emergency meeting to discuss his future. Drawn and pale Mr Barton insisted: "I do not accept that I have acted improperly," stressing, defiant to the last, that he had done nothing wrong and that all he now wanted was to "spend time with my family and get away from media and press intrusion." And he went on to apologise to his family publicly, who only last week were gathered together on the green outside the Houses of Parliament for a press photo-shoot aimed at shoring up Mr Barton's crumbling popularity and hiding his scandalous treatment of his son Nigel Laing, born through Barton's earlier profitable and prolific sperm donations – a son whom he had initially tried to discredit, branding him a blackmailer.

'Mr Barton went on to scornfully dismiss reports that the actions of his medical school contemporary, Giles Strumpshaw, had in any way influenced his vote in the recent Scientific Research Bill, and he brushed aside claims that his gambling, and sperm donations as a method of paying off those debts, was in any way improper or ill-judged.' The news report went on to say:

'This is the culmination of ten disastrous days of turmoil and embarrassment for the government which has been seized on by the Opposition; it is a crisis fatally compounded, of course, by Mr Barton's handling of the row and by the way he changed his story. He has both enraged and dismayed members of the party establishment, not least James Logan, the Prime Minister's press secretary, who indicated that he himself had been misled. Long time friends did not even attempt to defend their colleague: "It raises serious questions about his judgement," said one. Another friend and trusted minister did not try to support Mr Barton either: "His fatal mistake was the inability to see how others would interpret and judge his actions, not least, given that he was The Minister for the Family."' In the article, Gideon Wentworth had spared him nothing and the leader column was equally damning.

The disgrace and resignation of the Minister for the Family was featured across several pages in all the national press. Some even published a diary of the unfolding events and entitled it 'Diary of Donor Disgrace and Downfall'. All of Michael's past triumphs, misdemeanours and failures were raked over, and the consensus was that he was a maverick who could never really have been relied upon by the Prime Minister. Although he was talented and passionate about the health service and he had done a lot for working parents, he was a man who had ultimately lost his way and had never lived up to his early promise.

The centre colour spread featured a sombre, though elegant, photograph of Julia. She explained the pressure on her family and her shock at discovering her husband's former sperm donations and the numerous offspring that were likely to exist. She expressed sympathy for Nigel Laing's plight, but defended Michael who she explained had found himself trapped and confused as events spiralled out of control, adding that he was essentially a good and honest man. Julia went on to say that her faith, above all, had sustained her through the darkest hours and that she hoped some good would come out of it all, concluding that:

'A lot of good people have been very hurt, and even I have been guilty in that. Now we all need to be left alone to heal.' On her plans for the future Julia simply stated that she intended to take up some form of study at Wynshore University in the autumn. Sally-Anne concluded that Julia Barton was a woman of admirable character who would triumph despite the recent shocking revelations.

*

The police, who were keen to charge Breeda with breaking and entering and criminal damage, had to be persuaded by Moya that, because she was a well known local solicitor, the resulting publicity would be in no one's best interests. After some wrangling she pulled a few strings and all the charges were dropped. Finn was relegated to the attic room while Breeda, having been treated for depression, recovered. Andrew, who unknown to Moya, had for some time been enjoying the attentions of a pretty theatre nurse, behaved with indulgent forgiveness which his wife could only be grateful for.

Rosalind resolutely refused to believe that Michael could have been party to any wrongdoing, never once wavering in her staunch support of her beloved son-in-law.

"I really cannot see how Michael, with such a punishing schedule, could possibly be expected to monitor every dubious donation to the local constituency party. It's quite ridiculous that they can hold him responsible." And she was right; Westminster's anti-sleaze watchdog, when investigating Michael Barton's alleged misdeeds, finally concluded:

'The Minister could not have possibly have known that any such donation had been received from 'StemShaw'. In fact a simple administrative error by a temporary member of staff recruited from a local agency to cover absence had mistakenly processed the cheque, and sent out the standard letter of thanks bearing Mr Barton's computer generated signature.' It went on, 'Michael Barton has submitted himself and his actions to the necessary scrutiny appropriate to his office. The commissioner has been in possession of full and frank explanations of the relevant circumstances, and has concluded that no further investigation was warranted.'

Sir Julius Pink declared: "There wasn't a shred of evidence that anything improper took place." On the matter of the meetings with

Giles Strumpshaw, Sir Julius stated: "Certainly on the occasion of the scientific conference it is quite clear that their meeting was nothing more than pure chance." And of Strumpshaw's brief visit to the department he added, "Both Giles Strumpshaw and Mr Barton vehemently deny any impropriety and no evidence has been presented to me to alter their assertions." The national press were not swayed by this high-powered endorsement of the ex-Minister, calling it a whitewash; as far as they were concerned, a stain on his character remained.

Michael released a statement, saying:

'I am grateful to Sir Julius for clearing my name and I now feel that I can draw a line under these events. I am intent on winning back the trust of my Wynshore constituents, whom I wish to continue to represent with vigour and enthusiasm.'

It was the shock outbreak of a particularly virulent strain of Asian flu that ended the press debate about the alleged misdeeds of Mr Michael Barton. As the government struggled to control the spread of the virus and schools closed and hospitals were inundated, Michael was provided with some much-needed breathing space.

He greeted the postponement of the spring general election with relief. It gave him an opportunity to regroup and take soundings from Tim Nash and others. Finally the constituency party agreed that he would stand again for Wynshore. Politics was all he knew now. His only other option was heading up some toothless quango. He hoped his constituents would remember that he was a good MP who took their concerns seriously and worked hard on their behalf. With luck his majority would hold and carry him through to the next parliament.

Reluctantly Michael agreed to Julia's request for space and time to think things through. He moved into the London flat. Every other weekend he had the sad task of collecting Tess and Katherine for a weekend in London. They were sullen and uncooperative. Which was probably, Michael reasoned, just what Julia wanted. He felt the girls' burning resentment for him keenly. They were trapped for two days in a dull flat with none of the usual sustaining paraphernalia: CDs, videos and friends. His attempts at enjoyable educational excursions, to the Science museum and Greenwich, were a dismal failure.

"Do you think you can ever forgive me?" He asked Tess one Sunday.

"Only when you understand how horrible everything is for us."

"Tell me." Michael said softly. And she did.

Tess told her father how at school she had had to become Katherine's protector because her little sister was constantly ridiculed and picked on by bullies. They surrounded her in the playground asking, "How many kids has your dad got then?" They taunted both girls with snide remarks and disgusting gestures relating to sperm donation, taunts that the teachers apparently never heard nor saw. Some of Tess's friends had dropped her completely, their parents didn't want them playing with the children, others were over kind. Katherine, being younger, had felt this most keenly and, even when they weren't openly picked on, they were pushed to the back of the dinner queue and never chosen for team games. School was an ordeal to survive as best they could. Some of the parents didn't speak to Mummy any more either. Auntie Breeda hated them now and they were never asked round to play. It was an appalling list of indignities that her father's actions had brought upon his family.

Michael fell into a black depression. He made a supreme effort to keep in contact with Nigel and Sarah, ringing and visiting. They found him a changed man – stooped and gaunt.

"Poor Michael, just look at him." Sarah had remarked and then added, "Julia and he will be reconciled won't they? I wouldn't want to have been part of breaking up his family, Nigel, that would be dreadful."

Michael in turn was afraid that events would settle it and finally sabotage his relationship with his son, just as it was getting onto a more normal and relaxed footing. Fearing that Nigel still believed everything he had done was a set up job, he was delighted when they invited him to the christening together with Julia and the girls.

He liked Nigel and told him so. His grandchild, a boy, Maxwell Gerald Michael Barton-Laing, equipped with a double helping of family names, and called Max for short, was a lusty infant who shared the same large hands and strong chin that marked him out immediately as a Barton. Michael found himself unaccountably nervous at the thought of meeting Gerald and Barbara, but the path was smoothed by the easy charm of both Sarah and her parents.

"We must put it all behind us, Michael," Gerald had said charitably. "We've got little Max to think of now. He's the future."

And Michael had readily agreed.

"Can we talk?" Julia asked, as they stood in the churchyard after the ceremony. Walking away from the family group they sat on a bench framed by white roses. "I've been thinking that it is time you came home Michael. The girls miss you. I miss you. And I don't think I have been very fair."

"Julia."

"Let me say this, Michael. I was terribly angry, particularly for the girls. But what sort of person am I if, in accepting Nigel into our family, I push you out? I realise you weren't deliberately trying to hurt us, rather the reverse actually. I may have lost you for a time but I have never really stopped loving you."

"I am so sorry Julia for all the mess and pain I have caused. It's surprising how strong the preservation instinct can be – even when it's wrong, hanging on is the last thing I should have done. I see that now. It's been a sort of test, I failed it." Michael spoke honestly at last. "Nigel is a young man I am proud to call my son, he has the qualities I seem to lack; his tenacity and integrity are remarkable. I always wanted a son, and you were right, Nigel is very much how I imagined he might be. I'm actually very fortunate because, despite my best efforts, he hasn't completely disowned me, although I'm sure he's come close to it. " Julia slipped her hand into Michael's. Across the churchyard Tess and Katherine were taking turns to hold the baby.

"I love you very much Julia, I'll do everything I can."

"I know you will."

Hand in hand they walked back to their family.

Sundays in the Barton household were now simple affairs – no more lunches with friends. By the summer Breeda and Finn were packing up to move to Ireland, where Finn took up a well-paid job as a computer consultant. Julia sent a card asking to be forgiven and enquiring as to a forwarding address, but she received no reply.

As she passed their house the removal van was being loaded. Julia slowed the car to a crawl. Breeda, who was anxiously supervising the removal of the life sized statue of the Blessed Virgin now swathed in bubble wrap, looked up for an instant. Their eyes met and Julia thought Breeda might speak...

But the moment passed and Julia drove on.